Harlequin Cowboy Christmas Collection

Family and friends gathered around the tree, exchanging gifts and good food, sharing the warmth of the season…there's no place like home for the holidays. Especially after spending their days tending the ranch and riding the range, the rugged men in this special 2-in-1 collection value the place they hang their hats.

And this Christmas, these cowboys could be coming home to a few surprises in their stockings! They may not be looking to find that special woman, but romance has a way of catching solitary men under the mistletoe.

So join us as we celebrate these cowboys and the women who lasso their hearts!

If you enjoy these two classic stories, be sure to check out more books featuring cowboy heroes in Harlequin Special Edition and Harlequin American Romance.

W9-BID-719

New York Times Bestselling Author

Leanne Banks
and
Cathy Gillen Thacker

A PROPOSAL
AT CHRISTMAS

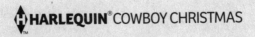

HARLEQUIN® COWBOY CHRISTMAS

Recycling programs for this product may not exist in your area.

ISBN-13: 978-0-373-60989-5

A Proposal at Christmas

Copyright © 2014 by Harlequin Books S.A.

The publisher acknowledges the copyright holders of the individual works as follows:

A Maverick for Christmas
Copyright © 2011 by Harlequin Books S.A.
Leanne Banks is acknowledged as the author of this work.

A Cowboy Under the Mistletoe
Copyright © 2010 by Cathy Gillen Thacker

Printed in U.S.A.

www.Harlequin.com

CONTENTS

A MAVERICK
FOR CHRISTMAS

Leanne Banks

This book is dedicated to Susan Litman.
You know why.

Prologue

Abby Cates remembered the moment she fell for Cade Pritchett. She had been nine years old at the time, and he'd been giving swimming lessons at Silver Stallion Lake. At seventeen, Cade had been tall, strong and blond. He was nice to all the kids, but demanded they learn their strokes. Abby was pretty sure he didn't remember scooping her out of some too-deep water when she'd choked and panicked. In her little-girl mind, Cade was a god.

Despite her best efforts, Abby had never found any man who could top Cade in her mind, not even now that she was twenty-two. And that was a terrible shame, especially since he'd never noticed her and, on top of that, wedding fever was running through Thunder Canyon like a bad flu.

Now that her older sister Laila was engaged to Jackson Traub, the discussions of weddings were nonstop.

Her mother was usually so eager for Christmas that she began decorating plans in early November, but this year she was clearly distracted. If her mother didn't take a little break from wedding talk, then Abby was going to explode through the roof of her family's home. She tried not to listen to her mother's phone conversation as she finished cleaning up the kitchen after dinner.

"A double wedding for Marlon and Matt," her mother cooed. "Love is definitely in the air. And soon enough, there will be babies," she continued, her tone giddy with delight.

Abby glowered. *Love is in the air.* Yeah, for everyone except her. Her mother began to dig for more details on the double wedding of her cousins, and Abby turned the water on high as she washed the last pot. She wished she could wash out her brain as easily as she could clean the dishes.

Why in the world had she fallen for a man who couldn't seem to even notice her? Talk about unrequited love. Then it had gone from bad to worse when he'd dated her beautiful oldest sister, Laila, the town beauty queen. Then it went from worse to tragic when he'd proposed to Laila. At least her sister had turned him down, but she'd hated the idea that Cade would suffer from Laila's rejection.

The past couple of years it had been so hard to see Cade with Laila. Abby had felt as if she'd walked around with a permanent knot in her stomach. In love with her sister's on-again, off-again boyfriend? It was like a bad soap opera. Although she loved Laila, Abby had been torn between guilt and resentment. She'd successfully kept it hidden, but she didn't know how much longer she could manage it, especially since it felt as if everyone around her was finding love and getting married. And as far as Cade Pritchett was concerned, she might as well be invisible.

Irritated with her bad mood, she muttered to herself, "Suck it up. Wedding fever won't last forever, and Christmas is right around the corner."

One second later, the door opened and her sister Laila waltzed in wearing a smile and flashing a cover of a bridal magazine. "I guess I need to start planning for the big day."

Abby felt something inside her rip. The beginning, she feared, of turning into a rocket and shooting through the roof. If she didn't get out of here. "Gotta go," she said, tossing the towel she held on the counter. "I'll be back later."

Laila shot her a bemused look. "Where are you going?"

"I need to do some research for a paper," Abby manufactured, although it was partly true.

"Can't you do it online?" Laila asked.

"Nope. Tell Mom when she gets off the phone," Abby said and grabbed her coat. She jammed her hands through the sleeves and raced outside. Full of so many different emotions, she walked blindly away from the house. She skipped getting into her orange Volkswagen Beetle, hoping the cold air would freeze her feelings.

She was torn between swearing a blue streak and crying. She hated to cry, so she began to swear under her breath. Walking toward town, Abby whispered every bad word she could call to mind. At a younger age, she would have gotten her mouth washed out with soap, but there was no one to tattle on her unless she counted the bare November trees and whistling wind. Unfortunately she used up her repertoire very quickly, and despite her best efforts, her eyes filled with tears.

Chapter One

It had been a long day and it was colder than a well-digger's backside. Cade had been working like a dog and wanted a little reward. He wouldn't be getting it from a woman tonight, so Cade Pritchett looked inside the café, trying to decide whether or not to indulge in a slice of cherry pie.

Cade looked away. Since that insane moment he'd proposed to Thunder Canyon's beauty queen, the woman he'd dated casually the past few years, he'd become all too aware of his burning need for a family of his own. It didn't make sense because Cade wasn't interested in falling in love. He'd done that once and lost the woman to an accident. He wasn't interested in risking his heart, but he wanted more than what he had now. A partnership in his father's business, his own spread just outside of town and his hobby rebuilding motorcycles. Oh, and his hound dog, Stella. He should have listed her first.

From his side, he heard a sniffling sound. Curious, he glanced over and saw Abby Cates wiping her nose as she leaned against the café window. His stomach clenched. Abby, little sister of the woman he'd asked to marry him during the Frontier Days celebration. That had been a monumental mistake.

He heard Abby sniff again and Cade felt a surge of concern. He should check on the girl. The poor thing looked upset. He moved toward her.

"Hey, what's up? Or down?"

Abby glanced up in shock, her wide eyes blinking in surprise. "Hi," she said and gave another sniff and surreptitious wipe of her nose with her tissue. "What are you doing here?"

"Thinking about getting a piece of pie," he said. "Long day."

She nodded and blinked away her tears. "This is the beginning of one of your busy seasons, isn't it?"

"Yeah, how'd you remember?" he asked.

"Osmosis," she said. "I guess I eventually noticed during the last few years when you didn't hang around the house as much."

"Yeah," he said. "So, what's with the sniffles? I don't think it's allergies or a cold."

She shrugged and lowered her gaze, her eyelids hiding her emotions from him. "I don't know. Lots of changes going on at my house. I guess I'm going to miss Laila now that she's getting married," she said, then froze and met his gaze. "I'm so sorry. I didn't mean to say—"

He waved his hand in dismissal. "No problem. My

pride was hurt more than anything else. Laila and I were never crazy in love. I shouldn't have been such a darned fool by proposing to her," he said.

"You weren't the fool. Laila was. She should have never let you get away," she said.

Cade laughed and shook his head. It felt nicer than he'd like to admit for Abby to rush to his defense, but he knew more than most that romance and emotion could be fickle and elusive. He shoved his hands into the pockets of his sheepskin jacket. "You shouldn't be out here in the cold," he said. "Let me buy you a cup of hot chocolate."

She met his gaze for a long moment, and he saw a flurry of emotions he couldn't quite name except one. Defiance.

She licked her lips. "I'd like something a little stronger than hot chocolate."

Surprise punched through him. "Something stronger," he said. "You're a little young for that, aren't you?"

She gave a husky chuckle. "Are you suffering from a little dementia due to your advanced years? I'm twenty-two."

"Whoa," he said. "When did I miss that?"

"I guess you weren't looking," she said wryly. Her chocolate-brown eyes flashed with humor, and his gaze slid over her silky, long brown hair.

"I guess not," he said. "So you want to go to the Hitching Post?"

"Sure," she said with a shrug, and they walked down the street to the town's most popular bar and hangout. It was crowded when they walked inside, so he hooked his hand under her elbow and guided her to the far end of the bar.

"Hey, Abby," a young man said from halfway across the room.

She glanced up and shot the guy a smile.

"Hi, Abby," a young woman called.

"Hey, Corinne," she said.

"You seem pretty popular here," Cade said, finding a space next to the bar. "How often do you come?"

She shook her head and rolled her eyes. "I know those people from my classes at college. I'm usually too busy to spend much time here. They're probably surprised to see me here."

He nodded. "What do you want to drink?"

"A beer's okay," she said with a shrug.

He noticed her lack of enthusiasm. "What kind?"

"Whatever you're having is fine," she said.

He felt a twinge of amusement. "You really don't like beer."

"I'm working on it," she said. "At least once a year."

He laughed out loud. "I'll get you one of those pink girly drinks. Cosmo," he said to the bartender. "And a beer for me. Whatever you have on draft."

Moments later, she sipped her pink martini and he drank his beer. "It's loud in here," he said.

She stirred her drink with the tiny straw. "Yeah, I guess that might bother you older folks," she said with a naughty smile.

He shook his head. Her teasing gave him a kick. "Yeah, I'm thirty. Don't rub it in. What have you been doing lately?"

"School. College," she corrected. "I'm also working at the youth center. And as you know, my family can get a little demanding. I have a part-time job teaching skiing lessons at the resort when I can fit it in. What about you? How's that new motorcycle coming?"

He was surprised she'd remembered. "Close to perfection, but I'm still tinkering with it."

"You wouldn't know perfection if it slapped you in the face," she teased.

Cade liked the way her long eyelashes dipped over her eyes flirtatiously. Someday, Abby could be trouble, he thought. "What do you mean by that?"

"I mean you have that perfection complex. Nothing you do is ever good enough. Not with your woodworking. Not with your motorcycle."

She nailed him in one fell swoop, taking him off guard. "How'd you know that?"

"I've known you for years." She took the last sip of her cosmo martini. "How could I not know that?"

For one sliver of a second, she looked at him as if he was a dork then shrugged. "You want another one?" he asked.

She shook her head and smiled. "No. I'm a lightweight. Already feel this one. I'll take some water."

Cade ordered water for her and continued talking with Laila's little sister with whom he'd played board games and computer games when he'd been waiting for Laila. He was distracted by her mouth. Especially when she licked her lips after taking a sip of her water. Her lips were plump, shiny and sexy. He shouldn't notice, but he sure did.

"So you're busy at work," she said and took another long sip of water. "Bet your father's driving you crazy."

"Yeah," he admitted. "No need to repeat that."

She laughed. "I won't. That could be tricky working

with your dad. I mean, I love my own dad, but I can't control him."

"That's for sure," he said, thinking of his own father.

She clicked her half-empty water glass against his beer and dipped her head. "We agree. Cheers."

"So, what are you majoring in?" he asked.

"Psychology. I finish next spring, but I may need to get an advanced degree. I like working with the teens."

"I can see where you would be good at that," he said, thinking that although Abby appeared very young, she was pretty mature for her age.

"I don't know what I'll do after I graduate. I haven't decided if I'll leave Thunder Canyon or not," she said.

Her statement gave him a start. "You would leave town?"

"I may have to if I want to get an advanced degree. Plus, with everything going on with my family, it may be time for me to strike out on my own by then."

He nodded. "If you wanted to stay, you could get an advanced degree online. And just because you move out of your parents' house doesn't mean you have to move out of town."

She smiled. "You almost sound like you'd like me to stay. That can't be true. You barely notice me."

"You're a quality girl—" He broke off. "Woman," he corrected himself. "I hate to see Thunder Canyon lose a good woman like you."

"Ah, so it's your civic duty to encourage me to stay here," she said.

He felt a twist of discomfort. "Lots of people would miss you."

"Well, I haven't made any decisions yet. I need to finish my classes first. I'm just glad the end is in sight.

What do you think about the rivalry between Lip-Smackin' Ribs and DJ's Rib Shack?"

Cade would have had to have been deaf and blind not to know about the controversy between Thunder Canyon's longtime favorite barbecue restaurant DJ's Rib Shack and the the new rib place, which featured waitresses dressed in tight T-shirts. "I'm a DJ's man all the way. I don't like it that the Hitching Post started featuring LipSmackin' Ribs on the menu and I refuse to order them. I'll buy drinks here, but no ribs."

"So you've never even visited LipSmackin' Ribs?"

"I went a few times just to see what the fuss was about," he said.

"You mean the skimpy uniforms the waitresses wear," she said.

He shook his head and rubbed his jaw. "I pity your future boyfriend. He won't be able to pull anything over on you."

"Future? How do you know I don't have a boyfriend right now?" she asked. "I don't, but I certainly could. There are even some men who think I'm attractive, some who ask me to go out with them."

"I didn't mean it that way. And you be careful about those guys. You make sure they have the right intentions."

She shot him a playfully sly look so seductive he almost dropped his beer. "What would you say are the right intentions?" she asked.

His tongue stuck in the back of his throat for a few seconds. "I mean just that—you need to make sure they have the right intentions. You shouldn't let anyone take advantage of you."

"Unless that's what I want him to do, right?"

He choked on his beer. Where had this vixen come from? Although she'd been a spirited competitor whenever she'd played games and been far more knowledgeable about sports than most females he knew, Cade had always seen her as Laila's sweet little sister. "I think it's time for you to go home. I'm starting to hear things come out of your mouth that aren't possible." He waved for the bartender to bring the bill.

"Oh, don't tell me I scared big, strong Cade Pritchett," she teased as he finished his beer and tossed some bills on the counter.

"There's more than one way to scare a man. Let's go," he said and ushered her through the bar to the door.

Abby felt higher than a kite. She'd been waiting forever for the time when it was just her and Cade. She'd had a secret crush on Cade since even before her sister had dated him, and watching Laila's wishy-washy attitude toward Cade had nearly put her over the edge on more than one occasion during the past few years.

But now, she thought, her heart beating so fast she could hardly breathe, she had Cade all to herself, if only for a few more moments. "So is most of your work right now for people who want to get special Christmas gifts?"

"A good bit of it," he said. "But there's a potential for a big order. We'll find out soon." He stopped abruptly. "Is that old man Henson trying to change a tire on his truck?" he asked, pointing down the street.

Abby tore her gaze from Cade's and felt a twist of sympathy mixed with alarm. "I think it is. Isn't he almost eighty-five? He shouldn't be changing a tire during daylight let alone at this time of night," she said.

"Exactly," he said and quickened his pace. "Mr. Henson," he called. "Let me give you a hand with that."

Abby joined Cade as they reached the elderly man, who'd already jacked up the truck. "I'm fine," he said, glancing up at them, his craggy face wrinkled in a wince of pain. "It's these dang rusted bolts."

"Let me take a shot at them. Abby, maybe Mr. Henson might like a cup of that hot chocolate I was talking about earlier."

"I don't need any hot chocolate," Henson said. "I'm fine."

"I'm not," Abby said. "Would you keep me company while I drink some to warm me up?"

Henson opened his mouth to protest then sighed as he adjusted his hat. "Well, okay. But make it quick. I gotta deliver some wood in the morning."

Abby shot a quick look at Cade and shook her head. Mr. Henson was legendary for his work ethic. She admired him for it, but she also knew he'd gotten into a few situations where he'd had to be rescued. Flashing Henson a smile, she hooked her arm through his and walked to the café.

She made chitchat with the man while they sat in a booth and waited for their hot chocolate. She noticed Mr. Henson kept glancing out the window. "Your truck will be fine. It's in good hands with Cade."

"Oh, I know that," Mr. Henson said. "Cade's a fine young man. You'll do well with him."

She dropped her jaw at his suggestion then gave a wry laugh. "I think so, too, but I don't believe he sees me that way, if you know what I mean," she said and took a sip of the hot drink.

He wrinkled his already deeply furrowed forehead

and wiggled his shaggy gray eyebrows. "What do you mean? You're a pretty girl. I'm sure you turn quite a few heads."

"Thank you very much," she said. "That means a lot coming from you."

"It's true. I've never been known for a silver tongue. My Geraldine, rest her soul, would tell you the same. Although she *was* the prettiest woman to ever walk the streets of Thunder Canyon. I still miss her."

Abby slid her hand over Mr. Henson's. "I'm so sorry. How long were you married?"

"Fifty-three years," he said. "That's why I keep working. If I sit at home, I'll just pine. Better to be moving around, doing something."

"But you could afford to take a break every now and then. We don't want anything happening to you," she said and made a mental note to stop in and visit Mr. Henson. His loneliness tugged at her heart.

He shrugged. "I'll go when the good Lord says I'm ready, and not a minute before." He glanced outside the window. "Looks like Cade's finished changing my tire. We should go now. Let me pay the bill. And don't you argue with me," he said when she'd barely let out a sound. "I don't get to share some hot chocolate with a girl as pretty as you very often these days."

"And you said you didn't have a silver tongue," she said. "Thank you."

The two left the café and caught up with Cade, who appeared to be looking for a place to wipe some of the grease off his hands. Abby offered the paper napkin she'd wrapped around her cup of hot chocolate.

He made do with it. "Thanks," he said then glanced at the truck again. "It's no wonder you had trouble with those bolts. I had to bang on them to get them loose. You'll get that tire repaired soon, won't you?" he asked.

"I'll get to it. I'll get to it," Henson said in a testy voice as he inspected the job Cade had done changing his tire. "Thank you," he said with a nod. "What do I owe you?"

Cade shook his head. "Nothing," he said.

"Aw, come on. I gotta give you something for your trouble," Henson said.

"Okay, I'll tell you what you can give me," Cade said. "You can stay out of trouble."

Henson glared at Cade for a moment then laughed. "I'll see what I can do. Thank you again. And, uh—" He glanced at Abby. "Take care of that pretty girl. You shouldn't let a good one like her get away."

Abby shot a quick look at Cade's disconcerted expression. Her face flamed with heat and she quickly focused her attention on her hot chocolate—blowing on it, sipping. "Thanks for the hot chocolate, Mr. Henson. Good night, now," she said.

She stood beside Cade as the old man got into the car and drove away.

"I'll give you a ride home. My car's just down the street. That Henson is a character, isn't he?" Cade muttered, leading her to his vehicle.

"I have to agree. So are you," she said, wishing the evening wouldn't end.

He opened the car door and glanced at her. "Me?"

"Yes, you," she said. "You're always trying to stay in the background, but here you go again saving the day."

"What do you mean?" he asked as he started the car.

"I mean you're always rescuing somebody. It's just what you do. White Knight syndrome?"

He looked at her for a long moment with an expression on his face that made her breath stop in her chest. He looked at her as if he were seeing her as more than Laila's little sister. "I didn't think anyone noticed," he finally said.

"Of course I notice," she managed in a voice that sounded breathless to her own ears.

He glanced away and put the car in gear, driving toward her home. Abby was torn between relief and disappointment. She had wanted that sliver of a moment to continue, yet she could breathe a little better now.

"Is that an official diagnosis? White Knight syndrome?" he asked, his mouth lifting in a half grin of amusement.

"No. I don't think you're clinically maladjusted. You're just a good man," she said, although *good* was putting it lightly. Cade was much more than a good man.

He glanced at her and chuckled. "Thank you. I feel better."

"That will be five dollars," she said and laughed at his sideways glance at her. "Just kidding. I'm not licensed to practice."

They approached her street and her stomach knotted. She tried to think of a way to continue this special time. She didn't want it to end. "I always thought that was strange. A doctor practices medicine. An attorney practices law. What if they have a lousy day practicing?"

Cade pulled the car to a slow stop and shifted into Park. "Good point. I try to avoid both if possible."

Abby drank in the sight of him, meeting his watchful blue gaze and noting the vapor of his breath from his mouth. His strong chin matched his character and determination and his broad shoulders had always made her think he could carry anything life threw at him. He'd suffered some deep losses. She knew that beneath that sheepskin jacket, his muscles were well developed from the times he'd played touch football with her extended family in the backyard.

She knew a lot about him, but she wanted to know so much more. She wanted to slide underneath that jacket and feel him against her. Maybe it was time to take a chance. A crazy chance. Her heart raced so fast she felt lightheaded.

"I've always liked your eyes," she said in a low voice.

His gaze widened in surprise. "What?"

"I've always liked your eyes," she repeated. "They say so much about you. You have this combination of strength and compassion and the first place you see it is in your eyes." She bit her lip then leaned closer to him. "Of course, the rest of you isn't bad, either."

"It's not?" he echoed. She saw a lot of curiosity and flickers of sensuality in his gaze.

"Not bad at all," she said, sliding her hand up the front of his jacket. Taking her courage in her hand, she tugged at his jacket to bring his head closer to hers. Then she pressed her mouth against his, relishing the sensation of his closeness and his lips meshed with hers. He rubbed his mouth against hers and she suddenly felt his hand at her back, drawing her breasts against his chest.

His response sent a flash of electricity throughout her and she opened her lips to deepen the kiss. He took advantage, sliding his tongue inside her. Craving more, she gave what she knew he was asking. Despite the cold temperature, she felt herself grow warmer with every passing second of his caress. Warm enough to strip off her coat and…

Cade suddenly pulled his mouth from hers and stared at her in shock. "What the—" He shook his head and swore, taking a giant step away from her. "I'm sorry." He swore again. "I shouldn't have done that."

"But you didn't start it," she said, her heart sinking at his response.

He held up his hands. "No, really. I shouldn't—" He cleared his throat. "You go on home, now. I'll watch from here."

"But, Cade—"

"Go inside, Abby," he said in a voice that brooked no argument.

Still tempted to argue, Abby had pushed her courage as far as it would go tonight. She swung away from him, hopped out of the car and slammed the door behind her. Striding home, she was caught between euphoria and despair. He had kissed her back and he sure seemed to like it. For those few seconds, he had treated her like a woman he desired. This time she hadn't imagined the way he tasted, the way his lips felt against hers, his hand at her back, urging her closer. This time, it had been real.

But then the man had apologized for kissing her. The knowledge made her want to scream in frustration. Was she back where she'd started? Was she back to being Laila's little sister?

Chapter Two

Cade would have mainlined his third cup of coffee after lunch if it had been possible. He hadn't slept well last night and had felt off all day. He stripped another screw for the designer desk he was making for an entertainment hotshot in L.A., and swore under his breath.

His father and partner, Hank, was talking, but Cade was trying to focus on the desk instead of the way Laila's sister had kissed him last night. And worse yet, he thought, closing his eyes in deep regret, the way he'd kissed her back.

Cade tried to shake off the thoughts and images that had been tormenting him since he'd apologized and burned rubber back to his house. Thoughts about her had haunted him. Her wide brown eyes, her silky, long brown hair and her ruby lips swollen from the friction of his mouth against hers. His own lips burned with the memory, and he rubbed the back of his hand against them, trying to rub away the visual and the guilt. What the hell had he been thinking?

Impatience rushed through him and he grabbed a file. His mind torn in different directions, he stabbed his other hand. Pain seared through him, blood gushed from his hand. Cade swore loudly and stood.

"What are you doing, son?" his father demanded, striding toward him to take a look at Cade's hand.

"It's fine," Cade said. "I'll bandage it and it will be fine."

"You better be up-to-date with your tetanus shot," Hank said.

"I am," Cade said. "I'm not that stupid."

"Based on your performance this morning…" his father began.

"Lay off, Dad," Cade said, looking down at the man who had taught him so much about carpentry and life, the man who'd never recovered from the death of his wife several years ago. None of them had really recovered from the death of Cade's mother. She'd balanced her husband's stern taskmaster nature with softness and smiles.

"Son, I don't want to have to say this, but you need to snap out of your funk. Laila is getting married to someone else, and you're just going to have to get used to it," Hank said bluntly.

Shock slapped through Cade as he stared at his father. He opened his mouth to say he hadn't been thinking about Laila then closed it. He sure as hell didn't want to tell his father he'd been thinking about Laila's little sister Abby.

"You bandage up that hand and go check in on the

community center. They've requested a few things for their Thanksgiving program."

Cade shook his head. "We don't have time for me to go to the community center now. We have too much work."

Hank shook his head. "Get some air, do something different. You'll come back better than ever."

"You know that since we're equal partners, you can't be giving orders," Cade said.

Hank sighed and rolled his eyes. "Okay, consider it a request from your elderly father."

Cade felt a twitch of amusement. His father was still a hard driver, especially in the shop. "Elderly my—"

"Get on out of here," Hank said.

Cade pulled on his jacket and walked out the door, feeling his father's gaze on him as he left. He didn't want his father worrying about him. With a few exceptions during his teen years, Cade had made a point of not causing his parents much grief. Once his mother had gotten sick, his younger brothers had acted up, and Cade knew his father had needed to be able to rely on him. Work had gotten them through the rough times, and for Cade, the loss hadn't stopped with his mother. There'd been Dominique and he'd felt the promise of happiness with her before she'd been taken from him.

Stepping outside the shop, he walked toward the community center a few blocks away. He shook his head, willing the cold air to clear it. He shouldn't be thinking about Abby. It was wrong in so many ways. Putting his mind on the community center's Thanksgiving needs should point him in a different direction. He welcomed the change.

Cade walked inside the glass door of the community center and headed toward the gym at the back of the building. He pushed open the door and his breath hitched at the sight before him. The object of his distraction handed a baby to the community center's children's director, Mrs. Wrenn, and began to climb a ladder holding a humongous horn of plenty.

"What the hell?" he muttered, walking toward the front of the room.

Abby continued to climb the ladder while she lugged the horn of plenty upward. Cade couldn't permit her to continue. "Stop," he said, his voice vibrating against the walls.

Abby toppled at the sound of his voice and whipped her head in his direction. "Cade?"

"Stay right there," he said, closing the space between him and the ladder. He grabbed each side of the metal ladder. "Okay, you can come down now."

Abby's hair swinging over her shoulders, she frowned at him. "Why? I've just got a little farther to go."

"Not while I'm here," he said, his voice sounding rough to his own ears.

Abby shook her head. "But it won't take another minute for me to finish—"

"Come down," he said. "It's not safe. I'll handle it."

She paused long enough to make him uncomfortable. "Abby," he said.

"Okay, okay, but I was doing fine before you got here," she said, descending the ladder.

"That's a matter of opinion," he muttered under his breath as he watched her bottom sway as she wobbled.

She missed the last step and fell against him. He caught her tight and absently grabbed the horn of plenty, his heart pounding.

"Oops," she said after the fact.

Some part of him took note of the sensation of her breasts against his chest, her pelvis meshed against his as she slid downward. His brain scrambled, but he fought it.

"I really would have been fine," she insisted.

"Yeah," he said, unable to keep the disbelief from his voice. "I'll handle the rest of this."

"You're not being sexist, are you?" she demanded. "Because I really *can* do this."

Cade felt his heart rate rise again. "Not sexist," he said. "Just practical. I'm more athletic than you are."

"I don't know," she said. "I played soccer and—"

"I have more upper-body strength," he said, deciding to end the argument once and for all.

He felt Abby's admiring gaze over his broad shoulders. "I can't argue with that," she said.

He felt an odd thrill that he quickly dismissed. "I'll go ahead and hang this horn of plenty," he said. "Do you mind holding the ladder?"

"Not at all," Abby said cheerfully.

Cade climbed the ladder and hung the horn of plenty. He descended to the floor. "My father told me you need a few things for your Thanksgiving show."

Mrs. Wrenn jiggled the toddler and Abby extended her arms to the small boy. "Come here, Quentin."

The toddler fell toward her and Abby laughed, catching him in her arms. "Hiya, sweetie," she said.

The mocha-colored child beamed and giggled as Abby cradled him, clearly feeling safe with her. Cade saw a flash of Abby, laughing, burgeoning with pregnancy and another baby on her hip. Her brown eyes were sexy with humor and womanly awareness.

Cade shook his head, snapping him out of his crazy visual. "How can I help you, Mrs. Wrenn?"

The elderly woman beamed at him. "Thank you so much for coming. We need a ship hull and a table for the pilgrim and Native American dinner. It doesn't have to be too special."

"We can take care of that," Cade said. "We'll get a donated table and dress it up."

"That would be wonderful," Mrs. Wrenn said.

"And I'll work out something with a ship's hull during the next week. How many people do you want on it?"

Mrs. Wrenn winced. "Twenty."

"Whoa," he said. "Good to know. We can take care of that."

Mrs. Wrenn gave a big sigh and clasped her hands together. "Thank you. I knew we could count on you, Cade. We want to give all of the children a chance to feel like stars."

Cade nodded, catching Abby's eye and feeling a flash of kinship with her. He was surrounded by people who either were or felt as if they needed to be stars, but he couldn't be less interested. If he read Abby's wry gaze correctly, then she felt the same way.

"I can do that," he said.

"I knew you could," Mrs. Wrenn said.

He glanced at Abby and the sexy look in her gaze took him off guard. He fastened his gaze on the graying Mrs. Wrenn. "Any particular colors you have in mind?"

The director shrugged. "Harvest colors."

He nodded. "I'll take that back to the shop. Anything else you need?"

"Nothing else I can think of," Mrs. Wrenn said and

glanced at Abby. "Is there anything else that comes to mind? Abby has been nice enough to fill in since my volunteer helper Mrs. Jones had to have bunion surgery."

Abby glanced at the director, then looked at Cade. "Not a thing, but if you get lost, you can contact Mrs. Wrenn or me."

"I don't get lost," Cade said.

"That's a shame," Abby said under her breath, then lifted her shoulders. "Then if you need suggestions."

He shot her a sideways look. "Who does Quentin belong to?" he asked, unable to squelch his curiosity.

Abby's gaze turned serious. "His mother, Lisa, has passed her GED and has completed her LPN. She wants to get her RN. She's just nineteen and one of my ROOTS girls. I told her I would step in as often as possible during her education. She's halfway through her RN."

He felt a shot of admiration. "You're a good friend."

"She's a good mom. It's the least I can do."

Cade's respect for Abby grew. Big brown eyes, long brown hair, she was just Laila's little sister, but now she seemed like so much more. He glanced at the toddler and couldn't hold back a smile. "How are you babysitting with your courses?"

"Just call me Superwoman," she deadpanned. "Kinda like you're Superman."

He felt a crazy hitch in his chest and inhaled quickly. "I'm no Superman."

"Nobody else knows that," she said and shifted the baby on her hip.

His mind flashed. Body. Baby. Come-hither smile. Heaven help him.

Cade cleared his throat. "I'll get back to the shop."

"Thank you for coming, Cade," Mrs. Wrenn said in her squeaky voice.

"Let us know when you need a break," Abby offered, her eyes lowered to a sexy half-mast.

Cade felt a rush of arousal race through him. He swore to himself and turned away. "See you ladies later," he said.

"Anytime," Abby said, and the sexy invitation sent his blood rushing to his groin. Cade swore again, but he suspected the fresh air might not cure his distraction.

Abby was surviving at home, but barely. Although she was happy her sister Laila had found true love and wanted to marry, it was hard to deal with the constant wedding plans. Plus, her cousins were headed down the aisle, too.

Enough was enough and it felt like pulling teeth to get Cade to look at her as if she was more than a fourth grader. Reality beckoned, however, and Abby was forced to join her family for a dinner with Jackson Traub and his sister, Rose. Jackson had managed what many other men had tried by winning over her sister Laila.

"To Laila and Jackson," her father toasted, lifting his glass. "May your love be bigger than your wills."

"Here, here," Abby's mother said.

"Yeah," Abby muttered under her breath and took a big gulp of sparkling wine.

Laila beamed and looked at Jackson. The love between them sizzled. Laila lifted her glass to Jackson and her eyelids lowered in an intimate gaze. "Who would have ever known?"

"Who?" Jackson echoed and clicked her glass against his.

Abby felt a sliver of envy that traveled deeper than

her soul. What she wouldn't give to have Cade look at her that way. *Not in this lifetime,* she thought.

Thank goodness the Cateses understood their priorities. Food was near the top of the list. Soon enough, a platter of roasted chicken was passed her way, followed by mashed potatoes. After that, green beans and biscuits.

Abby took a small spoonful of each dish as it passed. Her mind was preoccupied with Cade. Her appetite was nearly nonexistent. The good news was that everyone's attention was focused on Laila and Jackson, so no one would notice the fact that she wasn't the least bit hungry.

Abby nodded and smiled and pushed her food around her plate then murmured an excuse to get her away from the table. She sought peace in her backyard. It was freezing, but that was no surprise. Abby enjoyed the freezing air that entered her lungs. Despite the fact that it was too cold for words, she was thrilled with the solemn quiet her father's ranch offered at moments like these.

She meandered past the porch and shoved her hands into her pockets.

Seconds later, she heard voices from the back porch.

"I know it's crazy, but Laila is my dream come true," Jackson Traub said. "I never expected it, and she took me by surprise."

"I'm so glad," Rose Traub said. "I was surprised, but happy when it happened. I love that you never thought it would happen to you."

"Thanks," Jackson said, unable to conceal his amusement.

"Humility is the beginning of wisdom," Rose said.

Jackson swore. "You're tough."

"You taught me. I'm just not sure I'll ever find my true love. Maybe he doesn't exist. I feel like I've dated every man in Thunder Canyon."

Abby swallowed a sound of frustration that threatened to bubble from her throat. Rose had been out with a *lot* of Thunder Canyon men. She'd even gone out with Cade, and that hadn't set well with Abby, at all.

"You haven't dated every man. There's still old man Henson and his friends," Jackson joked.

Abby resisted the urge to laugh, but Rose didn't. Her warm chuckle drifted through the cold air. "Thanks for the encouragement. Mr. Henson is eighty-five if he's a day."

"Just kidding," Jackson said. "But the truth is you can find your true love. I did. Don't give up."

"I'm not sure I can count on that," she said.

"Give it a little longer," Jackson said. "You might be surprised."

Seconds later, silence fell over Abby as she stood outside the deck in the dark. She wasn't quite sure what she should take away from the cold night and the conversation she'd overheard.

Abby stared into the horizon, feeling the stars from the sky watching over her. She should leave, she thought, but she felt the stars tracking her. She wanted—no, needed—to feel the stars guiding her to her future. More than anything, she wished a lucky star was shining down on her. A star of love. If not love, then an antidote for love.

Fixing her gaze on the brightest star, she felt a ripple of realization shimmy down her spine. She'd wanted Cade as long as she could remember. She'd pushed herself to flirt with him the other night. Abby felt as if her passion for Cade would never be returned. But she would never be sure if she didn't put herself out there.

Abby had never been much of a flirt, and she had no idea how to be a seductress, but maybe she needed to give it her best shot now. Maybe she needed to do everything she could to make Cade see her as a woman, a desirable woman who wanted him. At that moment, she made a promise to herself. No more shy little sister, hiding behind Laila. Abby needed to find her inner sexpot.

Abby cringed at the thought. Okay, maybe not *sexpot*, but *seductress* had an empowering ring to it…when it didn't make her snicker.

Two days later, Cade took a break from work at the shop and headed for the new bakery in town, the Mountain Bluebell Bakery. He was feeling deprived lately and figured giving in to his sweet tooth was the least of possible evils. Cherry pie or something better sounded great.

He exhaled and his breath sent out a foggy spritz. Noticing a crowd ahead, he slowed as he approached. A news team was interviewing several different citizens of Thunder Canyon.

"So, do you think a down-home ribs meal is good enough to keep customers happy?" the newscaster asked. "Or do you think tight T-shirts and short shorts are necessary in today's market?"

"Nothing wrong with short shorts and tight T-shirts," a man from the crowd yelled.

"But is it necessary?" the newscaster asked.

"Well," the man said, "I guess not. But it sure doesn't hurt."

The crowd laughed.

Suddenly a microphone was put in Cade's face.

"What about you? Do you think a tight T-shirt and short shorts are more important than a home-cooked meal?"

"No," he said without hesitation. "The food and service are great at DJ's. No need for tight T-shirts."

The reporter moved past him and Cade automatically searched the crowd. His gaze landed on Abby on the opposite side of the street. He wondered what she thought of all this. She'd seemed a bit skeptical of the skimpy outfits of LipSmackin' Ribs.

Her gaze met his, and he lifted his hand and gave her the hi sign. She nodded and moved toward him.

Cade noticed the way her long brown hair swung over her shoulders. Her cheeks were pink from the cold and her plump lips shiny and distracting. She had the kind of lips any man would want to kiss.

"Hi," she said as she approached him. "Can you believe this?"

He nodded at the crazy press. "Not really. Who would have thought a debate over ribs would bring national news to Thunder Canyon?"

"I'm with you," she said, glancing over her shoulder at the crowd behind her. "What are you doing out and about?"

"I'm taking a break and checking out the new bakery down the street. I hear they've got some good stuff," he said.

"Mind if join you?" she asked.

Something told him he should refuse, but he didn't give in to it. "What about school?"

"I don't have a class until tonight."

He frowned. "You take night classes? Why don't you stick to day?" he asked.

Her lips twitched. "Because not all of my classes are available during the day."

"Hmm."

"Are you going to buy me a chocolate tart or not?" she asked.

He blinked. "Yeah, I'll buy you a tart. Let's go."

He led the way to the bakery and they ordered their pastries and coffee.

Moments later, the two of them sat at a table with coffee, a chocolate tart and a slice of cherry pie à la mode. Like many of the shops around town, the bakery featured both Thanksgiving and Christmas decorations. The shop owners in Thunder Canyon weren't dummies. They would maximize the holiday season to get the most out of it. Cade, however, wasn't big on Christmas since his mother and Dominique had died years ago.

Abby took a spoonful of chocolate tart into her mouth and closed her eyes in satisfaction. "Now, that is good."

"Yeah," Cade said, fighting a surge of arousal as he took a bite of his cherry pie.

"No, really," she said, lifting a spoon toward Cade. "You should try this."

Cade glanced into her brown eyes then felt his gaze dip deeper to her cleavage. When had Abby Cates gotten cleavage?

Cade cleared his throat. "I'm game," he said and opened his mouth.

He felt her slide the spoon and decadent chocolate past his lips onto his tongue. His temperature rose. He swallowed.

"Good," he managed.

"Of course it is," she murmured.

Cade met her gaze and felt a wicked stirring throughout him. Something about Abby made him...hard.

She took a sip of coffee and looked at Cade from the rim of her coffee mug. "Coffee's not really my favorite," she said. "When it comes to hot drinks, I'd rather have hot chocolate or apple cider."

"I'll take coffee," Cade said.

"But what if you had a choice?" Abby asked. "What would you choose?"

"Coffee with cream and hazelnut," he said.

"Smells delicious," Abby said, closing her eyes and smiling.

"But do you want to drink it?" he asked.

"Not so much," she said. "But I would love to smell it."

He chuckled and she opened her eyes. "What's wrong with smelling?" she asked.

"Nothing," he said. "Nothing at all."

She got to the end of her tart and there was one bite left. "Bet you want it," she said, waving the spoon in front of his mouth.

The motion was incredibly seductive, and he found himself craving what she offered. Or maybe he was craving what he wanted. He couldn't quite tell what Abby was offering, but it was a big no-no. Or was it?

He clasped his hand over hers, the last bite of chocolate hanging between them.

"Take it," she urged.

Her voice was too sexy to ignore. He grabbed her hand and drew it to his mouth. Cade enveloped the chocolate with his mouth and swallowed it down. The motion was both carnivorous and sexual.

Abby's brown eyes widened in surprise.

"What did you expect?" he asked.

"I don't know," she said. "Something more..."

"Polite?" he asked.

Her eyes darkened. "Maybe. If so, I'm glad I was wrong."

His gut tightened. "You need to be careful. You're asking for trouble."

"Just from you," she said.

His heart hammered against his rib cage. "This is a bad idea."

"There are worse ideas," she countered.

He felt himself begin to sweat. How could Laila's little sister affect him this way? It wasn't possible.

"Go away, little girl," he said and pulled back.

"I'm not a little girl," she said.

"You're too young for me," he said.

"Says who?" she challenged.

Her defiance caught him by surprise. "Says anyone with any sanity."

Abby leaned toward him, her eyes full of everything he shouldn't be thinking. "Haven't you heard? Sanity's overrated."

"I don't know what game you're playing, Abby. But I'm not playing," he told her with finality.

Chapter Three

Abby's ego bruised *again,* she buried herself in her schoolwork and decided to follow up on her intention to visit Mr. Henson. She hadn't seen his old truck in town during the past few days and decided he might enjoy some leftover chicken and dumplings Abby and her mother had made last night. She also brought along a wreath to add a little holiday cheer to his home, hoping it might lift his spirits. She drove her orange VW toward his place and slowed as she turned onto his dirt driveway. The ground was too frozen to allow the dust to kick up the way it would in the summer, she thought as she pulled in front of the old white farmhouse.

Although Mr. Henson did far more than most folks thought he should, Abby knew he'd finally given up on ranching several years ago and leased his acreage to a local rancher. The old blue truck with peeling paint was parked next to the house, which meant he should be home.

Abby picked up the container of food and got out of her car. She noticed the steps to his porch were still crusty with ice and wondered if he had any salt she could throw on them for him. Knocking on the door, she paused and listened, but there was no response. She knocked again and heard a faint reply.

"Mr. Henson, it's Abby Cates. Are you okay?"

She heard the sound of slow footsteps and moments later, the door finally opened. Abby was surprised at the sight of him. His face was grizzly with white stubble, his hair hadn't been combed and his clothes were rumpled.

"What are you doing here?" he demanded in a cranky voice.

"I came to see you and I brought some chicken and dumplings," she said.

His eyes lit with faint approval. "Oh, well, that's nice of you. Come on in," he said and hobbled inside. "Where's that Pritchett young man? Aren't you two married?"

"No," she said. "Cade Pritchett barely knows I'm alive."

Mr. Henson glanced over his shoulder. "That's his mistake, I'd say."

She noticed his grimace as he took a step and her alarm buttons started to go off. "Mr. Henson, you're limping. What's wrong?"

He waved his hand. "Oh, it's nothing. Couple logs fell on my leg when I was delivering wood. You mind if I heat up those dumplings? I bet they're tasty."

"They are, but I think you might need to get your ankle checked by a doctor," she said.

"Doctors usually can't do anything. Medicine is just one more racket, I say."

"But—"

"You gonna make me beg for those dumplings?" he asked.

She sighed. "No. Sit down and I'll heat them up for you," she said and walked toward the kitchen, then turned as something occurred to her. "If you'll let me take you into town to see the doctor as soon as you finish eating."

He scowled at her. "I'm telling you, it's a waste of time and money."

"It will make me feel better," she told him. "I'm worried about you. You're not yourself."

His gaze softened. "Well, you're being silly," he said gruffly. "I'll go," he said, sinking onto the sofa. "But not until I eat those dumplings."

Thirty minutes later, he'd finished the food and she hung the wreath on his front door.

"What's that for?" he asked as he shuffled toward her car.

Abby adjusted the red bow. "To give you some Christmas spirit."

He muttered and got into her car. Abby drove toward town with Mr. Henson fussing the entire way about her car.

"What can you carry with this thing, anyway? Bet my lawn-mower engine is bigger than this. What keeps it running?" he asked. "Sounds like squirrels."

"The only thing I have to carry is me," she said. "I

don't haul wood, and this car is surprisingly good in the snow."

"Can't believe that," he said. "You'd get stuck in six inches."

"It's light, so it doesn't sink, plus the gas mileage is terrific. What kind of gas mileage does your truck get?"

He made a mumbling sound that she couldn't understand. "Excuse me? What did you say?"

"Fifteen miles to the gallon," he said. "But I could haul most of the houses around here if I wanted."

She bit her tongue, refusing to point out the obvious, that there was no need to haul houses. Turning off the main drive, she pulled next to the clinic door.

"This is a no-parking zone," he told her.

"I know," she said. "I just wanted to get you as close to the door as possible."

"Hmmph," he said and opened the car door.

"Just a minute," she said, cutting the engine and rushing to the passenger side of the car.

"Gotta be a darned pretzel to ride in that car," he grumbled, but leaned against her as she helped him inside the clinic. Two hours later, she helped Mr. Henson back to the car as he hobbled on crutches.

"Just a sprain," he said. "I told you it wasn't anything and I'm not taking that pain medication. It makes me loopy."

"It's not a narcotic," she said as she carefully arranged the crutches in her backseat. "Do you have plastic bags?"

"Yeah, why?" he asked.

"For the ice. The doctor said you need to put ice on your ankle."

Mr. Henson shrugged.

"Well, if you don't want to get better and you want to keep feeling rotten, you don't need to follow his instructions."

She felt the old man whip his head toward her. "I didn't say that," he said.

"The doctor said between the bad bruise and sprain it's a wonder you didn't break it. So you need to take care of it. RICE is what he said."

"Yeah, yeah," he said. "Rest, ice, compression and elevation."

"You can sit back and watch some TV," she suggested.

"Hate that reality stuff. Give me a book or a ball game instead."

"That could be arranged," she said. "I think my mother said something about fixing some beef stew. Maybe I could bring some over for you if you behave yourself."

The old man licked his lips. "That sounds good."

She smiled. "You'll get better faster if you do what the doctor says."

"Maybe," Mr. Henson said and paused. "You know, you would make a good wife. You nag like a good wife would."

Abby didn't know whether to feel complimented or insulted.

"Cade Pritchett will be chasing you sooner than you think," he said.

"Not in this lifetime," she said.

Mr. Henson lifted a wiry gray eyebrow. "You disrespecting your elder?"

"No," Abby said reluctantly. "I just can't fight reality."

"Girlie," he said, "I'm eighty-five and I lost Geraldine, my reason for living, eight years ago. I fight reality every day."

She couldn't argue with that.

After that, Abby focused on her schoolwork and her work at ROOTS, a community group founded for at-risk teens. Abby led her girls' teen group on Tuesday nights where they talked about everything from bullies and sex to cosmetics and higher education.

The truth was most of the girls in Abby's group were pretty cool. They were older than their years and saw Abby as the person they wanted to become. She was humbled by their admiration.

"So, we've told you about our guys. When are you gonna tell us about yours?" Keisha, a wise-to-the-world fifteen-year-old, asked.

"I don't really have a guy," Abby said.

Silence settled over the group and Abby felt an unexpected spurt of discomfort. "Well, I *could* have a guy. It's just that the guy I want doesn't see me."

Shannon, a sixteen-year-old with purple hair, frowned. "Is he blind?"

Abby chuckled. "Not in the physical sense. He used to date my sister, so he sees me as the little sister."

"Oooh," Katrina, who wore faux black leather from head to toe, said. "Drama. I love it. Does your sis know you like the guy?"

Abby shook her head.

"Does *she* like this guy?" Keisha asked.

"Oh, no. She's engaged to someone else."

"Well, then, you should definitely move in on him," Katrina said.

Abby laughed uncomfortably. "He sees me as the little sister."

"You should change that," Shannon said. "Maybe you could dye your hair pink."

"I'm not sure that's me," Abby said.

"Well, you have to do something different," Shannon said, her gaze falling over Abby in a combination of pity and disapproval. "You're, like, everything but sexy."

"She's not ugly," Keisha said.

"I didn't say that," Shannon said. "She's just not sexy."

"I don't know," Katrina said. "She's got that fresh, natural, girl-next-door look."

"But *not* sexy," Shannon repeated.

Silence followed.

"We could help you," Shannon said.

Alarm slammed through her. "Help?" she echoed in a voice that sounded high-pitched to her own ears.

"Yeah," Keisha said, clearly warming to the idea. "We can sex you up. Your guy won't be able to ignore you then."

"I'm not sure…" Abby said.

"Hey, it's like you always tells us," Shannon said. "If you always do what you've always done, you'll always get what you've always gotten."

Abby blinked at the sound of her words played back to her. True, but how much of a change was she willing to make?

"If you won't do pink or blond hair, then we can do big hair," Shannon said, pursing her profoundly pink lips.

"And cat eyes," Keisha added.

"And a short, black leather skirt," Katrina added.

Abby winced inwardly. *Black leather skirt?*

Shannon nodded. "Kim Kardashian hair. He won't know what hit him."

Abby managed to redirect the conversation, but she knew her girls were determined to perform a drastic makeover. She ran into her fellow ROOTS volunteer, Austin Anderson, after the meeting. Austin was twenty-four years old and the two of them were good friends, thanks to their time spent working together.

"How's it going?" Austin asked and stepped beside her as she walked toward her car in the small parking lot.

"Okay," she said and knew her voice didn't hold the commitment it should have.

Austin laughed. "Let's try this again," he said. "How's it going?"

"I think I may have just gotten myself into a situation," she said as she drew close to her car.

"What kind of situation?" he asked, putting his hand against her car door before she could open it.

Abby sighed and turned to lean against the car. She reluctantly met his gaze. "I did a bad thing," she said.

"You sold drugs or killed a baby," he said.

She couldn't withhold a chuckle. "Neither. I did, however, get drawn into a discussion about my personal life with my ROOTS girls group. Now they want to perform a sexy makeover."

He laughed. "Hooker time."

She shot him a sideways glance. "Kinda. But they make an important point. They repeated my words of wisdom back to me. If you always do what you've always done, you'll always get what you've always gotten."

He nodded. "Okay."

"Well, if I go through with this makeover, I may need a cohort."

Austin stared at her for a long moment. "I'm not sure this is a good idea."

"It probably isn't, but I need to shake things up."

Austin gave a heavy sigh. "What do you have in mind?"

"I dress up in makeover mode. You and I hit the town in places where people will talk. My unrequited love wakes up and sees that I am the answer to his heart's desire."

Austin winced. "Abby, I'm really not sure this is a great idea."

"I'm sure it isn't," she said. "But I have to do something to shake up Cade's impression of me."

"Cade?" Austin echoed. "Cade Pritchett." He gave a low whistle and shook his head. "Isn't he the one who proposed to your—"

"Yes," she said in a flat tone.

Austin took a deep breath. "Okay, I'm in. Let me know when you want to do this."

"Apparently Saturday night," she said in a wry tone. "It's the most visible night."

Austin nodded and raked his hand through his hair. "All right. Text me with the time." Austin brushed his finger over her nose sympathetically. "You're a great girl. If he doesn't realize it, he's an idiot."

"So far, he's an idiot," she whispered, her heart hurting.

The following Saturday, the ROOTS teens performed their magic on Abby. As she stared into the mirror, she wasn't sure if it was magic or something more gruesome.

"Are you sure…" she began as she looked at her dark eye makeup.

"It's perfect," Keisha said.

"You are so hot," Katrina said. "You're going to knock every guy off his feet."

Abby was not at all sure. She squinted her eyes at her teased hair, trying to see a remnant of her usual self.

"Ready to go?" Austin asked from the back of the room.

Abby took a deep breath and turned to look at him.

"Oh. Wow," he said.

Abby felt a sudden spurt of panic. "What does *'Oh. Wow'* mean?"

Austin strolled toward her. "You look hot. You'll turn heads. Look out, Thunder Canyon."

Abby rose and walked toward him. "You're lying like a dog, aren't you?"

"Not at all," he said. "You're going to turn heads like nobody's business tonight. Are you ready?"

She met his gaze and quieted her crazy heartbeat. "Not really," she said. "But that first jump in cold water is the hardest. It may as well be now."

Abby and Austin visited the hottest bars and made sure she was seen by the maximum number of people. Their last stop was an old bar on Main Street. Surprisingly enough, Cade was at this bar watching a ball game. He didn't even notice her as she sashayed inside with Austin.

Austin, however, noticed Cade. He ordered Abby another soda water, her fifth of the evening. She countered with a martini.

Austin raised his eyes. "Lemon drop?" he asked. "I'd say you've earned it."

Abby propped on a bar stool and tried to look flirty as she sipped her lemon-drop martini.

It was a little bitter, so she switched off to ice water. She jiggled her leg from the bar stool and wondered if Cade would ever tear his gaze from the screen.

Suddenly, Austin gave a loud laugh that startled her and vibrated throughout the bar. He leaned toward her and nuzzled her.

Abby blinked in shock. *Holy buckets.*

"Play along," he said in a low voice.

Oh, yeah, she thought and nuzzled him back and giggled. That was what she was supposed to do. Right?

Out of the corner of her eye, she saw Cade looking at Austin and her. He didn't look happy. She forced a light laugh.

"He's looking, isn't he?" Austin said as he lifted his fingers to her cheek.

"Yes," she said in a low voice.

"It's what you wanted, isn't it?" he asked.

Abby felt torn. "I guess."

Austin shook his head. "Better make up your mind. He's right behind you," he muttered. "Cade," he said. "Old man, how ya doing? I see a friend on the other side of the room. I'll be back in a minute—darlin'," he added to Abby.

Abby turned to look at Cade. His face looked like a thundercloud. "Hi," she said. "How's the game?"

He shrugged. "It's California against Clemson."

She smiled. "Not close enough to care."

"I guess. What the hell have you done to your hair?"

Abby frowned. "Dressed it up. Dressed me up," she said.

"You don't need to dress up," he said. "You're asking for trouble dressed like that."

Abby frowned at him, feeling a double spurt of frustration and anger. "Some people might say I looked pretty."

"Some people would say anything to get you into bed," Cade said.

Offended, Abby narrowed her eyes at him. "You just need to butt out of my date. I'm having a good time. There's nothing wrong with that."

Austin appeared from behind Cade and lifted his eyebrows. "Ready to go, sweetheart?"

Abby frowned in Cade's direction. "Sounds good to me," she said and rose from her bar stool. It took every bit of her concentration not to look at Cade. "G'night," she said, without meeting his gaze, and hooked her arm with Austin's as she strutted out of the bar.

As she and Austin stepped into the cold night, she sucked in a clean breath of air. "I'm not sure that worked."

Austin chuckled. "Well, I think you showed him what he's missing."

His sense of humor lifted her spirits. "Thanks for being a good soldier."

"It wasn't so bad. It's not like I have anyone waiting for me," he said.

She studied his eyes, trying to read him. "I would almost think there was someone you want waiting for you."

"Don't worry about it," Austin said, opening the passenger door to his SUV.

"Hmm," she said, wondering if Austin could have a crush on someone. And for whom would he be pining?

Austin drove her home and she stepped outside the car. "Thank you for indulging my craziness," she said.

Austin shrugged. "We're all crazy in our own special way."

Abby laughed. "Thanks. You make me feel a little better. I think you may have been right from the beginning. This wasn't a great idea."

"You never know," he said. "He might surprise you."

"I won't count on it," she said. "But thanks, anyway."

She watched as he pulled out of her driveway then reluctantly turned toward her home, wondering if she could make it to her bedroom before any of her family saw her because they would give her a hard time for dressing so out of character. The house wasn't well lit. Abby suddenly recalled her mother mentioning something about a Brunswick-stew dinner being held at the local Knights of Columbus. Her father loved Brunswick stew and, if the dinners were cheap, she suspected the rest of her family was chowing down, too. Her mother must have been thrilled to skip meal preparation tonight.

She stomped through the frozen snow to the front door of her home and opened the door. She waited in silence, listening for signs of her family. Nothing. Thank goodness. She breathed a sigh of relief then suddenly heard a tap at the door.

Wincing, Abby eyed the peephole and got the shock of her life. She blinked to make sure she wasn't dreaming. It was Cade.

Taking a deep gulp of breath, she swung open the door. "Forget something?" she asked.

He narrowed his eyes at her. "You okay?"

"Of course I'm okay," she said, unable to conceal her impatience and a bit of witchiness.

His gaze fell over her. "I was worried about you," he muttered.

"Why?" she asked, leaning against the doorjamb.

"The way you were dressed. I didn't want your date to take advantage of you," he said.

"He was a perfect gentleman," Abby said.

"Yeah, well—" He sighed, his gaze falling over her. "You gonna invite me in?"

Surprised, Abby stepped backward. "Sure. Come on in."

The foyer was dimly lit by a lamp.

Cade stepped toward her and lifted his hand to her hair. "You don't need all this makeup and gunk clouding your natural beauty. What were you thinking?"

Abby swallowed over a lump of emotion. "Natural beauty?" she echoed.

"Yeah," he said and stroked her hair. "Why would you mess with this?"

She opened her mouth and stared at him. "Umm." She shrugged her shoulders. "I don't—"

His mouth descended onto hers.

Abby gasped, trying to swallow her shock.

"You're hot without all the makeup," he told her, and she felt her world turn upside down.

Somehow, the two of them stumbled to the couch in the den. She fell backward and he followed her down. His weight was the sexiest thing she'd ever felt in her life. She closed her arms and legs around him.

Cade devoured her mouth and slid between her legs. His hardness meshed against her, making her wish the clothes between them would dissolve. She wanted him inside her. There was no such thing as close enough.

He rubbed and she arched. His tongue tangled with hers. *Give me more,* she thought. *Give me all of you.*

Cade swore under his breath, but continued to kiss her. He kissed her as if she was the most important thing in the world. Abby was hot with want and need. She'd wanted him so long, so very long.

His hand slid to her breast and she stopped breathing. He rubbed her nipple. Abby arched toward him. He groaned into her mouth. The sound was so sexy she couldn't stand it.

"I want you so much," she whispered desperately.

"I want you," he muttered and thrust against her.

Abby heard, felt something in the room, but Cade overpowered her senses.

The sound of a gasp took her slightly away from Cade's spell. "What?" she murmured.

"Oh, my God. How perfect is this."

Abby blinked, hearing her sister's voice. She tugged her mouth from Cade's and felt him look in the same direction.

Laila smirked. "This really is perfect. Why didn't I see it before?"

Mere breaths later, he rose from Abby and stood. He glanced from Laila to Abby, but his gaze lingered on Abby. "Crazy," he said. "This was crazy. I can't explain it. I'm sorry. I should go," he said and left.

Abby stared after him, trying to compute everything that had happened. Why had he kissed her? She wondered what would have happened if Laila hadn't interrupted them. Abby felt a rush of frustration and met her sister's gaze.

"Oops," Laila said. "It could have been worse. Everyone else is on their way back from the Brunswick-stew dinner."

Abby rose from the couch. "Why don't I feel better?"

"It's not my fault I walked in on the two of you. It's not like you sent up a warning flare," Laila said.

Abby could have screamed. "Do you have any idea what it's like being your sister?"

Laila blinked. She winced. "That bad?"

"Beauty queen a gajillion times over, super success-ful. Worse, there's Cade."

Laila bit her lip. "How long…"

Abby shook her head. "Longer than you want to know."

Laila gave a slow nod. "Sorry," she said.

"Yeah," Abby said and rose from the couch.

"I gotta ask. What's with the outfit?" Laila asked, waving her hand toward Abby's leather skirt and tight top.

"It was an experiment," Abby said, not wanting to linger on her so-called makeover.

Laila laughed. "Bet you knocked Cade on his ass."

Abby bit her lip because she wasn't sure what Cade would do tomorrow. "I'd appreciate it if you wouldn't broadcast what you interrupted tonight," Abby said. "G'night."

Cade drove his SUV to his place outside of town. He was torn between arousal and the overwhelming feel-ing of insanity. What had he been thinking?

He had not been thinking. That was the point.

He'd seen Abby dressed like sex on a stick, felt pro-tective and chased after her, then gave in to some insane urges. He was still hard from kissing and holding her.

He had definitely gone insane and he needed to bring himself back to sanity, no matter how painful it was.

Pulling into his long driveway, he sucked in a deep breath and pulled to a stop. He cut the lights of his SUV and felt a sense of loneliness at the thought of nothing going on inside his house with no one waiting for him.

A sliver of Dominique slid through his mind like a ghost. He remembered her black hair and her laughing black eyes. He'd hoped she could heal him, but he hadn't been sure. When he'd finally gotten around to deciding to ask her to marry him, she'd died in an automobile accident. That seemed as if it had been a lifetime ago. Years earlier, his mother had died and his family was trying to dig their way out of their grief.

After Dominique he'd just closed the door on his emotions. It had been the easiest route. Then, Laila had seemed just like him. Emotionally closed off. After dating her off and on for years, it had made sense to Cade for them to marry. In many ways, they were the same. They were getting to the place where they should go ahead and do the baby thing, so perhaps he and Laila should get married.

In retrospect, it had been a crazy idea, and he deeply regretted pursuing the possibility. Cade wanted a family of his own, and he hated that he wanted it. Life would be so much easier without that strong desire. He could work at his family's furniture shop, build his motorcycles, contribute to the community, take a woman friend every now and then and his life would be fine.

Right?

Or not.

Cade swore under his breath and raked his hand through his hair. He'd just made out with Laila's little sister. How screwed up could this situation be? Shaking his head at himself, he stepped out of his truck and walked into his lonely-ass house. The dog greeted him at the door. Thank goodness for man's best friend.

Strolling to the refrigerator, he grabbed a beer. The sound of his footsteps echoed on the wood floor of his foyer and kitchen. Is that what he was going to hear for the rest of his life? The sound of his boot heels on his own kitchen floor?

What was wrong with that?

He took a long swig of his beer and headed for the den, his dog, Stella, trailing after him all the way. Cade found the remote and turned on his giant flat-screen TV. He flicked through a few channels. Thank goodness there was a college football game. He didn't care who was playing.

Sinking down on his leather couch, he took another long swig of beer then sucked in a deep breath. He stared at the big-screen TV and waited for the game to anesthetize him. The thought of Abby's lips against his slid through his mind. The sensation of her lips, soft, silky, swollen, slick.

Her breasts had felt so good against his chest. Her nipples against his chest, his palm. Lower, lower, he'd rubbed against her. She'd arched against him.

He'd given in to the urge to slide his hands lower, to seek out her secrets. He'd felt her damp arousal.

Then Laila had walked in.

Cade swore under his breath. He didn't want to think about this anymore. He should focus on the game and his beer instead.

An hour and a half later, he woke himself up with a snort. He blinked, staring at the screen. The game was over. An infomercial about an exercise machine was playing.

Cade stared at it for a few minutes then flicked off the TV. A soft lamp kept the darkness from completely enveloping him. In the past, the darkness had been comforting. But now…

Now he wanted more and now he wanted Abby. And that was insane. Super insane.

His body grew hard too quickly and he swore again. Rising from the couch, he headed for the shower. Cade turned the water on cool, stripped off his clothes and stepped inside. A hot shower would have felt a lot better, but he needed to get away from his need for Abby. A cold shower should cure him. That was all he needed to knock some sense into himself and Abby out of his mind.

Chapter Four

Cade did what he'd always done when he was bothered about something. He threw himself into his work. It was good timing because between the approach of the holidays and some new high-dollar custom orders, Pritchett & Sons were slammed.

He sanded a bed head in preparation for stain. A man had commissioned this piece for his wife for their tenth anniversary. It would be a nice piece when he finished it, Cade thought, feeling a nip of envy over the customer's good luck of having a woman and children in his life.

Narrowing his eyes, he refocused on the work at hand. A family just wasn't in the cards for him. At least, not now. Cade heard his brother using the electric screwdriver on a table he was making and glanced over at him. Dean was good company because he didn't talk all that much. Cade couldn't have abided much chattiness at the moment. He was too busy trying to quiet his own mind.

Dean met his gaze and nodded in the direction of the bed head. "That's looking good."

"Yeah, I think Mr. Winston will be pleased with it. Hopefully Mrs. Winston will, too," he said wryly. He'd learned through the years that women often didn't see things the same way men did.

Dean nodded and gave a low chuckle then got back to work.

Cade continued sanding. He found the rhythm of woodworking both soothing and absorbing. From an early age, when his father had taught him the basics, Cade had envisioned little touches he'd wanted to add in the pieces on which he'd worked. His father hadn't discouraged him, and although Hank was more focused on producing solid, basic furniture, Cade had taken an artistic bent.

Within the past few years, people had sought him out for his one-of-a-kind pieces, even asking for his signature on the finished furniture. At first, it had seemed silly to Cade, but the request for his signature had become so frequent, it was now almost a routine.

Nearly finished with the sanding, Cade heard the shop door open and glanced up to see their regular courier, Mike Jones, loaded down with boxes. "Hey, Mike, let me give you a hand with that," Cade said, rising from his bench.

"Thanks. I've got more in the truck."

"I can help," Dean said.

Cade took the boxes into the back room to sort them out later. Seconds later, Dean and Mike brought in more.

"You can tell it's the holiday season just by the number of packages," Cade said.

"For darn sure," Mike said, pulling out his electronic gizmo for Cade's signature. "Unfortunately, holidays can bring out the wackiness in people." He shook his head. "I just made a delivery to the Tattered Saddle and Jasper demanded that I wait while he opened the packages. He tore through them and apparently didn't find what he was looking for. I was waiting for his signature, and he called somebody on the phone yelling about some missing package. And then, I must not have heard correctly, but the old man said something about how the Rib Shack may not be as easy to take down as expected."

Clearly rattled, Mike shook his head again. "Gotta run. More deliveries. See you guys later and thanks for being *sane*."

The courier ran out the door, leaving a rush of cold air in his wake. Cade looked at Dean and saw the same mixture of alarm and confusion written on his brother's face that he felt. "What the—"

Dean lifted his shoulders in confusion. "I've always thought Jasper was odd, but I can't believe he's behind the problems at the Rib Shack. What would he have to gain?"

"You got me," Cade said. "Maybe it's like Mike said and he didn't hear the old man right. Jasper's been known to mutter and mumble."

"Hmm," Dean said, the sound short and full of suspicion.

Cade shrugged it off. "We need to get back to work."

"Yeah. Same for me if I want to make that poker game tonight," Dean said, heading back to the table.

"Just be careful who you're playing with," Cade said.

"I know better than getting in a game with a bad crowd," Dean said with a scowl.

"Just a reminder from someone who's bailed you out a couple of times," Cade said.

"Three years ago," Dean said.

"Some things you don't forget. Like being woken up at 3:00 a.m. because your younger brother has been left in the snow wearing only a pair of underwear and his socks because he bet more than he had."

"Three years ago," Dean repeated with a sigh. "Thanks for coming."

"There was never a doubt I would do anything else."

Dean nodded and they returned to work, but Cade felt his mind turning to thoughts of Abby. He didn't like surprises and he was damn surprised that he'd acted like he had with her. He'd always viewed her almost as a little sister or cousin. She was his little buddy, he'd thought. Not a woman with whom he wanted to share a bed. Now she was someone who made him feel so worked up and *hot*.

Irritated with his distracting thoughts, he tossed his brush aside and stomped to the back room to get a cup of coffee. It may as well have been tar since he'd made it this morning. Sipping it, Cade grimaced and walked out the back door of the shop, hoping the cold air would clear his head and cool his body. A couple minutes later, he walked back inside and returned to his bench.

"You okay?" Dean asked.

"Yeah," Cade said, taking another sip of terrible coffee.

"There's a lot of talk about Laila and Jackson getting married. It's enough to get on anyone's nerves, let alone—"

Cade swore under his breath. "I'm okay with Laila marrying Jackson. I wish them well. Laila isn't who's bothering me."

Dean's eyebrows rose in surprise. "Then who is?"

Reluctant to discuss the subject with anyone, Cade shrugged. "Nobody is. It's just work. I have a lot of work to do. So do you."

"Yeah, whatever," Dean said. "You aren't usually this much of a pain in the butt to deal with just because you've got a lot of work to do."

Cade sighed at his brother's words. He'd been trying so hard not to think about Abby that he hadn't realized he'd been hard on everyone else. "It's not Laila. It's Abby."

"Abby?" Dean echoed. "Abby who? The only Abby I know of is Laila's little sister." Dean must have seen the conflicted expression on Cade's face. "Really? Abby Cates?"

"I'm not sure how it happened. I saw her crying a few weeks ago and offered to buy her a hot chocolate. Somehow we ended up at the Hitching Post instead. I drove her home, and she kissed me."

"Whoa, that must have caught you off guard," Dean said. "It's always awkward when you have to tell a woman you're not interested." Silence followed. "You did let her know you weren't interested, didn't you?"

"Yeah, but then I saw her out with some guy, and she was dressed for trouble. I was worried about her, so I followed her home and we stopped talking and started—" He broke off. "Anyway, it's crazy. Abby's not my type. I can't see myself in a long-term relationship with her."

"Hmm," Dean said. "You don't think she's some kind of rebound fling for you, do you?"

"No," he snapped. "I wouldn't do that kind of thing to Abby. She's too good to be treated that way. And besides, I'm over Laila. I was never in love with her."

Dean lifted his hands. "Okay, okay. I'm on your side. Remember?"

Cade frowned. "Yeah, I know. I'm gonna take a walk. I'll be back in awhile."

In a town as small as Thunder Canyon, Abby was sure she'd run into Cade sooner or later, but it was as if he'd vanished. She knew he was putting in long hours at the shop, but still, she would have expected to see him out and about at one time or another. During the past week, she'd completed two papers, babysat for one of her ROOTS girls and endured hours of wedding-planning discussions from her mother and Laila. The good news was that her mother had started to set out snowmen and Santa figures inside the house. Abby could only hope the holidays would provide at least a slight reprieve from wedding talk.

Since she had walked in on Abby and Cade, Laila had tried to overcompensate by constantly remarking on how pretty and smart Abby was. Although Abby appreciated the sentiment, she wasn't interested in the extra attention. She really didn't want the rest of her family knowing about her unanswered quest for Cade. It was bad enough that Laila knew.

One of Abby's friends, Rachel, invited Abby to join her at the Hitching Post for a girls' night out. Ready for a break, she accepted. Although she didn't tease her hair like the girls at ROOTS had done, she realized she wanted to look more like a woman than a high-school girl, so she put on some mascara and lip gloss, changed into a sexy shirt and wore some high-heeled boots with her jeans. She looked in the mirror and shrugged at her reflection. No one would accuse her of being a beauty queen, but she supposed she looked a little better than usual.

"Abby," her mother called from the kitchen. "Rachel's here."

Grabbing her jacket, she headed for the front door where Rachel stood. Her father was sitting on the couch reading his paper. "Don't get into any trouble," he said.

Abby planted a kiss on his cheek and laughed. "Now, when have I ever caused you any trouble?"

"Hmmph," he said. "It's not too late. You be careful."

"You, too, Daddy. Too much bad news is bad for your health," she shot back with a cheeky grin. "Let's go," she said to Rachel and the two of them ran down the front steps to Rachel's six-year-old Ford Explorer. "Thanks for inviting me out," Abby said. "I need a break from everything," she said.

Rachel nodded. "Me, too. I turned in a ten-page paper this week."

"Multiply that times two," Abby said.

"At least you're getting near the end," Rachel said. "I'll have to take some courses in summer school to wrap everything up."

Abby knew Rachel and her boyfriend had recently decided to take a break and Rachel was very upset about it. "Heard anything from Rob lately?"

Rachel frowned. "Just some texts and Facebook messages."

"You could 'unfriend' him," Abby said.

"I'm not ready yet, but we're not going to think about Rob tonight. We're going to have fun. Jules and Char are meeting us there. How's the wedding planning going?" Rachel asked.

Abby groaned. "Can we put that in the same category as Rob tonight?"

Rachel laughed. "Fine with me."

The Hitching Post was hopping with business. With a football game playing on several of the flat-screen TVs, the bar area was crowded with guys rooting for their teams. Abby skimmed the bar/restaurant for Cade, and felt a pinch of disappointment when she didn't see him. *Get over it,* she told herself.

Jules and Char waved them over from a table on the far side of the room. "Woo-hoo," Char said, lifting her beer. "The chicks are out of the coop tonight." She lowered her voice. "Plus we've got a hot server. I think I should order a round for everyone, don't you?"

"I'm a lightweight, so I'll take water to start," Abby said.

"Me, too. I'm driving, so I don't want to take any chances," Rachel said.

Char frowned. "Okay, but I don't think he's going to like the tip he gets from water."

"We can order some food," Rachel suggested, grabbing a menu. "The ribs look good."

"Not for me," Abby said. "Those are LipSmackin' Ribs and I don't want to have anything to do with that company."

"Such passion about ribs," the server said from behind her and gave her a once-over, twice. "You could give their waitresses some competition."

Abby felt her cheeks heat with color. "I'm not interested in competing with LipSmackin' Ribs's waitresses. I would, however, like a hot-fudge sundae with whipped cream and nuts."

"Cherry on top?" he asked, and she saw a look of sexual interest in his gaze. After her recent depressing experiences with Cade, it gave her a little thrill. At least some males found her attractive.

"Yes, thank you," she said.

"What else can I get you lovely ladies?" he asked and took their order. "I'll be back," he said, looking deliberately at Abby.

"Ooh, he's definitely interested in you, Abby," Jules said. "And he's cute. Maybe you should hang out with him."

Abby felt conflicted. "I don't know. I'm really busy right now with school and ROOTS. This probably isn't a good time."

"When *is* a good time?" Rachel asked. "Come to think of it, you hardly ever give a guy a chance. Unless you're still holding out for—"

Abby shot Rachel the look of death, which thankfully caused her to close her mouth.

"Oops," Rachel said.

"Holding out for what?" Jules asked.

"Or who?" Char said.

A friend since junior high school, Rachel was one of the few people in the world in whom Abby had confided about her crush over Cade, and since Laila had started dating him, the two had made a deal not to discuss him unless Abby brought up the subject, which had been nearly never.

The server returned with their drinks and orders. He set her ice-cream sundae in front of her along with a piece of paper. "Text me," he invited, then turned to the rest of the group. "Anything else I can get you?"

"Three more just like you," Char said, flirting outrageously.

He chuckled. "I'll see what I can round up," he said and went to another table of customers.

"You have to text him," Jules said. "He's cute and I bet he would be a lot of fun. You could use a little fun."

"We'll see," she said. Maybe Jules was right. Maybe she shouldn't be spending all her time waiting for Cade. It's just that no other man had come close in her eyes.

"Speaking of fun, is anyone leaving town during the holidays?" Rachel asked. "I'm stuck here."

Abby shot Rachel a look of gratitude for taking the focus off of her, and the women discussed dreams of a trip to the Caribbean. It was all in fun. Abby visited the restroom and when she came out, her gaze collided with Cade's. Her heart immediately slammed into her ribs.

His gaze traveled up and down her and he gave her a slight nod before he turned back to the football game. She felt a shot of something like humiliation travel through her at his muted, unfriendly response. He might as well have snubbed her.

Indignation rose within her and she refused to let him get away with it. The last time she'd been with Cade, he'd been practically making love to her and she wasn't going to let him forget it that easily.

Stiffening her spine, she sauntered toward him and tapped him on the shoulder. "Nice to see you. How you been lately?" she asked and deliberately licked her lips.

"Okay," he said, barely sparing her a glance. "Been busy at the shop."

"Yeah, it's that season," she said. "It must get terribly *frustrating* being cooped up in that shop all day and night. I don't know how you do it."

"You do what you have to do," he said.

And she would, too, she told herself, taking her courage in her hands. "That beer looks good. You mind if I have a sip of yours?"

He glanced at her. "I thought you didn't like beer."

She shot him what she hoped was a seductive look. "I might like yours," she said.

He gave a muffled sigh and lifted the beer toward her. She lifted her hand at the same time and between the two of them, the mug was jiggled and cold liquid spilled onto her chest.

Abby gasped. She had not intended that to happen.

Cade swore under his breath. "Hey, give me some napkins," he said to the bartender. Seconds later, he was pressing them against her chest. "How the hell did that happen?" he muttered.

Abby's heart stuttered at his closeness, her body conjuring memories of how he'd caressed her and kissed her. "It's not the only thing that could happen again," she murmured.

He jerked his head upward and met her gaze. He looked at his hands and her chest for a long moment, then picked up one of her hands to give her the napkins while he backed away. "Go away, little girl."

His insistence on calling her a girl made her crazy. "You know very well I'm no little girl."

"This isn't going to work. Do you realize that I babysat for you once?" he asked.

Abby felt another wave of humiliation, but she pushed it aside. "That was one time and it wasn't really babysitting. It was a swimming camp and my mom asked if I could stay late because she had to take one of my sisters to the doctor."

"Close enough for me," he said. "You're too young and immature for me. I need a woman, not a girl."

Abby felt her anger explode like a Fourth of July firecracker. Straight through the roof. Her heart hammered like a shotgun that wouldn't stop. She narrowed her eyes at Cade, picked up his half-spilled beer and dumped the rest of it. In his lap.

His eyes widened. "What the—"

"That's what this woman does when she is roaring mad," Abby whispered. "Maybe you can remember the cold feeling down below when you start thinking about the fact that you want me more than you're willing to admit." Turning on her heel, she strode to the table where her friends were chatting and drinking.

Rachel glanced at her and her brow furrowed. "You okay?" she whispered.

"Never better," Abby said, adrenaline still coursing through her veins.

"You're lying," Rachel said, looking over Abby's shoulder. "What happened?"

"I just did something a sweet, good little girl wouldn't do," Abby said in a low voice, taking a sip of her water and wishing it was a martini.

"And that is?" Rachel asked.

"I poured half of Cade Pritchett's beer in his lap." The revelation was more satisfying than she could have ever expected.

Rachel gasped, then laughed—then laughed again. "You didn't?"

"I did," Abby said.

"Oh, I wish I could have seen that." Rachel lifted her hand for Abby to give a high five. "You just kicked butt. I can only hope I'll have enough guts to do the same thing to Rob."

"I didn't plan it," Abby said, feeling a sliver of guilt.

"Of course not," Rachel said.

"What are you two whispering about?" Char asked.

Abby paused a half beat, then manufactured an excuse. "I didn't want to tell everyone I was pooped. It's embarrassing."

"Hey, we're all overbooked with exams and papers," Char said. "We understand. Plus we can always insist you give a rain check. And maybe you can bring that server and a few of his friends with you."

For the first time in a long time, if not forever, Abby considered taking a chance on someone other than Cade since Cade was rejecting her completely. She didn't know how much humiliation she could take. Even now, she felt a twinge of regret for dumping Cade's beer in his lap. It wasn't her nature to be so impulsive and, well, aggressive.

Abby rubbed the piece of paper with her server's contact information between her fingers, wishing it were a lucky charm that would release her from her passion for Cade. "You never know," she finally said. "Anything is possible."

* * *

Cade couldn't believe sweet little Abby had dumped his beer in his lap. He stared after her as she returned to her table.

"Need some more napkins?" the bartender asked innocently.

"Yeah," Cade muttered. He didn't want to leave the bar with his pants so wet.

"And another beer?" the bartender asked as he gave Cade some napkins.

"Not right now," he said then swore under his breath. *Women.* Who would have thought Abby could be so impulsive? So emotional? So passionate and hot…

A slew of images and memories conspired against him, making him want to take her to his bed for at least a night. Or thirty nights.

All wrong, he reminded himself as he forced himself to remember that he had once been her babysitter. He had once been involved with her sister. Cade knew Abby would want more from him than he could give. Unlike Laila, Abby would want all of him. His mind, body and heart, and Cade had no intention of giving away all of himself to any woman.

A few days later, Cade walked toward the diner to get a decent cup of coffee since the coffeemaker at the shop had taken its last gasp. He ended up getting an extra cup for his brother Dean and headed back to work. Passing by the community center, he heard the sound of children singing. He remembered that the kids were preparing a Thanksgiving program and wondered if this was part of it.

He'd successfully avoided Abby since the incident at

the Hitching Post. Her words, however, grated on him. It still wasn't acceptable for him to get involved with her. Abby had a soft heart and he would hurt her. Hell, he already had.

He hated himself for it, but he missed seeing her. He'd spent a lifetime not thinking about Abby, and now thoughts of her crept up in his mind at the oddest moments. Cade should just continue on his way back to the shop. No detours.

Or he could stand in the back where no one would notice him. Just to see if the props from Pritchett & Sons were working out okay. Sipping his coffee, he stepped inside the center and nodded at the woman at the desk as he made his way to the gymnasium.

It must have been a dress rehearsal because the kids were in costume. He had to admit they looked cute. A bunch of little pilgrims stood on the bow of the faux ship singing their little lungs out. One of the pilgrims pulled off her hat and started playing with it. In front of the ship, a group of mini–Native Americans wearing headdresses squirmed and wiggled. One little Native American started tugging on his neighbor's headdress.

He spied Abby stepping toward the tugger and shaking her head. The boy immediately stepped in line. He chuckled. The boy must have learned, as Cade was learning, that despite her sweet smile and nature, Abby had a kick to her personality. The song about making friends and sharing ended, and Abby and the director applauded the children's efforts.

Cade knew that most of these preschoolers came from disadvantaged homes. Their time at the community center provided a hot meal, early education and exposure to learning all kinds of things they might never experience otherwise. With all her other activities, he had to admire Abby for helping the children.

As she bent down to untie a headdress, the children swarmed around her like bees to a flower. No surprise that she was good with kids. He felt the dark longing for his own family yawn inside him again and tamped it down. Maybe someday, but not with Abby. He would only hurt her.

Chapter Five

Between school, her work at ROOTS and filling in at the community center, Abby's schedule switched into high gear. In theory, she was too busy to think about Cade, but that's why theories were only theories. Real life was something else. The good news, however, was that she was too busy to be overly bothered with Laila's wedding. Sure, she felt a twinge every now and then, but with her current demands, it was easier to push aside.

After one of her night classes, she grabbed a hot chocolate with marshmallows at the diner while she sat in a booth and reviewed notes for an upcoming exam. A shadow fell over her and she glanced up to see the server from the Hitching Post looking down at her.

"You didn't call or text me," he said.

"I've been crazy busy with school and other things," she said.

"Too busy for a little fun?" he asked, sitting across from her.

"Too busy for any fun," she said.

"You don't remember my name," he said.

She searched her memory. *Started with a* D. "Daniel," she managed.

He raised his eyebrows. "Well done."

She shrugged, knowing she'd just gotten lucky and tried not to squirm at the way he studied her.

"I'm not just a waiter for the Hitching Post," he said. "I'll be studying law in the fall."

"I wasn't judging you," she rushed to say, although she was somewhat surprised.

"But you couldn't be less interested," he said.

She was impressed by his perceptiveness. "You're good," she said and pushed a strand of her hair behind her ear. "The truth is I'm cursed," she confessed.

His eyebrows lifted. "Cursed? That sounds a bit dramatic," he said.

"Well, it is dramatic, and I am, indeed, cursed. I fell head over heels for a man when I was a teenager, and even when I tried my very best not to care for him, I did. I failed at ignoring him. I failed at not thinking he was the best man in the world."

Disappointment flitted through his gaze. "Oh. Damn. How come no one like you went crazy for me as a teenager and couldn't be seduced away?"

"Ha, ha. I'm sure there were plenty of girls falling for you. You just probably didn't notice them because there were so many. You're not exactly hard to look at, and you're full of charm."

"Not enough charm to turn your head," he said.

Abby sighed. "I'm just sick. It's a sad thing, but I'm sick."

"You should give me a chance," Daniel said. "Maybe I could cure you."

She laughed, wishing she felt remotely tempted, and shook her head. "Maybe not me, but I could refer you to at least eight of my friends if you promised not to break their hearts."

"Eight at once and no hearts broken? That's a tall order," he joked.

She laughed, again wishing her heart were as free as it should be. Free enough to enjoy and exchange interest with another man. Darn Cade Pritchett. Why had he captured her heart if he would never return her feelings?

The weather forecast was wicked bad. Blizzard coming. Fifteen inches. Zero visibility. Abby thought about Mr. Henson. She'd packaged several meals from the Cateses' freezer and taken them to him several days ago, but she hadn't checked on him recently.

Guilt slashed through her. She should have visited him. She should have… Well, no more should haves. She would go check on him now before the storm hit full force.

Abby drove her VW Beetle as the snow was flying. She pulled in to Mr. Henson's driveway with more food and rushed up the steps to knock on his door.

"Coming," he called from inside.

Abby waited impatiently, glancing at the snow pouring sideways.

Mr. Henson opened the door and smiled. "What are you doing here?" he asked, his grumpy tone at odds with his expression.

"I wanted to make sure you're okay," she said. "A blizzard is coming and I brought you some more food."

"I like your mama's cooking," he said. "Yours isn't too bad, either," he added, waving her inside. "You shouldn't have come out in this weather."

Abby stepped inside. "I was worried about you."

"No need to worry about me. I'll go when I'm supposed to and—"

"—not a day before," she finished for him. "I just don't want you rushing things."

He met her gaze. "Why is that?"

"I like you."

His lips lifted in a small, craggy smile. "You shouldn't get too hung up on me. My Geraldine told me I was dangerous to women. I never believed it, but—"

Abby stifled a laugh, but smiled. "Geraldine was right. How's your ankle?"

"Damn slow healing," he said as he shuffled toward the kitchen. "If I was just a few years younger, I'd be better fast, like that," he said and snapped his fingers. "This one is taking a while. Gotta say the ice and meds help a little. A *little*," he added with emphasis. "It's no miracle."

"I hope you'll turn a corner soon. I'm glad you're not hurting quite as much. In the meantime, I want to make sure you're ready for this blizzard headed our way."

Mr. Henson lifted his head as if he were offended. "I've lived through more blizzards than years you've been alive, missy."

"I'm sure you have," she said. "But I'm a neurotic whippersnapper who wants to make sure you make it through this one, too."

He stared at her for a long moment. "This younger generation is strange."

A knock sounded at the door, startling both of them. "I'll get it," she said and strode toward the door. She opened it, stunned to see Cade staring back at her. Her heart felt as if it lodged in her throat.

"What are you doing here?" she and Cade said at the same time.

Abby blinked, reining in her heart, mind and soul. *Oh, not soul,* she told herself. Not soul. That was too much, too deep. "I'm here because of the blizzard."

"So am I," Cade said. "You shouldn't be here. It's already started."

"My car is good in the snow," she said, lifting her chin.

Cade gave a short, humorless laugh. "In this weather? I don't think so."

"It is," she insisted. "I wouldn't have come out here if my car couldn't have made it."

"Yeah, well, good luck making it back. The visibility is already shot," Cade said.

Abby frowned. Now she was dealing with two grumpy old men.

Cade walked past her. "You need some wood? What's your flashlight and candle situation?" he asked Mr. Henson.

"What's wrong with you two? I've been through blizzards before. I can do it again," he said.

"But your ankle," she said.

Cade glanced back at her. "What about his ankle?"

"He sprained and bruised it. I took him to the doctor last week."

"It's nothing," Mr. Henson said. "But the ice and meds helped. I'm fine."

"Why didn't you tell me?" Cade asked.

"You weren't talking with me," she retorted. "I'm too young to know anything. Remember?"

Silence fell over the room. They could have heard a pin drop.

"Hmm," Cade said and turned back to Mr. Henson. "Let's double-check your supplies, heat and cell phone. I need to make sure Abby gets home okay."

"I'm good. You get your woman home," Mr. Henson said.

Abby groaned.

"*My* woman?" Cade echoed. "She's not my woman."

"Well, she would be if you had any sense," Mr. Henson said. "Do you know what a good cook she is? She's brought me some meals."

Cade shrugged his shoulders. "I didn't know. Glad she's been feeding you."

"You know, it's a mighty fine thing when a woman can cook like she does. That's part of what makes a good wife. Plus she's doggone pretty. Have you taken a good look at her? She's—"

"Mr. Henson," Abby said, feeling her cheeks blaze with embarrassment. "We really do want to make sure you're going to be okay during this storm." She cleared her throat. "Batteries," she said. "I'll check the batteries."

Within a few moments, she and Cade had Mr. Henson armed and prepared for the storm. "Now, you take care and I'll check on you again. Call if you have any problems," she said, squeezing the elderly man's shoulders.

"I won't have any problems," he told her.

"Then call for any reason," she said. "I should go." Resisting the urge to meet Cade's gaze, she pulled on her gloves and strode out of the house.

Cade had been telling the truth about the weather. The white stuff was pouring down with a vengeance. She adjusted her cap and swiped the snow out of her eyes as she stomped to her car. Her VW started up with its usual dependability and she flipped on the windshield wipers to the fastest setting. Putting the car into gear, she pushed the accelerator and slowly moved forward.

The visibility was terrible, but Abby figured if she went slow and steady, she would be okay. Fishtailing up Mr. Henson's driveway didn't build her confidence, but she soldiered on. It was only about twenty miles between Mr. Henson's house and her home, she told herself and kept a light foot on the accelerator.

Soon enough, she saw Cade's SUV in her rearview mirror. Certain she was moving too slowly for him, she opened her window and waved her hand for him to pass, but he didn't. Of course not, she thought. He had to look after her the same way he would look after his little sister. Having him at her backside just made her more edgy, especially when her little VW pulled left when she was holding the steering wheel straight.

Moving at a snail's pace, she wrapped her hands around the steering wheel with a death grip. Suddenly another car appeared out of nowhere and headed straight for the driver's side of her VW. Her heart raced and panic rushed through her. Abby swung the steering wheel to the right and mashed on the accelerator. The snow was so thick she was driving blind. She felt it the second her car lost traction with the road and pitched

downward, then collided with something that brought
her car to a halt, her seat belt jerking her tightly against
her seat. She held her breath and squished her eyes together, waiting for the air bag to slap her.

When it didn't, she slowly opened her eyes and took
a careful breath and did a quick physical evaluation. She
jiggled her arms and legs and—

A thump sounded on her window, scaring the bejee-
zus out of her. Abby looked out the window into Cade's
concerned gaze. Her heart turned over. Blast it.

"Are you okay?" he yelled.

She nodded. "Fine. Really," she called in return. "I
can handle it. I'm okay."

He shook his head and motioned for her to roll down
her window.

"I'm fine. Really," she repeated as she lowered her
window. "I can handle this."

"You're in a ditch," he said.

"Oh," she said. "Oops."

"Unlock the door. I'll help you up to my car," he said.

She didn't like the put-upon sound in his voice. "I
could call my father," she said.

"There's no need for him to come get you when I'm
here," he said.

"I don't want you to feel obligated," she said. "You
feel obligated to rescue everyone. I don't want you to
feel obligated about me."

"Open the door," he said. "It's damn cold out here."

"Charming," she muttered under her breath, but did
as he said. He extended his hand and she accepted it,
wishing he was reaching for her in entirely different
circumstances. That was a dream that wasn't going to
come true anytime soon.

Pulling her hand from his, she climbed up the side of the ditch. She tripped once and he reached out his hand, but she ignored it. She trudged upward and made it to the top where Cade's SUV blinked its emergency lights at her in an almost mocking way. Abby resisted the urge to stick her tongue out at the vehicle, knowing her attitude was ridiculous.

Cade led the way to the passenger side of his vehicle and opened the door. She stepped inside, reluctantly grateful for the warmth. Cade climbed into the driver's seat.

"You shouldn't have gone out to old man Henson's house in the middle of a blizzard," he said.

"It wasn't the middle of a blizzard," she retorted. "It was the beginning."

"Same thing," he said. "Why didn't you call me?"

"Why should I?" she asked. "You told me I was too young. That means nothing I say is valid."

"I didn't say that," he began.

"Same thing," she countered and crossed her arms over her chest.

Silence followed, and she refused to fill it, though she wondered if it would kill her. This was going to be the longest ride of her life.

He could smell her perfume. It wasn't strong, but soft and flowery with a hint of spice. Cade told himself he should ignore it, but his nose must have thought differently because he inhaled more deeply. Lord, she smelled good. He stole a sideways glance at her and immediately caught the stubborn set of her jaw so at odds with her soft, overly full mouth.

Her lips could conjure wicked images in a man's

mind. Not his, of course, he told himself. Abby was the equivalent of his second little sister. Off-limits.

He saw her lick her lips and his gut tightened. Those wicked images began to seep through his brain like smoke through a keyhole. Cade gritted his teeth and focused on the road.

"I would listen to you about Mr. Henson. I know you've got a good head on your shoulders," he said.

"Hmmph."

"Really," he said. "Look at all you're doing for the community center and ROOTS. You're close to graduating." He paused and took a breath. "You're an intelligent young woman."

She shot him a gaze full of doubt.

Cade tore his gaze away from her sexy mouth. "You are," he insisted and took a deep breath. "You and I just shouldn't get involved."

"And why is that? If I'm an intelligent young woman?" she asked in a quiet voice.

"Because—" He bit his tongue to keep from saying she was too young and inexperienced. "Because underneath it all, I'm a heartless sonovabitch and I'll hurt you."

Her shocked silence was so thick he could have cut it with a knife.

"I find that difficult to believe," she finally said. "I've known you for a long time and I don't know anyone who would call you a heartless sonovabitch."

"You don't know anyone I've ever fallen in love with, do you?" he challenged, tightening his hands on the steering wheel.

Another silence stretched between them. "Laila," she finally said.

"No. Laila and I were never in love. I haven't been capable of love for a long time, Abby. You're not rough and hard like me. You should have someone who can love as freely as you can."

Abby didn't say anything in return as she appeared to digest his words. Instead of talking, she turned on his radio to a classic-rock station and turned up the heat in his SUV a notch.

Aeons later, he pulled into her driveway. Abby turned to him. "You wouldn't want me to make decisions for you. Don't make decisions for me," she said in a soft voice. "And I'm sorry I poured that beer in your lap the other night. It was impulsive, even though you kinda deserved it." She leaned toward him, close enough to kiss him.

He felt a crazy, wicked expectancy swell inside him and waited. And wanted.

"Thanks," she whispered, pulling back and getting out of his car. He looked after her, swearing at himself because he was hard with wanting her. Forbidden fruit was a pain in the butt.

He had warned her off. If anyone was advising Abby, they would say to stay away from Cade Pritchett, but her thoughts gravitated toward him despite the fact that she was crazy busy. He should have been the last thing on her mind, but he wasn't. Abby did her best to make sure he wasn't the first, but he was right up there.

Even though he'd warned her away from him, she'd seen the way he'd looked at her mouth. He'd almost wanted her to kiss him. Almost. So, he *was* attracted to her. She had to keep reminding herself because he'd discouraged her every time she'd approached him. Every time she'd tried to seduce him. Which had felt like a joke because she didn't know anything about seduction. The only thing Abby knew was that she had wanted Cade as long as she could remember.

But she wasn't sure she could put herself out there again. It was so humiliating wanting him to notice her as a woman, wanting him to want her just half as much as she wanted him. She'd seen the spark, though, and a part of her couldn't help but hope that spark could turn into a fire between Cade and her. If only the two of them could get together again with no one else around. Just the two of them and maybe, just maybe she would get the chance she'd been waiting for since forever.

Abby waited several more days, hoping she would run into Cade, but that didn't happen. At this rate, it looked as if she would have to seek him out if she was going to see him before next year. Taking matters into her own hands, she headed for Pritchett & Sons near closing time. Just before 6:00 p.m., she walked into the display area and found Cade putting holiday decorations into the window.

He met her gaze then looked away. "Hey," he said.

Abby shoved her hands into the pockets of her jacket at his cool tone. She had her work cut out for her. "Hey to you. Bet you've been busy lately," she said and walked toward him.

"Always busy this time of year," he said, carefully placing a nutcracker on the middle shelf.

She nodded. "Yep." She bent down and picked up another nutcracker. "My mother loves these. She collects them."

"I know," he said.

Of course he knew, she thought. He'd dated Laila for several years that had included several Christmas seasons. "I think there's something creepy about them."

He glanced at her in surprise. "Really? Why?"

"I think it's the combination of inanimate eyes and a jaw that can crack nuts. It reminds me of Chucky in that horror movie *Child's Play.*"

"They're not that spooky," he said and bent down to put another nutcracker on the shelf.

"Easy for you to say," she said. "Did one of your older sisters ever whack you on the head with one of them?"

He shot her a sideways glance. "Not Laila," he said.

"Yes, Miss Perfect Laila," she said, revealing a bit more bitterness than she intended.

"She's not perfect," he said in a mild voice. "That wasn't why I proposed to her."

"You proposed because she was the most beautiful woman in Thunder Canyon," she said.

"Most beautiful is relative. I proposed because I thought she was strong enough to deal with me. You know, despite getting whacked with a nutcracker, you're lucky you have your family. Especially when the holidays come around."

"I guess," she said and picked up an ornament that resembled a snow-covered church. She giggled as she held up the ornament.

"What?" Cade asked.

"Do you remember when Reverend Walker's mother blew up her kitchen just before Christmas?"

Cade nodded with a smile. "She was making moonshine."

"My mother didn't stop talking about that for months," she said and giggled again. "I love Christmas."

She felt his gaze on her and looked up at him. He glanced away. "What about you?"

"It's a mixed bag," he said with a shrug. "I have some happy memories, but ever since my mother died, it's hard. Sometimes it's just a day to get through."

Abby's heart twisted at the pain in his voice. "That's got to be difficult."

"That's why I said you're lucky. You still have your family intact."

Grabbing hold of her courage, she took a quick breath. "You could have your own family if that was what you really wanted. You just have to reach out for it."

Cade met her gaze for a long moment, and she saw the hunger in his eyes, the same hunger she felt for him. He leaned toward her and lifted his hand, then pulled back at the last second as if coming to his senses.

"You don't know what you're talking about. I'm not right for you," he said.

Frustration roared through her, making her want to stomp her foot and scream, which she suspected wouldn't help her cause. "Says who? Shouldn't I get a say in the matter? I'm starting to wonder if you're afraid of how you feel for me."

"I'm not afraid," he said in a low voice, but she saw something different flash through his gaze. A strong flicker of passion she hadn't seen before. Abby took a step closer, then another and lifted her hand to his arm, sliding it upward to his shoulder. She gently pressed her chest against his and watched him close his eyes and take a quick, sharp breath.

"Doesn't this feel right?" she whispered and lifted her other hand to his other shoulder.

Moving in achingly slow increments, he slid his hands around her, pulling her into his arms. Her heart pounded in her chest and her lungs refused to work. Cade's stormy gaze met hers and she could tell he was still fighting his feelings. "I shouldn't be the one to take your innocence."

"You won't be. I'm more grown-up than you think," she assured him and lifted on tiptoes to press her mouth against his. She slid her tongue over the seam of his lips, and he immediately took her mouth in a hungry kiss.

It was as if a dam inside him broke loose. She felt his hands on her hair, against her back, pushing her into his hard crotch. Breathless, hot and filled with need, she matched him kiss for kiss, caress for caress.

He pulled back slightly and swore. "Are you sure about this?"

"Yes," she said before he could finish the question.

He took her mouth again in a quick, hard kiss that promised so much more. "I'd better lock the door."

Chapter Six

Cade cut the lights and led her to a room in the back. "We can have some privacy here," he said and closed the door behind them. A big sofa faced an old television, and at the far end of the room sat a small table and chairs with a refrigerator and microwave. "This is where we rest when we're pulling all-nighters," he said.

Her heart skipped as he laced his fingers through hers and guided her toward the sofa. She couldn't help hoping they would be pulling a different kind of all-nighter tonight.

He slid his fingers through her hair and she automatically lifted her mouth to his again. He kissed her deeply, and the fire between them flared again. Now that he was so close, she couldn't get enough of him fast enough. She tugged at his shirt, pulling the buttons free, dipping her open mouth against his throat to catch a breath. His ragged breathing was music to her ears.

With his assistance, she finally peeled off the layers covering his upper body and slid her hands over his muscular chest. He was all man. She wanted to feel all of him against all of her. She rubbed her chest and mouth over his bare skin and he shuddered.

Unable to fight her impatience, she pulled off her sweater and tossed it over her head. When she reached to remove her bra, his hands replaced hers and that barrier was gone in seconds.

She moaned in pleasure at the sensation of her bare breasts rubbing against his chest. His groan joined hers. "You feel so good."

"I'm gonna make you feel good, too," she promised and slid her hands down to unbuckle his belt and undo his jeans. She filled her hands with him and he whispered another oath.

"Where did you learn—"

She pressed her mouth against his and began to stroke him. Now was not the time for questions. Now was the time for pure pleasure. The heat between them built so quickly she would have sworn it was summertime. When he grazed her nipples with his thumbs, she felt a corresponding tug low between her thighs.

She bit her lip at the sensations ripping through her. "I want you."

"Not too fast," he said. "Not too—"

She stroked him intimately again and he sucked in another sharp breath. "What are you trying to do to me?"

"The same thing you do to me," she said. "Fast isn't fast enough."

With a rough groan, he stripped off the rest of her clothes and nudged her onto the sofa. He stood directly in front of her and she pushed his jeans and underwear down then gave him an intimate kiss.

It didn't last long. Seconds later, he followed her down on the couch, pushing her legs apart with his thigh. He dipped his fingers into the place where she was aching for him.

"You're already wet," he said in approval as he caressed her and made her more restless for him. Each stroke made her a little more crazy.

"Inside," she whispered. "Come inside."

Three more delicious, mind-bending strokes and it seemed he couldn't wait any longer. He thrust inside her and she arched toward him. She felt his gaze fall over her like liquid fire. The want in his eyes nearly pushed her over the top. When he began to move, she moved in return. The sensations inside her built and she clung to him. He thrust again and she felt herself spin out of control. A heartbeat later, she felt him stiffen with his own climax and she relished the fact that for this moment, this night, he was finally hers.

Cade stared at the lithe temptress in his arms while he tried to catch his breath. Little Abby Cates. Who would have known she was wild in bed? She met his gaze and her lips lifted in a sensual smile that reminded him of a cat who'd just licked a bowl of cream. Her hands slid over his skin with sensual strokes that indicated she wouldn't be adverse to going round two with him.

Cade, however, wanted to get control of himself and he was curious as hell about Abby Firecracker Cates. She was a lot more experienced than he'd expected and not at all shy about going after what she wanted. It made him wonder how many men… A shot of jealousy burned through him, taking him by surprise. He shifted, sitting up slightly, and pulled her onto his lap.

"You took me by surprise," he said, sliding his fingers through her hair, which skimmed the top of her breasts. Gazing down her naked body, he thought about everything he still wanted to do to her.

"How is that?" she asked.

"Well, I don't know. I didn't think you'd be so—" He broke off. "I thought you would be more shy. Not so experienced."

She licked her lips. "Are you saying you didn't like—"

"Hell, no," he said and raked his hand through his hair. "I just— How many guys have you dated, anyway?"

She smiled. "Oh, well I've been out with a lot of guys, but I've only really been with one other guy. First year in college. One time," she said and turned her head away as if she embarrassed to discuss it.

"One time?" he echoed, incredulous. "You didn't make love with me like you'd only done it one other time."

Abby sighed and looked at him, sliding her hands over his chest in a way that made him begin to get aroused again. "Okay, I'll tell you my secret," she whispered and rubbed her mouth against his. "You inspire me."

A ripple of pleasure raced through him like lit gasoline. No one had ever said anything so sexy to him in his life.

An hour later, after they'd made love again, Cade knew he would sleep well tonight. In fact, he could fall into a half coma given half a chance.

"I should take you home," he said, sliding his hands through her hair. He could get addicted to the silky sensation.

"No need. My car's parked down the street," she said.

"I can't let you drive home by yourself," he said, his innate sense of protectiveness rising to the surface.

"That would be crazy since I have my car," she said, rising and beginning to put on her clothes. "But it's a nice thought."

Cade felt a strange combination of feelings. He didn't want her to leave, yet he needed to get himself together. This had been a wild few hours that he hadn't expected.

"This doesn't seem right," he said, pulling on his own clothes.

"It's okay," she said, then paused and a flicker of vulnerability flashed through her eyes. "Is this a one-night stand?" she asked in a low voice.

Cade paused. It should be a one-night stand, he thought. But it wouldn't be. Abby had burrowed her way inside him and he couldn't let her go. Right now, anyway. "No," he said standing. "It's not a one-night stand."

Relief trickled through her expression, and he could practically feel the tension ease from her frame. "Then everything's okay," she said and pulled on her boots. "And I, um, guess I'll see you when I see you," she said, meeting his gaze with a smile.

She was fully dressed and somehow much more grown-up to him than she had been mere hours ago. She was a woman.

"I'll walk you to your car," he said and pulled on the rest of his clothes. He grabbed his jacket and led the way out the back room, then out of the shop. The frigid air hit him like a slap in the face.

"Whoa," he said. "It's doggone cold."

"Can't disagree," she said, snuggling inside her coat.

He reached over and put his arm around her. "Sure you're okay driving yourself home. This doesn't seem right."

"I'll be okay," she said.

"So, you wanna get together Wednesday?" he asked.

"Not good for me. I have a study group that night."

"Thursday?"

"Babysitting for my ROOTS mom Lisa," she said.

"Well, can you squeeze me in on Friday?" he asked in a half-mocking voice.

"Maybe," she said, fluttering her eyelids in a flirty way.

His gut clenched. Frowning, he wondered where that sensation had come from. "Friday," he said firmly.

"Where?" she asked.

"My house," he said. "And I'll pick you up."

"It would be better if I drive. That way I won't get any questions."

"I can handle questions," he said.

"There's no need right now," she said and before they knew it, her orange VW was in sight.

"You should be driving a more substantial vehicle," he grumbled.

"My car gets me around," she said.

"And into ditches," he said.

"One ditch," she corrected. "During a blizzard. I've never gotten stuck before."

"If you say so," he said as they stopped beside her car. He lifted his hands and cradled her hand between them. "I'll see you Friday," he said and lowered his mouth to hers. Her lips were swollen from their passion. They quickly grew warm. He did, too. He slid his hand lower to the small of her back to draw her against him where she made him ache for her. Even after all their lovemaking.

That kiss went on and on, and he would have extended it longer if he hadn't needed oxygen. He drew back and they both gasped for air. Cade laughed uneasily. He couldn't remember the last time a woman had affected him this way. Had Dominique?

"All righty," she finally said in a sexy, husky voice. "I guess I should go."

"Yeah," he said, but still held her in his arms.

"I don't really want to," she confessed in a whisper.

"That makes two of us," he said. "I'll get my SUV and follow you home."

"Not necessary," she said.

"It is for me," he said and gave her a brief, firm kiss and pulled back.

"G'night," she said softly, and he helped her into her car.

Jogging back to the shop, Cade got into his SUV and quickly caught up with Abby on her drive toward her home. As he drove, he remembered all the other times he'd taken this same route to get together with Laila. That seemed centuries ago. Although Cade had never been in love with Laila, Abby had completely wiped Laila out of his mind.

He turned onto her street and watched as she pulled to a stop. Lowering her window, she peeked outside. "See you soon, Cade," she said with a wave.

Cade waved in return, feeling a little crazy.

* * *

Abby sauntered into the warm kitchen of her home where Laila and her mother were making lists and looking at photographs of bridesmaid dresses. Humming under her breath, she tried to withhold her giddiness over the evening she'd shared with Cade. Plus, she would see him again soon. She was so happy she almost couldn't contain herself, yet at the same time, she wanted to keep the fantastic news to herself a bit longer.

"Hey, Abby," Laila said. "What do you think of this bridesmaid dress? It's not too fussy, is it?"

It was horribly fussy and the color was hideous. "Oh, it's pretty."

"What about this one?" she asked, pointing to a pink dress with lace.

"Oh, that's pretty, too. Is there anything around here to eat?"

"You didn't have any dinner, did you?" her mother asked, frowning. "Where have you been, sweetie?"

Abby felt her cheeks heat and swiped at her hair. "Regular thing. Studying."

Feeling Laila scrutinize her, Abby turned away. "I'll just fix myself a peanut-butter-and-jelly sandwich."

"There's some chicken potpie in the refrigerator," her mother said.

"The wind must have picked up outside," Laila said. "Your hair's a mess."

Her hair was a mess because Cade couldn't keep his hands out of it, she thought, remembering how he'd tugged at her hair to draw her mouth against his. She bit her lip and began to make her sandwich. "It always gets difficult to manage when I wait too long to get a haircut. I should make an appointment."

"Hmm," Laila said. "Hey, do you mind taking a look at just one more dress and telling me what you think."

"No problem," she said, licking a dot of grape jelly from her finger. She looked over Laila's shoulder at the photo where Laila's perfect fingernail pointed at a putrid green dress with rainbow-colored lace and a bustle. It was one of the most hideous dresses she'd ever seen in her life. *But who cares?* she thought. She'd be happy to wear a burlap sack as long as Cade held her the way he had tonight. "Pretty again," she said and took a bite of her sandwich.

Laila shot her a look of complete suspicion. "What have you been smoking? That dress is awful."

Abby shrugged. "I hear it's bad luck to disagree with the bride."

"And what is your honest opinion?"

"My honest opinion is that this is your wedding and you should be happy with all of it," Abby said. "I'm going to grab a glass of milk and hit the sack soon. I'll see you later," she said and kissed her mother on the cheek.

Her mother sniffed. "Is that a new perfume you're wearing? I can't quite place it."

Abby felt a nervous twist and giggled. "Eau de *pbj*? G'night. Love ya."

Abby gulped down her sandwich and milk, then washed her face and brushed her teeth. Stripping out of her clothes, she put on her pj's. She picked up her shirt and inhaled, smelling a hint of Cade's scent—a delicious combination of aftershave, leather and pure man.

Her bedroom door swung open and Laila stepped inside, studying her. "What are you doing?"

Abby glanced away. "Smelling my shirt to see if I can get another day's wear out it. What do you think?"

"I don't know," Laila said. "There's something about you. I can't quite put my finger on it. You're practically—hmm—glowing. What's going on?" she demanded.

"Nothing. How are you doing? You seem to be making progress with your wedding plans," Abby said.

Laila furrowed her brow. "Don't change the subject." She frowned then her eyes rounded. "You've been with Cade. *What* have you been doing with him, Abby?"

"Nothing terrible," she said, because it had all been wonderful. "Why do you care? It's none of your business. You don't want him anymore. You never did," she said, her stomach clenching nervously.

"I care because you're my sister." Laila crossed the room and sat on Abby's bed. She lifted her hand to push a strand of Abby's hair from her face. "I know I said it was perfect if you and Cade got together, but I hope you won't move too fast with him. Or expect too much from him."

"What do you mean?" Abby asked, feeling a yucky sensation in her stomach.

"I mean, you're not that experienced."

"Oh, don't you start with that, too," Abby said, pulling back and rolling her eyes.

"Ah, so Cade has said the same thing," Laila said.

"I'm really tired," Abby said, not wanting to hear what her sister had to say. She'd had a magical evening, the most wonderful evening of her life, and she didn't want anyone, especially Laila, to spoil it. "I need to get some rest."

"Just be careful," Laila said. "Cade is a wonderful

man, but when it comes to his heart, it may as well be locked up in Fort Knox."

"How would you know that?" Abby asked. "You never really took him seriously, anyway."

"But I've known him a long time," Laila said. "Like I said, Cade's a good man, but I don't want you to get hurt."

Abby sighed and put her hand over Laila's. "You had your chance with Cade and you didn't want him. Maybe that's why he never really opened up his heart to you. You didn't love him as much as—"

Laila's eyes rounded. "Oh, Abby. You may have a bad case of hero worship, but you can't be in love with him. You're too young."

Abby's frustration ripped through her. "I realize you're in love, but that doesn't make you an authority on my feelings, or Cade's." She smiled. "Be happy for me. I am. Just please don't tell anyone else. It's still too new," she said and sank back onto her pillow.

"What does *too new* mean?" Laila asked.

"Exactly what I said. Can you please keep it to yourself?" Abby asked.

"Yeah," Laila said in a reluctant but gentle voice and stroked Abby's head. "Just be careful with your sweet heart. And remember you deserve a man who can give you all of his heart, too. G'night, sweetie," she said and turned off the lamp beside Abby's bed.

In the darkness, Abby closed her eyes, wanting to close her mind to everything Laila had said. Laila may have dated Cade off and on for several years, but their relationship had never been deep. Abby shoved her sister's warnings out of her mind and focused on how Cade had felt in her arms, and how much he had wanted her.

Surely, that had to mean something. With all his reservations, Cade wouldn't have given in to his feelings for her if those feelings weren't strong. Abby clung to that thought, but her sister's voice played through her mind like a song she wanted to forget.

Cade's fingers itched to call Abby several times during the next few days. He was torn between wanting to get together with her before Friday and telling her that the two of them together was not a good idea. He held off until Friday when his father came down with a virus, which wouldn't have been a big deal if a reporter for a major decorating magazine wasn't coming to town to interview his dad.

At the last minute, Cade was stuck answering three thousand questions from a snap-happy journalist. In the back of his mind, he noticed the time passing, but the journalist was fascinated with their specialty pieces and the stories behind them. At six o'clock, the journalist/reporter, Ellie Ogburn, offered to take him to dinner. Cade sent a text to Abby canceling their date, telling her he had a big work issue.

At the Hiching Post, Ellie continued to interview him. She was a lively, confident woman in her late twenties with an inquisitive mind. "So, how did you become such an artist? From my initial phone interview with your father, he said you were artistic from the beginning."

Uneasy with the woman's flattery, he scrubbed his chin with his palm. "My dad was being kind. In the beginning, my creativity didn't always mesh with functionality."

"Yes, your father encouraged you. So he must have seen a spark of genius?"

Cade winced. "I think *genius* is pushing it. You need to remember my family is all about hard work. All of us show up every day to get the job done."

"But you're the one in demand now. You're the one who makes the specialty pieces that everyone wants signed. Why?" she asked.

He shrugged. "I can't explain it. I just listen to the stories of why these clients want specialty pieces, and then I go to work. Sometimes it's about family. Sometimes it's about work, but it always involves some kind of passion. I think about the personalities of the people who are requesting these specialized pieces. The woodworking is important to them or they wouldn't be seeking me out. If you want something basic, you can go to a big-box store to take care of it. There's nothing wrong with that. This economy is squeezing all of us. But if you come to me asking for a customized piece, then I'm going to do my best to give you something unique that fits you and your needs."

Ellie smiled. "That's pretty impressive. You mentioned the word *passion.* Where's the passion in your life? Do you have anyone special that inspires you?" she asked, batting her eyelashes at him.

Her flirty response gave him a jolt, and his mind slid to thoughts of Abby. He couldn't help remembering when she'd told him that he inspired her. "I keep my personal life private," he said and just let his statement sit there. He could deal with the silence, but he'd learned that many other people couldn't.

Ellie nodded and finally said, "Okay, well, is there a Mrs. Cade Pritchett?"

"Not gonna discuss my private life," he said firmly.

"That's just a status," she protested. "Single or married."

"Last time," he said. "I'm not discussing my private life."

"That's a shame. Any chance you'd like to come to New York for a long weekend?" she asked.

"I wouldn't want to cloud the article you're going to write from this interview," he said.

She pursed her lips. "You're no fun."

"True," he said. "Ask anyone. I'm no fun."

"Why do I think that's a front?"

He shrugged, his mind sliding toward Abby. "No idea."

An hour later, he escorted Ellie to her hotel, but left before she entered the lobby. He drove home and entered his too-silent house. His dog greeted him with a bark and a wag then followed him as he walked to the kitchen to grab a beer. If things had ended out differently, as he'd planned, he wouldn't have spent the evening alone. His body warmed at the thought. She would have gotten him hot and taken him up and down and all around. She would have made him needy, but left him satisfied.

She was nowhere close, right now, though. He checked his cell phone for the tenth time for her response, but there was none. He wondered why she hadn't replied and decided he should shrug it off.

Cade took a beer from the fridge, popped it open and took a long gulp. What a day. He felt as if he'd been probed and prodded every which way. In any other situation, he would have walked away, but this had been business. This article could bring in big business. He especially hadn't liked it when the discussion had veered toward his personal passion. Cade didn't spend a lot of time thinking about personal passions. In fact, he avoided anything or anyone that got him too worked up. He'd fallen in love once, and that woman had died. On top of that, the woman who had made family happen for his brothers, sister and father, had died suddenly, taking away the whole concept of family happiness with her. Since then, Cade had felt half-dead inside. He'd still longed for his own family, but without the terrible pain he'd experienced when he was younger.

He checked his phone one more time. No messages, text or voice from Abby. Maybe it was for the best.

Cade worked all day with his brother Dean on Saturday to make up for the time he spent with the reporter on Friday. The two of them finally took off for a late dinner at the Hitching Post after seven.

"I'm getting too much of this place," he said. "I'm going to DJ's for some good ribs next time I eat out."

"You didn't like Ellie?" Dean asked. "I thought she was hot."

"She was tiring," Cade said, sipping his beer and surveying the bar. "I'm glad you and I made good progress today. Her interview really cut into my time yesterday."

"Man, you're getting old if you think she was tiring. I wish you would have handed her over to me," Dean said.

"That interview could mean a lot for us. I wouldn't want you cluttering it because you wanted a good time. You can get a good time with a lot of women. No need to piss off this one," he said.

"And you think you didn't piss her off?" Dean asked,

starting his second beer. "She looked like she wanted more than dinner with you."

"I dropped her off at her hotel and went home. I'm not a complete fool," Cade said.

"Tell the truth," Dean said. "You wouldn't have minded going up to her room, would you?"

The truth was Cade hadn't been at all interested, but he wasn't going to tell Dean that. "You gonna come into the shop tomorrow after church?"

Dean blanched. "I gotta go to church?"

Cade laughed. "Leona Moseley was asking about you the last time I went."

Dean groaned. "No way. She's been after me for two years. Why do you think I don't go to church without someone to protect me? It's enough to make a man lose his religion."

Cade laughed again. "We all have to take turns. I took a turn two weeks ago. Dad is sick, so someone else needs to step up."

"Have some pity, Cade," Dean said. "I don't want to face Leona."

Cade groaned, but heard the sound of a familiar laugh from across the room. He tilted his head then searched the room. Nothing. Nothing. Noth— Cade's gaze collided with the sight of Abby with a group of girls and a guy with his arm wrapped around her waist.

A wicked twist of jealousy wrapped around his gut and throat like a python. What the hell was she doing here? What the hell was that guy doing touching her like that?

Chapter Seven

Abby forced herself to laugh at everyone's jokes. The sound she made was hollow to her own ears, but she focused on being amused instead of heartbroken. She laughed at another comment one of her friends made, although she couldn't repeat what made it so funny.

Daniel squeezed her waist. "You want to meet me after my shift?" he asked. "We could go out."

"That's too late for this schoolgirl," she said. "I have a ton of work to do."

"So you're blowing me off again," he said. "I could give you a good time."

"Maybe she doesn't want to have a good time with you right now. Or anytime," Cade said, taking Abby completely by surprise.

She dropped her jaw in surprise.

"Hey," Daniel said. "The lady can decide for herself."

"Well?" Cade said expectantly.

She narrowed her eyes at him for a long moment. How could he be so arrogant when he'd stood her up last night?

"You were pretty busy last night," she said then lowered her voice to a whisper. "With another woman."

"What did you say?" Cade asked, wrinkling his brow in confusion.

"You heard what I said," she hissed.

"I didn't," Cade said.

"Well, use your imagination. You were having dinner with a woman. One of my friends sent me a cell-phone photo of you enjoying a meal with a pretty woman last night when you told me you were working."

Realization flooded Cade's face. "That was the reporter. My father was supposed to handle this interview, but he got sick."

"Uh-huh," she said, unable to conceal her disbelief. "It must have been a real hardship to spend the evening with her."

"Hey, maybe I'd better take Abby home," Daniel said. "She seems upset and you're not helping any," he said to Cade.

Cade's face hardened with anger. "Not tonight, or any night for that matter." He took Abby's hand in his and tugged. "Abby and I need to talk. Have a good night," he said and led her in a swift trot outside.

"That was rude," she sputtered as they stood a few steps outside the back door of the Hitching Post. "He was trying to look after me, which is more than you can say. Besides—"

Cade shut her off when he pressed his mouth against hers. She made an unintelligible sound of protest that turned into a moan, when he changed the tenor of the kiss and slid his tongue past her lips.

Abby sighed and lifted her hand to his shoulders. She pulled back and stared into his eyes. "What the hell were you doing with that woman last night?"

"Exactly what I told you. My dad got sick, so I had to take the interview. The reporter's questions were nonstop. She insisted on dinner. That was when I sent you the text."

"Hmmph," she said, still suspicious. "You could have called me after the interview ended."

"I thought about it, but I figured you might be busy with classwork and I didn't want to interrupt your sleep if you'd hit the sack," he said.

She stared at him silently.

"Why are we arguing when you and I both know we want to go back to my place and be alone?" he asked in a husky voice that touched her in secret places.

"Is that what you want?" she asked.

"It was what I wanted last night," he said.

Her heart tripped over itself. "Then let's go."

She got into his SUV with him, and at every stop sign he reached across the console to kiss her. Their stops grew longer and hotter. At the next-to-last stop, he gave her a long French kiss. It must have been a very long one because a car behind them beeped.

Cade swore under his breath and raced forward. He glanced at her at the next stoplight, but set his jaw as if he were trying to steel himself from kissing her again. Finally, he pulled into his driveway and stopped the car just outside his front porch. He jumped out of the driver's side of the car and rounded the vehicle to open her door. Then he helped her out and rushed her up the steps and inside his house, slamming the door behind them.

Pushing her against the wall, he tangled his fingers through her hair and took her mouth. "Who was that guy back there? Is he important to you?"

"No," she admitted. "He's just been asking me out for a week or so. I've turned him down."

"Except tonight?" he asked, and she could feel the tension in his strong body. The hint of possessiveness in his tone made her feel as if he'd turned her upside down.

She took a deep breath. "How would you have felt if you'd received a text photo of me having dinner with another man when we were supposed to get together?"

She felt him hold his breath then he released it. "I wouldn't have been happy."

"Well, I wasn't, either," she said, meeting his gaze dead-on.

"You didn't have anything to worry about," he told her.

"How was I supposed to know that?" she challenged.

"I'll show you," he said and took her mouth again.

They tugged off each other's clothes, and soon enough she felt her naked skin against his. He kissed her and touched her as if he couldn't get enough of her. Abby could hardly breathe with the passion he expressed to her.

As if he could no longer wait, he pulled on protection and took her against the wall. Abby wrapped her legs around his waist and clung to him. It was the most exhilarating experience of her life. She almost couldn't believe it was happening, but then he thrust high inside her, groaning his release.

Abby had never felt so desired and so desirable. She'd

dreamed of being with Cade, but the reality was so much more powerful than she'd ever thought possible. A burst of emotion rolled through her, stinging her eyes with its intensity and to her horror, tears began to fall down her face.

Trying to shield her tears from Cade, she turned her head away, praying she'd moved fast enough.

"What's wrong?" he asked, still holding her tightly against him. He slid his hand up to her cheek and felt the telltale wetness. "Did I hurt you?" he asked, sounding horrified.

"No, no," she insisted, swiping at her tears as he lowered her unsteady feet to the floor. "It's ju—just—" She sniffed, damning her emotions. "When I saw that photo of you with her, I thought the other night had been a one-night stand, after all, and—"

"It wasn't," he told her, cradling her against him. "I'm sorry you got that picture. You can check out the feature when it hits the stands. It was really important to the business."

Abby took a deep breath and tried to get herself together. She was appalled that she'd cried.

"I promise," he said, lifting her face to his. "Don't cry anymore. It kills me."

She made herself smile. "No more crying," she promised.

He lifted her up and carried her down the hallway into his bedroom. Placing her gently on his bed, he followed her down. "You are so beautiful," he told her. "You're so much more than I realized."

Her swollen, battered heart eased just a little with his words and she curled into him. "You can skip the condoms," she told him.

"Why?" he asked, looking intently at her.

"I'm on the pill for bad cramps and I'm pretty sure neither one of us has a social disease," she said.

He groaned in anticipation of pleasure. "You just made my day even better," he told her and began to make love to her again.

Two hours later, she pulled on one of his shirts and joined him in the kitchen. "Let me fix you some scrambled eggs and toast," he said. "I'd like to offer you more, but I'm running low on groceries because it's our busy season."

"I don't need any—"

"You're not hungry?" he asked. "Because I'm starving."

Now that he mentioned it, she pressed her hand to her stomach. "Scrambled eggs sound good."

He pulled bread from the freezer and popped four slices into the toaster while he turned on the gas stove. She watched him, naked from the waist up, as he cracked eggs into a bowl and beat them silly. After pouring a little oil in the skillet, he tossed in the eggs and stirred them. Minutes later, both the toast and eggs were ready.

Cade put the food on plates and nudged her to the table. "There," he said, setting a plate in front of her. "I'll have something better for you next time. And there will be a next time," he said, meeting her gaze as he bit off a piece of toast.

Abby took a tentative bite of eggs, surprised to find them cooked perfectly.

"What? You don't like the eggs?" he asked.

"Actually you did a great job with them, not overcooked, not undercooked."

"You sound surprised," he said.

"Well, you're a bachelor carpenter. You haven't mentioned taking cooking classes," she said and scooped another mouthful.

"You thought I was completely useless in the kitchen?"

"I didn't say that," she said. "I just didn't think it was your forte," she said. "Delicious. You didn't even burn the toast."

He chuckled. "That's because it was frozen. You can probably cook circles around me, but I can fix a few things worth eating. Steak, barbecued chicken, fish on the grill."

She smiled. "If it involves fire, you're there. Right?" she asked.

He met her gaze and grinned. "Stop looking at me and finish your eggs before they get cold."

Abby bit her lip and looked at him, anyway.

He looked at her and his gaze held an irresistible mix of sensuality and Cade. "I mean it, Abby. Stop looking at me or I'm going to haul you off to my bed again."

"Would that be such a bad thing?" she asked.

He shook his head and scrubbed his hand over his face. "Finish your eggs. I don't want to be responsible for making you faint."

"Then you should have put on a shirt," she told him and ate her eggs.

Although they got a little distracted, Cade managed to help her get dressed and he bundled her up and led her to his car. "I don't want you having to answer a lot of questions about where you've been," he said and he drove toward her parents' house.

"I don't mind if people know you and I are seeing each other," she said. "Do you?"

"I don't like people poking into my business. I don't want either of us to have to deal with gossips. I just want us to be for us right now," he said and covered her hand with his. "Is that okay with you?"

Warmth flooded her. When he looked at her that way, she would say yes to anything he asked. Plus he made an important point. Even though she had known Cade forever, they hadn't shared an adult relationship very long. After what Laila had said to her the other night, Abby didn't want to hear the opinions of any detractors. She was glad Cade felt the same way.

He stopped in front of her house and pulled her against him once more. "You feel so good it's hard to let you go," he said.

Her heart skipped over itself at his words, and she sighed. "That makes two of us."

"It's supposed to be unseasonably warm for the next day or two. If the weather matches up with the forecast and you're caught up on your classes, maybe I could take you for a spin on my Harley."

"I'd love that," she said, remembering how envious she'd felt all those times Laila had ridden off with Cade on his motorcycle.

"You'll still need to dress warm," he warned her.

"Call me," she said, knowing she would be pulling a late night for her classes in order to make time for a ride with Cade. It would be worth it, she told herself. She could sleep some other time.

The following afternoon, Abby drove out to Cade's house to meet him for their motorcycle ride. The temps were supposed hit the mid-fifties. For Montana in the winter, that was considered a heat wave. She was so excited she felt like a kid at Christmas. He approved her warm clothing. "Good job with the ski mask and gloves. Just hang on and lean with my body on the curves," he said and put a helmet on her head.

She mounted his prized Harley behind him and wrapped her arms around him as he started the engine. "You ready?" he asked.

"I was born ready for this," she said.

He laughed and they were off. Cade steered the motorcycle toward the countryside. Although the roads were perfectly dry, some stubborn snow packs remained here and there. Abby knew this jump in temperature was just a tease. They would get snow again before the week was done. That knowledge made her all the more determined to enjoy the ride.

The moutains loomed with dramatic beauty over the plains, providing breathtaking vistas. A half hour later, Cade pulled into a small diner and parked the Harley near the door. He helped her off the motorcycle and Abby pulled off her helmet and ski mask. She was surprised to feel a little wobbly.

Cade must have noticed because he laughed as he steadied her. "Still feel like you're riding?" he asked.

She nodded. "I can still hear the buzz in my ears, too."

"You'll get used to it," he said. "You just need some practice. I figured we could grab a bite to eat here. If you're not hungry, they make good coffee and hot chocolate."

"Yes to the second," she said and shook her hair as they walked inside. "I bet my hair looks crazy," she said, raking her hands through it self-consciously, feeling it crackle with electricity.

He sat across from her in a booth and shook his head. "You look beautiful. Your cheeks and lips are red and you hair reminds me of what it looks like after we—" He broke off as a waitress approached them.

"How ya doin', Cade?" the thirtysomething red-haired waitress asked with a wink and a smile. "It's been a while, but I guess you don't ride that Harley through a blizzard."

"It's true, Dani. I'll take a club sandwich and coffee. What about you, Abby?" he asked.

"Hot chocolate," she said.

"You sure like 'em young these days, don't you? Are you sure she's legal?" Dani asked with another wink.

Slightly irritated by the waitress's remark, Abby smiled. "I look younger than I am. Must be all that clean living. I guess I need to dirty up my lifestyle a little so I can catch up," she joked.

"No need for that," Cade countered.

The waitress laughed. "I like her sense of humor. Got a little kick behind that sweet face. Good for you. I'll get your coffee and hot chocolate," she said and walked away.

"You handled her pretty well," he said. "Dani's known for ribbing people."

"I have a feeling she's trying to get your attention. She looked at you like she wanted to gobble you up. I guess I can't blame her," she said with an exaggerated sigh.

He chuckled at her. "You keep surprising me. I just never would have expected sweet little Abby to have a wild bone in her body."

"I'm pretty sure I have more than one. I just haven't discovered all of them yet," she said.

He groaned. "Heaven help me. What do you think of the ride so far?"

Dani delivered their beverages and scooted to another table.

"It's glorious," she said. "We are spoiled with all these beautiful views and I think we see them so much we stop really looking at them. You can't avoid it when you're on the motorcycle. The mountains and hills and lakes are right there in your face."

"That's one of the things I like about riding. Nothing between me and nature," he said. "Did you get too cold?"

"No," she said, taking a sip of her hot chocolate. "You kept me warm."

His eyes darkened in sexual awareness. "You're asking for trouble again," he said. "Do you say these kinds of things to other men?"

"No. Why would I do that when it's you I want?"

Cade felt the need ripple through him at the look in her eyes. It was amazing how such an innocent girl—woman, he mentally corrected himself—could get him stirred up with just a side comment or the way she looked at him. Even the way she sipped her hot chocolate was sexy to him. Abby Cates was looking like a lot of trouble, but he didn't feel like running the other way. At least, not yet.

After he talked her into sharing a few bites of his club sandwich, they hit the road again. He slowed as they drew close to Silver Stallion Lake. The lake served as a recreation area for local families and visitors. He'd spent a few summers lifeguarding during the summers.

He pulled to a stop and cut the engine. "I have a lot of memories from here."

"Me, too. It was the first time you held me in your arms," she said.

He swung his head to look at her and pulled off his helmet. "What?"

"Yes," she said, pulling off her own helmet and the ski mask. She had an impish gleam in her eyes. "You were giving swimming lessons. Some water went down the wrong way and you rescued me," she said in a melodramatic tone.

Cade rolled his eyes.

"You don't remember?"

"I can't say I do," he said, racking his brain. "In my defense, I pulled a lot of choking kids out of the water. How old were you?" he asked, then shook his head and lifted his hand. "Don't tell me."

She laughed and swatted at his shoulder. "Feeling old?"

He thought of everything that had happened in his life since those carefree summers at Silver Stallion Lake and the truth was he did feel old. Between the loss of his mother and Dominique, and his work at the shop, he'd felt gutted and empty more often than not.

"You're not old, Cade. You just need to get out and have a little more fun," Abby said. "I can help with that," she offered in that sexy voice that made his blood heat. She squeezed her arms around him and he felt a surprising corresponding squeeze on the inside, somewhere near his heart.

"I might just take you up on it," he said and started the engine. "Get your helmet on," he said and followed his own advice. He accelerated, leaving the lake behind him, but he longed for that lighthearted young man he'd once been.

* * *

Abby sat on Cade's sofa wrapped in his arms. A fire blazed in the fireplace and they both sipped hot cider. She couldn't imagine anything better. She leaned her head against Cade's chest and stroked his hand. After several more moments passed, it occurred to her that Cade hadn't spoken for quite awhile.

"You're quiet," she said. "What are you thinking about?"

He sighed. "Nothing," he said. "Lots of stuff."

She smiled at his response. "I think I'll go with your second answer. What kind of stuff?"

"Oh, what things were like before my mother died. How quickly it all changed. My father changed overnight. My younger brothers went a little wild. I considered it, but I saw how much my dad was hurting. I didn't want to add to the pain. My sister, Holly, she just seemed lost. Dad doted on her, but for a while, there, he was a dead man walking."

"I know that was hard for you," she said.

He nodded. "It was," he said. "And the holidays were the worst. My mother was the one to make holidays happen, so when she was gone, we didn't know what to do. The holidays would hit and we didn't plan for them, so we would fumble around and throw something together." He chuckled. "I can't tell you how many cooking disasters we had. Lesson number one, you need to thaw the turkey."

Abby stroked his hand and studied his face. "Well, at least that's a funny memory."

His smile faded. "Yeah. One of the few."

"I bet there were some other funny ones," she said.

Cade nodded. "The gifts we bought. One of my

brothers bought Holly bubble bath that made her break out. My father gave us savings bonds and stale chocolate my mother had bought a long time ago. He forgot to buy the new stuff, so he gave us the old chocolate. We all ate it, wanting to feel like we had when we were younger, when she was alive, but it didn't work."

"I'm sorry," she said. "I'm sorry she died."

"Yeah, I am, too. And then there was…Dominique," he said.

Abby's stomach clenched. She'd heard very little about Dominique, the woman who had stolen Cade's heart. Her family had lived in town briefly and she'd attended the same local university as Abby. Abby had heard Dominique had been a one-of-a-kind dark-haired beauty. A lot of guys had chased her, but she'd liked Cade best.

"You were serious about her," Abby said.

He nodded.

"Everyone said you were going to propose to her when she returned from her trip to California," she added.

"Everyone was right about that," he said. "She took off between Christmas and New Year's to meet some friends in California. I figured I would surprise her when she got back. I'd bought the ring."

As much as she wanted Cade for herself, the thought of his loss stabbed deeply at her. "I can't imagine how horrible that must have been."

"Pretty damn bad," he said. "And her parents partly blamed me because I didn't propose before she left. They were convinced she would have never gone if I'd asked her first."

Her breath stopped in her chest. "They blamed you? That's horrible."

He shrugged. "Maybe they were right. I wanted her to have a break. She'd been working hard at school. She was looking forward to the beach."

Abby shook her head. "It's just wrong. You were being sweet and—" It was hard for her to say the words, but she swallowed back her own pain. "And loving. Couldn't they see how hurt you were?"

"They were devastated. They couldn't see past their own pain," he said. "I can't blame them."

"So all of this is why the holidays suck for you," she said.

He paused a moment then nodded. "Yeah, I guess so."

Abby took a deep breath and slid her hand to Cade's jaw. "I would if I could, but I can't bring back Dominique or your mom. I can't make things the way they were, but if you're open to it, I can probably make things happier than they have been."

He lifted an eyebrow at her. "You think?"

"Only if you're open to it. If you're not open, I can't do anything. I'm no Houdini."

His lips twitched. "And if I'm open?" he asked, lifting his hand to push a strand of hair from her face.

"I'll surprise you," she said.

"You've already done that."

"Well, I'll do it again."

Chapter Eight

The following night, Cade arrived home and was surprised to find a Christmas wreath hanging from his front door. *What the—* He opened his front door and smelled the delicious scent of something he definitely had not cooked. His dog greeted him with a wagging tale and anticipation of a few bites of whatever was cooking.

"I love you, darlin'," he said, rubbing her soft, furry head. "But the vet says you should only get dry dog food. And this smells so good I may not be able to share."

Cade walked farther into the house, noticing the sound of his television playing the sweet music of Monday-night football. "Hello? I hope you're not an ax murderer, but if you are, can I eat before you kill me?"

Abby poked her head from the kitchen doorway and

smiled. "No plans to kill you," she said. "Unless you complain it's overcooked. Have you looked at the time?"

"You need to remember I had to make up for all the time I lost doing that stupid interview instead of my real work," he complained.

"Yeah, eating a meal at the Hitching Post with a pretty woman making eyes all over you," she said. "Pure agony."

"I guess I shouldn't have brought that up."

"I guess you shouldn't have," she said. "But we could change stations if you're interested in some beef stew."

"Do I have to beg?"

She gave a slow smile. "That's a tempting image," she said. "But I think I'll save it for another time. Come on and I'll pour a bowl. I have biscuits, too."

Cade's mouth drooled. He tried to remember the last time he'd had homemade biscuits and couldn't. Striding into the kitchen with the dog at his heels, he blinked at a turkey decoration, this one hanging from one of his kitchen lights.

"That's something," he said, pointing at the bird.

"Pull his foot," she said, arranging biscuits on a small plate.

Curious, Cade pulled it. Nothing happened.

"Other foot," she said as she placed his meal on the table.

Cade pulled the other foot and the turkey gave a *gobble-gobble* sound. Cade stared at the stuffed bird and couldn't resist pulling the leg again. The turkey gave another *gobble-gobble*.

"I don't know what to say," he said, tempted to pull the foot again, but the aroma of the beef stew called to him at a cellular level. He sat down at the table. "Where the hell did you find it?"

"Addictive, isn't it?" she said with a lone biscuit in front of her. "Seems silly, but it's hard to resist pulling the turkey's foot."

"Is that all you're going to eat?" he asked, his spoon poised over the stew.

She gave a gentle, crocodile smile. "I ate hours ago."

He growled then took his first bite. "Food of the gods," he said. "Who fixed this? Your Mom?"

Quicker than he could take his next breath, she pulled his bowl away from him and he realized he'd made a huge mistake. "Because you're too busy to cook. You have a wicked-crazy schedule. No time for cooking something this amazing." He paused. "Is this when I beg?"

She slid the bowl back in front of him. "Your habit of underestimating me is getting a little old. Even old Mr. Henson tried to tell you I was a good cook."

"You're right," he said, taking another bite and swallowing a moan of pleasure and satisfaction. Cade was a bachelor, all too familiar with frozen dinners and restaurant meals. A home-cooked meal was a thing of wonder to him. "I will never underestimate your cooking again."

"That's good to know," she said, as she leaned her chin on her palms and watched. "Is that the only way you won't underestimate me?"

Cade thought of how she'd made love to him and desire thudded through him. "No, but I won't finish this meal if you keep reminding me."

She smiled. "So, are you rooting for the Eagles?"

He met her gaze and felt his heart lift at her effort

to let him enjoy the meal she'd prepared for him. It occurred to Cade that with the exception of that turkey hanging from the light in the kitchen, he could get used to Abby greeting him with a hot meal and a welcoming smile. Tension eased out of him. She kept surprising him, and he wasn't inclined to ask her to stop.

After he finished his second bowl, he built a fire and they watched the game. In a manner of speaking, anyway. Cade couldn't tell you the score at halftime because he'd been too busy taking off Abby's clothes and making love to her. He pulled her on top of him and she rode him, bringing herself and him to climax. He watched her smooth, creamy skin shimmering in the firelight. Her face glowed with arousal. The expression in her eyes called to him. At the same time, it frightened the hell out of him.

A half hour later, he cradled her in his arms.

"I should head home soon," she said. "It's getting late."

"It would be nice if you could stay all night," he said, brushing his mouth over her soft jaw.

She gave a soft sound of pleasure. "It could be arranged, but it would take some planning."

"Oh, really," he said. "How's that?"

"I've pulled all-nighters with study groups before. I've gone out of town on girl trips."

"If you stayed overnight with me, you wouldn't be studying schoolwork, I can promise you that," he growled.

She laughed. "No, I would just say something along those lines to my parents."

"I don't like the idea of you lying to your family about me," he said.

"Well, you want to keep it on the down low. And I'd just as soon not get grilled about it, either." She sighed. "Maybe I can figure something out. But I should head out now."

"See you tomorrow night?" he asked reluctantly, standing with her, pulling on his jeans as she got dressed.

"No. Tomorrow night I'm with my ROOTS girls. During the day, I'm helping with the community-center Thanksgiving production. Thank goodness, they'll be giving their performance soon. Then they'll be out on break. That reminds me, I should stop by and check on Mr. Henson, too." She glanced up at Cade. "So tomorrow I'll be slammed. Do you want to try for lunch on Wednesday or is that too public for you?"

"I can do lunch on Wednesday," he said, but was surprised at his eagerness to spend more time with her. Maybe it was the sex. Lord, he hoped so because a big part of him wanted to occupy all of her free time.

"You'll have to keep your hands off of me," she warned him with a sexy tilt of her lips. "You'll have to pretend we're just friends. Are you sure you can do that?"

With the way she was looking at him, he suspected it might be more difficult than he would have expected, but Cade had a long history with self-restraint. "I guess I'll just have to buck up and do my best," he said, pulling her back into his arms. "We'll make up for it some other time."

Cade insisted on following her home. It didn't feel right to have her drive home by herself. If they'd been officially dating, he would have always walked her to her door. As she got out of her car, she waved at him and walked into her family home.

Cade stared after her. She was so young, tender and sweet. He knew she was stronger than he'd originally thought, far more of a woman, but he still feared that he would hurt her. He couldn't help believing that eventually Abby would want all of him, and Cade had lost part of himself a long time ago, and that part would never come back.

Abby helped at the community center and spent the afternoon in class. Afterward, she squeezed in some time at the university library. Since she'd been spending so much time with Cade, she was really having to maximize her study time. Sipping a bottle of water, she made notes for yet another paper she was writing.

"One of your friends told me I might find you here," a male voice said.

Abby glanced up to find Daniel looking down at her with a smile. "Uh, hi," she said, completely surprised. "Who—"

"Char," he said and sat down next to her. "You disappeared the other night at the Hitching Post. I was concerned about you. That guy looked pretty intense."

"Cade?" she said. "Cade would never hurt me. No, I've been crazy busy and I can't talk now because I need to work on this paper."

"Rain check?" he asked and, when she paused, he covered her hand with his. "You gotta give me a rain check after I tracked you down."

Uncomfortable, she moved her hand away from his. "You really shouldn't have."

"I see a woman who makes me curious and I gotta

find out more," he said. "But I can wait. Take care. I'll keep in touch," he said and strolled out of the library.

Abby frowned after him. She would definitely need to speak to Char about passing any further personal information on to this guy. The more often she saw him, the more uncomfortable he made her and he didn't seem the least bit discouraged. She shrugged off her uneasiness and refocused on her paper, wondering what Carl Jung would have to say about Daniel.

A half hour before her meeting with the ROOTS girls, Abby left the library and grabbed a fast-food burger and soda. She usually skipped caffeine this late in the day, but she could feel herself starting to fade. From her first visit at ROOTS, Abby had learned she had to be on her toes with the girls.

The group started out small and quiet, so she helped the girls with their homework. Since many of the girls came from such disrupted homes, it was often difficult for them to find a quiet place to concentrate. Thirty minutes into their meeting time Katrina and Keisha burst into the room.

"You have to report him. You have to. What if it gets worse?" Keisha asked Katrina.

"Shut up," Katrina hissed. "If I ignore him, he'll go away."

Abby stood, alarmed at the bruises she saw on Katrina's face. "Girls," she said.

Keisha looked at Abby and lifted her chin defiantly. "You talk to her. She won't listen to me."

"Katrina?" she said. "Would you like some water or hot chocolate? We can talk over there if you like," she said.

Katrina was a sixteen-year-old with bleached blond

hair who did her best to make herself look tough with the black leather and kohl eyeliner she wore. Abby knew that beneath her tough exterior, the girl had a mother who was rarely at home and Katrina was struggling to stay away from a bad crowd at school. She'd been suspended for smoking in the girls' room.

"It's no big deal," Katrina said as she swiped her damp face with the back of her hand. "It's my mother's new boyfriend. He's been staying over and he gets pissed when I spend too much time in the bathroom. I'll just spend the night with one of my friends. He'll cool down."

Abby didn't like the sound of this at all. She handed Katrina a cup of hot chocolate. "Does your mother know?"

Katrina shrugged, but her hand was shaking as she held the cup. "She's too busy. She's working three jobs. He says he was laid off," she said, but her tone suggested she didn't believe him.

"How long has he been around?" Abby asked.

"A couple months. He was okay in the beginning, but once he started staying overnight, he thought he could tell me what to do when my mom wasn't around. He really likes his whiskey. Seems like he drinks a bottle every day."

"I'm so sorry you've had to go through this," Abby said.

"Don't feel sorry for me. I can take care of myself."

Abby nodded. "If Keisha was in this situation, what advice would you give her?"

Katrina gave a short laugh that almost sounded like a sob. "Keisha wouldn't be in this situation. She would kick his butt out of the house."

"Okay. What about Shannon?"

Katrina paused. "Shannon's different."

"What would you tell her?"

"As much as it sucks, I would tell her to rat on him. It's such a pain to deal with child protective services. If only we were eighteen," she said. "Everything would be easier."

"Not so much," Abby said. "But that's not the point. I want you to give an official report. I could do it, but I want you to care enough about yourself to do it for yourself."

Katrina sighed. "I'll have to stay with some super strict people I don't know," she said.

"Maybe not," Abby said. "Plus it wouldn't be forever. Do you really think your mother would keep this guy around if she knew he was hitting you?"

Katrina shrugged. "She doesn't want to deal with it."

"Which means you have to," Abby said. "You deserve to live in a situation where you are not abused and neglected. If I've helped you learn anything, you've learned that."

"I don't want to be with people who are always telling me what to do. You know I'm not used to that," she said.

"It's temporary," Abby said. "That's what you have to remember. You're a strong young woman and this is one of those times when you need to be your own best friend. I'll go with you to make the report."

Katrina swore under her breath. "You really think I have to do it?"

"You've been around here long enough to see what happened with other girls in this situation. You are a very smart, very capable young woman. I think if you end up with someone who wants to know where you are and when it may not be fun, but it will be a lot better than worrying about whether you'll be beaten. And I repeat, it won't be forever."

Katrina sighed. "Okay, okay. Can we do it now? Believe it or not, I don't want to miss school tomorrow. I have an exam."

"Let me take a few more minutes with the other girls, then you and I can head out," she said.

Abby talked to the other girls while Keisha walked over to give Katrina a big hug and shook her finger at the girl. Abby felt a surge of warmth at how the girls were supporting each other.

Hours later, Katrina was safely tucked in bed at her temporary foster parents' home while her mother's boyfriend was brought in for questioning and would soon be charged with assault on a minor. Before that, the drama had intensified: Katrina's mother arrived in a sad state, apologizing profusely to her daughter and promising to do a better job.

Although it was nearly 2:00 a.m. when Abby arrived home, she felt a sense of temporary relief that she knew Katrina was safe, and she was so proud of her ROOTS girl for choosing to stick up for herself. These girls came across as tough, but many of them had been abused, and one of Abby's biggest goals had been to help them grow away from a victim mentality.

Abby said a little prayer, and just before she drifted off to sleep, she thought of Cade. She wished all of those girls at ROOTS could find a man as strong and gentle as Cade.

Cade met Abby at DJ's for lunch on Wednesday. He arrived a couple minutes early and ordered coffee for

himself. He didn't mention that anyone would be joining him, but sat in one of the booths at the back of the
restaurant. He saw her open the door and glance around,
pushing her hair behind her ear. Instead of waving, he
simply stood, and within an eye blink, she saw him and
moved toward him.

"What a surprise to see you here," she said in a mocking voice and gave him a far-too-quick hug before she
sat down. "Nice to see you," she said.

He drank in the sight of her, noticing the dark circles
under her eyes and the slight pallor of her skin. "Did
you sleep at all last night?"

"Why?" she asked. "Do I look like a hag?"

"I would never call you a hag," he said.

"Well, something must have made you say that,"
she said.

The waitress showed up then. "Lunch ribs with coleslaw for me," he said. "What about you?" he asked Abby.

She gave a quick glance at the menu and shrugged.
"Barbecue sandwich and fries. I need some grease."

"And to drink?" the waitress asked.

"A chocolate milk shake," she said.

The waitress smiled. "Excellent choice. I'll be back
soon."

"So I look like a hag," she said to Cade.

"I did *not* say that. You just look very tired. Circles
under your eyes, your skin is pale—"

"I need to get better with concealer. I think it's a required skill. Think about it. If you can hide dark circles,
then no one will know that you spent the last night with
a girl who'd been beat up by her mother's boyfriend."

"Oh, my God. Who's the girl?" Cade asked. "Who's
the guy? If you want me to talk to him—"

She finally smiled, and it was like the sun broke through. "I knew you'd say something like that. That's one of the reasons I—" She broke off. "One of the reasons I like you."

Warmth spread throughout his chest, but he tried to shrug it off. "Is the girl okay?"

"For now," Abby said. "I had to talk her into reporting the incident and the guy. I stayed with her thoughout the whole experience and the poor girl was put through the ringer. The temporary foster parents seem pretty nice if they can deal with her independence. She's used to doing everything for herself, which means she's not used to taking orders or filling anyone in on her whereabouts."

"That's a rough way to live," he said. "You do a good job with those kids at ROOTS."

"Sometimes I wonder if they do more for me. But I have to tell you when someone has been physically abused, it really draws the line about what needs to be done. Her sweet face was bruised all over. I was just glad I could be a tiny part of getting her to a safe place."

"I bet you're a much bigger part than you think you are," he said, wishing he could take her hands in his, pull her against him so she could relax for a little while.

She shrugged. "What's important is that Katrina is safe. I hope things will continue to be on the upswing for her. I'll be watching, that's for sure."

"Hmm," he said.

She shot him a sideways glance. "What does that mean?"

"It means you're always talking about me having a hero complex. I'm starting to wonder if you don't have the same problem," he said.

Her lips tilted again. "Very funny," she said.

"I'm not being funny," he said.

"Sure you are," she said and the waitress delivered their food. "Thanks," she said to the woman.

"My pleasure," she said. "You two let me know if you need anything else, okay?"

Both of them dug in to their food, creating a comfortable silence. Abby took a few sips of her milk shake. "Brain freeze," she said, squeezing the bridge of her nose then shaking her head. "How have things been at work? Any more gorgeous reporters?"

"No more reporters at all. It's back to me and the wood. Sometimes I make art. Sometimes I make furniture. I do a lot of knocking, sawing and sanding, but no one needs to call the police because of it, thank goodness."

"That's a funny thought," she said. "You sawing on a piece of wood and a bunch of wood specialists come in and arrest you."

"Very funny," he said, clearly disagreeing with her. "But the truth is it's pretty satisfying. I'm sure it's not as big as having a kid, but it's been good for me. You really look like you could use a nap. If I were in charge, I would take you off to bed so you could get some rest."

"I'll survive. I'm a young college student. We exist on adrenaline, right?"

"If you say so," he said. "I'd still like to drag you off and make you take a nap."

She paused a half beat, studying him. "I may not wake up for a long time if you did that, and today, I've still got a long ways to go."

"Don't burn the candle at both ends too long. Mother

Nature has a way of kicking you on your butt if you push her too far."

"Sounds like you're speaking from experience," she said and swallowed more of her shake.

"Unfortunately," he said in a wry voice.

The waitress delivered the check and when Abby glanced up, Cade noticed she cringed and sorta hunched down. As soon as the waitress left, he studied her. "What's up?"

She lifted one shoulder, glanced over it then looked back at Cade. "Probably nothing. It just seems like this guy keeps showing up everywhere I am. It's like he has a GPS on me or something."

His sense of protectiveness shot up inside him. "Who is he?"

"He's a server at the Hitching Post. He was flirting with my friends and me the night I was out with them, but I wasn't all that impressed. I think he's one of those guys who is attracted to a girl because she's not interested. I think he sees it as a challenge."

"What's his name?"

Abby lifted her gaze as if she were searching her brain. "Um. *D* something. Daniel."

"Daniel what?"

She shook her head. "I have no idea."

"Is he the guy who was hitting on you the other night? Do you think he's stalking you?" he asked, his gut tightening. He didn't like the idea of anyone bothering Abby.

She paused a half beat and shook her head again. "No, he can't be. It's just that he showed up at the university library and he doesn't even go there, so that creeped me out a little. It's probably nothing. I'm probably freaking out because I need sleep," she joked. "Don't worry."

But he would. If he didn't worry, he would think about it. "Let me know if he pops up anywhere else during the next few days."

"It's really nothing," she said.

"Then it won't be a big deal for you to tell me if he shows up," he said. "Deal?"

Her lips lifted in a slow smile. "Deal." She took another sip of her milk shake through the straw and gave a quick, soft sound of approval that reminded him of... *No need thinking about that,* he told himself.

"Where are you headed? I'll walk you to your car," he said.

"Are you sure you want to do that? People may talk," she said, her eyes glinting with flirty challenge.

"I'll keep my hands to myself," he said, barely containing a growl.

"Well, darn," Abby said and stood, and Cade was treated to the sight of the sexy sashay of her sweet, round bottom as they walked from DJ's.

Friday couldn't come soon enough, Abby thought as she sat in the diner waiting to meet two classmates to discuss their presentation for class the following Tuesday. In charge of the Jung presentation, she filled out a few more note cards as she waited.

"You never stop, do you?"

Abby's stomach knotted at the voice that was becoming all too familiar. She reluctantly glanced up. "Daniel. What a surprise," she said.

He smiled. "It's not that big of a surprise. I know you

like this place and you frequent it at night. You know I'd like us to spend more time together."

His smile was a little too practiced. It bothered her. "I hate to be blunt, but us spending more time together? It's not going to happen."

"Sure it is. You'll catch a break soon, be ready for some entertainment." He bent his knees and braced himself on the table so his face was level with hers. "I'm more than ready to provide it."

"No," she said, wishing she didn't have to be even more blunt. It was as if he'd completely forgotten the other time she'd turned him down. "You don't understand. I'm not interested in having a relationship with you."

He shrugged. "No problem. We can start out having fun."

Abby was tempted to scream, but she swallowed the urge. "You know how there are girls who say no and mean yes?" she asked. "I'm not one of those girls."

Chapter Nine

"I'm on my way," she said after Cade picked up his cell phone. "Can we have some sort of fabulous take-out for dinner?"

"Such as?" Cade asked.

"Lobster, filet mignon, asparagus, au gratin potatoes, chocolate mousse, followed by some time in a hot tub and maybe one of those martinis you got me at the Hitching Post. Nothing too complicated," she said.

He chuckled. "Right."

"Pizza and soda. I hardly ever drink soda, but tonight I want to be bad."

He laughed louder. "If soda is your version of bad…" he began.

"Don't mock me. At least I kept it simple."

"I'll see what I can do," he said. "Stella will be glad to see you when you get here."

"Anyone else around there who'll be happy to see me?" she asked.

"Me," he said.

Twenty minutes later, she pulled into Cade's driveway, stopping as she drew close to his porch. Normally, she would jump out of her car and bound up the steps, but she was seriously dragging tonight. She hoped she didn't embarrass herself by falling asleep unexpectedly. It didn't help that just as she left the community center this morning, Daniel had been waiting in front of the building. She hadn't said anything to her friends yet, but she thought she was going to have to have a conversation with Char. Her friend probably was just trying to nudge her into giving in to a fun time with a hot guy. Char had no idea that Abby was involved with someone else.

Frustration nicked at her. In one way, she chafed at the idea of keeping her relationship with Cade secret. In another way, she agreed with him that she didn't want to endure anyone else's thoughts or assessments of her and Cade. So, for now, she just had to be evasive. Not her best talent.

Sighing, Abby got out of her car and stretched. The wind whipped over her, reminding her that it was still winter. The warm day last weekend had been a quick little treat and it was gone now. Bundling her collar upward, she climbed the stairs and knocked on the door.

Stella barked, and within seconds Cade opened the door. "Well, look what the wind blew in. Very nice," he said, tugging her inside and pressing his mouth against hers. "You're cold," he said.

"That's why I mentioned a hot tub," she said and

glanced behind him. "You have one in your back pocket?"

"Very cute," he said. "I don't have a hot tub, but I have a tub filled with hot water. If you're interested," he said.

She stared at him in disbelief. "Really? A tub? For me? A bath? Omigosh, I can't believe it. An early Christmas gift."

"It's just a tub," he warned, guiding her toward the hall bathroom.

"Haven't you noticed how many sisters I have? Do you know how often I get to take a bath? Take a guess," she said, staring at the steaming water. It was all she could do not to instantly strip and jump in the tub.

"Not often. Go ahead. Get in. Just don't drown," he said.

She smiled and squeezed his arm. "Oh, I won't drown. I had an excellent swimming teacher."

He shook his head. "Shut up and take a bath."

"Really? Are you sure I don't need to wait for the pizza?" she asked.

He shook his head again. "No need," he said. "But don't fall asleep."

Abby shut the door behind him, stripped out of her clothes, twisted her hair into a knot on top of her head and put her foot in the steaming water. It was *hot*. Which made it perfect. She eased the rest of her body inside the tub and leaned her head against the back of the tub. Abby was in heaven. Her long showers rarely lasted over eight minutes, so soaking in Cade's bathtub felt like the most indulgent luxury possible.

She felt the muscles in her body relax, tendon by tendon. From some point in her brain, she thought she heard Cade's doorbell ring. Pizza? she wondered, but couldn't find it in herself to move more than a millimeter. Had her bones turned to butter? She hadn't felt this relaxed in...how many years?

Mentally playing a jazz song, she closed her eyes and just floated.

Seconds later, she heard Cade knocking on the door and instantly sat up, startled. "What?" she asked, wondering when the water had turned cold. She shivered at the temperature. It had been so lovely and hot, like, two minutes ago.

"Abby, I'm starting to get worried. Answer me. Are you conscious?" Cade asked from the other side of the door.

"I'm here. I'm awake." Beginning to shiver, she stepped out of the tub. "Is the pizza here?"

"In a manner of speaking," Cade said, opening the door and extending a terry-cloth robe in her direction. "You want this?"

"That would be perfect," she said, grabbing the robe and clutching it against her.

"Don't drag your feet. I don't want the pizza to get cold," he said.

"Okay, okay," she said to herself then spoke louder as she towel dried herself. "I'll be out in a minute."

She pushed her hands through the sleeves of the robe, tied the sash and bent over to pull the plug out of the drain of the tub.

Stepping out of the bathroom, she headed down the hall to the kitchen and found a table spread with steaks, shrimp, baked potatoes, *asparagus*—she noted in shock—and bread. She looked at Cade in surprise. "I thought we were having pizza," she said.

"You don't want it?" he said.

"No," she said. "Of course I do. I'm just so—" She was both amazed and touched. "How did you do this?"

"A little help from my brother. I couldn't pull off the lobster. This time," he added, rubbing his chin thoughtfully.

Unable to stop herself, she threw herself against him and wrapped her arms around him. "I can't believe this. Aren't you Mr. Hotshot?"

He squeezed her against him. "You get this excited about a nice meal?"

"It's not the meal. It's the fact that you would go to the trouble to make me happy," she said. As soon as the words were out, she feared she should have kept them in.

"It wasn't that much trouble," he insisted, clearly uncomfortable.

"It was nice. Very nice," she said. "Thank you."

She lifted her lips upward, and he paused a half beat, then kissed her. The pause bothered her, but then he kissed the bother out of her.

Cade pulled back. "I can't let you distract us from eating this meal."

"Even if I tried my very best?" she said, sliding her fingers down the neck of the robe to the belt.

"Stop," he said. "Or Stella will get this while I'm hauling you off to my bed."

He pulled out a chair for her and she took the seat, reveling in his attention. Abby and Cade ate the steak and vegetables, nibbled on the bread. She sipped a fruity martini he'd concocted for her and poured into a beer mug. "This is fabulous. I haven't had a meal like this in—" She broke off. "I can't remember when I had a meal like this."

"I'm glad you asked for it," he said, nodding. "I should do this more often."

"I didn't ask for it," she said. "I was joking. I told you I was joking. I never expected you to actually to do this."

"So I surprised you?" he asked, a wicked glint in his eyes.

"Yes, you surprised me," she said. "And it's all wonderful, but I'm so full I don't think I can eat one more bite."

"Better make some room," he said, taking another bite of his steak. "There's something chocolate in the fridge."

Surprised again, she shook her head. "You're joking."

"Not me. I guess I can let you take a little break if you need to. Want to sit in front of the fire?"

"As long as you promise to keep me awake," she said.

"Burning the candle at both ends again," he said. "I warned you about that."

"It's temporary. My schedule should ease up soon. Besides, I have to ask you, what time do you get up and go into the shop?"

"That's different," he said. "I'm used to getting up at 5:00 a.m. I've been doing it since…" He shot her a dead-serious look. "Since you were ten."

"You are wicked and horrible. People don't know," she said. "They all think you're this super amazing, wonderful upstanding citizen, but I know the truth."

"And what is the truth?" he asked, his eyes glinting with the devil again.

"You are quite simply the devil," she said. *And I'm*

falling out of my crush on you and into love with you.
She bit her tongue to keep from saying the words. She'd
always known she had a crush on Cade. In her more
melodramatic moments, she'd insisted it was a lifelong
passion. But real forever love? Oh, no, this wasn't good.

Cade's hand shot out to grip her arm. "Are you okay,
Abby? You look a little squeamish. Did the food bother
you?"

Abby shook her head. "Not at all. It was wonderful,
and you know it. Thank you for arranging such a fabulous meal. I'm very touched," she said, feeling her throat
grow swollen with emotion. Oh, heaven help her, she
couldn't cry. "I'm also very full, so I'd like to take you
up on that offer to sit in front of the fire." She stood.
"Let me help you clear the table first."

Moments later, he linked his hand through hers as
they walked into his den. It was Friday night, so there
wasn't much on television. Abby sank onto the sofa.
"Oh, what a day and now what a wonderful night."

"Rough day?" he asked.

"Just busy. Went to the community center, visited
Katrina, took an exam and got fitted for a bridesmaid
dress." She winced when she realized what she'd said.
"I'm sorry. Really sorry."

"It's okay," he said. "I'm happy for Laila."

She searched his gaze and saw that he was telling
the truth. A sliver of ease slipped through her and she
sighed. "That is really good."

He nodded and pulled her against him. "Anything
else?"

"Not really. My car is working great. I'm not behind on my papers. I have a group presentation next
week, and I'm ready for my part." She paused. "Um,

I guess I should tell you this. I don't have to stay tonight, but I told my mom I might be staying overnight with a friend."

"I don't want you lying to your family about us," he said.

"But you also don't want me telling them the truth about us, either," she pointed out, lifting her hand to his chin. "That makes it kinda tough, so I told her the truth when I said I might be staying with a friend. You are my friend, aren't you?" she asked, leaning toward him and pulling his head down to hers. "A very, very good friend, right?" she asked and he kissed her.

Abby fell asleep just before ten o'clock, which told him she was continuing to burn the candle at both ends. He'd have to wake her up to fuss at her, though, and she looked so tired he couldn't bring himself to do it. He picked her up and carried her to his bed. She semi-awakened then immediately fell back asleep. Cade slid into the other side of his bed and tried to remember the last time a woman had spent the entire night. His house was his private domain, so he rarely invited a woman to stay longer than an evening. He looked at the outline of her feminine form beneath the covers and knew she was naked underneath. It wouldn't take much for him to want to wake her and make love to her. He knew she wouldn't protest, either. He couldn't remember a woman who had matched his sexual appetite, but Abby did.

He couldn't explain it and sure as hell didn't want to overthink it, but he liked seeing Abby in his bed. She was the last thing he saw before he fell asleep and the first thing he saw when he awakened the next morning. Sometime during the night, she'd snuggled up against him. Her legs were laced through his and one of his arms was curled around her waist. Her eyelids were fluttering and she blinked as her eyes opened as if she weren't sure where she was.

"You're here with me," he said. "In my bed."

"I was getting there," she said. "I'm not always speedy quick in the morning. I don't remember coming into your bedroom," she said, lifting her head to glance around. "I haven't spent a lot of time here before, so I was curious…"

"You didn't get here under your own steam. I carried you," he said.

She looked at him in surprise. "Well, darn, I wish I hadn't missed that." She gave a sheepish smile. "I must have fallen asleep very early. Sorry."

"It wasn't that early," he said and lifted a finger to her nose. "If you're nine years old."

She swatted his hand away. "Thanks a lot. I was a regular box of Cracker Jack last night, minus the popcorn and the toy."

He laughed. "You made up for it before," he said and pulled her against him. "And today you're all mine."

When Abby finally looked out the window, she saw that it had snowed several inches during the night. So much for another motorcycle ride. Not today. They still managed to share a glorious day without leaving Cade's property. After breakfast, she joined him in his workshop as he tinkered with the motorcycle of a friend who had asked him to pimp it out. During the afternoon, he watched part of a college game while she put the finishing touches on her brief PowerPoint presentation. Afterward they went outside and tossed the ball with Stella. The dog couldn't get enough of the game.

When it began to turn dark, they went inside and ordered pizza.

"You're quiet," Cade said after a few moments of silence. "And you're not eating much of the pizza."

"I hate to see the day end," she admitted. Her stomach was clenching at the prospect of returning home and having to pretend that she still wasn't involved with Cade. Plus, the day had been so wonderful and they hadn't done anything monumental. They'd just been together.

"Me, too," he said. "But it will be easier this way if we don't have other people knowing our business."

"I guess," she said.

She saw him stiffen slightly. "You don't agree?"

"Well, I'm one of six children. My mother is all wrapped up in planning Laila's wedding, so I'm not sure she has any time to think twice about who I'm dating as long as he's not a recently released convict."

He chuckled. "I guess I could pass muster on that one. I just don't want to deal with the gossip and uninvited opinions. I don't like people talking about my private business."

"Except when you asked Laila to marry you in front of the whole town," she said, because it popped out of her mouth before she could bite her tongue. She bit her lip instead—way too late.

"That was strictly a moment of insanity invoked by a combination of a stupid discussion with my brothers, whiskey and the fact that I'd recently turned thirty," he said.

Abby gaped at him and covered her mouth. "You were having an age crisis?"

"I figured she probably was, too, since she's the same age as me. I figured I need to start a family sometime. May as well be sooner than later."

Cade could start a family with her, Abby thought, but although he had come around to seeing her as a lover, he didn't seem to view her as a viable option as a wife. The knowledge stung, but her ego had taken a beating more than once with Cade. "So that was a phase," she said. "You're not interested in having a family anymore."

"I didn't say that, but it's got to be the right time with the right person," he said.

A stab of pain shot through her. She'd already hinted that Cade could have what he wanted with her, but he seemed determined not to hear her. She refused to beg. "I hope you find exactly what you're looking for."

He blinked at her response. "What does that mean?"

"Exactly what I said. I think people get into relationships to meet different needs. We all have to figure out who can really meet our needs and who can't," she said and picked up her slice of pizza and prayed she would be able to swallow the bite she took.

Cade seemed more thoughtful than usual during the next hour. He watched her carefully. "I'm thinking you're going to have another busy day tomorrow since you played hooky today."

"You're thinking right," she said, mentally reviewing her insane schedule.

"How's Monday since you'll be busy Tuesday night?" he suggested.

She was impressed that he remembered her standing ROOTS commitment, but didn't allow herself to get too worked up over it. "Monday is better. What did you have in mind?" she asked.

"I'll come up with something better than Monday-night football. Will that work?" he asked.

"Yes. I love surprises," she said.

"It's a good thing one of us does because I hate them," he muttered, then pulled her against him. "What's going on in that pretty head of yours?" he demanded.

"You mean you can't read my mind? I would have sworn that was one of your superpowers," she joked.

"You must have me confused with someone else," he said.

"Nope," she said, shaking her head. "I would swear it was you."

"Well, you're wrong, and I've noticed you still haven't told me what's going on in your brain," he said.

"Good for you," she said, still not revealing her thoughts and feelings. "Observant, too." She lifted her hands to his shoulders and sighed. "When are you going to stop talking and kiss me?"

Between the impending holidays, her cousins' upcoming double wedding and Laila's wedding planning, things at the Cateses' household were moving at a fever pitch. Her sisters were busy with their jobs and social lives, and it always seemed as if one or two of them were moving in or out of the house. Her brother, who still lived at home, provided ample companionship for her father since they were both football freaks and her brother would choose to root for the team opposing her father's choice just to up the ante.

All the busyness made Abby wonder if anyone would really notice if she were gone for a few days, or more.

A tempting thought when she daydreamed about taking a trip with Cade… As if that would happen. Maybe in her next life.

On Sunday, her mother encouraged all the kids to go to church. "It won't hurt you. You may even learn something," she'd always said.

Abby often enjoyed the worship service on Sunday morning. It was a quiet slice of time that offered her the opportunity to calm down and remember what was important. Today, however, as she sat with her mother, father, Laila and Jackson, she found herself checking her watch and resisting the urge to squirm. Just two weeks away from Thanksgiving, the sermon topic focused on sharing with both friends and those less fortunate. The pastor pointed out that even though our friends may not seem to need anything, many of us keep our vulnerabilities hidden. He also said that we should especially keep people in mind who have suffered losses during the holidays.

Abby couldn't help thinking of Cade. People thought of him as the man on whom everyone could depend. He was, but Abby had caught a glimpse of the pain of loss he suffered, pain he rarely let anyone see. It frustrated her that he would only let her so close when she was certain she could make some of his pain go away. Even though he clearly had passion for her, she knew he didn't view their relationship as long-term, and that hurt her every time she thought about it. Something inside her kept her from giving up just yet. During the last hymn, she thought about how to help Cade through the holiday season. Christmas was right around the corner and she wanted him to feel joy instead of dread.

After church, she helped her mother put a big Sunday lunch on the table. Roasted chicken with vegetables, mashed potatoes and biscuits. Her entire family, along with Jackson, made it for the meal.

Abby's father gave a quick grace, and a second after he said "Amen," her brother was reaching for the mashed potatoes.

"I'm glad all of you were able to join us for lunch," Abby's mother said. "I'm sorry you missed church. The minister gave an excellent sermon. Don't you agree, Abby?"

Abby hated being put on the spot, especially when her mother was using her as the example, especially when she was not the least bit perfect. "Very good sermon. The minister reminded us to be generous and thoughtful to everyone because we don't always know when people are suffering. Mom, you and Dad have been such good examples in this area, I'm sure the rest of us will be thinking about this." She searched for a change of subject and glanced at Laila. "How are the wedding plans coming?"

"I can't believe all the details," she said. "It's not just choosing my dress. It's also choosing the bridesmaids' dresses and what the men will wear, the decorations for the church, what the theme will be."

"Vegas sounds like a great theme to me," Jackson muttered. "Eloping."

Abby's mother gasped. "Don't you dare think of it."

"Too late for thinking," Jackson said. "But don't you worry, Mama Cates. I want everyone to know Laila is off the market."

Everyone at the table except Abby laughed. Jackson's comment was in stark contrast to Cade's determination to keep his relationship with her a secret. One more little stab, but Abby brushed it aside.

Speed-cleaning the dishes and kitchen after the meal with a couple of her sisters, Abby mentally planned her afternoon and evening.

"You sure are quiet," Jordyn, one of her sisters, said as she dried a pot.

"And you're cleaning like a bat out of you-know-where," Jasmine agreed, as she dried a pan. "What's the rush? Aren't you gonna hang around for the football game?"

"Not today," Abby said. "I have too much to do. I'm behind on my schoolwork."

"Well, don't work too hard," Jordyn said, shooting her a look of concern. "You're looking a little thin and rough. Circles under your eyes."

"If it were anyone but you, I'd wonder if you were lovesick," Jasmine said just as Laila walked into the kitchen.

"Lovesick?" Laila echoed. "Who's lovesick?"

"No one," Abby said firmly. "I've just got a lot of schoolwork to do. Add that to working at the community center and ROOTS and I'm swamped."

"Hmm," Laila said, clearly unconvinced.

"Like I said," Jasmine repeated. "I'd think you were lovesick if I didn't know you better. You've always been more into your grades than dating."

"And you've always been more into dating than anything else," Abby said with a laugh.

Jasmine swatted at her with the towel, but Abby successfully dodged her sister. "I gotta run. Hope you guys win your bets this time."

"Fat chance," Jordyn said with a mock scowl. "Brody almost always manages to win."

Abby headed for her bedroom to gather her laptop and books. Just as she turned around, Laila appeared in the doorway. "Lovesick?"

Abby's stomach sank. She really didn't want to have this discussion. "Not me," Abby said. "I don't have time to be lovesick."

"But Jazzy had a point. You look like you've lost weight and you have circles under your eyes," Laila said. "I can't help thinking Cade is responsible."

"Cade is not responsible. You know I have a crazy schedule," Abby told her, grabbing her coat from the back of her chair, mentally scolding herself for almost forgetting it. She needed to get her head together. She was far too distracted.

"I also know you're crazy for Cade," Laila said.

"So what if I am?" Abby tossed back at her sister. "You don't quiz Jazzy about all her boyfriends. Why me?"

Laila hesitated. "Because you're different," she said. "Your heart is softer. I'm afraid you could really get hurt."

Her sister's concerns slid past her defenses and Abby fought the sting of tears in her eyes. She dumped her stuff on the desk and wrapped her arms around Laila in a hug. "I'm lucky to have a sister who cares so much about me, but you can't stop this. You can't keep me from getting hurt. This isn't the same as when I was learning to ride a bike and I scraped my knees. I can't turn away from the most amazing man in the world."

Laila groaned. "Oh, no. You really do have it bad."

Abby pulled back and forced a tiny laugh from the

back of her tight throat. "Well, it's about time, isn't it?" she asked. "However it turns out, I'll survive. I've got the backbone of a Cates."

Laila sighed. "That's true. I just hate—"

"Stop," Abby said. "Be happy for me. When I'm with Cade, I'm happier than I ever dreamed possible."

Laila gave a slow nod. "But if you need anything from a hug to a place to stay for the night, you let me know."

"I will. Thanks," Abby said. "Now, I've really got to go."

"And don't forget to eat," Laila yelled as Abby flew out the door.

That night at the library, Abby typed notes on her laptop for two more papers with a deadline before Thanksgiving. She took a sip from a bottle of water as she scanned one of her research books for more facts pertinent to her topic. She'd been so distracted by her time with Cade that she'd slipped up and forgotten about these papers. Plus she'd checked on Katrina today just before her mother showed up for a parental visit. That situation was looking up since Katrina's mother had kicked her boyfriend out of her house and life.

She scratched a note on her notebook and decided to look for another reference. Glancing at the time on her cell phone, she winced. The library closed at midnight and it was already ten-thirty. She searched for a couple more titles that looked promising and headed back to the section that held those books. "Not that, not that, not that," she murmured then found one of her books. "There you are."

"Exactly. There you are," a male voice said from behind her.

Abby swung around to find Daniel standing just a few feet away from her. "Oh, you startled me."

"Gotta keep a girl like you off balance to keep you interested."

Except, she had never been interested, she thought, irritated, as she turned back to the bookshelf. "I really can't chat tonight, Daniel. I've got to find one more book to make some notes."

"You're always busy, Abby. You need to take a break. You know what they say. All work and no play is bad for your health."

"My health is fine. It will be a lot better when I get through this semester," she muttered as she surveyed the shelves.

Daniel stepped between her and the shelves she was searching. "C'mon, Abby. I've been chasing you for weeks. What's it take to get your attention?"

She noticed the smell of alcohol on his breath and her irritation intensified. "Daniel, I told you I don't have time for this tonight. I don't have time for this at all. I'm not interested in you," she said bluntly. Surely that would make him leave.

"Why not?" he asked, moving toward her, so that she backed against the opposite shelf. "Your friends tell me you need to get out more. You're not involved with anyone." He lowered his head. "I think we could be good together. Very good," he said as he lowered his mouth.

Shocked, Abby turned her head and tried to step away, but Daniel closed his arms around her. "You ought to give me a chance. Just one. I could change your mind."

"Let me go, Daniel," she said, her heart beating with a combination of surprise and fury.

"You smell so good," he said. "I've had dreams about you."

"Daniel!" she yelled, not wanting to alert the entire library over his foolish behavior, but he had crossed over the line.

He slid his mouth over her forehead.

"That's it. I warned you," she said and jerked her knee sharply upward into his groin.

Daniel yelped in pain and doubled over. His whimper made her feel sorry for him, for about a half of a second then her anger came back full throttle.

"What the hell did you do that for?" he asked. "I was just trying to give you a little kiss."

"I didn't want a little kiss," she told him. "I didn't want any kisses from you, and if you ever put your paws on me or anyone else I know in the future, I'm calling the police. When I say no, I mean no. And here's a news flash, that goes for all women. Do you understand me?"

He looked behind her, still grimacing. "Yeah, me and everybody else," he said and limped past her.

Abby whirled around and found at least twenty students, along with the librarian, staring at Daniel, then her. Her face flamed with embarrassment. She made a habit of not calling attention to herself, and to have everyone observing her in this situation was, oh, humiliating. She cleared her throat. "Sorry for the interruption. I, uh, need to get back to work."

Chapter Ten

Another jam-packed day. Abby worked with the kids at the community center, went to two classes, worked more on her two papers and squeezed in a little surprise shopping for Cade. She would have been more excited about her purchases, one of which was burning a hole in her pocket, if she hadn't gotten a late start for his house because her mother had phoned her cell to ask her to pick up some groceries.

She pulled into his driveway and bolted out of the car. Before she could make it up the steps to his porch, he opened the door and leaned against the doorjamb. "Well, well, well, if it isn't the nutcracker herself."

Abby blinked at him and her mental to-do list fell into a pile of dust. "Nutcracker?" she said. "What are you talking about?"

"I'm talking about your new nickname," he said.

Confused, she walked up the steps, noticing a couple sleds propped against the house. Her gaze was drawn back to Cade, and she lifted her shoulders. "What do you mean?"

"As of last night, there are stories going around that a young man named Daniel Payne suffered bodily injuries that you inflicted," Cade said. "Stories I'm certain are not true. Because you would never let a guy get to the point of no return in the college library."

Anger soared through her. "He walked into that library past the point of no return. He'd been drinking. I told him I wasn't interested and never would be, but he wouldn't stop. Crowded me against one of the bookcases. I yelled. I warned, but he wouldn't listen. There was only one thing left to do."

"Did it occur to you to call me?" he asked, something dark flicking through his blue gaze.

"I didn't have my cell phone on me when I was reaching for the book on abnormal psychology. It was very embarrassing. By the time I stopped yelling, a crowd of people were watching and listening. For a minute there, I was afraid I might get banned from the library, but this was not my fault. I have *not* encouraged that guy in any way."

"You still should have called me," he said, scowling at her.

"I told you I didn't have my phone," she said.

"Afterward. You should have called me afterward. You had to be shaken up and I could have paid this guy a visit to make sure he didn't bother you again," he said.

She felt a rush of warmth at Cade's protectiveness. "That's nice of you," she said softly. "But I don't think there's any danger of him coming anywhere near me again."

"He better not or he's going to have to answer to me," Cade said, pulling her inside his foyer. He opened the closet door and grabbed a hat.

"There's no need to get physical, Cade. You're a lot bigger than he is. You could squash him with one of your feet," she said.

"Look who's talking about not getting physical, *nutcracker*," he said. "And I've rarely needed to resort to violence in my life. I'll just reason with the guy."

Her stomach began to lurch. Abby had tried not to think about the incident, but down deep it really had bothered her. She knew, based on her studies, that she would have to work through it sooner or later, but later just sounded better to her right now.

"Can we talk about something else? It's not a happy subject for me," she said.

His gaze softened. "Sure, and I have just the thing to take it off your mind," he said, pulling on the hat he held in his hand then following up with his gloves. "We're going sledding."

"Now?" she asked, the idea appealing to her in a surprising way.

"Now," he said. "The hill behind my brother Dean's place is perfect."

"Aren't you worried he'll see us and ask questions about you and me?" she asked.

"Dean knows about you and me," he said, guiding her out the door.

She gaped at him. "He does?"

"Yeah, I told him about it a couple weeks ago. He knows not to discuss it," he said and grabbed the sleds.

Abby was so stunned she didn't know what to say, until a thousand questions entered her mind. *Exactly what did you tell Dean? How much does he know? Two weeks ago? You were still saying I was too young then. Did you tell him you've fallen desperately in love with me and can't live without me?* She rolled her eyes at the last one because she knew the answer to that. *No and no.*

Within an hour, she felt seven years old again. Flying down a snow-covered hill shrieking with joy. Cade dared her to race him. She won once. He won the second time. Then he double-dared her to ride down the hill on his back. Unable to resist, she joined him and they took a tumble in the snow.

"Are you okay?" he asked, his voice anxious as he rolled her from her front side to her back in the snow. "I must have hit some ice."

"I'm fine," she said and started to laugh. "I'm going to be so wet by the time we get back to your house." She laughed again. "And it's all your fault because you are a reckless sled driver."

He frowned with consternation. "I'm not reckless. I just hit some ice. Are you sure you're okay?"

"Fine except for all the snow that's gone all the way down my neck to my back. I never dreamed that perfect Cade could be reckless," she teased.

He looked as if he were trying to be stern with her, but her giggles must have gotten to him. "Sit up, so you don't get any more snow down your sweater," he said, pulling her up. "Look at you. You've got snow all in your hair. You're a mess," he said, shaking his head.

"All your fault, Mr. Reckless," she said and smiled up at him. "I have an early Christmas present for you."

He looked at her in confusion. "Christmas? We've got a whole month to go," he said.

"You wouldn't know that by your display window at Pritchett & Sons," she said.

"True," he said. "So what's this Christmas present? A lump of coal?" he asked with a wary expression.

"Nope," she said and pulled a mistletoe packet out of her pocket. She lifted it above her head. "Oops. Kiss me quick or it's bad luck."

He shook his head and snatched the mistletoe from her. "Trust me, you don't need mistletoe for me to kiss you." He lowered his head and his warm lips took the cold away from her within mere seconds. As he deepened the kiss, her temperature heated up and she wrapped her arms around his neck. She loved his strength. She loved his wisdom and sense of humor. Being with him made her feel so much more than happy. She couldn't think of one word to describe all the ways he affected her. Abby kissed him with all her heart and passion.

Cade responded. A moment later, he finally pulled back, his eyes dark with wanting. "We'd better head back to the house or I'm going to strip you and we're going to give my brother an eyeful. And I would never hear the end of it."

Cade led the way back to his house and they both stomped the snow from their boots before they stepped inside. He glanced at Abby and spotted her teeth chattering and her blue lips from the cold and swore.

"Why didn't you tell me you were freezing?" he asked, pulling off her gloves and coat. "Hold on to me while I help you ditch these boots."

"It wouldn't have done any good. We still had to walk back to your house. It's no big deal. I'll warm up. By next week," she said, smiling through her chattering teeth.

He chuckled despite himself. He didn't like being responsible for her getting this cold. He was surprised at how protective of her he felt. When he'd heard about that Daniel guy molesting her at the library, he'd wanted to go after him but, from what he'd heard, the guy was planning on leaving town for a while. Good riddance, Cade thought and gave up on pulling off the rest of Abby's soggy clothes in the foyer. She needed warm water. He ditched his own jacket and boots.

"Here we go," he said, picking her up in his arms and carrying her down the hall.

"What are you doing?" she asked.

"You need a hot shower," he said, carrying her into the bathroom. He turned on the jets to the shower then pulled off the rest of her clothes and his. "Ready?" he asked, already distracted by her naked body. It felt as if it had be aeons since he'd made love to her.

He hauled her into the shower and she shrieked. "Are you trying to scald me to death?"

Cade dialed the temperature back a little bit and pulled her against him. She was still cold. He pressed his mouth against her shivering mouth and she put her arms around him as she sank into the kiss. He felt a couple of chatters, but he knew he'd knocked off the worst of the chill when she sighed against his mouth. Her sigh said so much. If her sigh could talk, it would say she trusted him and wanted him. Her sigh said she was already feeling pleasure, but there was more to come.

That sigh coupled with her naked body against his was the most wicked and wonderful sensation he'd ever had.

"You can turn up the water temperature now," she said.

He liked the way she heated up, he thought, and he had every intention of making her blood boil with pleasure. Lowering his mouth to her again in a deep, wet kiss with the water streaming over them, he lowered his hands to her breasts, focusing on her responsive nipples.

Abby made a sexy sound and wriggled against him, making him stiff with wanting her. This time, he wanted to make her want and wait. This time he wanted to make her crazy. He lowered one of his hands between her silky thighs and found her warm and wet. He continued to stroke and she began to wiggle against him.

"Cade, I want you," she whispered. "I want you inside me."

"Soon," he promised and dipped his lips to her breasts, taunting her nipples then sliding lower and lower.

Mere minutes later, her body flexed and she climaxed, letting out a high-pitched moan of satisfaction. Taking her with his mouth had nearly put him over the edge. The ability to wait burned to cinders. He picked her up and with her back propped against the tile wall, he took her.

Her sexy gaze burned into his with each stroke he took and somehow in the middle of taking her, he felt as if she had taken him.

After they got out of the shower, Cade wrapped Abby in his big terry-cloth robe and pulled on a pair of jeans and a sweater. "Soup and sandwiches okay with you?" he asked as he pulled from the refrigerator the premade deli sandwiches he'd bought from the grocery store on the way home.

"Perfect. You want me to heat the soup?" she asked, walking into the kitchen. She pulled the foot of the turkey still hanging in his kitchen.

"Gobble, gobble, gobble," said the electronic voice.

Then she pulled it again. "I didn't want him to feel neglected," she said to Cade.

"He hasn't been," Cade assured her. "His foot is pulled every morning and every evening when I get home from work. Whether he needs it or not."

She gave a low chuckle. "Glad you're taking care of him." She glanced through his cupboard and pulled out a can of soup and poured it into a pot on the stove. "You really do cook like a bachelor, don't you?"

"How's that?" he asked, unwrapping the deli sandwiches and putting them on paper plates.

"I mean you don't cook anything like chicken or soup or stew," she said.

"I cook barbecue pork. Does that count?" he asked.

"On the grill?" she asked.

"Yeah."

"If it's on the grill it doesn't count for real cooking. The grill is great, and I love food cooked on the grill, but sometimes you have to turn on the oven," she said.

He glanced down at the petite woman with wet, mussed hair and big brown eyes who was trying to give him instructions on cooking. He knew that she could cook circles around him. "That's when I turn on the microwave," he said.

"Good for you," she said and laughed.

A few moments later, the soup was heated. She served it with some crackers she found and they sat at the table. "Bean 'n' bacon soup. Excellent choice," he said.

"It's not rocket science. You could have done the same thing," she said. "All it takes is a can opener, a pan and a stovetop."

"That's two steps too many for me," he said, lifting another spoonful of soup to his mouth.

She laughed. "Well, I'm glad I could help out."

He looked into her amused brown eyes and watched her take a bite of her sandwich and felt something inside him ease. What was happening to him? When had canned soup and deli sandwiches felt like a gourmet dinner with Abby sitting across from him.

She met his gaze and glanced away then back at him. "What's wrong? Is there mustard on my chin or something?"

"No. I was just thinking how pretty you are," he said.

Her cheeks flushed. "Thank you. After being hounded by my sisters for looking too thin and having circles under my eyes, that's very nice to hear."

He frowned and studied her. "Now that you mention it," he began.

She shook her head. "Don't you start," she said. "The circles are temporary because of the increased schoolwork at this time of the semester."

"Plus there's the matter of you spending all your extra time with me. I don't want to keep you from your schoolwork," he said.

"Oh, please do," she joked.

"Really, Abby. You're too close to let anything get in your way. Including—" He broke off when his house phone began to ring. "That doesn't happen very often," he said. "Everyone who knows me calls my cell." He paused for a moment then let the call go to voice mail. "What were we talking about?"

"The Jacuzzi you're planning to install," she said.

He chuckled, although the image of Abby naked in a tub of bubbling water was all too appealing. "I've actually thought about it, but never got around to it…"

The phone rang again and he frowned. "Maybe I should check it," he said, rising from the kitchen table. He glanced at the caller ID and felt as if he'd been punched. He immediately picked up the phone.

"Cade Pritchett," he said and waited.

The silence stretched for one, two, three seconds. "Cade, this is Marlene, Dominique's mom."

"Hello," he said. "How are you?"

"Bill and I are doing well. We're actually in Montana visiting some relatives. We wondered if we could drop by and see you tonight," the woman said.

Cade nearly choked on the next breath he drew. "Tonight?" he asked, glancing at Abby, sitting at the table in his robe. She shot him an inquiring glance.

"I know it's short notice, but I think it's important. We won't stay long," she promised.

Hearing the twinge of desperation in the woman's voice, Cade felt compelled to respond. "Okay. I'm finishing up dinner. When do you think you'll be here?"

"In fifteen minutes or less. And we've already eaten, so you don't need to feed us. See you soon," she said.

Cade hung up the phone and stared at it.

"Can you give me a vowel?" Abby asked after a long moment of silence.

"Dominique's parents are coming. They'll be here in less than fifteen minutes."

Abby gaped at him and dumped her spoon in her

soup. "Oh, wow, I need to get out of here," she said, rising form her chair. "But we forgot to put my clothes in the dryer, didn't we? Darn," she said. "I could borrow something from you if I wrapped it around me twice."

He chuckled at the image. "Not necessary. You can stay here. We'll throw your clothes in the dryer now."

"I'm not greeting your former girlfriend's parents in your robe," she told him.

"I wasn't suggesting that. You could finish your sandwich in my robe and watch the television in there."

"Oh, hide out in your room," she said. "That could work."

"There's no need for you to hide," he said, frustrated that their evening was being interrupted by people who had held him responsible for the death of their daughter when his biggest crime had been loving her. "If you want to meet them, I'm fine with it."

"I'm not," she said and picked up her plate. She pressed her lips together and looked at him in sympathy. "Good luck, Cade," she said and gave him a kiss. Then she skedaddled toward his bedroom and closed the door behind her.

Cade raked his hand through his hair, wondering why the Gordons had chosen this time to visit him after all these years. His appetite gone, he dumped his soup in the sink and put the remainder of his sandwich in the fridge. He threw Abby's clothes in the dryer and the doorbell rang. Stella barked and ran to the door. Cade brought up the rear and opened the door to the mother and father of the woman he had once planned to marry.

"Hi," Marlene said and timidly stepped inside. "I'm sorry this is such short notice."

Bill extended his hand. "Pritchett," he said with a nod. "Nice to see you. You're looking good."

"Thanks, Bill. Come on in, both of you. Can I get you something to drink?"

"Oh, we won't be staying that long," Marlene said, making him curious as hell. The Gordons looked a little worn around the edges considering their age. Cade supposed he couldn't blame them. They'd had two children and one had died way before she should have.

"How's Bill, Jr.?" Cade asked.

"Doing very well," Marlene said. "He's working for a computer company about an hour away from here. He got married two years ago and he and his wife had a baby six months ago. She's gorgeous."

"Looks like Dominique at that age," Bill said.

Cade's gut tightened. "That's gotta be great for you two," Cade said. "Come into the den."

The two Gordons did as he asked and sat gingerly on the sofa. Silence stretched between them for a long moment.

Bill cleared his throat and adjusted the collar of his coat jacket. "The reason we wanted to see you is because Marlene and I realized we were hard on you when Dominique died."

"We weren't just hard on you," Marlene said. "We weren't fair."

"Dominique was determined to go to California during her break and nothing was going to stop her, even you," Bill said. "You probably knew that. Even if you didn't, you knew what kind of nature Dominique had. She needed to travel every now and then. It was in her blood. She probably got it from me. I went into the air force to see the world."

"We would have done everything to keep her alive, and we believe you would have, too, but who could have predicted that terrible accident?" Marlene asked with a shudder. "We'll never get over the loss, but holding you responsible was wrong and cruel. You were grieving for her, too."

"But we couldn't see that because we were hurting too much," Bill said, lacing and unlacing his fingers.

"So, we're here to apologize," Marlene said. "We were wrong to blame you. We hope you'll forgive us. More important, we hope you don't hold yourself responsible for Dominique's death."

Cade was stunned by all the Gordons were telling him. "I don't know what to say except that I still miss Dominique's presence in my life."

Marlene bit her lip and reached out to pat his hand. "We know you do. Because of that, we'd like to give you the necklace she wore. I believe you gave it to her," Mrs. Gordon said as she pulled a small box from her purse and handed it to Cade.

Cade opened the box to the diamond-accented sparkler pendant he'd given Dominique all those years ago. He'd told her she was a firecracker and that she lit up his life. The memory squeezed his chest again.

"This was a perfect example of her personality. She was a dynamo. That's one of the reasons we felt such a void when she died," Bill said. "I couldn't stand it. So we moved back to California and tried to make ourselves feel better."

"In some ways, it helped to move away," Marlene said.

"In others, it didn't. How do you explain to people you're meeting for the first time that you had the most beautiful daughter in the world and she would have accomplished amazing things if she hadn't died way too young?"

Cade nodded. "I hear you," he said, his mind suddenly flooded with images of Dominique.

Bill took a deep breath. "We'll never stop missing her," he said.

"Never," Marlene agreed. "But Dominique wouldn't want us to hold a grudge. She would want us to get as much out of life as possible. She would want the same for you, Cade."

Cade felt jolted by Marlene's last comment. "I'm living. I miss her like you do, but I'm living."

"Did you ever get married?" Marlene asked gently.

"Marlene," Bill said. "That's none of our business."

Marlene extended her hand to Cade's again. "Well, I just want to tell you, Cade, that I hope you will find another woman to love. You have a lot to offer and it shouldn't be stuck in the past." She took a deep breath. "That's all I have to say except to thank you for being so good to Dominique. You were a solid, stable force that made her feel safe enough to fly. You were exactly what she needed at that time in her life."

Cade took in Marlene's words, but he would have to digest them later.

"We should leave now," Bill said to Marlene. He stood and helped his wife to her feet. "Thank you for seeing us. Thank you for being a good man to our daughter and to us," he said and shook Cade's hand again.

"God bless," Marlene said and threw her arms around his neck. "God bless and good night," she said and the two of them left his house.

Cade stared after them, looking at the tire tread marks their vehicle left in the snow. The words from both of the Gordons felt as if they jumbled together in his head. What did all this mean? Did it mean anything? He rubbed the necklace he'd given Dominique all those years ago between his fingers. He felt his lungs constrict. What was he supposed to do with this? As much as he'd loved Dominique, he didn't carry anything of hers around on a daily basis. Nothing material, that is. Her attitude about life had often haunted him. He'd been more practical. She'd enjoyed the unexpected. She'd looked for the magic. Cade didn't believe in magic. But surprises—lately he was changing his mind about those. Or maybe it was Abby who was changing his mind.

The dryer buzzed, signifying the end of the cycle, and Abby stepped outside the bedroom. "All clear?" she asked in a hushed voice.

When he nodded, she walked toward him, searching his face. "Did it go okay?"

He gave a slow nod. "Yeah. Better than I expected," he said and rubbed his fingers over the pendant in his hand.

Abby glanced down at the necklace. "Did that belong to her?"

"Yeah. I gave it to her when we were dating. They wanted me to have it," he said, still stunned by the conversation he'd had with her parents.

Abby lifted her eyebrows. "Sounds like they had a turnaround."

"Yeah." He paused a moment. "They apologized for blaming me for her death."

"Wow," Abby said. "That's huge." She smiled. "And wonderful. Even though you knew you weren't responsible, it's got to feel great knowing they don't resent you anymore."

He thought about that for a moment. Practically speaking, he'd known he wasn't responsible, but some part of him had thought there must have been something he could have done to prevent Dominique's death. "Sometimes I've wondered if I could have done something to keep her safe. It was my job. It felt like my job, anyway."

"Ohhh," Abby said. "Your superhero complex coming out again. You have the power to save everyone and everything?"

He shot her a sideways glance at her light jab. "It's more that I felt responsible for her."

She nodded. "You were responsible for keeping her safe," she said. "Twenty-four-seven even though you weren't with her and your superpowers are unfortunately limited." She sighed and wrapped her arms around him. "As happy as I am to be with you now, I'm sorry you've had to suffer such a terrible loss."

Her words felt like soothing water on a sore place inside him. He held her close and felt comforted in a way he couldn't remember. Her sweet honesty made a tightness inside him ease. Cade couldn't help wondering if Abby was the one with superpowers.

Chapter Eleven

When Cade went to work the next morning, he felt like a different man. The trees looked prettier, the snow was beautiful, the crisp air felt good to breathe. He hummed along to the country music tune playing on the radio in his SUV. He waved a car in front of him at an intersection. The sun was shining. He would see Abby tonight. Anticipation hummed through him. Today was going to be a good day.

He pulled into the parking lot and got out of his car, ready for a hard, productive day at work followed by an evening with Abby.

"Hey, Cade," his brother Nick said as he walked into the shop. He gave a broad wink. "I hear you've been busy robbing the cradle with another Cates sister."

Cade blinked. Where had Nick heard about him and Abby? Nick had been on a hunting trip for the past ten days, so this was the first time Cade had seen his brother in a while. Wondering if his other brother, Dean, had been talking, he called for him. "Dean!"

Dean poked his head out from the back room and held up his hands. "It wasn't me. I didn't tell him anything. He went to the Hitching Post last night and apparently the gossip has already started." Dean shot him a sympathetic look. "Sorry, bro."

"I'm not robbing any cradles. Abby's twenty-two." He walked toward the back room. "Welcome back," he added as an afterthought, his mood plummeting. Cade was a private man and hated being the subject of gossip. He was just getting past the fallout from his public proposal to Laila Cates and sure as hell didn't want to stir up anything else.

"So you really are seeing her?" Nick asked, following him to the back room. "It's none of my business, but this isn't a rebound thing because of Laila, is it?"

Cade turned and shot Nick a deadly glance.

"Hey, it's wasn't my idea. One of the waitresses said she wondered if that's what's going on since you lost out on Laila," Nick said.

A month's worth of his patience shot in five minutes, Cade ground his teeth. "Here's a news flash. I don't feel like I lost out on anything with Laila. I'm glad she and Jackson are happy together."

He could tell by his brother's expression that he wasn't convinced. "You've known me a long time. Am I the kind of man to go out with a woman for the sake of a rebound?"

Nick paused then pressed his lips together in a slight wince. "Sorry. I was just surprised to hear it. Are you serious about her?"

Cade clenched his jaw again. His feelings were nobody's business but his own. "I'm not about to get serious with a woman after two weeks."

"Sure," Nick said. "That makes sense."

Cade sighed and put Nick out of his misery by changing the subject. "So, how was the hunting?"

"Oh," Nick said. "You wouldn't believe the rack on the elk I bagged."

The subject of Abby was blessedly dropped. Cade worked in complete silence without stopping until after lunch and decided to get a breath of fresh air and a cup of coffee and a sandwich to go at the diner. Old man Henson waved at him from a stool as he ate a piece of pie.

Cade placed his order then walked toward him. "How's that ankle?"

"Pretty good. I'm getting around good. Mildred here at the shop has been dropping off some goodies for me after she gets off work. I think she's sweet on me," he said in a lowered voice. "But she's a nice woman. A bit young for me but my Geraldine would approve of her."

Cade smiled. "Good for you," he said.

"I saw your little lady in here this morning. She loves her hot chocolate, doesn't she? Won't touch the coffee. I asked her about you and she said she had seen you a few times." Mr. Henson gave him a nudge. "I knew you would come around. Pretty, sweet and can cook. What's not to like about that?" he asked. "She's a looker and a cooker. You'll do good with her."

"Abby and I aren't serious, so there's no need to be thinking about the future," Cade said.

Mr. Henson shook his finger at him. "Don't you wait

too long to get her in your corral. I'll tell you there's plenty of other young bucks right behind you."

Mr. Henson's hearing wasn't the best, so he tended to speak loudly. Cade felt the small crowd in the restaurant watching him. The whispers would start any minute, he realized, and his gut began to churn. "How's that pie?" he asked, pointing toward the pastry on the old man's plate.

"Oh, it's good," Mr. Henson said. "But you know everything here is good."

"How's your truck?" Cade asked. He wanted to provide everyone who was listening with a mundane conversation, so they would turn their attention elsewhere. Away from him.

"Order for Pritchett," the waitress at the register said.

"That's mine," he said to Mr. Henson and slapped the man on the back. "You take care of yourself."

He paid for the order and picked up the bag. "Thanks," he said.

"You're welcome. We all love Abby here. You're a lucky man," the waitress said shyly, then whispered, "I gave you a piece of pie."

Cade clenched his jaw and nodded then left the diner.

After helping at the community center and going to one of her classes, Abby paid a visit to Katrina since she had just been returned to her mother's apartment. "Everything okay?" Abby asked, sitting across from her on a couch in the modest room.

"It's all good. The foster family was really nice, and they invited me to stop in anytime."

"So you got some new friends out of this," Abby said. "Not bad. You think you would ever visit them?"

"I might," Katrina said, nodding. "They really were nice to me. They always wanted to know where I was, but they were nice."

"And no sign of your mom's boyfriend, right?" Abby asked.

Katrina's eyes darkened. "Ex. My mom's ex. He's gone for good. She promised, and I think she means it. She's talking about dropping one of her jobs so she can spend more time with me."

"That would be great. You know I'm so proud of you, don't you?" Abby said and pulled Katrina into a big hug.

Katrina resisted for half a second then returned the hug. "Yeah. It wasn't fun, but it had to be done. I like that you didn't *make* me do it. You just made me think I deserved to be treated better."

Abby gave her another squeeze then pulled back. "Never, ever forget that," she said.

Katrina met her gaze. "I won't. See ya tomorrow night?"

"I'll be there," Abby said and stood. "Call me if you need anything."

Katrina nodded. "I'll do that."

After going to another class, Abby received terrific grades on an exam and a paper she'd turned in two weeks ago. She was flying high by the time she was scheduled to meet Cade at DJ's for a quick early bite. Just as she entered the eatery, her cell rang. It was Cade.

"Hey," she said. "Everything okay?"

"I decided to pick up ribs and bring them back to the house. Is that okay with you?" he asked.

"Sure, sure," she said, but wondered about something she heard in his voice. "I should be there in about fifteen minutes."

"See you then," he said and hung up.

His tone bothered her, but she had no idea what was wrong. She would ask when she got to his house. The important thing was that they would be together. She'd been looking forward to seeing him since she woke up this morning, she thought, smiling to herself.

Pulling into his driveway, she bounded up the steps, knocked on the door and stepped inside. Stella immediately came to greet her, wagging her tail. "Welcome me here, darlin'," she called. "I've had a crazy-good day and it's just gonna get better."

Cade appeared in the doorway with an inscrutable expression on his face. "What happened during your crazy-good day?" he asked in a subdued tone.

"Are you okay?" she asked, studying him.

"Tell me your good news," he said.

She rubbed Stella's soft, furry head and stepped toward him. "Where do I begin?" she said and looped her arm in his. "I got As on my exam and one of my major papers. Katrina moved back in with her mother and that's looking good. And the best thing is I get to see you." She stood up on tiptoe and pressed her lips against his.

He gave a brief response. "Good for you. Congratulations."

She looked at him in confusion. "Something's wrong. Tell me," she urged.

"Some things happened today that made me start thinking," he said.

"About what?" she asked.

He took a quick breath and narrowed his eyes. "About us."

"What about us?" she asked, his expression making

her stomach knot. "Have you been happy when you've been with me?"

"Yeah," he said. "I've been happy."

"That's good, because I've been unbelievably happy. The only thing that would make me happier is if we didn't have to keep it a secret. My feelings for you seem to be growing exponentially every day. Every time we're together, I feel closer to you. I—" She bit her tongue, but could no longer hold back the words. "I love you, Cade. You're such an incredible man. Being with you is a dream come true for me."

Cade looked at her for a long moment then looked away.

Her heart fell at his lack of response. *Oh, please, Cade, don't bail on me now.*

He lifted one of his hands and cleared his throat. "Sweetheart, you may think you want me. You may think you love me, but you haven't been around me enough to really know that."

She stared at him in disbelief, then shook her head. "Yes, I have. I've known you forever."

"You haven't known me as a man," he said. "Even you would say you've been carrying around a heavy dose of hero worship for a long time."

"And it was valid. You've been a hero to a lot of people. You've been the man that so many people knew they could depend on, especially if they needed help," she said. "I could meet a hundred other men and it wouldn't make any difference to my feelings. I know my own heart."

"Just listen to me. I think we need to slow things down," he said, meeting her gaze.

Shock rushed through her. "Slow down? Now?" She

laughed in disbelief. "It's too late for that. I'm in love with you, Cade." She paused and the silence that followed was deafening.

She shook her head. "You can't say it, can you?" She felt as if her world had been turned upside down. "You obviously have feelings for me, but you can't say them. It's just you, me and Stella, and you can't say anything about what I mean to you."

He clenched his jaw and she could see he was wrestling with something inside him. But it looked as if she wasn't on the winning side.

Insidious, ugly doubt crept inside her. Her sister's words of warning played through her mind. Maybe Cade didn't really love her. Maybe he couldn't.

She bit her lip as her chest twisted so tightly it hurt. "I don't know what to say. You can stand up in front of hundreds of people and ask Laila to marry you, but you can't give me any words at all. None," she said and waited through another agonizing silence.

"I need to go," she said, feeling the pressure of tears build behind her eyes. She ran for the door. She stumbled down the steps and blindly climbed into her car. The first sob racked through her and she tried to keep another at bay as she started her car. If she could just get away from his house, off his property, away from him…

She barreled down the driveway, tears falling heedlessly down her cheeks. She swiped at them so she could see to turn onto the road. Abby felt as if her heart was being ripped from her chest. She couldn't remember hurting this much, feeling this much pain. Her throat ached from holding back her sobs. She pulled into a church parking lot and killed the engine of her little car and cried until she wore herself out with her grief.

Gutted from her emotional outburst, she knew this wouldn't be the last time she would cry. Putting her car into gear, she began to drive and hated that Laila's prediction had become true. Cade, her beautiful, wonderful, caring Cade, wasn't capable of giving his heart anymore. Abby had come into his life too late.

Instead of driving home, she found herself heading for Laila's apartment. She couldn't face her family. She really didn't want to face anyone right now, but she thought Laila might understand her feelings. Laila's heart had never been broken, but she'd seen Abby's broken heart coming from a mile away.

She closed her eyes and sighed. Was there any way she could have prevented this? It would have been the same as trying to prevent a blizzard. She debated going to Laila's apartment. Her sister might not even be there. Jackson could be there. Abby almost decided to drive away, but punched her sister's cell-phone number. One ring. Two rings. Three— Abby lifted her finger over the stop button.

"Hey, Abby, what's up?" Laila said.

"Are you busy?" Abby asked.

"No. I was going to meet Jackson for dinner, but he has a special conference call. You want to go somewhere for dinner?"

"I'm not very hungry," Abby said, cursing the waver in her voice.

"Abby, are you okay?" Laila asked, concern threading through her voice. "Where are you?"

"In your parking lot," Abby said, her voice caught between tears and laughter.

"Get your butt up here right now," Laila said. "Or I'll come out there and get you myself."

Her sister's scolding warmed her heart. "Okay. I'm coming, but it's not gonna be pretty."

She made her way to her sister's apartment, and Laila was holding the door open before Abby even arrived. Laila scooped Abby into her arms and ushered her into her apartment. "What happened, sweetie?"

Unable to bear the sweet worry in her sister's gaze, Abby looked down. "You were right," she said, the terrible knot growing in her throat again. "You were right. Cade can't love me," she said and began to sob again.

"Oh, Abby," Laila said and guided her to the sofa and just held her while she cried.

Abby finally felt her tears wane. "Sheesh," she said, taking a deep breath. "You would think I wouldn't have any more water left in me."

Laila gave a soft smile. "Let me fix you a cup of tea."

"I don't really like tea," Abby said.

"You will right now. I'll add a little honey and booze. Lean your head back on the sofa and take some deep breaths."

While Laila made her tea, Abby closed her eyes and felt as if the room were spinning. Laila gave her a cool, damp washcloth for her face then doctored her cup of tea and brought it to her.

"Wait a moment or two then just sip it," Laila said and pushed Abby's hair from her face. "I was so afraid of this happening. You never got involved in the games with guys. You weren't interested in stringing along a bunch of guys just for the fun of it. You were saving your heart for the real thing. I knew that when you decided to love someone, you would love with all your heart. When I first saw you and Cade getting involved, I thought it could be good for both of you. But the more

I thought about it, the more I became afraid, because you're so emotional and Cade is not."

"But he is," Abby said. "That's the thing. He's very emotional. He's talked with me about losing his mom and Dominique."

Laila widened her eyes in surprise. "Whoa. Dominique? That surprises me. He was always a clam when it came to that subject."

"He is an emotional man," Abby said. "But I'm afraid you're right that he can't give his heart again." She felt the terrible sensation of tears backing up behind her eyes again and groaned. "Not again. I don't want to cry again."

"Sip your tea," Laila said.

Abby did as Laila instructed.

"And another," Laila said.

Abby took another sip. "This isn't bad."

"The honey and the booze help. Keep on sipping. I wish I could tell you that it's a magic drink and you'll never cry again, but I would be lying," Laila said. "You love too hard for it not to hurt a lot when it doesn't work out. But listen to me," Laila said, dipping her head to look straight into Abby's gaze. "You deserve a man who loves just as hard as you do and nothing less."

"I'm not sure such a man exists," Abby said hopelessly.

"You don't have to think about whether he exists or not tonight. You just need to know that you deserve a man who can give you all his heart. Now, I'm going to call Jackson and tell him not to come over."

"Oh, no, I don't want to interrupt—"

"You're not interrupting. I can see Jackson tomorrow. You and I will drink spiked tea and watch something stupid on television." She gave Abby another hug. "I'm glad you came to me. It means a lot. Now let me put on some more tea."

Laila provided a much-needed diversion from Abby's misery, and after another cup of tea, Abby had no trouble falling asleep the second her head hit the pillow. When she awakened in the morning, though, her pain hit her first thing. Her impulse was to pull the covers over her head, but she knew she couldn't.

Forcing herself from bed, she took a shower and the water felt like a healing spray on her face and body. Afterward, she walked into the kitchen where Laila was fixing eggs and bacon. "There you are. Good morning, sunshine," she said.

"Yeah, sunshine. That's me," Abby said. "Impressive breakfast."

"Feel the love. You better eat it," she said spooning the food onto a plate. "Orange juice? Coffee? Oh, that's right. You don't drink coffee."

Surprised, Abby took a bite of bacon. "I'm surprised you knew I didn't like coffee," Abby said, sitting down at the kitchen table.

"Why wouldn't I?" Laila asked, joining her at the table. "You're my sister."

"I'm one of six. You can't know the preferences of all of us," she said.

"You'd be surprised. You may think no one notices you, but we're all proud of you. We know you make straight As. We talk about you behind your back and wonder if you're going to be the first one to get an advanced degree."

"I've got to get this one first," she said. "But it's

nice to know you're rooting for me even if it's done in secret."

"Right. Now you're going to need a strategy so you don't burst into tears every other hour," Laila said. "You need to keep busy, but also take lots of naps."

"How do you know about this? You've never had a broken heart," Abby said.

"I've gotten close a couple times, but I've nursed a few friends through some terrible breakups. And," she said, putting her hand on Abby's arm, "I couldn't stand it if Jackson and I broke up now. The very thought of it makes my heart stop. It would be too terrible."

Abby nodded, the yawning sadness stretching inside her.

"But you don't have to do it alone. I want you to call me anytime. If you don't call me, I'll harass you. And remember, you have the Cates backbone," Laila said. "Now eat your breakfast. You need nourishment."

Abby left Laila's apartment and went home to change clothes. Thank goodness she had a busy day. She worked at the community center, gave her presentation for class, finished a paper and forced down a sandwich before she left for ROOTS. The girls were wired tonight because Thanksgiving was less than two weeks away. They sorted donated food into bags for families in need. By the end of the evening, all of them were pleased with how much they'd accomplished.

"You guys did great," Abby said. "Tell your parents what you did tonight, and if they could use a bag because growing teenagers eat food like they have holes in their legs, send them over. We're still collecting food."

"You'll be here next week, right?" Katrina asked.

"Absolutely. Wouldn't miss our before Thanksgiving get-together. But I have to tell you I've got a ton of work right now with my classes. So you won't get much sympathy from me if you're not staying on top of your schoolwork," Abby said.

There was a collective groan. "Whatever happened with that guy you liked? When we fixed your makeup and hair so you could get his attention?" Keisha asked.

Abby felt a sudden stab of pain and took a quick breath. "Didn't work out. I guess he wasn't the right one."

"Stupid guy," Keisha said. "You're the best."

"Thanks," Abby said. "I needed that."

Abby successfully made it home, made a cup of herbal tea with a heavy dose of honey and let it cool while she took a shower. She took a few sips and climbed under her bedcovers and cried herself to sleep.

Cade worked around the clock on Tuesday through Wednesday. Work was a solace. He felt as if he'd smashed a butterfly. Every time he closed his eyes, he saw Abby's hurt face. The devastation he'd seen in her gaze, heard in her voice, made him feel like the worst human being on the face of the earth. The truth was that he did have feelings for Abby. The truth was also that he couldn't give Abby what she needed. He'd known that from the beginning and it had only become more clear with each time he'd shared with her.

He never should have given in to his feelings for her, but she'd made him greedy for her passion and lightness. She'd made him want what he hadn't had in too long, maybe what he'd never had.

"Take a break," his father said. "We're all going to the community center to watch the kids do their little show."

"I'm not in the mood," Cade said.

"Well, get in the mood," his father said. "We have to be good examples. The director invited us, so we have to go. You look like hell. Brush your hair, wash your face. Do something to yourself, then come over. It won't last that long."

Cade washed his face, brushed his teeth and tried to avoid looking in the mirror. He had done what he was determined not to do. Hurt Abby.

Pulling on a jacket and putting a hat on his head, he walked over to the community center. It was a cold night and the scent of oncoming snow was heavy in the air. The merchants were mixing Thanksgiving and Christmas lights and decorations in anticipation of the holiday season. As usual, he felt no joy at the season. Abby would, though. She would find a way to get him to smile, use something like that dang gobbling turkey still hanging in his kitchen or hold some mistletoe over his head.

He tried to shake off the thoughts as he stepped inside the community center to the sound of children singing. Standing in the back, he watched the kids perform their well-practiced show. One little pilgrim forgot his words and he heard Abby give a prompt. His gaze automatically flew in her direction.

The room was more dark than not, so he had to focus to find her, but he did, standing on one side in the front, encouraging the kids. She would be a great mother, he thought. Loving and fun-loving, she would make growing up an adventure, just as she would make marriage an adventure for the right man. She would find him, he knew. The knowledge brought a bitter taste to his mouth.

He stayed through the rest of the show, but left as soon as the audience applauded. He needed to get home.

With his mind being tortured nonstop, he needed the escape that sleep could provide.

After arriving home, he turned on the TV to drown out the silence, then downed a peanut-butter sandwich and a glass of milk. The TV quickly annoyed him, so he turned it off. Stella watched him wander around from the den to the kitchen and back. Little bits of Abby mocked him. The turkey hanging in his kitchen, mistletoe she'd hung in three different doorways. It was more painful for him to look at that turkey than it was for him to look at Dominique's necklace.

Craving the need to escape his thoughts of her, he took a shower, praying it would wash thoughts of Abby from his head. He went to bed and tossed and turned, then finally fell asleep.

Cade heard the collision and the crunch of metal and glanced behind him. What he saw filled him with horror. Abby's cute little VW was a twisted mess. A truck had ran into her little car just outside his driveway.

His heart pounding in his chest, he raced to help Abby. She had to be okay, he told himself. She had to be. He got to her car and saw her slumped in the seat, unconscious. A trickle of blood slid down the side of her cheek.

"Abby," he yelled at the top of his lungs as he beat on the VW's window. "Abby!"

The sound of his own voice awakened Cade. His body drenched in a cold sweat, he shook his head, still locked in the terrible nightmare where he couldn't get to Abby, where he couldn't help her.

Sucking in deep breaths of air, he blinked his eyes

and turned on his bedside lamp. It had been a dream, he told himself. A dream. Still, he reached for his cell phone and his finger hovered over the speed dial for her phone number. He just wanted to hear her voice, to make sure she was okay. That was all he needed.

Reality finally began to penetrate his brain, and he scolded himself. He needed to get control of his emotions. He was totally out of hand. He was going to have to work harder at reining in his feelings. When he'd let his heart get away from him in the past, it had always led to pain. This time was no different.

On Thanksgiving morning, Cade went to DJ's along with what seemed like everyone else in the community to pack up turkey and rib dinners for the less fortunate. He walked into the diner and nearly walked straight into Abby.

He reached out to steady her, but Abby put up her hands and stumbled backward as if she would do anything to keep him from touching her. The knowledge stabbed at him. "Hey," he said. "How are you doing?"

She bit her lip and didn't meet his gaze. "I'm okay. Busy as usual. Oh, look, there's Austin," she said, gesturing toward a familiar-looking young man.

Cade studied the guy for a few seconds and realized this was the young man who had taken Abby out that night she'd been dressed to thrill. He felt a twist of jealousy even though he knew he had no right.

Abby glanced at one of several sheets of paper she held in her hand. "Austin," she called. "Rose," she said to the Traubs' sister and waved them toward her. "Do you two mind riding together to deliver the dinners? We want to start making deliveries as soon as possible because they're all spread out." Abby paused a moment then gave a slight smile. "Oops, maybe you two haven't met."

"I can take care of that," Austin said and extended his hand. "Austin Anderson. I've seen you around, but was never lucky enough to meet you."

Rose smiled. "Rose Traub. I believe my brothers are better known than I am," she said wryly.

"I can't imagine why," Austin said. "They can't be nearly as pretty."

Rose glanced at Abby. "Thanks for putting me with someone who has a sense of humor. It will make the day go faster."

"Have fun," Abby said to both of them and gave them a sheet of paper. "Here are the names and addresses for your deliveries. Thanks so much for your help."

Cade forced himself to move away from her even though he wanted nothing more than to be close to her, even in this room full of other people. Spending the past week without her had been pure hell. But necessary, he told himself as he joined an assembly line putting together the food boxes. He loaded a box of ribs into each package of food.

The room was full of conversation and purposeful activity. He heard a few people chuckling and wondered when he would feel like laughing again.

Suddenly an unfamiliar young woman approached Zane Gunther, the country music star who had made Thunder Canyon his home and recently fallen in love. "Mr. Gunther, I'm Tania Tuller. Ashley was my sister."

The whole room turned quiet because everyone knew that Zane was fighting a lawsuit over a fan dying at one of his concerts. The tragedy had apparently forced

Zane to reconsider his career in the fast lane. The poor guy had been horrified that such a thing could happen at one of his concerts.

"Mr. Gunther, if there's one thing I've learned from my sister's death, it's that none of us knows how long we have here to live our lives. That means we've got to go after our dreams and make the best out of the time we're given. Holding grudges is a waste of precious time. Ashley died going after her dream of seeing her hero. You were her hero," Tania said, her voice breaking.

Zane stepped toward Tania and put his arm around her to support her. Tania leaned against him. "My parents' lawsuit is an idea. Ashley would be horrified by it. Your music was the light of her life. I'm going to try my best to talk my parents out of this lawsuit, and I really believe I can."

Murmurs spread throughout the room like wildfire. Cade watched Zane speak quietly with Tania, but he found Tania's words sticking him like needles. Almost everything she said could have been directed at him. Life is short. He might not be holding on to a grudge, but holding on to fear was just as bad or worse.

He looked at Abby, who was struggling to put on a brave face, but he could tell she was miserable, and he was the cause of it. An overwhelming wave of realization swept over him. Abby was the woman of his dreams. She made him feel as if anything were possible. Being with her gave him the deepest sense of peace and happiness he'd ever dreamed possible.

Hard facts slammed into him. Fear had been holding him back. Fear might be why he wasted so many years dating Laila. Deep down, he knew that spending time with her was safe. He was so scared he would lose Abby that he was pushing her away before he could get hurt. Cade couldn't wait one more minute to talk to her.

Striding across the room, he stood directly in front of her and looked into her sad brown eyes and wanted to kick himself. "I've been a fool," he said. "You've misunderstood my reaction to you and I've been fighting my feelings like a bull in a china shop. I love you so much it freaks me out."

Abby blinked in surprise. "What?"

"Yeah, and I think deep down you suspected it. When I wanted to back off, I confused you. I'm so sorry for that," he said, shaking his head. "I love you so much that the thought of losing you scares me to death."

"But you didn't lose me. You pushed me away."

"I didn't lose you, but I've lost others. What I feel for you is stronger than anything I've ever known before. What if I lost you, too?" he asked, the sound of his voice gruff to his own ears.

"Oh, Cade," she said, stepping into his arms. "I wish you had talked about this with me before. I never want you to suffer like this. Never."

The sensation of her body against his was so sweet he had to catch his breath. "I've been a total hard-headed fool. You're everything I've ever wanted. I just hope you can forgive me."

She bit her lip as if she wasn't sure she could trust him. That possibility tore at him and he was determined to regain her confidence in him.

"You know that people will talk about us. Are you sure that's not going to bother you? Are you sure you're not going to change your mind?"

"Not in a million years," he said. "Let them talk. The most important thing in the world to me is you."

Cade wasn't given to wild impulses, but Abby brought out all kinds of surprising things inside him. He climbed on top of a table. "Listen, everybody. I love Abby Cates."

A heartbeat of silence passed before the room exploded with applause. Cade jumped off the table and pulled Abby back into his arms. Her face was full of shock and happiness. "Cade?" she said in surprise.

"Better get used to it, Abby. This is the effect you have on me," he said and took her mouth in a kiss for all the world to see.

Epilogue

Abby experienced the most thankful Thanksgiving day in her history. Every time she thought about Cade standing up on that table in DJ's to profess his love for her in front of everyone, she pinched herself to believe it was true. Of course, it helped that everyone in Thunder Canyon wanted to replay the scene with her over and over. Old man Henson chuckled over it every time she saw him, and the servers at the diner thought it was the most romantic thing they'd ever heard. Even her ROOTS girls wanted to hear the story over and over like a fairy tale from when they were little girls.

Her parents had always loved Cade, so they were thrilled, and Laila was pleasantly surprised to hear that Cade had stepped up the way he should. After Thanksgiving, the days passed with the speed of light and suddenly it was time for the Cateses' double wedding.

Cade was taking her to the wedding, of course.

They'd spent every possible moment with each other, and both freely admitted, every possible moment just wasn't enough. Abby followed in her mother's footsteps by putting Christmas decorations in every room of Cade's house, including the bathroom. At first Cade had thought it was ridiculous, but she'd heard him humming the Christmas song from a music box she'd placed in his bedroom on more than one occasion.

Although her friend Austin Anderson had originally planned to escort her, he'd graciously bowed out and Abby had heard he was taking Rose Traub.

Abby wore a navy velvet dress in honor of the holiday season, curled her hair and applied her makeup with care. This was the event of the season but, more importantly, she wanted to impress Cade. She wondered if there would ever be a time when she didn't want to impress him and just couldn't imagine it. At the same time, though, Cade made her feel as if she were the most beautiful woman in the world even if it was the end of the day and she knew she looked as tired as she felt.

"Abby!" her father called. "Cade's here."

Abby grabbed her coat and walked into the living room where Cade stood in a dark suit that set off his light hair and blue eyes. All she could do was stare.

"You look amazing," he said.

She laughed breathlessly. "I was just thinking the same thing about you."

"All right, you lovebirds, get on your way. I'm going to have to push my wife out the door soon. Never seen so much primping in my life," her father said. He'd been ready for a half hour.

"What do you expect, Daddy? It's a double wedding in a ballroom. We all want to look our best," Abby said and pressed a kiss on her father's cheek. "We'll see you there."

Cade led her to his SUV and helped her into the car. They talked during the entire ride about how they'd spent their morning. Soon enough, they arrived at the wedding. A line of guests formed, waiting to be seated for the ceremony of two of Thunder Canyon's most beloved couples. Abby could feel the excitement and anticipation in the air.

"Oh, look," she said. "There's Zane Gunther with Jeannette. She looks so pretty."

"Did you hear that the Tullers dropped their lawsuit against Zane?" he asked.

"No," she said. "That's wonderful news."

Cade nodded. "He's started a special foundation in Ashley's honor and he's naming it The Ashley Tuller Foundation."

"He's a good guy. It's amazing how fast he and Jeannette got together. They're already engaged."

"When it's right," Cade said, looking into her gaze, "you know it. And there's no need to waste time."

Her stomach dipped and she squeezed his hand. She stood on tiptoe and whispered in his ear. "I love you more than anything, Cade Pritchett."

He snuck a quick kiss and sighed. "This may be bad timing, but—"

"What?" she asked, confused by the nervous expression on his face.

"Come here," he said, pulling her away from the crowd. He led her to a quiet, private place on the other side of the building. The wind fluttered through his hair, making her want to touch it.

"I had wanted to wait to give this to you for Christmas, but I can't. Everything is right with you. You make me feel more complete, more at peace, more happy than I have in my entire life. I don't want to wait another minute without taking the next step," he said.

Her heart beating like a helicopter's propeller, she stared at him. "What are you talking about?"

Abby watched as Cade knelt down on one knee and pulled a small velvet box from his pocket. He opened it and lifted it for her to see a beautiful diamond ring. Abby gasped at the sight of it, but she couldn't keep her eyes off of Cade. Was this really happening? She was certain she was having an out-of-body experience.

"Abby, I love you with all my heart and soul. You are my true soul mate. There is nothing that would make me happier than to spend the rest of my life with you. Will you marry me?"

Abby's hands began to shake. She couldn't believe this was happening. Yes, she'd had a crush on Cade for as long as she could remember, but her crush had grown into a woman's love. Knowing that he wanted her to be his was so powerful she nearly couldn't comprehend it. "Could you repeat that last bit?" she managed in a husky whisper.

Cade stood and pulled her into his arms. "I love you, darlin'. Say you'll be mine forever."

With his arms around her, the reality set in. Cade Pritchett had just asked Abby Cates to marry him. "Yes," she said. "Yes, I will."

Cade placed the ring on her finger and sealed their promise with a kiss that sent Abby around the world. She knew she and Cade had found the love of a lifetime, and they would always cherish each other.

* * * * *

Cathy Gillen Thacker is a popular Harlequin author of more than one hundred novels. Married and a mother of three, she and her husband resided in Texas for eighteen years, and now make their home in North Carolina. Her mysteries, romantic comedies and family stories have made numerous appearances on bestseller lists, but her best reward is knowing one of her books made someone's day a little brighter. Visit her online at cathygillenthacker.com.

Be sure to look for more books by Cathy Gillen Thacker in Harlequin American Romance— the ultimate destination for romance the all-American way. There are four new Harlequin American Romance titles available every month. Check one out today!

A COWBOY UNDER
THE MISTLETOE

Cathy Gillen Thacker

Chapter One

"You're early."

And not for good reason, Ally Garrett thought, pushing aside the memory of her unsettling morning. She stepped out of her sporty blue Audi, ignoring the reflexive jump of her pulse, and glanced at the ranch house where she'd grown up. The aging yellow Victorian, with its wraparound porch and green shutters, was just as she remembered it.

Unfortunately, she couldn't say the same about the handsome Texas cowboy standing beside her. At thirty-three, the ex-marine was sexier than ever.

Ally got a handle on her mounting tension and turned back to the Mesquite Ridge Ranch's caretaker. Looked beneath the fringe of rumpled, dark brown hair peeking from under his Stetson, and into his midnight-blue eyes. Aware that he was just as off-limits to her as ever, she paused as another thrill coursed through her. "I wanted to get here before dark."

Hank McCabe tipped the brim of his hat back with one finger of his work-glove-covered hand. He regarded her with a welcoming half smile. "You accomplished that, since it's barely noon."

He was right—she should have been at work. Would have been if...

Determined not to let on what a mess her life was suddenly in, Ally bent her head, rummaging through her handbag for her house key. "I gather you got my message?"

Hank pivoted and strode toward his pickup truck, his gait loose-limbed and easy. "That you wanted to talk?" He hefted a bundled evergreen out of the back, and hoisted it over one broad shoulder. "Sure did." As she headed for the ranch house, he fell into step beside her.

The fragrance of fresh cut Scotch pine was nearly as overwhelming as the scent of soap and man. "I'd planned to have the tree up before you got here."

Which was, of course, the last thing she wanted on this last trip back home. Shivering in the bitter December wind, Ally ignored the stormy, pale gray clouds gathering overhead, and held up a leather-gloved hand. "I hate Christmas." The words were out before she could stop herself.

Hank set the tree down on the porch with a decisive thud. "Now how is that even possible?" he teased.

Ally supposed it wouldn't have been—had she been a member of the famously loving, larger-than-life McCabe clan.

Aware that her fingers were suddenly trembling, she paused to unlock the front door, then stepped inside.

The foyer of the 1920s home was just as plain and depressing as she recalled. "My parents weren't big on celebrating any of the holidays. On this ranch, December 25 was just another workday."

Hank hefted the tree over his shoulder again and followed her into the adjacent living room. His blue eyes flickered briefly over the sadly outdated thrift store furniture and peeling horse-and-hound wallpaper, which was at least forty years old. Then he plucked a pair of scissors from the scarred rolltop desk and cut through the webbing on the tree. "That's sad."

Ally shrugged. "That's just the way it was," she said flatly.

Hank shook out the tree and set it in the waiting metal stand. "It doesn't have to stay that way." He moved closer and briefly touched her arm, prompting her to look him square in the eye. "People have the power to change."

Not in her experience, Ally thought.

Although in her own way, she had tried, by leaving Laramie, Texas—and the ranch that had been the root of all her troubles—as soon as she was old enough to do so.

Oblivious to her feelings about the property, Hank strode into the equally depressing kitchen and returned with a beaker of water. He filled the stand, then stood back to admire his handiwork. One corner of his mouth crooked up, as he pivoted back to her and continued his pep talk, with all the enthusiasm of a man who was used to accomplishing whatever he set out to do. "I'm pretty sure you've got what it takes to infuse Mesquite Ridge Ranch with the yuletide spirit it deserves."

That wasn't really the point, Ally thought, as she inhaled the fresh, Christmasy scent. What did it matter if this was one of the most beautiful trees she had ever seen? "To tell you the truth, I'm not really into colored lights and presents, either."

Hank knelt to make sure the tree was settled securely in the stand. He gave one of the metal pins another twist. "Christmas is about more than just giving gifts, and trimming a tree."

"Let me guess." Ally paced over to the white stone fireplace. She turned so her back was to the mantel and took in what otherwise would be a cheerful tableau. "It's about family." Which was something else she no longer had, thanks to the fact that she had been an only child, as had each of her parents. Ally's only remaining link was to the house and the land, and soon that would be severed, too.

"And friends," Hank added, grabbing a cranberry-red throw off the couch and settling it around the base of the tree, like a skirt. "And wrapping up one chapter of your life, celebrating the bounty of it, before moving on to the next."

Unfortunately, Ally thought, she did not have much of anything positive to reflect on…especially this year.

"Although…" He paused, clearly thinking back to the events of last summer that had landed him here, in her absence. He straightened, then closed the distance between them, setting a comforting hand on her shoulder. The warmth of his palm penetrated her clothes, to reach her skin. "…I imagine it's pretty rough for you now, since this is the first holiday since your dad passed."

Ally didn't want to think about that, either. She stiffened her spine and deliberately lifted her chin. "No need for pity."

He studied her with a gentleness that threatened to undo her. "How about a little empathy then?" he insisted softly.

She shook off his compassion, and his light, consoling grip. Taking a deep breath, she gestured carelessly toward the eight-foot-tall symbol of Christmas. "So...back to the tree. If you're doing this for me—" she pressed her lips together, aware all it was going to do was remind her of what she'd never had, and likely never would "—don't."

Something in Hank hardened, too, at the harsh, unwelcoming tone of her voice. "I live here, too, now," he countered. "Or have you forgotten?"

She wished.

Time to get back on track.

To undo all those reckless promises she had made in the throes of an emotion that couldn't possibly have been grief.

Ally sighed, certain that Hank McCabe wasn't going to take the news any better than she was facing the upcoming yuletide. She drew a bolstering breath. "That's what I wanted to talk to you about."

Hank had known from the tone of Ally's terse email at seven-thirty that morning that the meeting was not going to be good. Hoping to delay the inevitable, he followed her down the hall that led to the rear of the sadly neglected ranch house. When they entered the kitchen, he observed, "You must be tired from the drive."

She stepped toward the sink in a drift of orange blossom perfume, her elegant wool business suit and silk blouse in stark contrast to his own comfortably worn jeans and flannel-lined canvas barn jacket. She took a glass from the cupboard and filled it with tap water. "Houston is only four hours from here."

Which meant she'd left moments after she'd sent the email.

Wondering why Ally had dressed so inappropriately for a day at the ranch, he watched as she drained the glass and then continued checking out the rest of the place, her ridiculously high heels making a clattering sound on the wood floor. Ambling after her, his body responding to her nearness, he took in the slender calves, trim hips and alluring thighs. She was five foot nine to his six foot three. Graceful and fit, with a sophisticated cap of sleek, honey-blond hair that framed her piquant features. And a body designed for lovemaking. But it was the sassy cynicism—coupled with the almost unbearable sadness in her wide-set, pine-green eyes—that always drew him in.

Ally rarely said what she was really thinking. She worked even harder to conceal what she was feeling.

Hank respected the need for privacy. He rarely shared his most intimate thoughts, either. But there were times, like now, when he felt she would be a lot better off if she confided in someone. To his knowledge, she never did, but remained determined to prove herself to everyone who crossed her path.

She wanted everyone to know that she was smarter, better, tougher.

That she didn't *need* anyone.

And that she couldn't wait to hightail it out of her hometown of Laramie, Texas.

Which was, Hank noted ironically, where *he'd* finally come back to stay.

Having completed her brief, wordless tour, Ally

swung around to face him. Up close, he could see the shadows beneath her eyes. The brief flicker of uncertainty and vulnerability in her expression.

She wasn't as over her grief as she wanted him to think.

He understood that, too.

The need to move on, even when moving on felt impossible.

"I'm putting the ranch up for sale on December 24," she said, leaning against the desk in the study.

Hank had figured this was coming. It was why he'd offered to take care of the place in her absence.

He'd wanted first dibs when it came time for her to let go of the four thousand acres she had inherited from her folks.

Ally folded her arms. "You've got two weeks to vacate the ranch house and move your herd off the property."

Two weeks to place his bid…

"In the meantime, I'm moving in," she added.

The thought of them encountering each other at all hours of the night and day wasn't as intrusive as Hank would have figured. Maybe because she was so damn pretty…not to mention challenging.

"I plan to start emptying the house immediately," she said.

Ally had donated her parents' clothing to a local church. As far as Hank could tell, all their other belongings remained. "You're sure you want to do this?"

"Why wouldn't I?"

Figuring he'd better word this carefully, he shrugged. "Sorting through a loved one's possessions can be difficult." You never knew what you might find…. "The fact that it's Christmastime is only going to make it harder."

Ally curled her hands around the edge of the desk. "I don't plan to celebrate the holiday. I thought I'd made that clear."

Hank wondered how long it had been since someone had engulfed her in a nice, warm hug. Or made love to her slowly and thoroughly. Or shown her any affection at all, never mind made a segue way into her heart. "In other words," he guessed, mocking her droll tone, "your way of dealing with something painful is not to deal with it at all."

Her green eyes flashed with temper. "Thank you, Dr. Phil." She paused to give him a withering once-over. "Not that any of this is your business."

Hank knew that was true. Nonetheless, it was hard to stand by and watch her make a huge mistake that she was bound to regret, maybe sooner than she thought.

Having learned the hard way that some events couldn't be undone, no matter how much you wished they could, later on, he pointed out, "Mesquite Ridge Ranch has been your home since birth."

A flicker of remembrance briefly softened the beautiful lines of her face, before disappearing once again. "I haven't lived on the ranch for eleven years. My life is in Houston now." She swallowed visibly. "Not that what I do with the property is any of your concern, either."

Hank stepped closer. It was time to put his own intention on the line. "Actually," he murmured, "it is very much my business, since I made it clear when I took over the ranch last summer that I wanted to purchase the land from you, if and when you were inclined to sell." He hadn't been sure at the time that would ever be the case.

Ally gestured apathetically, all-business once again. "If you come in with the best offer, it's yours."

That wasn't possible—at least right now, Hank thought pensively. He did his best to stall. "Sixty days is the usual notice given for vacating a property."

Brushing past him, Ally hurried out the front door. He followed her lazily as she crossed the porch and headed toward her shiny red sports car. "If we had a written contract instead of an oral agreement, that would be correct. May I remind you we don't?"

Hank watched her punch the electronic keypad twice and open up the trunk.

"In case you've forgotten, in these parts, a man or a woman's word is good enough for any business deal."

Ally hefted two suitcases over the rim and set them on the ground. With a grimace, she slammed the lid shut. Her honey-blond hair swirled about her pretty face as she pivoted to face him again. "If you remember, I said you and your cattle could stay here *until* I put the property up for sale."

And he'd agreed, not getting into details, because he had known she hadn't been ready to make a decision of that magnitude last June. And in his estimation, she wasn't ready now. Not during the holidays, when she was still clearly grieving the loss of her family.

"The general rule of thumb is not to do anything major until at least a year has passed. Your dad died just six months ago, your mom eight months before that," he reminded her gently.

In hindsight, if Hank had known Ally intended to

act this soon, he would have had his business plan all ready to go.

She sighed dramatically. "And it's Christmas again, or it will be in two weeks, and I don't *want* to be here for the holiday."

Hank wrested the suitcases from her hands and, ignoring her frown of disapproval, carried them to the porch for her. "Then why not wait until spring to put the property on the market?" he pressed.

She shrugged. "I have vacation days that need to be taken before the end of the year."

Something in her expression said that wasn't the whole story. Curious, Hank asked, "The company you work for wouldn't let you hold them over to the new calendar year?"

Ally's eyes became even more evasive. "The one I used to work for, before the merger, would have. The financial services firm I work for now is a lot more hard-nosed."

Clearly, she wasn't happy with her new bosses. "You could always quit," he pointed out. "Work the ranch instead."

He may as well have suggested she take a bath with a skunk.

"Not in a million years," she retorted, stomping around to the passenger side. "Besides, there's no way I'm voluntarily giving up my management position."

She removed a heavy leather briefcase on wheels and a shoulder bag from the front seat, then headed toward the steps.

Hank strode down to help her with them, too. "No doubt you've risen fast in corporate America. And worked hard to get there." He lifted the heavy briefcase onto the porch and set it beside her suitcases. "Your mom used to brag all the time about how well you were doing in the big city."

Hurt turned down the corners of her soft lips. "Just not my dad," she reflected sadly.

Hank opened the front door and set her belongings in the foyer. "We all knew how he wished you'd returned to Laramie to work, after college. But parents don't always get what they want in that regard. Ask my mom. She about had a fit when I told her I was joining the marines."

Ally lingered on the porch, turning her slender body into the brisk wind blowing across the rolling terrain. "Your dad understood, though."

Hank tracked her gaze to the small herd of cattle grazing in the distance, then glanced at the gloomy sky. "Dad rodeoed before he settled down. He understands risk is a part of life, same as breathing. Mom, once she had kids, well, she just wanted to protect her brood."

Turning back to face him, Ally leaned against the porch column. "Yet you came back for good last summer, anyway."

Hank shrugged, not about to go into the reasons for that, any more than he wanted to go over the reasons why he had left Texas as abruptly as he had. "Laramie is my home," he said stubbornly.

Ally's delicate brow furrowed. She jumped in alarm and squinted at the barn, pointing at the open doors. "What was that?" she demanded, clearly shaken.

Hank turned in that direction. "What was what?"

Shivering, Ally folded her arms again. "I thought I saw some animal dart into the barn."

Hank saw no movement of any kind. "You sure?"

"I'm positive!" she snapped, visibly chagrined.

Her skittish reaction clued him into the fact that she was definitely not the outdoorsy type—which did not bode well for ranch activity of any sort.

"What kind of animal?" he persisted. "A fox? Weasel? Snake? Armadillo?"

Ally shivered again and backed closer to the house. "None of the above." She kept a wary eye on the barn.

Hank was about out of patience. "Describe it."

She held her hands out, about three feet apart. "It was big. And brown…"

Which could be practically anything, including a groundhog or deer. Unable to help himself, he quipped, "We don't have grizzly bears in these parts."

Color flooded her cheeks. "I did not say it was a grizzly bear! I just don't know what kind of mammal it was."

Realizing the situation could be more serious than he was willing to let on, particularly if the animal were rabid, Hank grabbed a shovel from the bed of his pickup truck. "Then you better wait here."

Ally had never liked taking orders.

But she liked dealing with wildlife even less.

So she waited, pacing and shifting her weight from foot to foot as Hank strode purposefully across the gravel drive to the weathered gray barn. Seconds later, he disappeared inside the big building. Ally cocked her head, listening…waiting.

To her frustration, silence reigned. Hank did not reappear.

Which could not be good, since she had definitely seen something dash furtively through those wide doors.

When yet another minute passed and he hadn't re-emerged, she decided to head over to the barn herself. There was no need to worry, Ally told herself. Hank was probably fine. Had there been any kind of trouble, he would have let out a yell.

He probably had whatever it was cornered already—or was trying to figure out how to prompt it to run out the back doors, assuming he could get them open....

Her heart racing, Ally reached the portal. Looked inside. Hank was twenty feet to her right, hunkered down, the shovel lying by his side. With his hat cocked back on his head, he was peering silently into the corner.

"What is it?" Ally strode swiftly toward him, her heels making a purposeful rat-a-tat-tat on the concrete barn floor. And that was when all hell broke loose.

Chapter Two

Hank had seen his fair share of startled animals in the midst of a fight-or-flight response. So the commotion that followed Ally's rapid entry into the shadowy barn was no surprise.

Her reaction to the cornered creature's bounding, snarling brouhaha was.

She stumbled sideways, knocking into Hank, and screaming loudly enough to alert the entire county. An action that caused their unexpected intruder to lunge forward and frantically defend its temporary refuge.

In the resulting cacophony, Hank half expected Ally to scream again. Instead, like a combat soldier in the midst of a panic attack, she went pale as a ghost. Pulse leaping in her throat, she seemed frozen in place, and so overcome with fear she was unable to breathe.

Afraid she might faint on him—if she didn't have a

heart attack, that was—Hank gave up on trying to soothe the startled stray. He vaulted to his feet and grabbed hold of Ally. "It's all right. I've got it under control."

Although she barely moved, her frantic expression indicated she disagreed.

"Just stay here and don't move," he told her, as the frantic leaping, snarling and snapping continued.

He started to move away, but Ally clutched his sleeve in her fist and gave him a beseeching look.

Unfortunately, Hank knew what he had to do or the situation would only get worse.

"Stay here and don't move," he repeated, in the same commanding voice he had used on green recruits.

He pried her fingers from his arm and stepped closer to the other hysterical female in the room. He approached confidently but cautiously, hand outstretched.

"Come on, now. Let's just simmer down." He regarded the mud-soaked coat studded with thorns, looked into dark, liquid eyes. "I can see you tangled with a mesquite thicket and lost," he remarked in a low, soothing voice.

He stopped just short of the cornered animal and hunkered down so they were on an equal level.

As he had hoped, the aggressive growling slowed and finally stopped.

Another second passed and then his fat-bellied opponent collapsed in weary submission on the cold, hard cement.

Ally watched as Hank slowly stood and, talking gently all the while, closed the distance between himself and the intruder. Confidently, he knelt in front of the beast.

The muddy animal lifted its big square head off

the concrete and ever so gingerly leaned over to sniff Hank's palm. While Ally stood frozen in place, still paralyzed with fear, Hank calmly murmured words of comfort to the wild animal.

The beast answered his kind welcome with a thump of its straggly tail, then dropped its big nose and licked Hank's palm. A broad smiled creased the cowboy's handsome face. Chuckling, he lifted his other hand to the back of the filthy animal's head and began to scratch it consolingly behind the ears, his touch so obviously gentle and tender Ally wished she could experience it.

Apparently their trespasser felt the same, because it thumped its tail even harder.

Ally stared at the long creature with the drenched and filthy coat and unusually round middle. As she calmed down, she could see that the "savage beast" was actually a big, scraggly dog that had just been looking for shelter from the approaching winter storm. She knew she had just made a pretty big fool of herself in front of the ex-marine. Unfortunately, her fear, irrational as it might have been, was not entirely gone yet, despite the fact that their barn crasher was now putty in Hank's large, capable hands.

Telling herself she would not give Hank McCabe reason to think less of her than he probably already did, Ally willed herself to take several deep breaths. Suddenly he turned his head to look at her. Although he didn't speak, he seemed to be wondering why she hadn't budged from where he had left her.

Good question.

"How did you know that dog wasn't going to bite you?" she asked eventually, hoping to turn McCabe's attention to something other than her embarrassing display of cowardice.

"First, it was scared and upset, not rabid. Second, it's a golden retriever."

Her heart still pounding erratically, Ally discreetly wiped her damp palms on the skirt of her suit. "So?"

Hank regarded her with the ease of a man who was clearly in his element. "Golden retrievers are one of the gentlest breeds." He beckoned her with a slight tilt of his head. "Why don't you come over here and say hello?"

Ally swallowed and eyed the two warily. Hank continued to smile with encouragement. The dog lifted its big head and stared at her, considering.

The memory of another stray dog who had stared silently—then sunk his teeth into Ally's ankle—welled up inside her, followed by yet another wave of uncertainty and fear. "She didn't sound gentle when she came barreling out of the corner," Ally pointed out, taking another reflexive step back.

Hank shrugged his broad shoulders in exasperation. "You startled her. This pretty girl didn't know if you were friend or foe. You'll both feel better if you take the time to make peace with her."

Pretty? He'd called this filthy beast with the large jaws and wary eyes pretty? "And how would you suggest I do that?"

"Pet her. Talk to her. Show her a little kindness," he said as he rubbed the dog's head and neck.

Ally watched as the powerfully built retriever luxuriated in the massage. There was no doubt she was putty in Hank's hands, but animals sensed when humans were scared. And right now Ally was full of fear. Grimacing, she hugged her arms to her chest, not about to let herself be made vulnerable in that way. "I don't think so."

Hank lifted an eyebrow. "I'd ask why not," he replied drolly, "but it's pretty clear you're still as frightened of this big ol' sweetheart as she initially was of you."

His quiet disapproval rankled. "I don't like dogs."

Hank's eyes sparkled with devilry. "Dogs *and* Christmas. Wow. Sure your name isn't Ebenezer Scrooge?"

Ally gave him her most repressing look. "Very funny," she snapped, more annoyed now than embarrassed. "I was bit by a dog that strayed onto our ranch when I was five. I've been leery of them ever since."

Comprehension lent compassion. "That's a shame," Hank said sincerely, shaking his head in regret. "You're really missing out."

Still keeping a cautious eye on the suddenly docile creature, Ally remained where she was. She didn't care how friendly the big mutt looked now—there was no way Hank was getting her to venture over there. "I'll have to take your word for it."

A car motor sounded in the drive behind them. Ally turned to see a Cadillac pulling up in front of the barn. An elegantly dressed, silver-haired man in a gray Western suit, and a Resistol hat emerged from the car.

"Expecting someone?" Hank asked curiously.

She nodded as the stranger strode over to meet them. *I am doing the right thing,* she assured herself.

The short, slim man extended his hand and flashed a smile. "Ally Garrett, I presume? I'm Graham Penderson, of Corporate Farms."

So that was why Ally had arrived so early, dressed in a business suit, Hank thought, a mixture of disapproval and disappointment welling up inside him. She'd known she was taking the first step to sell the ranch that had meant everything to her mom and dad.

And now that Corporate Farms was involved, there was no doubt in his mind who would be the highest bidder.

Ally pivoted to face him, her expression as coolly commanding as her voice. "I take it you can handle this situation?" she inquired, gesturing toward the filthy stray.

Hank lifted his free hand to tip up the brim of his hat. If she wanted him to act like the hired help, he'd do just that. "Yes, ma'am," he said, putting as much twang as he could into the words, just to rile her, "I shorely can."

Ally narrowed her eyes and smiled at him deliberately. "All right." She pivoted once again. "Mr. Penderson. This way…"

Hank watched as she led the slick representative toward the ranch house. They were inside the sadly neglected domicile less than two minutes, then walked back out—maps of the property in tow—and climbed into the older man's Cadillac.

Hank looked down at the soaked, shivering dog cuddled against his side. "Well, I didn't expect that, at least not today." He rubbed some of the dirt off a fancy pink rhinestone collar hidden in the fur, which spelled out the first clear hint to the pet's identity. "But I'll deal with it. Meantime, what do you say we get you cleaned up?"

An hour later, Hank was kneeling in the big, old-fashioned bathroom upstairs, toweling off his canine companion, when Ally came down the hall.

She stopped in her tracks when she saw the mess of mud and hair and occasional spots of blood that had been left in the claw-footed tub, the pile of thorns and burrs heaped in the wastebasket.

It had taken some doing, but Hank finally had the animal in decent shape.

He noticed that Ally didn't come any closer than the door frame when she set eyes on the golden retriever. "What's that thing doing in here?"

"Getting a bath," he said shortly.

Ally propped her hands on her slender hips and wrinkled her nose. "And that smell?" she asked.

"Wet dog and my shampoo," he explained.

Ally studied the heap of wet towels next to the tub and made another face. "Ugh."

Hank passed up the opportunity to reassure her he planned to clean everything. Instead, he leveled a matter-of-fact glance her way. "Where's your pal Penderson?" he asked.

She tensed. "He left."

Slowly, Hank got to his feet and braced his own hands on his waist. "Tell me you're not selling to Corporate Farms."

Ally flushed uncomfortably. "I'm not selling to anyone until I've had a chance to have the property appraised," she told him quietly.

That made sense from a business point of view, he noted. "When is that going to happen?"

Her pretty chin took on a stubborn line. "A broker from Premier Realty in Laramie is coming out later this week, once I've had a chance to get the ranch house in order."

Wishing she'd stop looking so damn kissable, Hank pushed his desire aside and forced himself to concentrate on the very important business at hand. "And once you know what the property is worth?"

Ally swept a hand through her sleek cap of honey-blond hair. "As in all competitions," she replied, tucking the silky strands behind her ear, "the highest bid wins." She let her hand fall to her side and regarded the retriever with a disgruntled frown. "I really wish you hadn't brought him up here."

"First of all—" Hank leaned past Ally "—it's a *she*. And according to the rhinestone-studded collar she was wearing—" he lifted said collar out of the cleansing bubbles in the sink "—her name is Duchess."

Ally leaned closer and inspected the fancy collar without touching it. Then once again her gaze met Hank's. "Who does she belong to?"

"I don't know yet." Ignoring the quickening of his pulse, he knelt and fastened the pink leather strap around Duchess's throat. This was no time to want to bed a woman. Especially when she was his landlord. "It had no ring for metal identification tags." And hence was strictly decorative. But that confirmed Hank's guess that Duchess was a beloved house pet, not your run-of-the-mill stray.

He gave her fur one last rub, then dropped the towel and stood, motioning for the dog to do the same.

Abruptly fearful once again, Ally moved back into the hall. "So what are you going to do next?" she demanded.

"Feed her. Get her a bowl of water." *Come back and clean up this mess. And most of all, stop feeling attracted to you.* Hank moved through the door, and Duchess trotted by his side.

"And then?" Ally pressed.

He paused in his bedroom to remove his damp shirt and pull a dry, long-sleeved henley over his head. He grabbed a pair of jeans and slipped into the bathroom to change. "I already put in a call to my cousin Kurt."

When he emerged, still zipping up his pants, Ally

was staring at him as if she'd never seen a man disrobe. Her mouth agape, she watched him fish a pair of wool socks from a dresser drawer.

Hank sat down on the edge of the bed and pulled on the socks. Conversationally, he continued. "Kurt is a veterinarian here now."

Scowling, Ally shook her head as if to clear it. "I know that," she stated irritably.

"Anyway—" ignoring Ally's sudden pique, Hank headed down the stairs, Duchess by his side "—Kurt can't recall a golden retriever named Duchess, but he's having his staff go through the clinic's records to make sure she isn't a patient of one of the other veterinarians in the practice."

Ally followed slowly, her arms clamped defensively in front of her. Giving Duchess and Hank plenty of room, she finally reached the foyer. Lingering next to the newel post, she asked, "And what if that's not the case? Then what?"

Hank shrugged. "Kurt'll put out the word to other veterinarians in the area. I'll notify the Laramie County animal shelter, the newspaper and any other organization I can think of, till we figure out where she belongs." He strode past Ally into the kitchen, with Duchess right on his heels.

Ally followed, again keeping wide a berth from the two of them. She watched Hank pull a stoneware bowl out of the cupboard, fill it with water and set it on the floor in front of the dog.

Duchess lowered her head and drank thirstily.

Ally lounged against the aging laminate counter. "How do you know she wasn't just dumped in the country because her owners decided they no longer wanted her?"

Hank shot her an astonished look. "Seriously?"

He went to the fridge and, for lack of anything better, pulled out a package of smoked ham and several slices of bread. He crumbled them on a plate and set that in front of the dog, too. It was just as quickly and efficiently demolished.

"Seriously," Ally replied in a flat, no-nonsense tone.

Hank debated giving the dog more food, then decided to wait an hour, rather than overdoing it initially and having the food come right back up.

He headed for the living room, and motioned for Duchess to follow. Once there, he glanced out the window at the increasingly gloomy sky, then walked over to build a fire in the grate. The retriever collapsed beside him while Ally lingered in the doorway once again. "Well, for starters, I can't imagine anyone no longer wanting such a beautiful, loving dog," Hank said. "Duchess's temperament and behavior indicate she has been very well cared for up to now, wherever her home was. So it follows that whoever bought her the collar must be missing her desperately, wondering what's happened to her. *Especially* now."

Ally blinked. "What do you mean, especially now?"

Hank glanced at the dog's drooping, barrel-shaped belly. "You really don't know?" he asked in amazement.

Ally waved an impatient hand. "Don't know and don't care. The point is, Hank…" she paused and stared at him defiantly "…the dog can't stay here."

As if on cue, a cold rain began to beat against the windows. After lighting the fire, he looked out at the gloomy sky again and knew the winter storm they had been anticipating had finally arrived. He turned back to Ally, not about to throw out into the elements the dog he had just painstakingly cleaned up. "I don't know why not. It's not as if I'm asking *you* to do anything, Ally. I plan to take care of her." He lit the fire.

Crossing her arms yet again, Ally watched the blaze take off. "I don't want a dog in the house," she stated.

Hank moved his gaze away from the contentious stance of her shapely legs. "Well, I do. And since we have no formal written legal agreement in place banning a pet of any kind—and you already gave me another two weeks before I have to vacate the property—it looks like Duchess *will* stay. You, on the other hand…" he paused to let his words sink in "…are welcome to find a room at the inn."

Ally did a double take. "You're seriously trying to kick me out of my own home?" she asked, aghast.

Hank gave the logs another poke and replaced the screen. Slowly and deliberately, he rose to his feet. Noticing how his large body dwarfed her much smaller, delicate one, he murmured. "I'm just saying you have a choice, Ally. You can stay. Accept that it's Christmas— a time of giving—and that this golden beauty landed on our doorstep, in need of shelter and some tender loving care prior to the big event. Or…"

"*What* big event?" Ally interrupted, her brow furrowing yet again. "What are you talking about!"

Hard to believe this woman had grown up on a ranch. With a sigh of exasperation, Hank took another step closer and spelled it out for the gorgeous heiress. "Duchess is going to have puppies. And judging by the size of her belly, it's going to be soon."

Chapter Three

Ally stared at Hank and the rotund golden retriever curled at his feet, already half-asleep. "Puppies," she repeated in shock.

Crinkles appeared at the corners of Hank's eyes. He gestured magnanimously. "Merry Christmas."

Ally pressed a hand to her temple and sagged against an overstuffed club chair in a hideous floral pattern that clashed with the yellowed horse-and-hound wallpaper.

"This is surreal," she gasped.

Hank strode past her and went back up the stairs, leaving Ally to follow. He went into the bathroom. "More like one of those holiday commercials you see on TV, with all the cute little golden puppies running around. Or it will be, once Duchess delivers her brood."

He grabbed a bottle of spray disinfectant and liberally spritzed the floor and tub. With the ease of a man used to doing for himself, he tugged another clean towel off the shelf and used it to wipe down the dampened areas.

Aware that she was close enough to touch him, Ally stepped back to let him work. "She can't do that here!"

He gathered up the wet, filthy towels and mat, and dumped them into a plastic laundry basket he pulled from the bottom of the linen closet. His sensually shaped lips twisted cynically. "You keep saying that…" he chided softly. He gave her a long considering look, then brushed past her once again, headed purposefully back down the stairs.

Duchess barely lifted her head as he strode by to the mudroom beyond.

Ally worked to retain her outward composure as she watched Hank dump the soiled linens into the washing machine. She clenched her teeth while he added detergent and set the dials. "I mean it," she insisted.

He pulled the knob, then leaned a hip against the washer, and folded his brawny arms in front of him. "Listen to me, Ally." The water rushing through the pipes forced him to raise his voice slightly. "Hear what I'm saying. There is *no way* I'm putting that sweet lost dog in an animal shelter during the holiday season. Or at any other time, for that matter. Not when I've got the capacity to take care of her myself."

Ally had never encountered such fierce protectiveness. Despite the fact that it countered her current request, she couldn't help but admire Hank's gallantry. Or wish, just a little impractically, that one day someone would feel that way about her.

"Fine." She swallowed, struggling to hold her own

with this very determined man. "But the dog doesn't have to stay in the house."

Hank took a moment to scowl at her before he replied. "Where would you have me put Duchess? In the barn?"

That was exactly what her father and mother would have done, had they not run the pregnant dog off the property first. Ally forced herself to hang on to the Garrett family's unsentimental attitude just a little while longer. Coolly, she pointed out, "That was where Duchess was initially headed."

Hank's handsome features tightened in reproof. "Only because it was the best shelter she could find in which to deliver. Fortunately, we spotted her, and came to her rescue. Because if Duchess had given birth out there in the elements sometime in the next few days, with the temperature falling into the twenties at night, there's no way she could have kept her offspring warm enough. All her pups likely would have died—maybe Duchess, too."

Ally's eyes welled with tears at the thought of yet another completely avoidable tragedy. She was responsible for a lot of bad things that had gone down on this ranch. She wouldn't be held to account for this, too. "Fine." She finally relented, throwing up her hands. "But when you're not with her, you're going to have to figure out how to contain the dog so she's not in the way."

Hank shrugged his powerful shoulders. "No problem."

He regarded her in silence.

Another jolt of attraction swept through Ally. Suddenly, the dog wasn't the main danger to her well-being—the sexy cowboy in front of her was. "Well..." She gathered her composure around her like a shield.

"I've got to change and go into town...for a preliminary meeting with Marcy Lyon at Premier Realty."

Hank's eyes softened unexpectedly. His assessing gaze took her in head to toe, lighting wildfires everywhere it landed. "No business suit for that meeting, hmm?" he chided.

She fought back a self-conscious flush. "Everyone wears jeans in that office. You know that. Since they deal primarily in ranch property and are always climbing over fences and what not."

Hank nodded and said nothing more.

But then, Ally thought sadly, he didn't have to. He did not approve of her decisions and actions any more than her parents had, when they were alive. Now, as then, she told herself it did not matter. And still knew that some way—somehow—it did.

An hour later, Kurt McCabe stopped by, vet bag in tow. "You were right," he told his cousin, when he had finished his examination of Duchess. "Those puppies are coming soon."

"How soon?" Hank asked.

Kurt shut off the portable ultrasound and folded the keyboard back against the monitor before latching it shut. "The next twenty-four, forty-eight hours."

Hank figured they had time to prepare. "Any idea how many?"

His cousin slid his stethoscope back into his vet bag. "Looks like ten, from what I could see on the ultrasound, but the way they're packed in there, there could be one more."

Hank knew that was standard for the breed. "You have no idea who she might belong to?"

Kurt shook his head. "My staff and I all asked around. Got nothing. And…" he paused to use the transponder wand that would have detected surgically implanted information beneath the skin "…unfortunately, she's not outfitted with a microchip that would reveal her identity."

"Bummer," Hank said with a frown. Kurt put the portable transponder away, too. "I can tell you that Duchess is definitely purebred. Show quality. On her own, she'd be worth a pretty penny. If those puppies are purebred, too, the whole litter could easily be worth twenty thousand dollars or more. So if that is the case, someone will definitely be looking for her." He stood and shrugged on his yellow rain slicker. "The real question is, how is Ally Garrett taking this? She still as standoffish as I recall her being when we were all in school?"

"Probably more so." Hank slipped on a long black duster.

"A shame," Kurt remarked. Together, they headed out to his covered pickup truck to get the rest of the gear. "She was one good-looking woman." He reached inside the passenger compartment and brought out a whelping kit with printed instructions, and a warming box, handing both to Kurt. Then he picked up a bag of prenatal dog food and two stainless steel bowls. "And since you're in the market for a good-looking woman…" he teased, as they carried their loads back up to the porch and set them inside the front door.

Hank held up a silencing palm. "Just because you are happily married now, cuz—" He turned his back to the cold, driving rain blowing across the wraparound porch.

Kurt grinned even as water collected on the brim of his hat. "Paige and the triplets changed my life."

"Yeah, well," Hank muttered, "save the Hallmark card for later, will you?"

"Can't help it, buddy." Abruptly, Kurt sobered. "I remember how happy you were with Jo-anne, before—"

Again Hank lifted a palm. "That was a long time ago." He had spent ten long years, working to counter the loss. "I'm over it," he stated flatly.

"Glad to hear it." Kurt slapped him on the shoulder. "So maybe you'll start dating again."

The thought of opening his heart to the possibility of pain like that had him clenching his jaw. "I've dated."

His cousin lifted a skeptical brow.

I just haven't found a woman who could take Jo-anne's place. Hank cleared his throat and focused on the situation at hand. "Right now I have to figure out how to hang on to this ranch before Ally Garrett sells it out from under me."

Kurt blinked in amazement. "She's really going to let the Mesquite Ridge go, given how her folks felt about the ranch?"

Hank shook his head in silent censure. "The sooner, the better, in her view." As they headed back to Kurt's truck, Hank told him about the interest thus far from Corporate Farms and the local realty.

"Better get your bid in soon, then," Kurt advised.

He nodded, accepting the advice. *If only it was that simple.*

His cousin headed for the driver's seat. "Meantime, I suggest you read through the handouts in the folder I brought you. You and Ally are going to want to be prepared when Duchess tells you it's time...."

The rain was still falling when Ally drove up to the ranch house early that evening. Telling herself she was relieved to see that Hank's pickup was no longer parked next to the barn, she grabbed her briefcase full of information from the Realtor, her handbag and two small bags of groceries. Lamenting her lack of an umbrella, she headed swiftly for the back door.

The mudroom was as dark and gloomy as the rest of the house as Ally made her way inside. She promptly tripped over something warm and solid, and what felt like a pile of blankets.

A high-pitched yelp matched her own.

Belongings went flying as Ally threw out her arms and attempted to catch herself.

Another high-pitched yelp followed, plus the scrambling of feet on linoleum then a second crash as something hit the opposite wall.

Ally flipped on the light.

Found herself face-to-face with Duchess.

Only this time, instead of looking ferocious, the golden retriever looked hurt and stunned. And to Ally's surprise, very, very sad.

What was it Hank had said? *You'll both feel better if you take the time to make friends with Duchess. Pet her, talk to her, show her a little kindness....*

Ally supposed there was no time like the present to call a truce, especially since the two of them were alone. The last thing she wanted was to get bitten by a dog again.

Swallowing, Ally hunkered down the way she had seen Hank do. Trembling with apprehension, she held out her hand and took a deep, bolstering breath. "I'm sorry, girl. I didn't know you were in here." Which was something else she'd have to talk to Hank about. She had expected him to leave Duchess in his bedroom, not downstairs....

Her back against the wall, the dog stared at Ally and remained very still.

Ally gulped. Determined to establish peace with the lost animal, she forced herself to move closer and continue to offer her palm. After another long hesitation, Duchess dipped her head slightly and delicately sniffed Ally's skin.

Then she lifted her head and looked into Ally's eyes, seeming to want peace between them, too.

Which meant, Ally knew, she had to take the next step and pet the dog, too.

With Duchess watching as cautiously as Ally was watching her, she moved her hand once again.

Ally gently stroked first one paw, then the entire leg, before ever so tenderly moving her hand to the dog's chest, and then the sensitive spot behind her long, floppy ear. Oddly enough, the action was almost as soothing to Ally as it was to the canine. Noting how good Duchess looked with her clean, silky-soft coat, and dark liquid eyes, Ally smiled. And could have sworn the dog smiled back at her.

Maybe this experience would help her—if not actually like dogs, then at least tolerate being around them. And vice versa, Ally thought.

Which, of course, was when the back door opened and Hank strode in.

Pleasure lit his midnight-blue eyes. "Well, now, what have we here?" he boomed in a baritone worthy of ol' Saint Nick. Clearly unable to resist, he teased, "A softening of that stone wall around your heart?"

The heat of embarrassment swept her cheeks. Ally dropped her hand and stood. "Obviously, I had to do this."

Hank took off his wet rain slicker and hung it on the wall, then his hat. "Obviously."

Ally watched Hank run his hands through his disheveled hair. "I startled her," she explained.

He scanned Ally from head to toe, lingering on her rain-splattered trench coat. "And you didn't want to get bitten."

She shrugged out of her own coat and hung it on the hook next to Hank's. "No, I did not."

He kneeled down to pet the reclining retriever. "Hmm."

Ally scrambled to pick up the things scattered across the floor. "Why didn't you tell me you were going to put her in the mudroom?"

He looked at the full food and water dishes in the corner, then gallantly lent a hand. "You weren't here when I left."

Together, they carried Ally's belongings to the kitchen counter. "You could have left me a note."

"I did." He pointed to the message on the blackboard, next to the ancient wall phone. "I assumed you'd come in the front door."

He went back to arrange the pile of blankets in an inviting circle, then motioned for Duchess to come toward him. She moaned as she got up and ambled stiffly forward to collapse on the soft, makeshift bed.

Hank petted her briefly, then came back into the kitchen.

He smelled like winter rain.

"How did your meeting with the Realtor go?"

Not good. Ally unpacked the groceries she'd bought to get her through the next few days. "Marcy Lyon gave me a whole list of things that need to be done to the ranch house before the property goes on the market, if I want to get top dollar."

"Such as…?"

Ally opened the fridge and saw a delicious looking slab of beef from Sonny's Barbecue, a restaurant in Laramie. "Removing all the wallpaper and painting the entire interior, for starters."

While she put items away, Hank got out containers of restaurant coleslaw, potato salad and beans. "You could sell it as is." The mesquite-smoked brisket followed.

Ally ignored the scent of fine Texas barbecue and kept out a container of yogurt, and a crisp green apple, for herself. "And lose thousands of dollars and the potential of a quick and easy sale? No." She rummaged through the drawer for a spoon and filled a glass with tap water. "The look of this place has got to be updated before it officially hits the MLS listings. Marcy gave me a list of contractors to call. Hopefully, one of them will be able to help me out."

Hank added barbecue sauce and a package of freshly baked wheat rolls to the spread on the kitchen table. He shut the fridge door and swung around to face her. Amiably, he offered, "I could help you out if you'd agree to delay the sale for a short while."

Beware unexpected gifts in handsome packages. "And do what?" Ally challenged, ripping off the foil top to her yogurt.

He lounged against the counter, arms folded in front of him. "Give me a chance to pitch my plan to turn this ranch into a money-making operation."

Ally swallowed a spoonful of creamy vanilla yogurt and held up one hand to stop him. There was no way she was ever going to be as impractical and starry-eyed about the land as her parents had been. "I've heard enough plans," she stated simply.

Hank's dark brows lifted. Ignoring his skeptical look, she stirred her yogurt and pushed on. "That was all my father ever did—was come up with one scheme after another. None of which, mind you, was ever implemented…at least not effectively." Hence, the Mesquite Ridge Ranch had become a giant money pit rather than a paying investment.

Hank turned and reached for two plates. "There's a difference. I grew up on a ranch. I come from a family of ranchers. I know I could make this work—to the point I'd be able to pay all the taxes and operating expenses in the meantime—and eventually buy the ranch from you outright. All you need to do is just give me a chance."

Ally couldn't deny it was what her parents would have wanted—for her to sell Mesquite Ridge to someone who loved the land as much as they did. That is, if they could not get her to keep it herself. Which she didn't want to do. She watched as Hank set the table for two.

"Fine," she snapped, irked by his presumption. "If you think you have all the answers and can turn this place around?" She set her yogurt aside and sauntered up to him. "Then show me the numbers on paper. 'Cause I'm not interested in any pipe dreams or half-formed plans. Only the cold, hard facts."

Hank's gaze scanned Ally's face and body, lingering thoughtfully, before returning ever so deliberately to her eyes.

"How long do I have?" he drawled finally, in a way that left her feeling she had somehow come up short yet again.

"Until I officially put the property on the market,"

Ally answered, mocking his take-charge demeanor. "December 24."

"Fair enough." Hank's broad shoulders relaxed. He stepped back, smiling as if he'd already won her over with his brilliance and the deal was done. "In the meantime, you're more than welcome to join me for supper. As you can see, there's plenty."

There was indeed.

Unfortunately, sitting down with him like this would add yet another layer of intimacy to a situation that was becoming far too familiar, too fast. Ally stiffened her spine. She had come back here, against her will, to end this unhappy saga of her life. No way was she getting sucked back in again, with small town kindness or friendly overtures from handsome men with designs on her family's property.

"No, thanks," she said politely.

"Sure?" His genial expression didn't falter.

Ally chose the one avenue she knew would turn him off—a hit on his legendarily fine character. Ignoring the flutter of her pulse, she stepped away from him and stated in a coolly indifferent tone, "Supplying me with dinner will not give you an edge over any other prospective buyer."

As she expected, he remained where he was. The room was suddenly still enough to hear a pin drop.

His irises darkened to the color of midnight. He stepped closer. "Is that so?" His voice was silky-soft, contemplative. And somehow dangerous in a deeply sensual way.

Ally could see she had insulted him—just as she had intended—and created a real rift between them, simply by making the allegation. Refusing to back down, she folded her arms in front of her. "Yes."

"Then how about this?" Hank demanded.

Before she could do more than draw a quick, startled breath, he had pulled her into his arms. One hand pressed against her spine, aligning the softness of her body to the hardness of his. His other hand threaded through the hair at the back of her neck and tilted her face up. Slowly, he lowered his head toward hers. "And this?" he dared softly, a wicked grin curling the corners of his delectably firm and sensual lips.

As his breath warmed her face, she drew in the scent of wintergreen, and beneath that something masculine...brisk...like the chill winter rain falling outside. His mouth dipped lower still, until it hovered just above hers. "Will this give me an edge?" he taunted.

More like a demerit.

Refusing to let him know how much the near caress was affecting her, Ally smiled at him cynically and narrowed her gaze. "Go ahead and kiss me," she challenged sweetly. "It won't matter, either way."

"Good to know," Hank murmured, lowering his head all the more, until the only way to get any closer was to kiss her. "Because if I wanted to seduce you into selling the ranch to me," he informed her softly and patiently, "I'd do this." His lips brushed hers. Tentatively, then wantonly, as a thrill unlike anything Ally had ever felt swept through her.

"Not just once," he promised, kissing her hotly, "but again and again and again."

Hank kissed her with the steady determination of a marine, and the finesse of a cowboy who knew how to make happen anything he wanted. He was at once masculine and tender, persuasive and tempting. Seducing her in a way that left no room for denial. Ally caught her breath as her hands moved involuntarily to his shoulders and she tilted her head beneath his....

Hank hadn't figured he'd be putting the moves on Ally Garrett, now or ever. It wasn't that he wasn't physically attracted to her—he was. But he knew the two of them were all wrong for each other. And always would be. Yet the coolly provoking way she stared into his eyes, combined with the way she was testing him, made him want to haul her into his arms, and challenge her right back. And damned if instead of getting angry and slapping him across the face—and putting an end to this ludicrousness—she was pressing her body against his and kissing him.

As if she meant it.

As if she hadn't been kissed in a good long while.

As if she needed to feel close to someone again.

And wasn't that the kicker? Hank thought, as his lingering kisses continued to knock her for a loop.

They shouldn't be doing this, and yet he couldn't seem to summon up the urge to put an end to it, either. Not without indulging for a few minutes more....

Who would have thought a totally ill-advised make-out session with a self-serving cowboy could make her feel so good? Ally wondered as Hank wrapped arms around her. He gathered her so close she could feel the hard, hot muscles of his chest pressing against her breasts, and his heart slamming against his ribs.

He opened his mouth, exploring every inch of hers with his tongue, encouraging her to do the same to him.

Whoever would have thought she and the land-loving Hank McCabe would have anything in common? Especially when she intended to go right back to the city, as soon as her task was done....

When he finally came to his senses and released her, he looked as stunned by the passion that had flared up between them as she was.

Hank stepped abruptly. "Fortunately for you—" Hank's jaw tightened with the implacableness she expected from a McCabe "—the only way I'm interested in securing this property is by triumphing over the other bidders, fair and square."

Of course he was thinking about the ranch!

Mesquite Ridge was probably the *only* thing he'd been thinking about during the last five minutes.

Whereas she, Ally noted sadly, had foolishly romanticized Hank McCabe's pass to the nth degree. Damn her foolish heart! "Well, that's good, because 'fair and square' is the only way you'll get it!" she retorted, relying on her inherent cynicism for self-preservation. Legs trembling, she swept up her dinner and her soft leather shoulder bag. She cast him one long, scathing glance before storming past him. "Now if you'll excuse me, I've got some calls to make."

And some incredibly hot, passionate kisses to forget.

Chapter Four

An hour and a half later, Hank was in the mudroom, checking on Duchess, when he heard Ally come back into the kitchen. The sound of cabinets opening and closing followed.

Curious, he stood and ambled in to join her. Ally did not look as if things were going her way. "Need something?"

She rocked back on the heels of her red cowgirl boots. With her honey-blond hair in disarray, she looked prettier than ever. "Coffee. And I can't even find the coffeemaker."

Trying not to notice how nicely the crisp white shirt and gold tapestry vest cloaked the soft swell of her breasts, Hank admitted, "It bit the dust a while back." Briefly, he let his gaze drop to the fancy belt encircling her slender waist, and the jeans molding her hips and long, luscious legs. Just that quickly, he wanted to haul her into his arms and kiss her again.

Knowing that would be a very unwise idea, if he wanted to keep them out of bed, he pointed to the metal pot on the back of the stove instead. "I've been using that."

Ally blinked in surprise. "You're kidding."

So she had forgotten how to rough it, Hank concluded. He quirked a brow. "It works fine."

Clearly unconvinced, she sighed.

"I'll make you some," he offered.

Ally lifted her hands in quick protest. "No—I've got it." She brushed past him in a drift of orange blossom perfume, and checked the freezer. "If I could only find the coffee."

"It's in the brown canister next to the stove."

"Okay. Thanks." All business now, Ally reached for the pot and peered inside. Frowning, because it still contained the remnants of the morning brew, she carried it to the sink, rinsed it thoroughly, then filled it with two pints of cold water. She swung back to him, a self-conscious blush pinkening her high, sculpted cheeks. "Where do I put the coffee?"

"In the bottom of the pot."

Before he could explain further, a quietly grumbling Ally had opened the canister and dumped six tablespoons of ground coffee into the water. She snapped on the lid, put the pot back on the stove, then turned the burner to high.

Aware she still looked frustrated and upset, after a string of phone calls in the other room, Hank asked, "Any luck finding someone to paint the interior for you?"

Ally paced back and forth. "None whatsoever! And I called all ten names on the list. No one will take on a job this big so close to Christmas. In fact, almost all the crews are taking time off from now till after New Year's." She whirled. "Can you believe it?"

"Bummer." He pinned her with a taunting gaze. "Or should I say bah, humbug?"

The corners of her lips slanted downward and she narrowed her green eyes. "You're a laugh a minute, you know that, McCabe?"

Hank shrugged, glad to have her full attention once again. "I like to think so."

Ally huffed dramatically. "So it's on to plan B."

Curious, he moved closer. "Which is?"

The fragrance of brewing "cowboy coffee" filled the kitchen.

"Stage the house to the best of my ability, without changing the way the walls look, and put a painting allowance into the contract, for anyone interested in purchasing the property."

Hank eyed the faded chuck wagon wallpaper in the kitchen. It was as bad as the horse-and-hound motif in the rest of the downstairs. Luckily, the rooms upstairs had just been painted many, many moons ago. "You really think that will work?" he asked.

"I'll make it work." Ally flounced back to the stove. Noting that the dark liquid had come to a rolling boil, she grabbed an oven mitt and removed the pot from the flame.

"You may want to—"

Ally cut him off with a withering look and plucked a mug from the cupboard. Lips set stubbornly, she told him, "I think I know how to pour a cup of coffee."

"I'm sure you do." That wasn't the point. But if she insisted on doing things her own way...

Ally filled the mug, then topped it off liberally with milk from the fridge. She lifted it to her mouth.

He watched her take a sip, pause, then walk back to the sink, where it took everything she had, he supposed, for her to swallow instead of spit.

Hank carried the pot to the sink and set it down on a folded towel. Now that she was listening, he said, "The secret to making it this way is to let it steep for a good four minutes or so after boiling."

"Really," Ally echoed dryly, dumping the contents of her mug down the drain.

He met her gaze. "Really."

She set her cup down with a thud and pivoted toward him. "And how would you know that?"

"Experience." Hank studied her right back. "I made campfire coffee over an open flame all the time when I was in the service. Not too many espresso makers where I was."

"What did you do in the marines?" she asked curiously.

"Flew choppers involved in rescue missions."

"That sounds...dangerous."

And fulfilling in a way that countered the loss he had suffered...

But not wanting to talk about Jo-anne, or the years he'd struggled with residual grief and guilt over his fiancée's death, he filled a cup with icy tap water and finished his tutorial. "Once the coffee has steeped, you add three or four tablespoons of cold water to the pot."

Ally wrinked her nose in confusion and disbelief. "To cool it off?"

He shook his head as he demonstrated the technique. "This settles the grounds to the bottom. And voilà! *Now* it's ready to drink."

She sniffed and tossed her head. "I can't imagine those two things make that much of a difference."

On impulse, Hank reached out to tuck a strand of blond hair behind her ear. "Oh, ye of little faith."

Her eyes flashed. "You're beginning to sound all Christmasy again," she accused.

He lifted his shoulders affably. "Sorry."

"No, you're not."

She was right—he wasn't. He liked teasing her, liked seeing the color pour into her cheeks, and the fire of temper glimmer in her dark green eyes. He poured her a fresh mug, got the milk out again. "Give this a try."

She made a face, but eventually took both from him. With a great deal of attitude, she lightened her coffee, took a sip. Paused to savor the taste on her tongue. Astounded, she met his eyes. "That *is* better," she announced in surprise.

At last, he had done something right. Hank lifted a hand. "What'd I tell you?"

Ally beamed. "I could kiss you for this!" She flushed again, as common sense reigned. "But I won't," she rushed to assure him.

Hank nodded, aware that he was already hard, had been since she'd walked into the room. "Best you not," he agreed.

Ally's cell phone let out a soft chime. She withdrew it from her pocket, looked at the screen. Immediately sobering, she informed him, "I have to take this." She put it to her ear and walked away.

But not far enough that he couldn't hear some of what she was saying.

"...Calm down, Porter. It's not like we didn't know this was going to happen. We have no choice. Stay busy. You're usually big on Christmas! Go see the boat parade on Clear Lake, or The *Nutcracker* or Handel's *Messiah*... I promise I'll call you if I hear anything at all. Yes! Okay. Bye."

She walked back in to retrieve her coffee.

"Everything okay?"

For a moment, Hank thought Ally wouldn't answer.

Her slender shoulders slumped dispiritedly. "All the middle managers from my firm were ordered to take the next two weeks off, so that the executives in the firm that took us over can decide who goes and who stays." She met his eyes and admitted almost too casually, "The general idea is to keep the same number of clients and financial analysts and advisors while cutting costs... and that means a number of the higher salary employees—like myself—are going to be laid off."

"I'm guessing Porter is a middle manager, too."

Ally grimaced. "He started the same time I did, right out of college. We've worked our way up together. He's going to be absolutely devastated if he is let go."

As would Ally, Hank thought.

He studied her crestfallen expression. "Do you think you're going to make the cut?"

She shrugged. Her expression became emotionally charged. "If life were fair," she stated, "I would. But..." she swallowed, her expression suddenly remote "...you and I both know it's not."

"Hence, the immediate sale of the property," Hank guessed.

Ally shrugged again. "It needs to be done, in any case. Right now I've got the time to get the property listed. After December 26, I may not."

"Because you'll either be very busy with the reorg at work…" He refreshed both their coffees.

"Or pounding the pavement, looking for another job." She added a little more milk to hers. "Obviously, Porter and I both hope it's the former, not the latter."

Hank felt an unexpected twinge of jealousy. Realizing he was more interested in Ally than he'd thought, he stepped closer and asked, "Are you dating Porter?"

She looked surprised, then bemused by the question. "Uh…no. We're just friends."

Hank was relieved to hear that. Yet…he still had to ask. "Are you romantically involved with anyone?"

She rolled her eyes as if the mere notion was ridiculous. "I don't have time for that. But what about you?" she asked curiously. "Has there been anyone since that girl you were engaged to when you graduated from college?"

Hank shook his head.

Ally walked over to test the wallpaper. She found it rigidly adhered to the wall in some places, practically falling off in others. She deposited a strip of paper in the trash, then knelt to examine the linoleum floor. The speckled yellow-green-and-brown surface was clean, but very dated and extremely ugly. "What happened to the two of you, anyway?" She ran her palm thoughtfully over the worn surface.

Hank lounged against the counter. "Jo-anne was killed in a terrorist attack overseas."

Ally stood to face him again. "I'm sorry," she said,

genuinely contrite. "I didn't know." She paused and wet her lips. "Is that why…?"

Hank guessed where this was going. "I joined the marines? Yeah."

Another silence fell, more intimate yet. "And since…?" Ally prodded softly, searching his eyes as if wanting to understand him as much as he suddenly wanted to understand her.

"I've dated," he admitted gruffly. He shrugged and took another long draft of strong coffee. "Nothing… no one's…come close to what I had with Jo-anne." He turned and rummaged through the fridge, looking for something to eat. He emerged with a handful of green grapes. "What about you?" He offered her some.

Ally took several. "I was engaged a few years ago, before my mother got sick."

This was news. Hank watched Ally munch on a grape. "What happened?"

"I brought my fiancé home to the ranch. Dexter was a real city boy and I expected him to share my lack of attachment to the place. Instead, he fell in love with Mesquite Ridge and thought we should both quit our jobs in Houston and settle here permanently."

Hank polished off the rest of the grapes in his palm. "Your mom and dad must have liked that."

"Oh, yes." Ally made a face. "The problem was—" she angled a thumb at her sternum "—I didn't. I'd spent my whole life trying to get away from here and—" She stopped abruptly and whirled around, staring toward the mudroom in concern. "Did you hear that? It sounded like…"

A low, pain-filled moan reverberated.

"That's Duchess!" Without a second's hesitation, Ally hurried toward the sound. "She's obviously in some sort of distress!"

You never would have known this was a woman who didn't like dogs, Hank thought as Ally knelt in front of the ailing pet. She looked alarmed as she watched Duchess circle around restlessly, paw the heap of blankets, then drop down, only to get up and repeat the procedure. "What's she doing?" Ally asked.

Hank gave Duchess a wide berth and a reassuring look. "She's trying to make a bed," he said in a soft, soothing voice. "Dams do that for up to twenty-four hours before they deliver."

Ally moved so close to Hank their shoulders almost touched. "How do you know that?"

He resisted the urge to put his arm around her shoulders. "Kurt came by to examine Duchess while you were out. He confirmed she's within twenty-four to thirty-six hours of delivering her pups."

The news had Ally looking as if she might faint.

Hank slid a steadying palm beneath her elbow. "Kurt gave me the handout he distributes to the owners of all his patients, as well as a whelping kit and a warming box. I read through the literature before I went out to take care of my cattle." Figuring Ally would feel better if she was similarly prepared, Hank walked back to the kitchen, with her right behind him. He found the folder and gave it to her to peruse.

She skimmed through the extensive information, troubleshooting instructions and explicit pictures with brisk efficiency. "We can't handle this!"

It if had been a purely financial matter, Hank bet

she would have said otherwise. He cast a glance toward the mudroom, where Duchess was still circling, pawing and preparing. "Sure we can." Knowing the importance of a positive attitude, he continued confidently, "It's been about fifteen years, but I've done it before. I helped deliver a litter of Labrador retriever puppies on our ranch, when I was a kid." That had been one of the most exciting and meaningful experiences of his life.

Ally put the pages aside and wrung her hands. "Can't your cousin do this? He is a vet!"

Annoyed by her lack of faith, Hank frowned. "There's no reason for Kurt to do this when I can handle it."

Ally lifted a brow, unconvinced.

Irritated, Hank continued in a flat tone. "Someone needs to be with Duchess during the entire labor and delivery process. Kurt has other patients and responsibilities. He couldn't leave Duchess at home while he's off working with other animals. And if he took her to the clinic, she and her litter would be exposed to the viruses other dogs bring in, and that could be lethal to the newborn pups."

That much, Ally understood. But she was still reluctant to participate. She threw up her hands as if warding off an emotional disaster. "Okay, I get that, but I still can't do this, Hank! It's just too far out of my realm of expertise!"

He had thought it was a bummer that Ally Garrett loathed Christmas. With effort, he checked his disappointment about this, too. "Fine. You don't have to help." Holiday or not, he couldn't magically infuse her with the spirit of sacrifice and giving. No matter how much he wished otherwise...

"Good," she snapped, appearing even more upset. "Because I'm not going to!" After taking one long, last look at Duchess, she handed the folder to Hank, and rushed out of the kitchen.

There was absolutely no reason for her to feel guilty, Ally told herself firmly as she went up to the second floor sewing room and checked out the bolts of upholstery fabric still on the shelves. Not when she heard the canine whimpering coming up through the heating grate.

Or when Hank ran upstairs to raid the linen closet, and hurried back down again.

Or when she heard him rushing back and forth below, his boots echoing on the wood floor.

But twenty minutes later, when a loud whimpering was followed by an unnatural stillness, she couldn't stand it any longer.

On the pretext of getting the tape measure from the drawer in the kitchen, she went back downstairs to find the table had been pushed to one side.

Duchess was settled in a child's hard plastic swimming pool in the center of the kitchen. Hank knelt next to her. "Come on, girl," he was saying softly, as the animal arched and strained. "You can do it."

Duchess let out a yelp, then looked at her hindquarters with a mixture of alarm and bewilderment. A dark blue water bag had emerged. "Get a couple of the towels. They're warming in the dryer," Hank directed.

Figuring that was the least important of the chores, Ally rushed to comply. By the time she returned, Duchess had heaved again, and the pup was out completely.

Duchess reached around, tore and removed the sack

with her teeth, and cut the cord. As soon as that was done, she licked her newborn vigorously. The pup let out a cry.

Ally's eyes welled with tears at the sound of new life.

Duchess turned away from the pup and began to strain again. Hank picked up the whelp, wrapped it in a towel and handed it to Ally. The pup was warm and soft to the touch. The joy she felt as she looked down at the pale gold puppy cradled neatly in the palm of her hand was overwhelming.

Hank set the warming box on the floor, made sure the heating pad was turned to low, positioned it on one side of the plastic incubator, then covered it with a white, terry-cloth crate pad. "We'll give this a moment to warm up," he said, "before we unwrap the pup and put him in."

Too overcome to speak, Ally nodded.

Seconds later, Duchess strained yet again, and the second pup was delivered.

Over the next two hours, eight more were born.

Amid the squeaking and the squirming, Duchess cared for them all.

Until finally, she collapsed with a sigh.

"Do you think that's it?" Ally asked.

"Only one way to tell," Hank said. He counted the pups. "Kurt said there were definitely ten...."

Duchess strained again, ever so slightly.

A dark blue sack, tinier than the others, fell out.

Only this time, Duchess merely nosed the pup and turned away.

Please don't let this last one be stillborn, Ally prayed. "What do we do?" she asked frantically.

"Do our best to save it," Hank muttered. He picked

up the sack, quickly figured out which end contained the pup's head, and tore the protective membrane open with his fingers. Amniotic fluid spilled out as he gave the pup's nose a squeeze.

There should have been a cry, as with the others.

But there wasn't.

Knowing there was no time to waste, Hank grabbed the bulb syringe, pressed the air out of it, and then suctioned mucous from the lifeless pup's throat and nostrils. Nothing happened. Again, he suctioned out the fluids. The puppy still didn't respond.

Hand pressed to her chest, Ally watched as Hank lifted the tiny form and made a tight seal by putting his own mouth over the pup's nose and mouth, gave two gentle puffs, then pulled back and assessed her. Again nothing, Ally noted in mounting despair. No visible sign of life.

Helpless tears streamed from her eyes as Hank repeated the puffing process, then rubbed the puppy's chest while holding her head down.

Still nothing, Ally noted miserably.

Hank used the bulb syringe again, then lifted the puppy and attempted mouth-to-mouth resuscitation once more. And this time, to Ally's overwhelming relief, their prayers were answered.

The sound of that small gasp, followed by a high-pitched, rather indignant squeak, was nothing short of a miracle, Ally thought.

With tears of joy rolling down her cheeks, she watched as Hank gently wiped the moisture from the tiny puppy and wrapped her in a cloth.

Ally drew a quavering breath and edged so close to

Hank their bodies touched. "That was...incredible," she breathed, not sure when she had ever been so impressed by a man's gallantry under pressure.

He nodded, looking as amazed and grateful as she felt. "I didn't think she was going to make it," he admitted in a rusty voice.

Ally studied the cute black nose and tightly closed eyes. The pup's ears were as small and compact and beautiful as the rest of her snugly swaddled form. "You saved her."

Yet a trace of worry remained in Hank's blue eyes, Ally noted as he passed her the newborn.

A ribbon of fear slipped through her. She cuddled the tiny pup close to her breast, relieved to feel its soft puffs of breath against the open vee of her shirt. The whelp was breathing nice and rhythmically now, and felt warm to the touch. Yet...Ally searched Hank's face. "What is it?" she asked quietly. "What aren't you telling me?"

His glance met hers, then skittered away, as if he didn't want to be the bearer of bad news. "She's really small," he said finally.

About a third smaller than the others, Ally noted. She nuzzled the top of the puppy's head as she followed Hank back to Duchess's side. "So?" She felt the tiny pup brush its muzzle against her collarbone and snuggle even closer. Unbearable tenderness sifted through her and she stroked the dog gently with her free hand. Was this the connection dog lovers felt? Why many considered canines not just pets but members of their family?

All Ally knew for sure was that she felt fiercely protective of this tiny being. And would do anything to help her thrive. "Isn't there usually a runt of the litter?"

Hank admitted that was so, then frowned. "But it's not just that." He bent down to tend to Duchess.

Ally watched him remove the placenta and gently clean away any remaining afterbirth with the skill of a veteran rancher. "Then what's wrong?" she pressed. She lowered her head and heard a faint purr emanating from the whelp's chest. "I mean, she seems to be breathing okay now." The other ten puppies were okay, too. All snuggled together cozily in the warming box, which had been placed inside the whelping pen, within easy reach of Duchess.

Hank brought a bowl of water to Duchess, and knelt down next to the golden retriever. Shakily, the dam got to her feet and lapped at the water, before sinking down once again. Surveying her with a knowledgeable eye, Hank said reluctantly, "It could just be that the pup you're holding was the last of the litter to be born. And Duchess was exhausted."

Another shiver of dread swept through Ally.

She watched Hank take a fistful of kibble and hand feed it to Duchess. Wondering what he still wasn't telling her, Ally prodded, "I hear an 'except' in there."

Hank's big body tensed. "Sometimes," he allowed wearily, deliberately avoiding Ally's eyes, "when a mother dog shows absolutely no interest in one of her whelps, it's because the dam knows instinctively there's something wrong with the pup. That it may not survive…"

Shock quickly turned to anger. How could he even say that, after all they'd already been through? Ally wondered. "But the littlest one did survive," she protested heatedly, still cradling the puppy to her chest.

Hank nodded. And remained silent.

"She's going to be fine," Ally insisted, and to prove it, placed the runt in the warming box with the rest of the litter.

Again, Hank nodded. But he didn't seem nearly as certain of that as she wanted him to be.

Chapter Five

Wary of fast wearing out his welcome at Mesquite Ridge in regards to Duchess and her puppies, Hank gathered up the soiled towels and cloths, and carried them to the washing machine. For the second time that night, he added detergent and bleach, and switched it on. He returned to the kitchen, spray bottle of disinfectant cleaner, paper towels and plastic trash bag in hand.

He hunkered down to clean out the plastic whelping bed.

While he worked, Ally knelt on the floor next to the warming bed that contained all eleven puppies. The whelping instructions Kurt had left for them were in her hands. She appeared seriously concerned and incredibly overwhelmed with the responsibility of caring for the dam and her litter. Duchess was right beside Ally, face on her paws, serenely keeping watch over her brood.

Hank knew there was no need to burden Ally with this, too—she had enough on her plate, with the sale of the ranch, the task of sorting through her parents' things and the possible loss of her job. "I think I can handle it from here," he said gently.

She stopped reading and looked up, as if she hadn't heard right. "What?"

Was that hurt he saw flashing in her eyes? Or just fatigue and confusion? It had been a long day for Ally, too. "I need to walk Duchess for a moment," Hank told her. "But then I can handle it." He paused, wishing Ally would hang out with them a little longer. She was turning out to be surprisingly good company. "Unless you want to stay," he added impulsively.

For a second, Ally looked truly torn about whether to stay or go. "I'll stay until you get them all settled," she said finally.

"Thanks." Deciding to leave her to her thoughts, he headed outside, with Duchess beside him.

The retriever quickly got down to business, then headed back inside. This time she walked straight to Ally.

Hank knew Duchess was waiting to be petted.

Ally didn't.

Recognizing it wasn't going to happen, at least not then, the dog sank down beside her, close enough that her nose was touching Ally's thigh.

Ally looked at Duchess briefly, tenderness flickering across her delicate features. Wordlessly, she smiled and went back to her reading.

Hank folded a clean blanket in the bottom of the whelping pen, then encouraged Duchess to climb back in. "Come on, girl. I need you to get in here so you can take care of your puppies."

Duchess just looked at him, clearly understanding, but in no mood to comply.

At the "standoff" between him and his canine pal, Ally did her best to stifle a grin. Which showed how much she knew.

"You want to try?" Hank asked.

Her eyes twinkling, Ally tilted her head to one side and said drily, "I don't think she's in a mood to listen to me, either. But…" She rose gracefully and moved to the makeshift bed, patting it firmly. "Come on, sweetheart. You'll be more comfortable in here."

Surprisingly, Duchess rose, climbed in and settled down immediately.

Hank was stunned—and grateful. "Thanks."

"No problem." Ally waved the papers still clutched in her free hand. "I think we're supposed to introduce the puppies to Duchess next."

That was indeed the protocol. The only surprise was that Ally—a confessed dog loather—wanted to be present for this, too. But maybe tonight, Duchess and her big brood were changing all that, as well as Ally's feelings about being at the ranch. Which only went to show that miracles did happen at Christmas, Hank thought.

Keeping his feelings to himself, he asked, "You want to do the first one?"

Ally bit her lower lip, abruptly appearing shy and uncertain once again. "Maybe you better."

Figuring the littlest pup needed her mama most, Hank picked her up and laid her ever so gently in front of Duchess.

Once again, the mother dog turned her nose away, prepared to go to sleep.

Hank tried again, with the same result.

For whatever reason, Duchess wanted nothing to do with her tiniest whelp.

Ally shot Hank a look that mirrored his own consternation.

The worry Hank had felt earlier, when they'd been resuscitating the pup, increased. "Let's see if we can get the little one to nurse." He put the tiny pup at a nipple. She suckled weakly and soon fell right back to sleep.

Hank frowned in concern. "Let's see how the rest of them do." He picked up the hardiest pup, a male, from the warming bed and put him in front of Duchess.

The retriever immediately nosed the whelp, kissing and licking him. Encouraged, Hank put him to a nipple. The pup immediately latched on and began to nurse.

And so it went with the remaining whelps, until finally, they were left with eleven pups and ten nipples. Reluctantly, Hank removed the littlest one from Duchess's side, and handed her ever so carefully to Ally. The last puppy took the little one's place and began to nurse vigorously.

Ally cradled the tiniest puppy against her chest. "What are we going to do if she doesn't nurse any better than that?"

Hank studied the sweet-faced golden retriever curled against the warmth of Ally's breast, and knew they were the castaway pup's last hope. "I'll tell you what we're not going to do," he stated firmly. "We're not going to wait. I'm calling Kurt right now."

To Ally's relief, Kurt McCabe came right out to the ranch, even though it was well past midnight. The personable veterinarian brought a digital scale and his vet bag and checked over the dam and her litter. "Duchess and the whelps all look great," Kurt said when he'd finished recording the weight and sex of all five males and six female pups.

"What about the littlest one?" Ally asked.

"She's definitely a little weaker—as well as tuckered out from her rocky start. That's probably why Duchess initially turned away from her—because she knows instinctively that this pup is going to need more care than the rest, if she's to survive. And on her own, Duchess can't provide that," the vet explained.

Ally glanced at Hank's face, to gauge his reaction. Obviously, this was something the handsome rancher already knew. Which was why he had looked so concerned, and insisted they ask his cousin to make a house call, even if it was the dead of the night.

Her respect for Hank grew.

Ally turned back to Kurt, watching as he gently lifted the littlest one from the warming bed. "Fortunately, the pup's heart and lungs are strong, and there are a lot of things we can do to help her out," he continued.

"Like what?" Ally asked, feeling as protective as if she were the mama herself.

Kurt handed her the puppy. As before, she held the tiny puppy against her chest, and felt it instinctively cuddle close.

"The first thing I'm going to do is give her an injection of replacement plasma to help boost her immune system." Kurt paused to give the puppy the shot.

The little one flinched and let out several high-pitched squeaks.

Ally took comfort in the whelp's strong show of indignation. Judging by the looks on Hank's and Kurt's faces, they also thought it was a good sign.

"It's important you keep her warm. She's going to need to be hand-fed every two hours or so, until she's strong enough to nurse alongside her littermates." Kurt removed several cans of formula and a bottle from his bag, along with another set of instructions. "Come morning, let her try nursing again. Even if it's for only a couple minutes, she'll get colostrum. And of course, keep introducing her to Duchess. Sooner or later they should begin to bond."

And what if they didn't? Ally wondered, exchanging concerned glances with Hank. How would that impact the tiny puppy? Would it alter her chances of survival? Would she grow up feeling like Ally had—as if she never quite fit? Not with her family, not on the ranch, not at school…and now, maybe not even at the job that had been her whole life for the last ten years?

The thought of the defenseless little puppy being rejected made her heart ache.

Mistaking the reason behind Ally's melancholy, Hank stepped closer and patted her arm. "I know this little gal is only twelve ounces—which, according to the weigh-in we just did, makes her roughly twenty-five percent smaller than her siblings. And definitely the runt of the litter." He paused to gaze into Ally's eyes before continuing in a consoling voice, "But often times the smallest one will turn out to be the scrappiest."

"That's true," Kurt agreed.

Realizing worrying about things she couldn't change wouldn't help anything, least of all the tiny puppy cuddled in her arms, Ally began to relax.

Only to see Hank frown again. "The bigger problem is...who do these dogs belong to?"

Kurt nodded toward the wriggling bodies in the warming bed. "These dogs are all definitely show quality purebreds."

Duchess was pretty enough to appear in the Westminster Dog Show, Ally thought, and her puppies were miniature versions of her.

Kurt continued, "Duchess was obviously bred deliberately."

"Which means someone has to be looking for her." Hank knelt down to pet the retriever. He rubbed her large shoulders and stroked behind her ears with so much tenderness Ally felt her own mouth go dry.

"The larger question is how she became separated from the breeder in the first place." The muscles in Hank's own broad shoulders tensed. "Since I'm sure some of these puppies, if not all, have got to be spoken for already."

Surely not the littlest one, Ally thought, then caught herself up short. What was she doing? she wondered in alarm. This puppy wasn't hers to keep! None of them were....

Kurt unhooked the stethoscope from around his neck. "Some dogs want their privacy when they give birth, and slip off to nest in secret. My guess is that's what Duchess did."

"But wouldn't someone have reported her missing by now?" Ally asked.

"You'd think so," the vet replied.

"It's a mystery," Hank concurred grimly. "But one I intend to solve."

Kurt packed up his vet bag. "I'll do everything I can

to help." He paused to pet Duchess and several of her puppies. Standing, he glanced wryly at Hank and Ally. "In the meantime, try not to get too attached."

"Easier said than done," Hank muttered beneath his breath.

And for once, Ally knew exactly how Hank Mc-Cabe felt.

"So how do you want to do this?" Hank asked her, after Kurt had left.

Ally handed him the littlest pup so she could prepare a bottle of canine milk replacement formula, according to the directions, and set it in a bowl of warm water to heat. Then she checked the items in the emergency kit Kurt had left for them, taking out the unscented baby wipes, cotton balls and petroleum jelly, and lining them up neatly on the table. Lips pursed thoughtfully, she went to the drawer in the kitchen where linens were kept, and pulled out several clean dish towels.

Trying not to notice how cuddly—and fragile—the little puppy felt, Hank followed Ally back to the table. He wasn't sure exactly when the tables had turned. He just knew that she was now the "professional" on the scene. Aware how comfortable she looked in the home she was determined to sell ASAP, he asked, "You want me to handle the feedings tonight?"

Ally shook a few drops of formula on the inside of her wrist, looking up from what she was doing long enough to say, "I can manage the bottle feedings tonight. If we do one now…" She glanced at the clock. It was two in the morning. "…then I'll do another at four, and at six."

Which meant she'd get practically no sleep whatso-ever, Hank thought in concern.

He watched her pull out a kitchen chair and sit down. "You sure?"

Ally spread one of the towels across her lap, then held out her arms for the puppy. "I don't mind." Her expression was incredibly tender as the transfer was made. Looking as contented as a new mother, she settled the puppy on her side and gently offered her bottle. "You've got other responsibilities."

No more eager to leave the brand-new litter than she was, Hank pulled up a chair beside them. "So do you."

Ally smiled as the puppy finally got the idea and began to suckle. "Yours are more pressing," she reminded him.

Hank couldn't argue that. It had been raining all night, and the temperature was near freezing. His cattle were going to need extra feed to successfully weather the elements. Plus there were Duchess and the other puppies to consider. They needed help now, too. "Okay." He rose. "I'll take the ten puppies to Duchess, so they can nurse again, and then get everyone settled for the night."

Fifteen minutes later, all eleven puppies had been fed, licked by Duchess to ensure they would go to the bathroom, and then been cleaned up by their mama. Because Duchess still had no interest in the littlest one, Ally had taken care of the runt. She'd rubbed a moistened cotton ball across her bottom, and after the desired result, had cleaned her up with more cotton balls, adding a protective application of petroleum jelly.

Amazed that a self-professed city girl like Ally could take so early to such a task, Hank moved the puppies away from Duchess and back into the incubator, one by one, where they would be certain to stay warm.

All except the littlest one.

"You want to put her in the warming box, too?" he asked Ally, before he went up to bed himself.

Her gentle smile beautiful to behold, she cuddled the tiny pup to her chest. "I think I'll hold her just a little while longer," she murmured, without looking up.

And Hank knew for certain what he'd only guessed before. Ally was in love. With the puppy whose life he had saved...

"Just a little while longer" turned out to be most of the night. Hank knew that, because Ally was still up, albeit nodding off, when he rose again at five-thirty. "You've really got to get to some sleep," he told her, as he put another pot of coffee on the stove.

Ally yawned and stretched. "You're up."

Hank took the puppies and placed them at Duchess's side, one by one, and made sure they all latched on. "I'm used to staying up all night to nurse sick animals."

Ally shrugged and began preparing another bottle of puppy formula. "Financial analysts pull all-nighters, too."

Hank didn't doubt that she gave her all to whatever she did. Tenacity was something he and Ally seemed to have in common. However, he still thought she needed a break. He closed the distance between them, wishing he could kiss her again. He put his hands over hers, stilling the movements of her fingers. "Seriously, I can handle all the dogs for the next two hours if you want to catch a little shut-eye."

Ally pulled away. "I can't hit the sheets just yet. Gracie is due for another feeding." Her kissable lips assumed a stubborn pout.

Hank pushed away the forbidden image her sweet, soft lips had evoked.

With effort, he concentrated on the problem at hand. "Gracie?"

Reluctant pleasure tugged at the corners of her mouth. "I thought she should have a name, other than 'the littlest one.'"

Their eyes met. Once again, Hank felt a mutual purpose, a bond. The same sort of connection he figured parents of a newborn baby felt. But then she lowered her gaze, and it was gone. He studied the newborn pup's velvety golden coat and scrunched-up face. "Gracie is good. It suits her."

"You're not going to argue with me?" Ally joked, only half-humorously. "Tell me that I shouldn't name a pup I'm only going to have to give away?" She snapped her mouth shut, as if worried she'd reveal even more of her runaway emotions.

Hank shrugged. "I figure you probably already know that. Besides," he said slowly, "Gracie is the runt of the litter."

"What does that have to do with anything?" she demanded, narrowing her eyes.

"Someone willing to pay top dollar for a show quality retriever may not want anything less than perfection. Cute as Gracie is, her size could be a deterrent."

Ally fumed. "Not to me!"

No kidding. Her intense reaction worried him a bit. Ally was becoming personally involved in the situation and was bound to get her heart broken if and when Duchess's owner showed up to claim the litter and their mama. She almost would have been better off if she had continued to loathe the canine species as much as she had when Duchess first showed up.

The sound of a truck motor in the driveway broke the silence. Ally wrinkled her nose and continued cradling the puppy like a newborn baby. "Are you expecting anyone?"

Hank shook his head. "You?"

She furrowed her brow. "At dawn?"

A knock sounded on the back door, and Hank went to open it.

His father was standing there, foil-covered plate in hand.

Hank figured he knew what this was about.

The blessing was, Ally didn't. And if he could help it, she would never have any idea.

Chapter Six

"Might as well get it over with," Hank told his father short minutes later. As the sun rose over the horizon, the two of them emerged from Hank's pickup truck and strode toward the back. Hank opened the tailgate so they could get at the supplemental feed for his herd, and shot his father a knowing glance. "'Cause I know you didn't come here just to say hello to Ally, see the new pups and help me tend my cattle."

"You're right." Shane hefted a big bale of hay and carried it into the mesquite-edged pasture where the hundred cattle had weathered the cold and rain the night before. "I did want to talk to you in private."

Hank cut the twine and separated the feed, scattering it about so the steers could get at it easily. "What about?"

The two of them got back in the truck and drove a little farther on before stopping and doing the same thing again.

"The word in town is that Corporate Farms is wooing Ally," Shane stated.

Hank shrugged. "She's talking to a Realtor about listing the property, too."

His dad lifted a silver brow. "I thought *you* had a deal with her."

I thought so, too. Which was what he got for letting the arrangement be as convenient as Ally had needed it to be, when he had volunteered to watch over the property for her last summer, in the wake of her dad's death.

Hank went over to check the water supply. Ice had formed around the edges of the trough, so he broke it up with a hoe. "She agreed to let me run cattle here and live in the house, in exchange for my help tending to the ranch." At the time it had seemed the perfect solution for both of them.

Shane studied the property with a horse rancher's keen gaze. "She knew you were interested in buying it?"

"Eventually." *When I had the money.* "Yes." Hank carried another bundle of feed across the rain-soaked ground. "She also figured—rightly so—that I couldn't afford it yet."

Shane followed with another bundle. "I wish you had talked to me before you struck that deal," he said with regret.

Hank's irritation increased. Tired of weathering his father's meddling in his affairs, he squared off with him. "We both know what would have happened if I had!"

"You'd be better off now," his dad countered, his disapproval as evident as his need to help.

"I'd be *better off* if you and the rest of the family stopped trying to coddle me!" Acting as if he were some damned invalid, instead of a decorated ex-marine embarking on the next chapter of his life.

His father grimaced like the take-charge man he was. "We're not doing that," he argued.

Like hell they weren't! "You've done nothing but that since Jo-anne's death," Hank countered.

Shane's jaw set. "You fell apart."

Hank turned his gaze away from the mounting concern in his dad's eyes. "And I've long since put myself back together again."

Shane sighed. Tried again. "The point is, son—"

"The point is," he interrupted curtly, lifting a staying hand, "we shouldn't be having this conversation. Not now. Not ever."

Ally was upstairs in the sewing room when Hank and Shane returned.

It didn't take a rocket scientist to know something had happened while they were gone. The two men appeared to be barely speaking as they parted company. Which was a surprise. Ally had thought the McCabes were a close-knit family through and through. Yet as Hank stood watching his father's pickup disappear from view, he looked as tense and bereft as she had usually felt when dealing with her own parents.

Not that it was any of her business, she reminded herself sternly, returning to the cutting table.

Seconds later, she heard him come in.

Footsteps sounded in the hall. The door to his bedroom closed.

Fifteen minutes later, Hank emerged, looking freshly showered and cleanly shaven. He paused in the doorway of the sewing room. A smile quirked his lips when he glanced at the puppies snuggled together in the warming bed, with Duchess lying on the floor next to it.

An eyebrow lifted in silent inquiry.

Self-consciously, Ally explained, "I needed to do work up here, and I didn't think I should leave them unattended so soon."

Hank nodded, a knowing light in his midnight-blue eyes.

"By the way, the candy cane shaped coffeecake your mother sent over was absolutely delicious." The festive gift had sported a flaky golden bread, cranberry-cherry filling and cream cheese frosting.

Hank folded his arms and propped one shoulder against the frame. "I'll tell her you said so." He nodded at the sophisticated ivory fabric she was measuring. "What are you doing here?"

Ally picked up the shears and began to cut. "Making new drapes for the downstairs windows, to dress up the space."

He came closer, in a drift of sandalwood and leather cologne. "You know how to do that?"

Her gaze flicked over his nice-fitting jeans and navy corduroy shirt, then rose in a guilty rush. "My mother taught me how to sew when I was eight. I helped her make custom slipcovers and draperies." And she needed to stop remembering what it had been like to be held in his arms, kissing him passionately.

Hank hooked his thumbs in the belt loops on either side of his fly. "I didn't realize she had a business."

Ally swallowed around the sudden parched feeling of her throat. "They needed the income she brought in to buy more land."

His gaze roved her face, settling briefly on her

mouth. A prickling, skittering awareness sifted through her. "And put you through college?" he added, almost as an afterthought.

Ally tensed and marked off another length. "I did that myself."

Hank did a double take. "Seriously?"

Ally picked up her shears once again. She bent her head, concentrating on her cutting. "They didn't want me to leave Laramie County. They would have preferred I stay on the ranch and build a life here."

He came closer. "But you went anyway."

She sighed. "Like I said, I was determined to do things my own way." She pushed the bad memories aside and turned her attention back to him. "And speaking of parents...what's going on with you and your dad?"

A muscle in his jaw flexed. "What do you mean?"

Ally eyed him pointedly. "I saw the two of you come back. Neither of you looked particularly happy."

Hank shrugged and averted his gaze.

"Does the discord have something to do with the ranch?"

His expression darkened. "Why would you think that?"

"I'm not sure." It was her turn to lift her shoulders. "I just do."

Silence fell. Hank looked as if he was about to say something, but didn't. The quiet continued, fraught with tension.

Aware this wasn't the first time she'd been summarily cut out of a situation—her parents had done it all the time—Ally turned her attention back to her task and cut along the last line she had marked.

Her feelings were hurt, but she wasn't sure why—
it shouldn't matter if Hank confided in her or not. She
cleared her throat, and added with as much indolence
as she could manage, "Anyway, if that's all…"

"Actually—" Hank's frown deepened "—it's not.
I've got something I need to do in Laramie."

Could he be more vague?

Could she be more nosy?

Honestly! What was wrong with her today? Just because she and Hank had bonded a little over the birth of
the litter, and exchanged one way-too-hot kiss, that was
no reason to think they were involved in each other's
lives. Because they weren't now, and definitely wouldn't
be once the ranch was sold!

"Can you watch over Duchess and the pups a little
while longer?"

Trying to hide her disappointment at his sudden re-
moteness, Ally nodded. "Sure."

And that, it seemed, was that.

"There's no way we can give you a mortgage on
Mesquite Ridge without at least ten percent down," the
president of Laramie Bank told Hank an hour later.
"And given the fact we're talking about a two and a half
million dollar loan…" Terence Hall ran a hand over his
close-trimmed beard.

Hank had already run the numbers. "I need two hundred and fifty thousand, cash."

Terence rocked back in his chair. "Plus an application fee, closing costs. Money for the survey, inspection and title search. And a real estate sales commission
if she lists with a broker, as she currently plans to do."

The situation was getting worse by the minute, Hank

thought, as he listened to the Christmas music playing in the lobby of the bank. Only there was no Santa Claus here. Only Ally Garrett, and Graham Penderson from Corporate Farms, who could easily become this year's Grinch, by stealing the property out from under him.

Aware that his holiday spirit was fading as fast as his problems mounted, Hank decided to be straight with the most influential banker in the county. The word in the agricultural community was that if Terence couldn't make it happen, no one could. "I've got only forty thousand saved."

Terence rapped his pen on his desk. "Maybe you could convince Ms. Garrett to do some sort of land contract or lease-purchase agreement."

Hank's hand tightened on the brim of his Stetson. "I doubt it. Besides, even then I'd have only a hundred eighty days max—to come up with the rest of the cash, or forfeit everything I've already put in."

On just the assumption this would work out as I hoped.

"Perhaps if you sell your herd..."

"I'd be all hat and no cattle, with no cash to replace 'em."

"Sometimes there are sources for cash that aren't readily thought of."

Hank knew where this was heading. He'd already had one argument today with his dad. He wasn't going to have another, with a banker. He lifted a palm and stood, not about to go down that road now. "Thanks for your time," he said curtly. "I'll let you know if anything changes."

Terence followed him to the door. "Maybe you

should have another talk with Ms. Garrett," he suggested hopefully.

As it happened, Hank planned to do just that.

The only problem was, when Hank got back to the ranch, a big Cadillac with a Corporate Farms logo was sitting in the driveway.

Frowning, he got out of his truck and walked inside.

Ally was standing next to a ladder in the living room, a spritz bottle in one hand, a putty knife in another. In worn jeans, an old Rice University T-shirt and sneakers, with her hair drawn into a clip, she looked younger—and more vulnerable than ever—as Graham Penderson harangued her.

"It's a good offer. Better than you'd get if you went the traditional sale route."

Snorting, Ally sent Graham a narrowed-eyed glance. "That's ten percent less than the asking price suggested by Premier Realty."

You go, girl, Hank thought, pleased to see her standing up to the pushy acquisition agent.

Penderson turned his back on Hank and continued his pitch in a you'd-be-crazy-not-to-accept-this-deal tone. "We subtracted out the real estate commission and other costs. You'd still get the same amount, only without all the hassle and expense of—if you'll forgive my candor—renovating this dog of a house."

It was also, Hank thought, the home in which Ally had grown up.

Not a smart move, criticizing it.

He looked over at her.

Ally's face remained calm, her emotions—whatever they were—camouflaged. She climbed back down the ladder and wordlessly accepted the written offer Graham Penderson was holding out. With a forced smile, she walked over and put the papers on the scarred roll-top desk. "I'll take that into consideration," she stated cooly.

Graham Penderson did not seem to know when to quit. "If you sell to us," he continued, "you won't have to worry about updating anything on the property, since we intend to tear down all existing buildings, including the ranch house and barns, and build something much more utilitarian."

Ally blinked.

She hadn't been expecting that.

"That seems like a waste," Hank interjected, in an effort to buy Ally time to pull her thoughts together.

The agent swung around to him. "It's good business," he countered matter-of-factly. He turned back to Ally. "The offer is good for forty-eight hours," he said impatiently, holding his Resistol at his side.

"So you said." Ally ignored the question in Hank's eyes and gestured toward the door. "Now if you'll excuse me, Mr. Penderson, I have work to do."

The smart move, Hank noted, would have been to take the hint. The agent did no such thing.

"Not if you sell to Corporate Farms. Then, all you have to do is sign on the dotted line, take the money and run."

Clearly unimpressed, Ally stared down the CF representative. "So you *also* said."

Penderson stepped even closer. "I'd hate to see you lose out on what has to be the answer to your prayers."

Ally remained grimly silent. Hank figured this was

his cue, and walked toward the agent. "I believe the lady asked you to leave."

Penderson turned. Whatever he was about to say was lost as Hank clapped a firm hand on the small man's shoulder, physically propelling him across the living room, through the dingy foyer and all the way to his car. Hank waited until Penderson drove off, then went back inside. Ally was back on the ladder, spritzing a piece of the loose horse-and-hound wallpaper. If she resented his macho interference, she wasn't showing it.

"You okay?" he asked gently.

Ally set the spray bottle on the platform at the top of the stepladder. Stubbornly pressing her lips together, she eased the putty knife beneath the paper. "Why wouldn't I be?" The wallpaper made a ripping sound as it separated from the ancient drywall.

Hank stepped closer. He grabbed a piece of dampened paper and pulled it off the wall. "Because that jerk was giving you a hard time."

Ally came back down the ladder, picked it up and moved it another two feet to the left. Resentment glimmered in her green eyes. "I was handling him."

Hank stood with legs braced, as if for battle. "You may *think* you were."

She stiffened. "What is that supposed to mean?"

Here was his chance to bring up what he'd been reluctant to discuss before. "Corporate Farms is more than just an outfit that buys ranches and farms nationwide, or a firm that is angling to create the largest single ranch in the nation. It has a reputation for ruining communities faster than you can imagine."

Ally sobered. "How?"

"Well, first they come in with a lowball offer. Like

what just happened. If they fail on the first try—and often they don't—they up the ante. And they *keep* upping it until they get what they want. In fact, they're happiest when they do have to pay more than the assessed value of a property, because that drives up the prices of all the neighboring ranches and farms, and with that, the tax values. A few acquisitions by CF coupled with a bad year agriculturally, and before you know it the neighbors can't pay their taxes."

"Go on," Ally said quietly, suddenly a captive audience.

Hank sighed heavily. "So then Corporate Farms comes in again, and buys the properties in distress, this time for much *less* than what they're worth. The point is, an outfit like CF has vast resources and can move awfully fast. You may not be prepared for how fast. Or the kind of temptation they can exert." His eyes hardened. "Especially since word on the street is they want to eventually buy up every single ranch property in Laramie County and turn it into one big entity."

Ally regarded him calmly. "So in other words, I shouldn't sell to them because they're bad guys. And they're likely to put everyone else around here out of business if I do."

"Exactly," he muttered.

"Which is why your dad was here this morning."

Her insight caught Hank off guard. "That was part of it," he allowed cautiously.

She stepped closer. "And the rest?"

Hank's jaw set. "It's not relevant to this."

Her gaze narrowed. "Why don't you let me decide that? Seriously. You want me to trust you? Then you need to reveal more about what's going on with your situation, too!"

Fair enough. "My parents think I need their help to succeed."

Ally let out a disbelieving laugh. "You? The guy who was Mr. Everything in high school? Student body president, star athelete, class heartthrob—"

Hank focused on the most important of the litany. "Class heartthrob?" he repeated. Was that how she'd seen him back then?

Ally flushed. "Never mind. Forget I said that." She drew a breath and settled on a step of the ladder, turning businesslike once again. "Back to your very implausible story."

Hank's gut twisted with the irony. "It's true," he said, just as quietly. He edged close enough to rest an elbow on the top rung of the ladder. "My parents think I flipped out after Jo-anne's death. That was why I joined the marines and stayed in for ten years."

Ally tilted her head to look up into his face. "Was it the reason?"

His voice was edgy with tension as he answered, "I admit I was depressed and angry after she died. You can't not be if one of your loved ones dies in something as senseless and unexpected as a terrorist attack. But..." He paused reflectively, then shrugged. "I got over it."

The tenderness in Ally's eyes encouraged him to dig a little deeper into his feelings. "I grew up, I guess, came to accept that bad things happen in life to everyone. And what counts is your ability to pick yourself up and make something good happen—even in the worst circumstances—and move on. And that's what my career in the marines was all about. I helped save a lot of lives. Now I'm out…and ready to move on with the next chapter of my life."

Ally stood and moved away from the ladder once again. "But your mom and dad can't accept that."

He watched her amble back to the wall where she had been working, and spritz an area within reach.

Hank picked up a scraper and walked over to help. "My parents blame themselves for my taking off in the first place. They think they failed me somehow, after Jo-anne died. They don't want to be caught short again. And they're afraid if this ranching thing doesn't work out, I'm going to leave again."

For a second, a flash of alarm appeared in her eyes. "Will you?"

Was it possible, Hank wondered, she wanted him to stay around, as much as he was beginning to want her to do the same? "No. Texas is my home and always will be. That's one thing I figured out while I was overseas."

She scowled at the piece of wall covering she was working on, then tilted her head up to his. "When you say Texas," she murmured, looking at him from beneath her fringe of thick lashes, "do you mean Laramie, or anywhere in the state?"

"I got a hundred head of cattle, and I have to find somewhere of my own to graze them." At the moment, Mesquite Ridge was the only ranch available for lease or sale in Laramie County.

"So if it's not here…?"

Hank studied the way she was biting into her lower lip. "It'll be somewhere."

"That's all very interesting." She ripped off the stubborn piece of wallpaper with more force than necessary and dropped it into the trash can. Then she whirled around and chided, "But it doesn't explain why you just acted so protectively toward me."

He'd been wondering when she would bring that up.

Hank refused to apologize for giving Graham Penderson the old heave-ho. "I wouldn't think I'd have to explain that," he answered drily.

She lifted a blond brow. "Apparently," she said, perfectly mimicking his deadpan tone, "you do."

Was it possible? Was he really that hard to read that Ally had no clue how he was beginning to feel about her?

"Then how about this for an explanation?" Hank said, leaning in for a kiss.

Chapter Seven

His move wasn't all that unexpected. The woman in Ally had known Hank was going to kiss her again. She just hadn't known when—or where.

The question was, Ally mused, as his arms wrapped around her and drew her close, what was *she* going to do? Was she going to acknowledge the rapid thudding of her heart and the weakening of her knees, and give in to the ever so slow and deliberate descent of his lips to hers? When the professional businesswoman in her knew she should not—at least until the matter of the sale of Mesquite Ridge was settled? Or would she go with her feminine side, and the instinct that told her to grab this opportunity to see if their chemistry was as good as she'd suspected?

Unable to keep herself from slowing things down a little and speaking her piece, Ally planted a palm in the center of Hank's chest. She drew in a quick, bolstering breath and looked him square in the eye. "This won't change anything, you know."

Grinning, Hank threaded a hand through the hair at her nape. "I know *you* think so," he murmured, just as confidently.

And then all heaven broke loose as his lips finally took command of hers....

My goodness, did this man ever know how to kiss! With finesse and depth and stark male assurance. He kissed her as if kissing was an end in itself, and there was no one but the two of them in the entire universe. He kissed her as if he meant it—and always would. He kissed her as if she was the most incredible woman he'd ever been privileged to know.

And darn it all, Ally thought, as she threw caution to the wind and rose up on tiptoe to meet him with every ounce of womanly passion she had. She felt the same!

She never wanted this moment to end.

She wanted to stay just like this, with his arms wrapped around her, his strong body pressed ardently against hers.

She wanted to savor the peppermint taste of his mouth, and the incredible heat that exuded from every sexy inch of him.

And she wanted more. Much more than she had ever wanted in her life...

Right now. Right here.

And since it was Christmastime, and she had no other gifts headed her way, why not present herself with the most thrilling experience of all?

Ally broke off the caress to murmur, "I want you."

Hank looked down at her with a mixture of affection

and longing. He threaded both his hands through her hair and tenderly cupped her face between his palms. "I want you, too, but only," he said soberly, "if you're sure."

Ally had never been impulsive. Until now. And darned if she wasn't enjoying the experience. "I'm sure," she said, just as earnestly.

He nodded and swung her up in his arms. "Then we're going up to my bedroom and doing this the way it should be done."

"And how is that?" Ally asked, her recklessness soaring with every step he took, until at last Hank set her down next to his neatly made bed.

"Slowly." He paused to kiss her again, even more deeply this time again. "And with great attention to detail."

She liked his approach. It kept her from thinking too much about her feelings. Emotions could be her undoing. Better to think about the task at hand....

"Detail's good." Ally let her head fall back as he nibbled his way down her neck, lingering over her collarbone. She shivered when he eased her old college T-shirt over her head, letting it fall to the floor. His eyes darkened as he took in the curves of her breasts, spilling out of the lace of her bra.

"Very good," Hank murmured thickly, as he eased the fabric from her arms and reached behind her to undo the clasp.

The lace slid away. He bent her backward over his arm. Cool air assaulted her nipples and her breasts tingled in anticipation. Unable to bear the excitement, Ally let her eyes flutter shut. She felt the warmth of his mouth, the caress of his tongue, the nip of his teeth, while his hands conducted a very thorough exploration of their own. Despite her efforts to keep this a purely physical experience, feelings welled up inside her, mixing with the sensations. The combination of the two was overwhelming and incredibly enticing....

Ally's heart slammed against her ribs and her breathing grew short. It was suddenly imperative, she decided, that they both get out of their clothes.

Hank seemed to have the same thought, because he was guiding her upright again so he could use both hands to unbutton and unzip, and help ease off her boots and jeans.

"You, too," she said, jerking the shirt hem free of his jeans, working at the fastenings, spreading the fabric wide. His chest was every bit as sleek and hard and masculine as she had imagined it would be. Swirls of dark hair covered his flat male nipples and arrowed down past his navel.

Anxious to discover more, she let her hands move to his belt buckle.

Hank kissed his way from the shell of her ear down her neck. "I thought we were taking this slow."

Ally eased both her hands inside the waistband of his jeans. He was throbbing, ready, full. Heat poured through her, curling her toes and she rose up to meet him. With her heart slamming against her ribs, she kissed him full and hard on the mouth. Given the way she felt... "We are."

He grabbed her close and kissed her back, just as ardently. The hot skin of his muscular chest pressed against her bare breasts. She felt his urgency. And still he kissed her thoroughly. As if she was the most beautiful, wonderful woman on earth, and he was the only man for her. It felt as if they were meant to be together, meant to celebrate the upcoming holiday in just this way. And though Ally had never liked Christmas, never let herself want presents, she did want this.

What did it matter if it wasn't destined to be anything but a fling? she told herself practically. Something that felt so good had to be right.

Hank must have felt so, too. Otherwise he wouldn't be letting go of her long enough to step out of his boots, jeans and briefs, wouldn't be ripping back the covers on his bed and lowering her to the warm flannel sheets.

Slipping both hands beneath her, he urged her knees apart and eased his weight between her thighs. More kisses came, slower and more sultry than before, and only when she was trembling and arching and gasping for breath did he release her lips and kiss his way down her body. Lingering over her breasts, moving past her ribs, to patiently explore her navel...

Seeming more content than she had ever imagined he could be, he explored the hottest, wettest part of her, through the lace of her panties. Holding her hips, he made her wiggle and moan. And then his hands were inside the elastic, steadily easing that last bit of cloth from her. The intensity of his exploration left them both shaking.

At some point the tables were turned and her hands were on him, causing him to inhale sharply and bury his head against her throat.

"Enough playing," Hank murmured. Turning her onto her back, he stretched out overtop, his hot breath scorching her neck.

"Agreed." She put her palms on his hips and wantonly pulled him toward her.

A second later they were one, fitting together as if they had been destined to join forces just like this, his fullness generating another roller coaster of want and need. Forcing her to open herself up and wrap her arms and legs around him and be closer yet. And still they kissed, the two of them moving together, burning hotter, until they were soaring out of control. The force of the pleasure consumed her, prompting her to arch and shudder and cry out. And Hank, sweet unbelievable gift that he was, found his pleasure, too, surging into her just as rapaciously, taking her along for the ride.

Ally lay on her side, her eyes closed. She wasn't sure when she had ever felt so completely, utterly fulfilled...or so drained. Physically, she was exhausted. Emotionally was another matter. Her heart was in as much of an uproar as her senses. Every inch of her felt alive, appreciated and more vulnerable than she knew what to do with.

With a long, luxurious sigh that sounded like pure contentment, Hank rolled so his body was cuddled up next to hers.

Spooning was something Ally had never done, either. Yet with Hank's arm clamped snugly around her, his strong body pressed against hers, she didn't have the will to move away.

So she lay there, eyes shut, trying not to think about what had just happened or what it might mean. Now or in the future.

And she was still "not thinking" about it some time later when she awakened and found herself naked and alone in Hank McCabe's bed. Ally sat up with a start, clutching the sheet to her breasts. Her naked state, and the just-loved tingling of her body, made it official. She hadn't dreamed this tryst with Hank. Or her newfound, never to be repeated, recklessness. Fortunately for both of them, *he* had apparently come to his senses, too, and left the room before she roused. Which meant she could get dressed in solitude.

With shaking hands, Ally pulled on her clothes and went into the bathroom to splash cold water on her face.

The woman staring back at her in the mirror, with the bright eyes, flushed cheeks and kiss-swollen lips, looked different.

One roll in the hay with Hank and she felt different, too.

But Ally wasn't going to think about that, either.

She was going to go down and see to Duchess and the puppies, because she should have done that a good half an hour ago. Ally ran a brush through her tousled hair, twisted it up into a clip and hurried down the stairs to the kitchen.

Only to find the puppies already curled up to Duchess's side, suckling sweetly. All except Gracie, who was cuddled on Hank's lap, taking her formula from a bottle in his hand.

His dark hair was mussed, his jaw lined with late-afternoon shadow, and he, too, had the glow of someone who had just been well and thoroughly loved.

Ally pushed aside the notion of what it might be like to have him home with her like this every evening. No matter how much she might fantasize that, or wish for it in her dreams, it wasn't going to happen, she told herself firmly.

She didn't care how sexy he was.

She was not going to return to the place that had held so much loneliness and uncertainty in her youth.

To a place that held nothing but bad memories for her now.

"Why didn't you wake me?" Ally asked.

Hank looked at Ally tenderly. "I know how hard you've been working. I wanted you to get some sleep."

She had to admit she did feel better for the rest. "You didn't have to do that."

Something shifted in his expression, though the affection in his eyes remained. Appearing as if he had half expected just this kind of reaction from her, he favored her with a reassuring smile.

"I know that," Hank returned, just as quietly. "But I wanted to."

Just as, Ally thought wistfully, he clearly wanted to make love to her again. She swallowed, her fear of being hurt stronger than ever. "The thing is," she reminded them both, "I'm only here temporarily."

The look in Hank's eyes said he clearly felt otherwise. "So you're telling me I'm nothing more than a fling to you?"

Ally wished it were that uncomplicated. She could already feel herself being drawn to him again, heart and soul. The problem was, they were all wrong for each other. "We want different things from life," she told him in a low, measured tone.

His gaze narrowed. "Ranchers marry city girls all the time," he returned casually.

Marry! Telling herself they were speaking hypothetically, Ally concurred. "But in those cases, the city girls move to the ranch." Which was clearly not going to happen here. She edged closer to make her point as gently and kindly as possible. She put up a staying hand. "I'm not saying it wasn't great…"

"That's good to hear," Hank interrupted, looking her straight in the eye. "Because it was—" he paused, letting the words sink in "—great."

Ally flushed at the new heat in his midnight-blue eyes. "But it's not going to happen again," she continued, standing her ground determinedly.

He lifted a skeptical brow. "Sure about that?" he teased.

Ally nodded. She did not want to be hurt and instinct told her that, whether he wanted to admit it or not, Hank McCabe had the potential to break her heart. She gulped, moved closer still and inclined her head toward the adorable puppy he held in his arms. "So what's going on here?"

To her relief, Hank let the discussion about their love-making end.

"Well," he drawled, his attention returning to Duchess and the puppies, too. "You're not going to believe what just happened," he said. He finished giving Gracie the bottle, then held her up tenderly, to look into her cute little face and still-closed eyes. "Is she, Gracie?"

Ally could have swore the pup gave a tiny squeak in response.

But maybe that was wishful thinking, too.

"What happened?" she asked in concern.

Hank smiled and gently set the littlest puppy down in front of Duchess, who promptly began nuzzling the runt of the litter affectionately and cleaning her, with her tongue. That much attention from her mother was new, Ally noted with a start.

Hank beamed like a proud papa, and languidly rolled

to his feet. "Gracie nursed at her mama's side for a good three minutes at the start of the feeding before she got too tired and fell off."

Nursing from the mother was much harder, physically, than taking formula from a bottle. Which meant that Gracie was not failing, after all, but getting stronger. "That's nearly three times as long as she did this morning!" Ally noted, impressed.

"Not only did she get much needed colostrum and immunity from her mama," Hank reported happily, "but she drank most of this bottle, too."

Finished, Duchess nosed Gracie away from her and turned to the next puppy who needed her attention.

Hank reached over and picked up Gracie, handing her to Ally to cuddle. As she held her, Gracie made the same sounds the other puppies were making—like the quiet purr of a well-tuned motor. The males were a little larger than the females. All the puppies, including Gracie, seemed a bit more adept at wiggling and scooting around today. Duchess seemed attached to every one of them, even the littlest one.

"Gracie is getting stronger, too." Ally could feel it in the way the little puppy nestled against her.

Hank regarded her seriously. "It won't be long at all—maybe the end of the week or so—before Gracie can take her nourishment with her siblings, and give up the hand-feeding entirely."

Which meant, Ally realized with a pang, that Gracie wouldn't need her.

"That's great," she choked out, telling herself that the pup's coming independence, as well as Hank's wordless departure from the bedroom, was to be celebrated, not mourned. Ever so gently, she pressed a kiss on the top of Gracie's head and handed her back to him.

Their fingers brushed during the transfer. The tenderness of his touch told her he knew just how vulnerable and exposed she felt. A humiliating sting of tears pressed against the back of Ally's eyes. She knew she had to get out of there. Now. Before she gave her heart away to more than just Duchess and the puppies.

Determined not to reveal herself even more, she whirled around. Reminding herself she could not stay in Laramie, no matter what happened with her job in Houston, Ally found her coat, purse and keys. *I'm a city girl now. And that being the case...* "I have to go into town."

Hank's eyebrows went up. "Right now?"

Not trusting herself to speak, Ally nodded.

He looked...disappointed.

The odd thing was, she was disappointed, too. But she knew it was for the best. Despite Hank's protests to the contrary, their fling was just that—a one-time event never to be repeated. Ally forced herself to hold Hank's steady, assessing gaze, and said in the most even voice she could manage, "Since I can't find a crew to do it for me, I've decided to go ahead and strip and paint at least the living room and foyer myself. Hopefully, the kitchen and mudroom, too. I'm going to pick up some paint samples before the hardware store closes, and decide on a color this evening."

Hank settled Gracie in the warmer and began adding the other puppies, too. "Want company?"

Yes, as a matter of fact, she did. Which was another part of the problem. She was used to weathering life's difficulties alone. Hank was going to be in her life for only twelve more days. It would be a mistake to count on him more than she already had. And an even bigger mistake to put herself in situations with him that could only lead to further intimacy.

"Thanks for the offer," she said briskly, "but no." For both their sakes, she flashed a too-bright smile. "I think we've imposed on one another enough."

Much more, and she'd begin to think they were in some sort of relationship. And that was not the case.

"And I thought the situation couldn't get any worse," Ally's coworker told her over the phone in an anxious tone two hours later. "Unfortunately," Porter continued unhappily, "I was wrong."

I'm not sure I want to hear this.

Ally stopped her car at the end of the road leading to the ranch and rolled down her window. She checked the post and took out several pieces of mail, all for Hank. She set them on the seat beside her and rolled up her window again, speaking into the microphone attached to her earpiece. "What do you mean?" she asked, doing her best to remain calm.

"The powers that be have decided to notify everyone of their job status—or lack thereof—by email!" Porter railed. "If we're laid off, we're not even going to be permitted back in the building. They're going to ship our personal belongings to us."

Ally turned her car into the lane, the golden arc of her headlights sweeping through the darkness of early evening. On either side of the gravel path were heavy thickets of mesquite that further obscured her view. In no hurry to get back to Hank, she drove carefully. "I'm sure the new CEO thinks it will be easier that way," she told Porter.

"Maybe for them," he argued. "For us, it's all the more humiliating! And *depressing,* since the messages are all going out simultaneously on the morning of December 23!"

Good thing I've never been much for Christmas, or my holiday would be completely ruined.

"Couldn't they at least have kept us around until after the holiday?" Porter complained.

Ally winced as her Audi bumped through a water-filled rut that spanned the width of the gravel lane.

Was there no place on this ranch not needing repair? she wondered. Then said practically, "For accounting reasons, the company has to wrap this up before December 31. You know that. Anyway, the last I heard, the plan was to keep at least a few of the old middle managers around, to help with the transition. So you could still have a job when the dust settles, as could I."

"I'm not counting on it, which is why I'm already sending out my résumé as we speak." Porter paused. "At least you have a substantial financial cushion with the ranch."

Not as much as people probably thought, given the size and value of Mesquite Ridge. Unless they had looked at her financials…

"All you have to do is sell to Corporate Farms or whoever and—"

Holy cow! Ally blinked in astonishment as she reached the clearing that surrounded the ranch house and barn. If she hadn't known, she would have sworn it wasn't her home! She'd been gone only a little over two hours, yet half a dozen pick-up trucks and cars were parked there.

Inside the 1920s domicile, lights blazed.

Clearly, a party was going on.

Why hadn't she been invited?

Or at least advised that it was happening?

"...Whereas I will probably end up having to sell my condo," her coworker continued. "Unless I end up getting another job right away. If we're lucky enough to get a little severance, along with our pink slips—"

"Porter," Ally interrupted, "I've really got to go."

"Okay. Call me."

"I will." She turned off her phone and dropped the earpiece into her shoulder bag.

Gathering up Hank's mail, she drew a bolstering breath. And emerged from her car just in time to see Hank stride out of the front door and head straight for her.

Chapter Eight

Grinning, Hank strolled toward her, one hand behind his back. "Ready for a surprise?"

Was she?

Before Ally could protest, he produced a red Santa hat and slid it over her head, so the white fur trim obscured her vision. Trying—and failing—to hold on to her pique regarding both his cheerful antics and the party obviously going on in her absence, Ally drawled sarcastically, "Is this necessary?" The furry brim tickled the bridge of her nose.

"Yes, ma'am," Hank bantered back. "If you want to get in the holiday spirit…"

Ignoring the tremor of excitement soaring through her, Ally let him guide her. "I thought I told you I wasn't big on holidays."

Hank's warm hands closed over her shoulders. Purposefully, he steered her in the direction he wanted her to go. "Yet," he interjected, as if he expected that attitude to fall by the wayside as quickly and easily as her resistance to him had.

Talk about a one-track mind! Determined not to let him know how much she hated having to rely on him to get anywhere, Ally scowled as he helped her up the steps, onto the front porch. Her skin tingled from the contact. "You're not going to be able to change me, you know."

His laughter had a masculine, confident ring to it. "Famous last words," Hank whispered in her ear. He propelled her through the front door, turned her toward the living room and whipped off her Santa hat.

"Merry Christmas!" everyone said in unison.

Ally blinked. Thanks to Hank and the twenty or so working guests, the ugly horse-and-hound wallpaper that had dominated most of the first floor was almost completely gone. The unadorned wallboard provided a clean slate. For the first time in her life, Ally had an inkling of what the space could be like. "Thank you!" she whispered, overcome by the unexpected generosity shown her.

"Don't thank us. Thank Hank. He's the one who pulled it all together on short notice!" Hank's baby sister, Emily, came forward. The feisty twenty-eight-year-old beauty was chef and owner of the Daybreak Café. She had one of Duchess's puppies in her arms. "Hank told me you're in love with the littlest one, Gracie, and I have to tell you, Ally, I completely understand! I'm in love, too. In fact, I think I'd rather have a dog than a man. They're *much* more loyal and dependable."

Ally couldn't help but laugh, as did everyone else gathered around.

Jeb McCabe, Hank's older brother, came down off a ladder and sauntered forward. "Hey, Ally," he said. "Good to see you!" The former rodeo star gave her shoulders a casual squeeze, then turned back to his sister. "As for you—you wouldn't have trouble in the love arena if you picked good guys to begin with."

Emily scowled.

Apparently, Ally thought, this was an old and familiar argument.

Holden McCabe, Hank's younger brother, joined the conversation. Serious and responsible to a fault, even before his best friend's untimely death a year before, the horse rancher regarded his baby sister kindly. "If you'd just let the men in the family vet your choices first..."

"He has a point," Hank said protectively. "There's no way you'd end up with losers if the three of us put them through the gauntlet first."

Emily glared at all her big brothers. "What you mean is there's no way I'd ever have another date in my life, if the three of you were involved! Although," she declared cantankerously, as the front door opened and closed, "I'm not sure that would be such a bad thing!"

Behind her, Lulu Sanderson swept in. Gorgeous as ever, the sophisticated former prom queen made a beeline for where Hank and Ally were standing. Unlike everyone else in the room, dressed for manual labor, Lulu was wearing a Stella McCartney suede jacket, skinny jeans and Jimmy Choo heels.

The petite brunette smiled at Ally. "Hank told me you were back! And here I am, too, doing what I said I'd never do—working for my dad's barbecue restaurant."

This was a surprise, given that Lulu had gone to an Ivy League college and business school and—last Ally had heard—was successfully climbing the career ladder on the East Coast.

"Anyway…" Lulu turned back to Hank. She reached into her carryall and pulled out a piece of paper. "You can kiss me now, because I found a crew, and they'll have half a dozen workers here tomorrow to paint the entire interior. They think they can do it in two days, as long as you email them before six tomorrow morning to let them know the color choice."

Ally blinked in surprise and scanned the information handed her. "How did you manage that?"

Lulu lifted her hand in an airy wave. "Oh, I have connections all over the place. The crew is coming from San Angelo." Correctly guessing the reason behind Ally's concern, she continued, "And don't worry about the cost. Hank has it covered."

Ally turned back to him in stunned amazement.

He reassured her with a sober glance. "I know you want it done, as soon as possible, and I figure it's the least I can do since you let me stay here rent-free the last six months."

"Don't let him fool you," Emily McCabe interjected. "Hank is just trying to soften you up so you'll let him buy Mesquite Ridge."

Was that the case? Ally wondered. Was that the only reason he was being so incredibly generous and nice? His expression gave no clue.

While Hank walked Lulu out, Ally retreated to the kitchen to see what she could do about rustling up some refreshments for all the people who had turned out to help her. Emily tagged along, the puppy still in her arms. She knelt to replace the little dog in the warmer and pet Duchess and the other pups for a moment. Then she went to the window overlooking the side yard, where Hank stood, hands in his pockets, conversing privately with Lulu Sanderson.

Moving to the sink to wash her hands, Emily inclined her head toward the window and muttered, "I wish I could figure out what's going on with the two of them."

Me, too. Ally pushed aside the whisper of jealousy and worry floating through her. Why should she care who Hank chatted up?

Emily stood on tiptoe to get a better view. "They're not dating, and yet…they seem almost intimate on some level. It's like they've got something secret going on between them."

Like Hank and me? Ally wondered, reflecting on the way they'd recklessly kissed…and later made love. No one knew about that, either, Ally thought uneasily. Not that it would have been appropriate to talk about, given the matter-of-fact way they'd hooked up.

Ally turned her attention back to Hank's sister. Clearly, Emily was worried about Hank in a way Ally had never seen her be with her other two brothers. Was Hank right? Did every member of his family still treat him with kid gloves and think he needed extra protection from whatever life threw his way? It certainly seemed so.

Curious, Ally dug a little deeper. "I gather that bothers you," she remarked casually.

Emily shrugged and turned away from the window. She knelt down to survey the puppies, many of which were twitching in their sleep, or squirming to get more comfortable. "I never thought Lulu was Hank's type." She smiled at the velvety soft little animals sleeping in a tangle, heads pillowed on each other's backsides.

Then she sighed. "Or that Hank was Lulu's type, either, since the guy she married was a very savvy investment banker. Of course, he cheated on her and they're divorced now. And the rumor is Lulu got quite the financial settlement. So maybe she's just looking for someone steady and dependable, who also wants to live in Laramie." Emily chewed her lip anxiously. "And heaven knows, Hank is that. Once he commits to a woman, he's hers, heart and soul. The only problem is, he hasn't actually *committed* to anyone since Jo-anne died...."

But he had hooked up. With Ally. And maybe other women, as well. Ally realized too late that she and Hank hadn't even discussed exclusivity, or the lack thereof. She had just assumed he was single and unattached when he made his move on her. And even though they didn't plan to continue their relationship past the next few weeks, and maybe not even then, the thought of him with another woman rankled.

Maybe she *was* getting in too deep. With Duchess and the puppies. The ranch. Hank.

Ally arranged fresh fruit slices on a tray. "He thinks the family worries about him."

Emily followed Ally's wordless directions and arranged cheese and crackers on another tray. "I think we all just want to see him settled again with someone, even if it's not the kind of wildly-and-passionately-in-love kind of relationship he had with Jo-anne." She frowned. "Because honestly, until he has another woman in his life, long term, who wants the same things that he wants, I don't think he is going to ever be really happy again."

If that was true—and Ally had no reason to think it wasn't—then she was definitely out of the running to be the next woman in Hank's life. So maybe it was best the two of them kept to friendship and, despite the temptation, didn't hook up again. Because Hank needed a woman who loved this ranch and the lifestyle that went with it, every bit as much as he did.

"So what do you think?" Hank asked Ally, nearly two days later. Late that afternoon the painters had packed up and left, their check from Hank in hand.

Ally couldn't stop looking at her surroundings. In many ways, it was like having a new house, 1920s style. All the old blinds and worn area rugs had been removed. As per her instructions, the entire interior had been coated in sophisticated shades of gray that soaked up the light pouring in from the freshly washed windows. The original wide plank floors contrasted nicely with the newly painted high white ceilings and trim.

"I have to tell you I wasn't sure about the colors you selected." Hank surveyed their surroundings with a keen eye. "But now…wow."

"I knew it would work," Ally replied absent-mindedly, as she hung the long damask drapes she had made at the front windows. "The varying shades of gray are neutral enough to appeal to a buyer of either sex, and support a rainbow of color schemes for the various rooms." Ally climbed back down the ladder. "I'd say we just upped the value of the property by a good twenty thousand dollars."

Abruptly, concern flickered in Hank's eyes.

Her usual hard-edged business sense gave way to an unexpected flood of guilt. Regretfully, Ally guessed, "Which puts the asking price even further out of your reach?"

Hank shrugged, confident once again. "Not necessarily."

What did he mean by that? Had he found a way to obtain the money, the same way Lulu Sanderson had managed to do the seemingly impossible and scrounge up a painting crew? Maybe through one of his many family or friends in the area? His expression gave no clue. Yet there was something on his mind. Something mysterious and suddenly...almost merry in intent.

"Want to go for a ride?"

Now they were back to the chase. With Hank pursuing her, and Ally wanting nothing more than to relent. What possible good could come of this? she wondered. But found herself asking curiously, "What kind of ride?" Why did he seem so happy, when she was another step closer to selling the ranch house out from under him? Without having to resort to a sale to the greedy, undercutting Corporate Farms?

Hank shrugged, all indifferent male again. "You haven't really seen the ranch in a while, and I need to put out some feed for my herd." He gestured widely with his large, capable hands. With pure innocence he looked her in the eye. "You could help, if you like."

Ally hesitated. There didn't seem to be a sexual motive in the invitation. She tilted her head and continued studying the inscrutable expression on his handsome face. "Are you asking me to be a cowgirl?" Was this his new approach? Get her to love the ranch so much she'd be unable to sell it?

Hank shrugged and hooked his thumbs in his belt loops. Holding her gaze, he rocked forward on his toes. "A windshield cowgirl, maybe."

What was she—a one-hundred-forty-pound weakling unable to hold her own with one of the indomitable McCabes? Or a strong independent career woman capable of handling herself in any situation? Figuring it was time to remind Hank who he was really dealing with, Ally allowed, "Actually, some fresh air would be nice. Just let me change and check on Duchess and the pups first...."

He nodded. "I'll do the same and meet you out by the barns."

Fifteen minutes later, Ally was still in the kitchen, kneeling next to the puppies.

Hank strode back in, impatient to get going. "I knew I'd find you here," he said.

She refused to be rushed. "Gracie needed some more cuddling before I put her back in the warming bed with her littermates."

"Um-hmm." Hank bent down to pet Duchess's silky head. He angled a thumb at Ally, then told the dog in mock seriousness, "That gal over there. She's showing favoritism. Which normally would not be cool. But your littlest one needs some extra attention, so we're going to forgive Ally for her blatant unfairness."

Ally rolled her eyes. "I can't help it. Gracie needs me."

Still keeping a hand on Duchess, Hank reached down into the warmer and lovingly petted each of the other pups in turn. "Keep it up," he warned, "and Gracie's going to think you're her mother, not Duchess."

His criticism would have been easier to take if she

hadn't caught him sneaking into the kitchen to do the same thing. Ally got down on the floor with Hank and, still holding Gracie close, used her free hand to pet the other pups, as well.

Deciding maybe now was the time, she broached what was on her mind. "I could be Gracie's mother if I were to adopt her."

"I thought you didn't like dogs," he teased.

Okay. It was time to come out and admit… "Obviously," Ally murmured, "I was wrong. I do like dogs. In fact…" she paused and cleared her throat "…I think I actually might…love them."

Hank grinned. "Me, too."

Which was another thing they had in common. Not that Ally was keeping score….

"The only problem is," Hank continued seriously, "that none of these dogs are ours to keep."

Ally wasn't convinced about that. "Kurt has used all his connections as a vet to put out the word, state-wide now. And no one has turned up to claim them." She knew, because she checked with the vet daily.

"Yet. They still could."

Ally watched Hank rise and give Duchess a final pat on the head. "Now who's got the bah, humbugs?" she prodded.

He frowned. "I'm just being realistic."

"Christmas is not about reality. Christmas is about hope and joy. And before you argue with me," Ally added, her voice ringing with emotions, "I'd like to point out that you are every bit as attached to Duchess as I am to Gracie!"

For once, Hank didn't deny it. "You going to help me feed the cattle or not?"

Ally kissed Gracie on top of her tiny head and reluctantly put her back in the warming box, next to her littermates. "I'm coming with you," she muttered as she shrugged on her old shearling-lined denim jacket. "How long is this going to take, anyway?"

Hank slipped a hand under her elbow as he escorted her out the back door toward the barns. "As long as we want it to take."

Ally looked up at him and smiled. It was a beautiful winter afternoon, with a slight breeze, crisp cold air and blue skies overhead.

And that suited her just fine.

The Mesquite Ridge Ranch property ranged along the Laramie and Mesquite Rivers, an occasional barbed wire fence setting it off from the surrounding six ranches. Hoping Ally would appreciate what she was about to give up, once she absorbed the rugged beauty around them, Hank drove slowly along the gravel road, past thickets of juniper and holly, through acre after acre of mesquite and cedar choked hills.

He half expected Ally to complain about their unhurried progress. Instead, she settled back in her seat, and studied their surroundings in silence.

Hank wondered if she had any idea how much work he'd done the last six months, or how much more was going to be required to turn this ranch into the showplace it should be. Her pensive expression held no clue; the only thing he was certain of was that the tour was as unexpectedly thought-provoking and important for her as it was for him.

Realizing they had only an hour or so before dark, Hank finally turned the truck and circled back around to the grassy pasture that housed his herd. Ranging in size from six hundred to nearly eighteen hundred pounds, the cattle grazed sedately.

"I've always liked black Angus more than long-horns," Ally murmured, with an appreciative glance at the healthy steers.

As he cut the engine and they got out of the cab, Hank realized how little he really knew about her, how much more he wanted to learn.

"How come?" He came to her side.

Ally thrust her hands in the pockets of her old farm jacket, one he recalled her wearing in high school. Now, it was something to work in. Back then it had been her one and only coat.

She grinned up at him. "Black Angus don't have horns, and that makes 'em look cuddlier."

"Not exactly a word I'd use for cows and steers," Hank countered drily, thinking that if anyone here was in need of a cuddle, it was Ally. And not because a cold winter wind was blowing against them, inducing shivers.

It was more in the vulnerable way she held herself.

Knowing how completely she could give, when it came to physical intimacy.

Emotionally…well, emotionally was another matter. For every step she took nearer to him, she seemed to take another one away.

Her cheeks pinkening in the cold, Ally lazily closed the distance between them. Unable to help herself, she taunted, "And here I thought you were the more roman-tic of the two of us."

As soon as the words were out, she blushed. "I

meant…sentimental…when it came to ranching per se…" she choked out.

Hank chuckled. "You might be a tad sentimental and romantic, too," he teased right back.

"I wouldn't count on it."

"I'm sure you wouldn't."

Looking more like a cowgirl than ever with one booted foot crossed over the other, Ally leaned against the side of the truck, while Hank opened the tailgate. "How many cattle do you have?"

"One hundred." He flashed a wistful grin, aware that for the first time in a very long time he actually cared what a woman thought about him. "Or two hundred less than required to have what is considered a working cattle ranch."

Ally shot him a respectful glance from beneath her lashes. "I have every confidence you'll get there," she said quietly.

Hank knew he would. The only question was where would his cattle be housed. Here on Mesquite Ridge, or somewhere else by default.

Ally tugged on the leather work gloves Hank had loaned her. "They look healthy," she observed.

Beaming with pride, Hank carried a bundle of hay out into the pasture and cut the twine. "I've had good luck so far."

Ally took handfuls of alfalfa and spread it around, so the cattle didn't have to fight for feed.

"It's more than luck," she remarked. A bitter edge underscored her low serious tone. "It takes skill. Dedication. The willingness to study up on animal husbandry and do all the things necessary to keep the cattle in top form."

Hank carried another bundle over and set it down. There was an undertone to her voice that bore exploration. "Why do I have the feeling we're not talking about me any longer?" he asked casually.

She sighed and shook out more hay. "It's no secret my dad was a lousy cattleman. All he and my mom ever cared about was expanding the ranch."

"He eventually owned four thousand acres. Given the fact he started from nothing, that's quite an accomplishment."

"But no surprise," Ally muttered resentfully. "Every cent we had went to buying more and more land. To the point that we wore sweaters instead of running the furnace in winter, and did without practically everything because every penny spent was a penny we wouldn't have to buy more land."

"And you hated it."

"Of course I hated it!" She stomped back to the truck and tried to reach another bale. "I couldn't participate in any of the extracurricular activities at school because I was expected to go home and help out with my mother's sewing business."

Hank reached past her to pull the hay to the edge of the truck bed. "Surely your parents were proud of you when you got that big scholarship to Rice University."

"Honestly?" Ally shrugged and walked with him back out into the pasture. "They would have preferred I stay and work the ranch with them. But I had to get out of here." When they reached another open space, perfect for feeding, she paused to cut the twine that held the hay together, and exhaled wearily. "So I left...."

Together, they threw out the shredded grain, as additional cattle ambled toward them. "And you never came

back, except to visit," Hank surmised when they'd finished their task.

Ally nodded grimly as they walked away. "And I
didn't do that much, either, until my mother was di-
agnosed with Parkinson's disease." Ally strode to the
fence, where she paused to examine the thick strand
of mesquite on the other side. Trees up to thirty feet
high and nearly as wide sported dense, tangled greenery studded with long thorns. The heavy rain a few
days before had brought forth another wave of fragrant
white flowers. In the spring, the mesquite would bear
fruit in the form of beanlike pods that wildlife and cattle would eat.

Right now, Hank could tell, the overgrowth was just
one more mess Ally would prefer not to have to deal
with.

"But you did come back, when she was sick." Hank
remembered his mother talking about that, and the fight
between Ally and her parents that had evidently ensued.

Sorrow turned down the corners of Ally's mouth. "I
told them about this new protocol being developed at
a hospital in Houston. I wanted them to come and live
with me, so Mom could get the best treatment." She
inched off her gloves and stuck them in the belt at her
waist. "I knew the isolation of the ranch was no place
for anyone with the kind of neurological disease my
mother suffered from, that as time went on she would
need more and more care, and that—like it or not—it
was time they gave Mesquite Ridge up, in favor of my
mother's health."

"But your parents didn't agree with that."

"No." Ally's low tone was filled with bitterness.
"They didn't. They insisted they didn't need my help,

unless I wanted to move back home and take over the sewing business. That, they would accept." Her eyes gleamed with moisture. "Anything else…" she recalled in a choked voice, "forget it."

Hank took off his gloves, too, and went to stand behind her, resting his hands on her shoulders. "That wasn't fair to you."

Ally tilted her head back and relaxed against him. "I had worked very hard to get where I was in the company. I was a first line manager, about to be promoted to the next tier…on the fast track to an early vice presidency…." She swallowed. "So I said no, and I sent them money to get a caregiver to help out with my mother, instead."

Hank didn't recall anyone saying anything about nursing care. He paused, then tensed. "Tell me they didn't…"

She looked as if she had just taken an arrow to the heart. "They bought another ten acres."

"You must have been devastated," he observed quietly.

"I was furious." Ally blinked back tears. "And scared." She pushed away from Hank. Hands balled into fists, she began to pace. "With as much difficulty as my mother was having, getting around at that point, I was afraid she was going to have a fall."

"Which," Hank recalled sorrowfully, "she eventually did."

Ally swept her hands through her hair. "Unfortunately, my dad was out on the ranch, tending to his cattle, when it happened, and it was hours before he found her. By then, Mom had lapsed into a coma and she never came out of it." Ally gestured in despair as more tears fell. "My dad never recovered. I think that's why he had the heart attack last summer. Because...he couldn't forgive himself."

Hank drew Ally into his arms. "The question is, can you forgive yourself?" he asked softly.

Chapter Nine

No one had ever asked her that. Could she forgive herself? Was it ever going to be possible?

Ally looked deep into Hank's eyes. "I'm not sure," she said finally, knowing it was past time she confided in someone. The understanding glint in his dark blue eyes gave her the courage to go on. "There are times I have so much guilt I feel like I'm suffocating. Guilt because I couldn't convince my parents to handle my mother's illness any differently. I would give anything to have gotten them the help they needed, when they needed it. Instead of failing them at the toughest, most crucial moment of their lives...."

"Do you think they would have been happy in Houston?"

Her face crumpled. "No." More tears flooded her eyes. Hank settled his palms on her shoulders. "Do you think if they'd known they were coming to the end of their lives, they would have wanted to be right here, on the ranch?"

A sob rose in Ally's throat. She was so choked up she could barely breathe, never mind get words out. "I don't think there is anywhere else they'd rather have been."

He threaded a hand through her hair. "I know you miss them."

Tears blurred Ally's vision as pain wrapped around her heart. "I do."

Hank's hands shifted to her back and he pulled her close. Unable to hold back a second longer, Ally buried her face in the solid warmth of his shoulder. And cried the way she hadn't cried when her parents had died. She cried for all the times she had had with them…and all the things that were left unsaid, for the way she had disappointed them, and the way they had disappointed her. But most of all, she cried because she loved them anyway, with all her heart, and missed them so much she felt her whole being would shatter into a million pieces. And through it all, Hank held her close and stroked her back, letting her sob her heart out.

Ally had no idea how long they stood like that. She only knew that when the storm finally passed and she lifted her head, he wiped her tears away with the pads of his fingers and gently lowered his head to hers.

The touch of his lips was everything she had ever wanted, everything she needed. Ally kissed him back, pouring her feelings into the sweetly tender embrace.

For the first time in her life, she was really and truly happy to be right where she was. And it was all due to Hank.

He made Mesquite Ridge a different place for her.

It was still a wilderness, with so much of the four thousand acres uncared for and untamed. But when she was with Hank and saw the ranch through his eyes, she also noted the richness of possibility of the house and the land.

She saw the wonder to be had in a life here, with him.

And that made her want to be held, to be loved, to love in return.

It no longer mattered how much was holding them apart. She wanted to be with Hank again, even if only for a brief period of time.

And he wanted her, too.

His kiss, the warmth and tightness of his embrace, told her that.

And that was, of course, when the purr of a car motor came up behind them.

Ally and Hank let each other go, turned in unison and saw Graham Penderson, of Corporate Farms, get out of his Cadillac and stride toward them.

"I haven't heard from you," the small man said, as slick and falsely charming as ever. "So I thought I'd stop by to get your answer in person."

Ally felt Hank tense beside her. Knowing it would be a mistake to show any weakness to the CF agent, she resisted the urge to take Hank's hand and hold on tight. Deliberately, she held Penderson's eyes. "Thank you for the offer—" which, technically, was about to expire "—but my answer is no."

Ally wasn't surprised to see Penderson's expression grow more conciliatory than ever. "You understand ours is a one-time offer. Six months from now, if you still haven't sold on the open market, we won't be back with anything near what we are offering now."

But Hank would still be there, Ally thought, wanting the land.

If his "plan" to acquire it had been put together by then…

She stopped herself. She could not allow herself to think that way; otherwise she'd be no better a business person than her father had been. And it was up to her to see the ranch sold—for a good price—so her own future would be assured, no matter whether she got laid off from her job or not.

This was her chance to obtain the financial security that had always eluded her in her youth.

But she was going to do it her way. Not Corporate Farms'.

"I understand," Ally said calmly. "The answer is still no. I'm not selling until I get an offer that matches what the land is worth."

Penderson's glance narrowed. "We already gave you that."

"No. You didn't," Ally countered equably. "Fortunately, I have every confidence someone else will."

Especially now that renovations on the ranch house are under way.

"Fine, then." Penderson gave one last disparaging look at the acres of untamed land, resettled his hat on his head and stalked back to his Cadillac. "You'll be waiting a long time to realize more than what we've already offered, for property that is in such poor shape. And I'm not just talking about the house, which we planned to tear down anyway. No one can run cattle on pastureland this overgrown! The mesquite thickets alone are a hazard."

Ally and Hank stood in silence, watching him drive off.

"He has a point about that," she said with a sigh, as her mind returned to business. "There is mesquite everywhere and the trees are covered with two-inch thorns that can do a lot of damage to people and cattle."

Hank wrapped a companionable arm around her shoulders. "First of all," he soothed, "cattle are smarter than you think."

"Is that so?"

"It is." Hank squeezed her warmly and continued his tutorial. "They know enough to stay away from anything that is going to injure them. Second, the trees don't just sport fragrant white flowers in the spring and summer, they also produce long bean pods that the cattle can graze on, and provide shelter when it's cold, and light shade in the hottest parts of the day. Mesquite adapts to almost any soil that isn't soggy. It's heat and drought tolerant, helps prevent erosion and fixes nitrogen in the soil."

Ally thought about what the untamed growth would do to the bottom line. "Mesquite is still not popular with ranchers, since it readily invades grazing sites, and is virtually impossible to get rid of once it takes root."

Hank tipped back the brim of his hat and gave her the sexy once-over. "And here I thought you didn't know anything about ranching."

"I know enough to realize that a controlled burn is needed on vast parts of the ranch, to ensure the long-term health of the land. But as much as I'd like to rid the ranch of all the old dead grass, cedar, mesquite and so on, to germinate different seeds and promote steady, even growth, I'm not sure blackened land would be the best thing for any property on the market."

Hank inclined his head. "Nonranchers might not understand."

"And since everyone who is anyone wants a ranch these days, just so they can say they have one—even if they never really visit it…"

"It makes sense to leave the land wild and untamed, for now."

"Right."

They studied each other.

Ally knew Hank still didn't want her to sell to anyone else, but to her surprise, he didn't look the least bit relieved about what had happened earlier.

"Aren't you going to tell me I made the right decision regarding Corporate Farms?" She didn't know why, exactly; she just wanted to have Hank's approval about that.

He shrugged and walked toward the back of his truck. "It's not over yet."

Perplexed, Ally trailed after him. The intimacy they'd felt earlier was gone, just like that. "What do you mean?"

Hank slammed the tailgate shut. "I know what it looked like just now, but Corporate Farms has not given up. They will wait a few days and go into phase two."

Oh, really? "And what the heck is that?"

"First, they tried to take advantage of you. That didn't work, nor did playing hardball with you. So, figuring the third time is the charm, the next time they'll come back to woo you. And give you an offer you'd be nuts to refuse, with absolutely no time limit on deciding."

Ally shook her head. "I don't think so. Graham Penderson was pretty clear just now, that this was it—they wouldn't be back."

Hank folded his arms in front of him. "We'll see who's right. The question is, what are you going to do if they come back with a much higher offer?" He scanned her face. "Will you sell to them, knowing what you do about their overall intent, and how they do business? Or wait for another buyer?"

Hank had hoped—unreasonably, he knew—that Ally would have had time by now to really think about what she was going to do, and commit to selling to him. If only because he had the ability and the drive to turn the ranch into the financial success it always should have been.

Instead, the hard-edged business person in her kicked back in. "If Corporate Farms were to come back with another offer, I would of course listen to what Graham had to say. Just like I will consider any and all offers that Marcy Lyon at Premier Realty brings to me, after the property is listed. And should you come to me with a serious offer that meets my asking price, of course I'll listen to that, too."

Hank's gut tightened with disappointment. "But in the end the highest dollar wins," he guessed.

Ally nodded reluctantly. "I may not have a job in another ten days. This property still has a mortgage on it. Up to now, I've been making the payments and paying the utilities out of my savings, but I can't keep doing that when I have no revenue of my own coming in. Even if I somehow manage to keep my job, it's still too much of a stretch to continue for very much longer."

Hank understood.

"I suspect the people at Corporate Farms suspect that, which is why they thought they could come in with a low offer and I'd jump on it."

Hank's cell phone rang. Frowning, he pulled it out of the leather holder attached to his belt. Looking at the screen, he saw his cousin was returning his call. "I've got to get this. Hi, Will…"

Hank listened as Will confirmed the details. "Yeah. Eight tomorrow morning. The usual deal. Okay, thanks, see you then." He ended the call.

Trying to figure out how much he could tell Ally, without betraying the confidentiality of the business deal under way, Hank explained, "My cousin, Will Mc-Cabe, owns a charter service out at the Laramie airstrip. It used to be just private jets, flying in and out of there, but since I came back to the area he's added a helicopter to his fleet. So whenever he gets a request—usually from a big oilman or one of the other prominent business people in the area—I fly the chopper."

"Sounds lucrative."

It was. "The revenue from those gigs is responsible for all the cattle I've bought thus far, and the additional money I have saved."

Ally eyed him with respect. "How long will you be gone?"

Long enough to get the deal done, Hank thought resolutely. But wary of telling Ally anything before the plan was set, he replied cautiously, "I'm not sure. The person I'm taking wants to go to Dallas, with a couple of stops along the way, stay overnight, and then do the same thing the following day, en route back. Which brings me to the next question. Are you going to be able to handle Duchess and the puppies, or do you want me to bring someone else in to care for them?"

Ally glowered. "Seriously?"

"I did promise it wouldn't be your responsibility," Hank reminded her.

"Yeah, well, it's not the first promise around here that hasn't been kept."

Hank let that one pass.

She lifted her hands in a placating gesture. "Sorry. It just seems that whenever something goes wrong in my life, it happens here at Mesquite Ridge."

Hank tugged Ally close for another long, thorough kiss. Only when she was putty in his arms did he lift his head. "Things have gone right here, too, Ally," he whispered.

Very right. And one day he hoped she would see that.

Greta McCabe appeared on the ranch house doorstep at six o'clock the following evening. Hank's mother smiled warmly as Ally ushered her in out of the cold. "I tried calling before I came over, but there was no answer."

Ally didn't mind her stopping by without an invitation. It had been a little lonely since Hank had left for his trip early that morning. "I must have been out walking Duchess," she explained.

Greta cast an admiring look at the newly painted woodwork and walls, then turned back to her and handed over a large paper bag bearing the insignia of Greta's restaurant in Laramie.

"You didn't have to do this." Ally beamed with pleasure.

"I figured you'd be too busy to cook, given all you have to do around here," Greta said.

She was right about that. Ally had been working hard all day, making washable canvas slipcovers for the living room furniture.

"I wasn't sure what you liked so I put in a couple of different entrées. Just follow the reheating directions on the foil containers when you're ready to eat," Greta said. "And of course, the salads and desserts are ready to go."

"Thank you. This is so nice." Ally basked in the thoughtfulness.

"So how are Duchess and the puppies?" Greta asked.

Ally gestured toward the kitchen. "Come and see for yourself."

While Ally put the food in the fridge for later, Hank's mother knelt to say hello to the golden retriever and all eleven of the newborns. Nearly a week had passed since Duchess had given birth. All the pups except Gracie, who still lagged a little behind, were now close to two pounds in weight. And although their eyes were still sealed shut, they were getting about with increasing mobility, rolling and squirming across the warming bed when they were awake. Right now, they were all sound asleep in a pile of puppy arms and legs.

Greta smiled at the sound of the soft, gentle snoring. "I can't believe no one has stepped forward to claim them yet," she said.

Me, either, Ally thought.

The woman stood and regarded her with a soft, maternal expression. "So. How are you doing, dear?"

Ally swallowed. "Good," she lied. Then added, more honestly, "Considering."

Greta gently patted her arm. "This must be really hard for you, coming home for the first time after the funeral."

Ally nodded—it had been. Happy to have some female company, she picked up the coffeepot off the stove. "Would you care for some coffee?"

"Love some," Greta said.

Relieved that Hank's mom appeared in no hurry to go, Ally poured two mugs of the fresh brew and brought out a tin of sugar cookies from the grocery store. As they enjoyed their snack, they talked about the progress Ally had made thus far, updating the ranch house.

Greta cast her an appreciative glance. "It's not just the house that has benefited from your presence. Hank seems to be really flourishing since he's been around you, too. Bringing in a Christmas tree…"

Which was still undecorated, Ally thought, a little guiltily.

Greta ran a hand through her silver-blond curls. "Organizing that wallpaper removal party…"

Ally rubbed the edge of her plate with her thumb. "I was really surprised." And maybe a little thrilled.

Greta studied her over the rim of her mug. "He feels for you," she observed tenderly. "Probably because he knows what it is to lose a loved one."

Was that all that was drawing him to her? A mixture of empathy and lust, with a healthy dose of property hunger, thrown in? Ally wondered.

Oblivious to the nature of her thoughts, Greta ran

a nicely manicured hand over the tabletop, lamenting, "We never thought Hank would get over losing Jo-anne. But the years in the marines, and now this ranch, have brought him back to life."

And Hank's mom was happy to see that, Ally noted.

"I know you're getting ready to put the ranch on the market...."

If I don't sell it to Hank first, Ally thought, wishing all the harder he would find a way to make a decent bid, so she could accept it and move on. She would have peace of mind knowing the property was in the right hands to make it thrive, the way it should have all along.

Greta patted Ally's hand. "I know the process can be difficult, particularly when it comes to sorting through your parents' belongings. It can be a lot to take on alone, as well as very emotional, so if you need help...let me know. And before I forget, Shane and I would very much like for you to come to the annual open house at our ranch, on December 23...."

The day she was supposed to hear about whether or not she still had a job. Ally hesitated. "I'm not sure that will be a great time for me," she said.

"Nonsense. You have to eat. In the meantime, if you need help with anything at all, you let Hank's father and me know. We're only eight miles down the road. And it's not just a family thing that has us making the offer—or the fact that Hank is temporarily absent. It's part of the code of survival around here. Ranchers help each other out." She smiled warmly at Ally. "But having grown up on Mesquite Ridge, surely you know that."

Actually, Ally didn't. Her parents had always kept pretty much to themselves, and never asked for help for themselves—or gone out of their way to assist anyone else, even their closest neighbors. But maybe it was time that changed, too, she thought. For as long as she stayed in the area, anyway...

She thanked Greta again and walked her to the door, then went back to get Duchess and take her out into the yard.

As she went back inside, she noticed the message light blinking on the answering machine. There were two calls from Premier Realty and the title company, another from Porter, wanting to know if she'd heard anything more about the layoffs, and finally, one that was definitely not for her.

"Hank, honey, it's Lulu. Are you ready for dinner?" the chic divorcée asked enthusiastically. "'Cause I'm starving after the day we've had together! Oh, wait, I think I just dialed your home number instead of your cell. Never mind. I'll just come and find you." *Click.*

Ally sat staring at the phone. The call had come in at six-fifteen, when she was out walking Duchess in the yard. The screen ID said the call had come from a luxury hotel in Dallas.

So that was where Hank had gone! Ally realized, stunned. Lulu Sanderson was the client he was flying around? And now they were in Dallas together, sharing a hotel, if not a room? What in heaven's name was going on?

Chapter Ten

Hank knew something was going on with Ally when he returned home the following evening. He just wasn't sure what had her suddenly ignoring his calls.

He shrugged out of his leather aviator jacket and walked through the downstairs. It was clear she had been as busy and productive in their two days apart as he had. Custom slate-gray canvas slipcovers now gave the sturdy but ugly furniture a classy new look. A new area rug, colorful throw pillows and lap blankets had been strategically added.

There was still no real feeling of Christmas in the ranch house, since the tree and mantel remained undecorated. Hank was determined that, too, would change.

Thinking Ally might be with Duchess, he walked into the kitchen. All the puppies were cuddled up together in the warmer, sleeping contentedly. Duchess was lying next to it. She lifted her head and wagged her tail when Hank approached. He petted her silky head and scratched her behind the ears. "Looks like all is okay here with you and the kids," he murmured. Was Ally okay, though?

Hank gave the sleepy Duchess a final pat and headed on up the stairs.

Ally was standing in her bedroom in front of the mirror, blow-drying her honey-blond hair. Her slender form was covered by a satin robe with a tie sash. Her feet were encased in fuzzy slippers. Beneath the knee-length hem, her legs were bare.

Hank's pulse picked up a notch.

Was this all for him?

He hoped so.

He strode into the bedroom. Ignoring her indifferent reception, he asked, "Did you get my message?"

Ally curved the ends of her hair around a brush, held it against her chin and moved the dryer back and forth. "All six of them," she answered, sounding distracted.

Okay, so maybe he'd been a little eager to talk with her. But it had been thirty-six hours since they had seen one another. He had missed her. Had she missed him?

Aware that Ally hadn't exactly invited him in, Hank folded his arms and lounged against the chest of drawers. He was beginning to feel a little defensive, which seemed unwarranted, given all he had been doing behind the scenes on their behalf. "Why didn't you call me back?" he asked quietly.

Ally brushed her hair into place and spritzed it with hair spray. She steadfastly averted her gaze. "The message that you were coming home by six this evening didn't exactly warrant a reply."

Annoyed that he'd fallen so hard and fast for a woman who seemed easily able to do without him, Hank lifted a brow and said nothing in response.

Still doing her best to ignore him—although he was pretty sure she could see him out of her peripheral vision—Ally grabbed a dress out of her closet. Chin high, she headed for the bathroom across the hall. Over her shoulder, she added, "And I was busy."

Irked by her swift, inexplicable change of attitude toward him, Hank waited for her to come back out.

She looked as incredibly sexy as he expected in a cranberry-red dress. The V-neck exposed the lovely slope of her throat and the hint of décolletage; the fabric clung closely to her breasts, waist and hips before flaring out slightly. Ally rummaged in a drawer and pulled out a package of panty hose. "As were you, I take it."

He had been, with extraordinarily good results.

Not that she wanted to hear about it. At least not yet…

Ally disappeared into the bathroom again. When she emerged, she wore a pair of black stilettos that made her legs look spectacular.

Which made him wonder what else she had on under that sexy dress. And how hard would it be to get her to take it off for him.

Ally applied lipstick in front of the mirror. Then mascara, eyeshadow and perfume.

She was so beautiful. And clearly, so determined to make him jealous.

Despite his pique, he couldn't stop watching her, couldn't draw his gaze from the loveliness of her features.

When she opened a velvet case and removed a gold

pendant necklace, he finally gave in to curiosity. "I presume you're going out this evening?" he drawled.

"Yes." Ally fastened the clasp around her neck and let the teardrop pendant fall between her breasts. She returned to the box for matching earrings and put those on, too. "My dinner companion should be here shortly."

"Dinner companion," Hank repeated.

Finished, she gave her hair a final pat and turned to him. Her green eyes held a glacial frost. "Was there something you wanted?"

Yes, Hank thought. *You.* But aware how that would likely go over, he decided to cut to the chase, and asked instead, "Just for the record. Are you angry with me?"

"Why would I be angry with you?" Ally replied sweetly.

I have no idea. Wanting peace between them, Hank guessed, "For leaving you alone with Duchess and the puppies?" *And not getting you extra help with them despite the fact you insisted you did not need it?*

Ally shot down that theory with a decisive shake of her head. "I adored being with them."

So... "It's me you'd rather not spend time with," Hank concluded.

"Bingo."

Another silence fell between them, and then the doorbell rang.

"That's for me!" Ally grabbed an evening bag and a black velvet jacket and headed for the stairs.

Hank ambled after her.

He was not happy when he saw her "date" for the evening.

Judging by the determined look on her face as she sailed out the door, Ally knew that.

* * *

"Everything okay?" Graham Penderson asked Ally as they took their seats in the Lone Star Dance Hall.

I wish you had chosen another place to dine, she thought. But it was no surprise—Greta McCabe's restaurant, with its lively atmosphere and superb food— was *the* place to spend a social evening in Laramie. And it was clear that Graham Penderson—and by extension, Corporate Farms—were now going all out to woo her, just as Hank had predicted they would.

"Everything's fine," she answered. *I just wish I'd had time to quiz Hank about his trip with Lulu. It would have been interesting to hear what he had to say.*

Not that she wanted or needed to know, since she and Hank were history.

Still…

"We've had a chance to review the initial property assessment on Mesquite Ridge and think we might have come up a little short in our first offer," Graham said.

No surprise there, either.

Ally turned her full attention on her dinner partner, adopting her most hard-edged business demeanor. "I'm not going to be pushed into responding to *any* offer from Corporate Farms."

"We realize that was a mistake."

"Any future offer that comes with a timeline will be immediately rejected."

"Understood," Graham assured her.

Ally folded her hands in front of her. "That said, I'd like to talk with you about what figure *might* be acceptable…."

The CFS agent pulled an envelope from his pocket, and handed it to her. Inside, typed on their letterhead, was an astounding figure. One that would leave her set for a good while, job or no job....

Throughout the rest of the meal, Graham spoke with her about the benefits of a sale to Corporate Farms, and the various ways they could accommodate her to make the transition easier. Despite herself, Ally was impressed.

She knew what the impact on the community would be, should the company get a toehold in the area with the acquisition of Mesquite Ridge. And while the sentimental, compassionate side of her would not even consider such an offer, the businesswoman in her knew she would be a fool not to.

What happened to the other ranches in the area was not her responsibility. Her own future and financial security was.

And yet...

"Naturally," Graham concluded with finesse, "although we want you to have as much time as you need, we are going to want to follow up on this...."

"And I," an oh-so-familiar male voice said, " would like to speak with you about your dessert options for this evening."

Ally's heart skipped a beat. She turned and saw the familiar red shirt, blue jeans and black Lone Star Dance Hall apron on a very fine male form. Already knowing which handsome face she was going to see, she lifted her gaze and looked up into Hank McCabe's midnight-blue eyes.

Hank ran through the options with the finesse of a guy who had grown up waiting tables in his mama's restaurant. "We've got a fine cranberry-cherry pie, as well as a chocolate peppermint torte that is out of this world. And of course, the traditional banana pudding, pecan pie and peach cobbler. You can have ice cream with all of those. Coffee, too."

"What are you doing here?" Ally snapped. And why did he have to look so superb? She couldn't help but note he had gone to the trouble of showering and shaving before coming in. He'd even applied the brisk, wintry aftershave she liked so much.

Hank ignored the glare he was getting from the agent, and pointed to the black change apron tied over his jeans, and the Lone Star Dance Hall badge that bore his name. His smile widened. "I'm helping out. My mom's shorthanded tonight."

Helping out, my foot! Ally lifted a brow in wordless dissension. It looked as if they had plenty of waitstaff, as usual. "Um-hmm," she said.

"Good to see you have a job to fall back on, *Mc-Cabe*," Graham Penderson said. "You're going to need it, since the ranch where you house your cattle is about to be sold out from under you."

Hank locked eyes with Penderson, all tough ex-marine and veteran cowboy.

Talk about a Renaissance man, Ally thought.

Hank smiled. "I wouldn't count on it if I were you."

Penderson ran a smug hand across his jaw. "I would."

Wincing, Ally squirmed in her seat.

Given the high-stakes volatility of the situation, she wouldn't have been surprised to see Hank forget his manners and pull Penderson out of his chair by the knot of his necktie.

But as it happened, his expression did not change— if you discounted the slight darkening of his irises. He merely stepped an inch closer. Flashed a dangerous crocodile smile. "Still waiting on that dessert order. *Penderson.*"

Ally swallowed. She could see this situation fast getting out of hand.

She stuffed the papers the agent had given her into her handbag and shut the clasp, then held up her hands. "Actually, I don't think I want any dessert," she told them both.

"I do," Graham said. "And I want McCabe here to bring it to us, since he's so eager to help."

Out of the corner of her eye, Ally saw Hank's mother step out of the kitchen. Greta sized up the situation, hands on her hips. Sighed.

"Why, it'd be my pleasure," Hank drawled. "But..." He turned with a flourish and signaled the DJ running the sound system.

The man nodded and promptly started a song by Lady Antebellum entitled "One Day You Will."

"Well, what do you know, Ally." Hank slid his order pad and pen back in his apron pocket. He reached down and took her hand in his, and in one smooth motion, drew back her chair and pulled her to her feet. He winked at her. "They're playing *your* song. Sorry, Penderson."

The next thing Ally knew they were on the dance floor. Hank's left hand splayed warmly across her spine, and his right hand clasped her fingers as he two-stepped them around the floor to the strains of the romantic ballad.

Ally tried but could not stop the thrill rushing through her. "Cute, McCabe."

He grinned, all confident male. "Like the lyrics?"

Despite her decision to remain unaffected by his chicanery, his sense of humor was contagious. "Especially the part about if I left town and never came back," Ally retorted drolly.

He leaned close enough to whisper in her ear. "Like the song says, you'd be missed." His warm, minty breath caressed her cheek. "But if you just hang in there…and wait awhile…"

"The sun will shine again and," Ally paraphrased, "I'll find love and peace and the real me."

The laugh lines around his eyes crinkled. "Exactly."

If only he knew how much she wanted to believe that. As it was, the powerful lyrics combined with the soul-stirring music were drawing her in, every bit as much as the wonderfully comforting and enticing sensation of being in his arms again. Deciding she needed to reestablish some emotional boundaries, Ally lifted her chin.

Now that he had picked her tune… "What's your song?"

"Coming right up." Hank again signaled the DJ. One tune segued into another.

Ally listened a moment to the lively beat, then looked down the bridge of her nose at him. "'You Take My Troubles Away'?" *Seriously!*

He two-stepped her around the dance floor. "Appropriate, don't you think?" His lips brushed her temple.

Another thrill swept through Ally. "If this is supposed to be a message for me…" she warned.

"It is." Hank's voice was low and hoarse. All the pent-up affection she ever could have wished for in his gaze.

Ally had spent her high school years wishing something this out-of-control exciting and romantic would happen to her. But that didn't mean it was a good idea for Hank McCabe to go all possessive on her in the middle of a business dinner at his mother's restaurant! Particularly after what he'd done in Dallas the day before. She blushed and attempted without much success to resurrect the protective barrier around her heart. "Everyone is looking at us."

Hank's arm tightened around her waist. Their thighs brushed as they moved to the beat. "That's no surprise. You look incredibly beautiful tonight. But then..." his voice dropped another inviting notch "...you know that."

She felt beautiful—in Hank's arms. Ally struggled not to give in to the overwhelming emotions rising up within her. "And for the record, what on earth possessed you to pick out his-and-her songs for us?"

He shrugged and brought their clasped hands even closer to his heart. "I wanted the excuse to dance with you tonight."

That sure had done the trick. She was here in his arms, feeling like there was no place she'd rather be.

Ally cast a look over Hank's broad shoulder. "Penderson is livid."

"He'll get over it. It won't stop Corporate Farms from making good on their latest offer, if that's what you're worried about."

"How do you know there's been another offer?"

"Because Corporate Farms sees what I see in terms of the rich potential of the ranch. They don't want Mesquite Ridge to get away."

"So that's why you're doing all this." Ally did her best to keep the sadness from her voice.

"No. I'm doing this because I want you to know I'm sorry for leaving you alone for two days. And I don't want you to do anything stupid to get back at me, just because you're mad at me."

So he sensed she was onto him! Figuring she'd use the opportunity to get the answers to all the questions she had, but hadn't asked, Ally inquired sweetly, "Why would I be mad?"

Hank paused, revealing nothing, then said finally, "You tell me."

For a second, Hank thought Ally wouldn't answer. Then something shifted in her expression. A little of the fight left her slender body. "I don't want to have this discussion here," she said quietly.

Neither did he, if it was half as intimate as it appeared it was going to be. "Then let's go home." Or at least where he wished their home could be. In another week, he was well aware, that might not be the case for either of them.

Another silence fell, as the song they were dancing to came to an end.

They stood there, not moving, still holding on to each other.

"And let me drive you," Hank murmured.

Ally glanced over at Penderson.

The agent looked even more incensed. And Hank knew, whether Ally realized it or not, the stakes for the ranch had just been raised. Corporate Farms would be more determined than ever to steal the property out from under him. Which was too bad, because they weren't going to get it; his new plan guaranteed that.

"All right," Ally said eventually. "Just let me say good-night to Mr. Penderson."

Hank returned his apron and badge while Ally walked across the dance hall.

Hank's mother pulled him aside before he could duck out. "Are you sure you know what you're doing?" she asked.

"Don't I always?" he quipped. He refused to entertain the notion of failure.

Greta blocked his way. "I don't blame you for going after Ally Garrett. She is a lovely young woman. But she deserves better than the shenanigans you pulled just now."

Hank thought that was a little like the pot calling the kettle black. His own father had called for a duel, in the street in front of the dance hall, while working to win his mother's heart. The outlandish maneuver infuriated—and captivated—his mom to this day.

Where women were concerned, there was one thing Hank knew. You had to go public with your feelings if you wanted a real chance with them. He figured he had done that tonight.

He gave his mother a perfunctory smile. "I know Ally deserves only the best, Mom."

Greta lifted an elegant silver-blond brow. "Do you?"

Hank was tired of family interference, no matter how well meant. "My situation with Ally is complicated." Too complicated, he added silently, for a regular courtship at a regular pace.

Greta patted his arm with maternal affection. "Life is always complicated, Hank. That's what makes it so interesting." She paused to make sure she had his full attention. "It doesn't mean that Ally deserves any less than your best. Especially given all she's been through the last couple of years."

And was still going through, Hank thought, watching her converse quietly with Penderson.

Was his mother right? Was he making a mistake by going all Texan on Ally? All Hank knew for sure was that Ally looked tense and unhappy now—and that she had appeared to be doing okay before she knew he was on the scene....

"Everything all right?" Hank's mother asked Ally kindly, as she joined them in the employees-only alcove between the dining room and kitchen.

Ally stepped aside to let a server prepare a tray of drinks, and flashed a too-bright smile. "I told Mr. Penderson to feel free to stay and have dessert and coffee without me, since our meeting this evening is concluded and I've got another ride back to the ranch. Thus far, he's refusing...."

Greta lifted a hand. "I understand, dear. I'll talk to him and see what I can do. In the meantime, I want you to know I've asked Hank to escort you to our open house out at the ranch, on the evening of the twenty-third."

Ally's mouth dropped open in surprise. "I—"

Way to go, Mom, Hank thought, even more resentfully. It wasn't enough she was advising him—without his consent—on his love life. Now she was arranging it for him, too.

Across the dining hall, Penderson lifted a hand as if to signal a waiter.

Greta patted Ally reassuringly on the arm. "I'll take care of that." She glided off.

Hank looked at Ally. She appeared as shocked and peeved as he felt. Which in turn prompted him to say matter-of-factly, "It looks like we have a date." One arranged by his mother, no less!

Ally knew the matchmaking could not stand. So the moment they started the drive back to Mesquite Ridge, she looked at Hank and blurted, "I know your mother feels sorry for me because it's Christmas and I have no family of my own."

"That's not it," Hank interrupted, with the arrogance of a man who always thought he knew better—at least where his own family was concerned.

Ally argued back, just as insistently, "It's exactly why she asked me to go to the open house yesterday. And why, when I hedged instead of just accepting her invitation on the spot, she put additional pressure on me tonight, by asking you to escort me. Because she knew it would be impossible for me to say no to the both of you. I'd be outnumbered and out...whatever."

Hank exhaled in exasperation. He pulled the truck off the road, into an empty parking lot at the edge of town. He put it in Park, leaving the lights on and the motor running, and turned toward her, draping his arm along the bench seat. "First of all...left to my own devices, I would have asked you to the party myself and provided transportation to and from the event."

Ally looked out the window. "You don't have to do that, either. I'm fine on my own."

Hank slid a hand beneath her chin and guided her face to his. "No doubt. I still want to escort you. It's a fun party. A lot of people come, and we always have a good time."

Exactly why I wouldn't fit in, Ally thought. *I've never*

been a party person. And certainly not on a scale with the famously loving and outgoing McCabe clan.

"Furthermore," Hank continued in a low tone that sent shivers up and down Ally's spine, "my mom arranging for me to escort you has nothing to do with the sympathy she feels regarding your loss."

"Then what is it?" Ally asked, her voice tight with apprehension.

"She doesn't trust me to be able to handle another romance, after the way I screwed up with Jo-anne."

"What are you talking about?" Ally demanded. "The two of you were engaged! Plus, everyone knows you were madly in love each other." Just hearing about it had made her envious.

Hank exhaled. "No one knows this, but we were on the verge of breaking up when Jo-anne left to go overseas. You see, I asked her to marry me the week we graduated from college. She said yes. The only problem was, she had already accepted a job at an American hotel abroad. She still wanted to go and work there for a year, *then* come back and marry me later."

"And that put a wrench in your plans...." Ally guessed.

He nodded. "Pretty much. But I didn't want to stand in her way. She'd never really been out of Texas, and this would have allowed her to spread her wings and travel through Europe, on her time off work, for very little money. She wanted me to try and get a job there, too, so I could get the same perks and discounts at other hotels in the chain, as she did. But I wasn't interested in being a bellboy...which was all they had available."

"So what did you do?" Ally asked curiously.

"After Jo-anne went overseas, I took a job on a ranch

in Colorado and started thinking about what I really wanted to do with my life, which was join the military and become a chopper pilot. And then eventually acquire my own ranch. When I told Jo-anne, she thought it would be great. After all, she was all for adventure and living life out of the ordinary. And we figured we could both request assignments overseas and see the world together that way..."

He swallowed hard. "Things were finally back on track between the two of us. I had almost saved enough money to go and visit her for a couple weeks and then... she got killed in that terrorist bombing."

Ally understood a lot about grief and guilt. "And you had a hard time forgiving yourself," she presumed softly.

He nodded. "We wasted a lot of time arguing about things that could have been worked out a whole heck of a lot easier, if the two of us had just figured out what we had to have to be happy and been willing to compromise sooner."

Ally bit her lip. "There's one thing I don't understand. If your parents knew you were already thinking about enlisting, then..."

"I hadn't told anyone but Jo-anne of my plans, or her reaction. After she was killed, I didn't want to talk about what might have been, just what I was going to do next."

That made sense. Ally studied Hank's tortured expression. "So your mother thinks..."

"The same thing my dad thinks—that I need the family's help if I'm going to achieve anything—whether it be in ranching or romance. And that's why Dad is always stopping by the ranch to see if I need his help

with anything, and why Mom is trying to help our relationship along."

"Because your dad wants to know you're okay, busi-
ness-wise, and she's concerned about your personal life,
and…for whatever reason…wants to see the two of us
together."

Or, as his sister had said, the family just wanted to
see Hank with someone again, settled down with a family of his own to love.

He grimaced. "It would appear so."

Ally thought about that on the rest of the drive home.
It was nice that she had the approval of the McCabe
family, or guessed she did—otherwise they wouldn't
be pushing Hank and her toward each other. However,
it was not so nice that once again she wanted what she
could never seem to get—the sense that she was more
important to those closest to her than Mesquite Ridge
ever would be.

As they walked into the ranch house, she and Hank
stopped in the kitchen to check on Duchess and the
pups. All were sound asleep.

They continued on into the living room, where Ally
saw the message light blinking red, and a big shopping
bag from Neiman Marcus underneath the unadorned
tree.

His expression abruptly serious, Hank shrugged out
of his coat. "We still haven't talked about what upset
you while I was gone," he reminded her kindly.

No, Ally thought, they hadn't. And at this point she
wasn't sure she wanted to. After all, she had no official claim on Hank, or he on her. It didn't matter that
the two of them had kissed a few times and recklessly
made love once. They were both single, and she'd made

it clear she was selling the ranch to the highest bidder and leaving Laramie on December 24. If Hank wanted to see someone else, especially with Christmas on the horizon, that was his business.

Hanging on to her pride by a thread, she fibbed, "I think I just had a touch of cabin fever. I'm not used to being out here all alone."

Hank looked at her dress, the way she'd gone all out with her hair and makeup and hooked his thumbs through his belt loops. "Now why don't I believe that?"

Anxious to keep from spilling the truth, Ally looked at the answering machine. "Maybe we better see what that message is about."

"Let's not."

Ignoring his frown, Ally stepped forward and pushed the button, anyway.

As she had feared, Lulu's voice rang out loud and clear. "Hank, where are you? *I'm so excited!* I want to know when we're going to get together next! Hopefully, tomorrow. Call me, will you, honey? And do it soon!" *Click.*

Jealousy reared its ugly head.

Hank lifted a hand in damage control. "I know how that sounds, but it's not what you think."

Ally sure as heck hoped not!

Nevertheless, before she could stop them, words came pouring out of her mouth. "Well, now that we're on the subject, *honey,* messages like that one might have something to do with my pique."

Astonishment mingled with irritation on his handsome face. "Lulu and I are just friends."

"Uh-huh." Ally folded her arms and pinned him with a withering look. "Such good friends you spent the night in a hotel with her in Dallas last night?" The minute the accusation was out, Ally regretted it. For the sake of her pride, she had never meant to let on that she knew. But now the reckless words were out, there was no taking them back.

Recognition turned Hank's eyes a deeper blue, and he deliberately closed the distance between them. "First of all, Lulu and I weren't together, not in the way you're obviously thinking. And second of all, how did you know that?"

"The machine. She called here, looking for you, last night at dinnertime." *Probably accidentally on purpose, so I'd know,* Ally thought resentfully.

"Is that why you went out with Penderson this evening?" Hank looked at her as if he wanted nothing more than to make love to her, then and there. "Because you wanted to make me as jealous, as you are obviously feeling?"

"I went out with Penderson because he asked me to go." Ally spoke as if to a dimwit. "So he could apologize for putting the pressure on me regarding the sale of the ranch."

"And make another offer," Hank added tersely.

"And make another offer," Ally confirmed. "Just as you said he would."

Hank paused and searched her face. Once again he seemed able to read her mind. "Did you accept it?"

"I'm still hoping something better will come in," she replied honestly.

"Me, too." He smiled as if he knew a secret.

Ally recalled what Emily had said about Lulu getting a substantial financial settlement from her divorce. She shifted uneasily. "Back to Lulu…"

Hank gave her a stern look. "I repeat, she is just a friend."

"Who had a crush on you all through high school."

The tension in his broad shoulders eased slightly. "We never dated."

"To Lulu's lament."

Hank scrutinized Ally with unremitting interest. "There's nothing for you to be envious about," he insisted.

She scoffed. "I'm not envious. Just curious." As to why he still hadn't explained what exactly what was going on between him and Lulu...and why they had been together in Dallas the night before. Was Lulu the client Hank had been ferrying about for the last two days? Or had the two of them just happened to be in the Metroplex on business at the same time, and decided to have dinner together? And what were he and Lulu going to see each other about next that had her so excited?

Hank studied Ally, looking impossibly handsome and determined in the soft light. He gestured amicably. "Okay. *If* that's the case," he challenged audaciously, "then prove it."

Ally pushed away another wave of desire and held her ground with effort. Why did she suddenly feel she had a tiger by the tail? "How?" she asked, just as casually.

Hank held his arms wide. "Come here and kiss me like you mean it."

Chapter Eleven

"Kiss you?" Ally echoed.

Hank came closer, until they were near enough to feel each other's body heat. "You asked me not to bother you with half-formed plans," he stated in a soft, decisive voice that coaxed her closer still. "I haven't and I won't. I'm asking you to trust that, given another week or two, I will meet my objective and make a formal offer on Mesquite Ridge that tops the one you've already received from Corporate Farms." He regarded Ally. "If you are willing to believe in me, in here—" he put his hand over his heart "—then demonstrate your faith in me and kiss me."

It was clear from the expression in Hank's eyes that the cynic in him expected her to do the opposite—assume the worst about his time with Lulu, and move away. And had she not spent the last week with him, and seen close up what a decent, loving and honorable man Hank had become, she would have done just that.

But she knew he was good and kind.

And although maddeningly self-contained at times— as his parents very well knew—not the kind of person to make promises he felt he could not deliver on.

Hank was not the only one who could take risks, Ally thought, as she went up on tiptoe and wreathed her arms around his neck. He promptly wrapped his arms around her and used the flat of his palm to bring her all the way against him.

Their lips met. She moaned softly, tangling her hands in his hair, never wanting him to stop. And he didn't. Their tongues intertwined and his hard body pressed resolutely against her. Ally surged forward, surrendering all, until she was kissing him back more passionately than ever before. She reveled in his warmth and strength and the myriad sensations soaring through her. She knew it was Christmas, and that before this she had considered their lovemaking an unexpected gift, a salve for her loneliness. But it was so much more than that. She wanted him so much—wanted the companionship and understanding, and yes, the feeling of belonging that he offered. She knew he hadn't said anything about loving her.

It didn't matter.

She loved *him*.

Loved him enough to trust him, to take his hand and lead him up the stairs to her bedroom. Loved him enough to undress him and kiss him again, long and hard and deep.

She wanted him…so much.

Wanted him to tumble her onto her bed and disrobe her just as playfully as she had just done to him.

Her body was as ready for him, as his was for hers, and she reclined on her side, taking this gift for what it was, a coming together that was also an act of hope and faith, a moment in time to be cherished.

Hank trailed a hand over her side, the indentation of her waist, the curve of her hip, the line of her thigh. Her breath grew ragged as he caressed her abdomen, going lower still.

"I missed you," he whispered as he explored the tip of her nipple with the pad of his thumb, and followed it with a kiss.

"I missed you, too," Ally said, her pulse pounding, her senses in an uproar.

Shifting her onto her back, he draped a thigh over hers and continued caressing her, studiously avoiding the part she most wanted him to touch. Until she moaned, arched her back and opened her thighs, aware that nothing had ever felt so right....

Hank had never imagined he'd be in a position to use the chemistry he had with Ally to break down that stone wall around her heart. But Ally was so guarded and her time on the ranch with him so short that he had no choice but to use whatever advantage he had to get close to her. He wanted her in his life. Not as some long distance or occasional lover, but as a real, viable part of his everyday existence. He wanted to go to sleep with her every night and wake up with her every morning. He wanted to roam the ranch with her, and then hunker down inside, before the fire. Spend lazy afternoons in bed, when the mood struck, and work side-by-side all night when that was necessary, too.

It was more important for him to get her to stay than for him to own the ranch. If she ended up selling Mesquite Ridge to someone else, so be it. There was always more land in Laramie County. There was only one Ally.

Only one woman who could make the impossible happen, make him ready and willing to love again. Not the selfish way he had in his youth, but in the completely giving way of a man.

And she sacrificed for him, too, drifting lower, giving him what he needed, letting him know with each soft, sensual kiss just how much she cared.

Loving the no-holds-barred way she surrendered herself to him, he knelt on the floor in front of her and guided her to the edge of the bed. She caught her breath as he nudged her legs farther apart.

"Oh, Hank," she whispered, shivering as he breathed in the sweet musky scent of her and explored the petal pink softness. Satisfaction unlike anything he had ever experienced roared through him. Tightening her hands on his head, she allowed him full access, letting him stroke the pearly bud again and again. Until she was calling his name and coming apart in his hands, and he was moving upward once again, not waiting, taking her the way she yearned to be taken, until there was no stopping. Until she was clamped around him, shaking with sensation, bringing him to a shuddering climax and then slowly, sweetly down again.

Hours later, dawn streamed in through the bedroom windows. Ally was curled up next to Hank, her head on his chest, his strong arms wrapped around her. Her thigh nestled between his legs, and the warmth of his body pressed against hers. She inhaled the masculine scent of his skin and hair, and reflected on the passionate lovemaking that had kept them awake—and aroused—most of the night.

Hank stroked a hand through her hair. "What are you thinking?" he murmured, kissing her temple.

Easy. Aware she had never felt so safe, or so cherished, Ally let her eyelids flutter shut.

"I never knew it could be like this." *Never knew I could fall in love so hard and fast...or want to be with someone so very much.*

Was it just that it was Christmastime—and she was leaving Mesquite Ridge for good—that had her in desperate need of a connection? Ally wondered. Or was it because she had never had anyone so invested in making sure she was okay? All she knew for certain was that Hank was as tender and considerate as he was sensual, and that he had brought out a side of her she hadn't realized existed. He'd made her feel it was okay to be vulnerable. He'd helped her realize it was all right to need to be touched and held and cherished, in the way only he could.

"I...hoped...it could." His touch grew more loving and his husky voice dropped a notch. "But for the record..." his expression radiated a soul-deep happiness that mirrored her own "...I never imagined anything could feel this right, either."

Ally had only to look into Hank's eyes to know how true that was.

Disconcerted by the intensity of her feelings and the fluttering of her heart, she reverted to her usual cynicism. "Maybe it's a yuletide miracle," she teased.

The corners of his lips lifted. "Or just a plain miracle," he drawled.

The raw affection in his tone made her catch her

breath. "Must you always have your way?" she murmured back.

He pressed his palm to hers. "Once a marine, always a marine at heart. And now I'm a Texas rancher, too."

With no ranch to call his own. Yet.

Where had that thought come from?

He wasn't using her as a means to an end! He was not like that.

Hank had a lot more in his life, and on his mind, than the need to acquire land. He was a McCabe, and McCabes valued family and the people they loved above all else.

And even though Hank hadn't said he loved her, any more than she had confessed she loved him, she felt the connection between them. Knew they were on the cusp of something very moving and profound....

Whether or not it would last, she couldn't say. But she was going to be here for another week. She intended to spend that time enjoying Hank's company, seeing where this would lead....

He disengaged his hand from hers and chucked her beneath the chin. "I wish you wouldn't worry so much."

She wished so much wasn't at stake. How much easier it would be if Mesquite Ridge wasn't standing between them. She squinted at him. "I'm not worrying."

"The wrinkle between your brows says otherwise." Hank leaned over to kiss her temple. "All you have to do is trust me and give me a little more time, and I promise you, everything will be all right."

Hank stayed to take care of Duchess and the puppies, then headed off to feed his herd and "do what he needed to do" to be able to make her a solid offer on the ranch.

Which meant, Ally thought, as she headed to her father's den to begin the task of going through his many papers, Hank would likely be spending time with Lulu Sanderson.

Ally knew she shouldn't be jealous.

Hank was an honorable man, and he had shown her how he felt about her, the night before.

She had to do what he had asked of her, and trust in his power to achieve his goals.

She reassured herself that, unlike her parents, Hank knew what he was doing when it came to the business side of ranching. Certainly he had the connections through his family to get any expertise, advice and probably even financing that he needed.

Yet as Ally plowed through her father's notes about one crazy, ill-formed plan after another to make Mesquite Ridge profitable, her mood went downhill fast.

She was close to putting her head down in despair when Hank strode into the den, a fistful of mistletoe in his hand, a grin as big as Texas on his handsome face. "You look…happy," Ally murmured. Really happy.

He set the mistletoe down and sat on the edge of the desk facing her, his long legs stretched out in front of him. "And you look like you just lost your prize cow."

Ally flushed. "I don't have a prize cow."

"Exactly." He swiveled slightly, so the side of his denim-clad leg pressed against hers. "But you could, if you hang with me long enough." He paused to survey her from head to toe, before returning his gaze ever so deliberately to her face. "Seriously…" his voice dropped to a compassionate murmur "…what's going on?"

Ally rocked back in the ancient wooden swivel chair

and sighed. "I was going through my dad's papers, trying to figure out if there was anything I should save."

Hank's brows knit together. "And...?"

"See for yourself." Feeling like she could use an impartial opinion, Ally handed over a folder. "These are his plans to put Mesquite Ridge on the map. First there was the dude ranch idea. He spent several years on that, when I was in elementary school, but learning how much it would cost to get an operation like that up and running eventually put an end to that notion."

She handed over another folder. "Then there was his grand idea to open up a rock quarry on one end of the property and harvest limestone for builders."

Hank frowned. "I imagine hauling the rock to the cities made the cost of that prohibitive."

Ally sighed. "Exactly." She picked up another box of meticulously kept folders. "For the next few years after that he tried to find a way to buy or build a giant telescope, and put a pay-per-view planetarium on the property for tourists or star lovers passing through."

"Hmm." Hank glanced through the pages and pages of papers. "That's actually kind of interesting."

"If completely impractical," Ally added impatiently. "Next up was the idea to build a wind farm and somehow connect it up to an electrical power plant."

Hank raised his hand in the age-old gesture of peace. "He was just ahead of his time there. That's the wave of the future."

That, Ally knew. She wet her lips. "The point is...in all of this, you know what you don't see?"

Hank shrugged. "What?"

Ally drummed her hand on the scarred wooden desktop. "Books on cattle or grass management. Data on the latest breeding practices. Or anything related to what he was supposed to be doing all along, which was building a cattle operation."

Hank cocked his head. "He had a herd."

"A small one that never amounted to much. You can see when you drive around the property how he let the land go to seed. There's mesquite and cedar everywhere. And everyone knows you can never get rid of mesquite. Cut it down, and it comes right back up."

"Hey. That's not such a bad thing." Hank set her father's folders in one neat pile, on the far side of the desk. "All of that untamed brush has not only kept the topsoil intact, it's added to the nutrient value."

Ally scowled. "You're just like him. You look at the land and you see value."

Hank grinned. Clasping her hands in his, he stood and drew her to her feet. "I sure do. And you know what else I see?" He winked playfully, refusing to allow her glum mood to spread to him. "A promise I need to keep."

The devilry in his blue eyes was almost as exciting as his lovemaking had been. "And what 'promise' would that be?" Ally found herself asking.

Hank picked up the half-dozen sprigs of mistletoe he had brought into the house, and clutched them in his fist. "Finding the perfect places to hang these."

"You're sure we need *six* sprigs of mistletoe?" Ally asked as she and Hank set off to find the perfect spots to hang the holiday greenery.

Hank followed, admiring the view. There was no question Ally looked good in her chic city clothing, but she really filled out a pair of jeans and a sweater, too.

"What number would you have us use?" He paused to secure one just inside his bedroom door.

Ally's heavenward glance told him what she thought about the subtlety of that. "One."

"But then—" Hank continued on down the hall, stopping at her bedroom door. He stepped inside the sanctuary that had been hers for the first eighteen years of her life, and tacked one there, too. "—You wouldn't have one here."

Merriment sparkled in her green eyes. "What makes you think I want mistletoe in my bedroom?"

Her teasing brought a smile to his face, too. She'd been so serious and bereft when she'd arrived at Mesquite Ridge the week before. It was good to see her loosening up and letting go of the grief and rigidity that had ruled her life prior to this holiday season. He winked again. "You never know when you might get the impulse to kiss someone. And need an excuse."

Ally sauntered past him, leaving a trail of orange blossom perfume. "If I want to kiss someone, I don't need an excuse."

"Ah," he said, thinking of the time when he would make love to her again, and get her to commit to more than just a momentary diversion or holiday fling. "Good to know."

Electricity shimmered between them. Ignoring his instincts, which were to make love to her then and there, Hank continued on down the hall. Determined to give her the emotional space she seemed to need, and show her they could have a good time simply hanging out together, he stopped midway down the staircase and put one there, too.

"Now that's an interesting place," Ally murmured.

"Isn't it?" Hank fantasized about having her beneath him, her arms and legs locked around his waist, and him so deep inside her he didn't know where he ended and she began. He continued to the front door and placed one just above it, in the foyer. One of these days, they'd make love without the sale of the ranch, and what that might or might not mean, between them.... One day soon, he'd be able to tell her how he really felt....

Oblivious to the passionate, possessive nature of his thoughts, Ally tilted her head. She studied the decoration over the portal, decreeing whimsically, "Not as original, cowboy."

Loving the way the unexpected endearment sounded rolling off her lips, Hank pressed the remaining greenery in her hand, relishing the soft, silky feel of her palm. "There's two left. Knock yourself out."

"Hmm." Accepting his humorous challenge, Ally sauntered off.

She paused next to the unadorned but fragrant Scotch pine and looked around. Then, grinning, she hurried across the room and stopped in the doorway between the living room and the hall that led to the kitchen and mudroom. "How about right here?"

"Expecting an earthquake?" Hank quipped.

"Door frames can be nice to lean against—" she batted her eyelashes flirtatiously "—should you want to lean, of course."

Hank liked this side of Ally. She was incredibly uninhibited and playful, deep down. The problem was that side of her didn't surface all that much. So far. If he had his way, that would change as readily as their relationship. "One left."

"Obviously, we know where that will go." Ally

sashayed on down the hall and into the big country kitchen.

The plastic baby pool that served as a whelping pen had been pushed to one side of the room. Duchess lay contentedly on the blanket lining it, her back against the side. The warming box, which contained all eleven puppies, was nestled beside the mother dog.

As Ally approached, Duchess lifted her head and thumped her tail happily.

Smiling in return, Ally handed the remaining sprig to Hank. "This should go in this room because you never know when one of us is going to want to kiss Duchess or a puppy."

Hank chuckled. He got out the step stool and fastened the mistletoe in the center of the eight-foot ceiling. "How's that?"

Ally stopped petting Duchess long enough to study the result. "Perfect."

"Maybe we should try it out."

"You're right." Ally gave the dog a final pat and turned her attention to the pile of slumbering puppies. She picked up the tiniest one and lifted her gently to her chest. "This one definitely needs a kiss."

Hank chuckled. "I'll make sure I give her one," he drawled. "But first this…" He wrapped his arms around Ally and, being careful not to squish Gracie, captured Ally's lips with a tender kiss that conveyed everything he was feeling and could not say.

She kissed him back just as ardently.

When he finally lifted his head and looked into her eyes, she nudged him with her knee. "You are so bad."

"You haven't experienced the half of it." They exchanged sexy grins.

Hank felt a surge of heat, content to wait. But it turned out his competition for Ally's attention was not.

The puppy lapped at her hand with her little pink tongue, let out a familiar squeak of hunger and began to squirm.

Smiling tenderly, Ally tore her gaze from Hank's. She glanced down, then gasped. "Oh my gosh, Hank! Look at this!"

Chapter Twelve

"Her eyes are open!" Ally cried in amazement. She had grown used to seeing the puppies in constant play, with their eyes shut tight. Being able to look into Gracie's dark eyes forged yet another unexpected yet highly emotional connection. To the point that Ally knew leaving her was going to be excruciatingly hard.

For Hank, too, judging by the depth of affection on his handsome face. He came closer and leaned in for a better look. "Right on schedule, too." He grinned triumphantly, then turned to Ally, his warm breath brushing her face. "I told you that Gracie might be little, but she's mighty."

Ally glowed with pride, knowing that just ten days ago the pup nearly hadn't made it, and now she was leading the pack in development. Except...Ally frowned. "She doesn't seem to be focusing."

Hank brushed a gentle hand over Gracie's soft head and scratched her lovingly behind the ears. "She won't be able to track an object for another two weeks, but between now and then, she'll see a little more every day."

Ally's spirits took a nosedive as the realization hit. "Unfortunately, I won't be with her when she can see more than a blur when she looks at me. I'll be back in Houston. With or without a job...trying to put together my life there." Ally's face crumpled as another wave of sadness moved through her. "Gracie will never really get to know me." She blinked back tears. "Not the way I've come to know—and love—her."

Hank wrapped a comforting arm about Ally's shoulders. He kissed the top of her head and flashed her a consoling smile. "She knows and loves you."

Ally luxuriated in his tenderness, even as she questioned his assertion. "How? Puppies' ears are closed when they're born, too. It takes several weeks before they can hear a loud noise. According to the handouts your cousin gave us, their lack of vision and hearing is Mother Nature's way of insuring they get enough sleep in the newborn phase."

Hank's eyes glimmered. "But their other senses— touch, smell, and taste—are there from the outset. Trust me on this, Ally." He tightened his grip on her protectively. "Gracie knows you, same as she knows her mama."

Ally supposed that was true.

Which made leaving the tiny puppy all the harder.

Ally blinked back a tear as Hank knelt beside the box. The other puppies were beginning to waken, squeaking and swimming and rolling around in the search for their mother. A few more were trying to open their eyes, too.

His expression unbearably sweet, Hank lifted them one by one and put them next to Duchess to nurse. Reluctantly, Ally settled Gracie against Duchess, too, then went to prepare a supplemental bottle of puppy formula.

Not that Gracie seemed to need the extra calories as much anymore, as she was able to nurse alongside her littermates, with nearly as much vigor…

Hank held the last puppy to wake up, cradling and petting him while he awaited his turn to nurse. Duchess lay contentedly, keeping one eye on the puppy Hank held, and watching over the others snuggled at her side.

"It's amazing how fast they're all growing," Ally murmured. Or how content she felt, watching them. She had never thought of herself as much of a ranch person. This experience was changing her mind. She liked being around animals more than she had thought.

Hank nodded agreeably. "In another week they'll be standing. A week after that running and scampering about."

Ally sighed. "Sounds lively." And she would miss that, too.…

The doorbell rang.

Ally looked at Hank. "Expecting anyone?"

He shook his head. "You?"

"No." She went to get the door. Seconds later, she returned with Kurt McCabe. He had his vet bag in one hand, a file folder in another. Encompassing them both with a friendly grin, Kurt told them, "I thought I'd stop by and check on Duchess and the puppies while I was out this way. And give you the news while I'm here.…"

* * *

That, Hank thought, could not be good. Trusting his cousin to be objective, in a situation where he might not be, Hank asked, "Did you hear something about Duchess and her puppies, and who they might belong to?"

"Maybe." Kurt set his bag on the table. "I had a call at the clinic a while ago that sounded a little sketchy. It was from a lady in Wichita Falls named Frannie Turner."

"That's two hundred miles from here!" Ally said.

Kurt obviously shared their consternation. "Anyway, Ms. Turner said she had agreed to watch Duchess for her sister-in-law, Talia Brannamore, who had been called off on an emergency with her great-niece's family in Nashville, Tennessee. Something about a house fire and Christmas and all the presents going up in smoke, and the family having small children and nowhere to go but a hotel, and it all being very short notice. Apparently, there was a lot of confusion, both before Duchess was dropped off with Ms. Turner, and during the first day Duchess was there."

Ally's eyes took on a cynical glint. "Kurt, this sounds like a hoax!"

Hank agreed.

"That's what I thought." Kurt knelt next to the whelping pen, stethoscope around his neck. "Except for one thing. This woman who claimed she was keeping the female golden retriever named Duchess, knew the retriever was pregnant and about to deliver eleven whelps. We didn't put that information in any of the flyers we sent out."

Ally blinked. "Why not?"

Hank explained, "The dogs are valuable. It's Christmas, and the demand for puppies—even those not quite ready to go home yet—is higher than at any other time of year. And these are purebred, show quality dogs. They're worth a lot."

Kurt started examining the puppies one by one. "So the fact that Frannie Turner in Wichita Falls knows that we have a golden retriever named Duchess is great. The fact she has no proof of ownership—no papers, or pictures of this dog—gives rise to a lot of question. She says it's because Duchess isn't hers, and she was just doing a favor. And that the dog got out of her house accidentally and ran away."

Ally pressed her lips together, clearly skeptical. "We're two hundred miles from Wichita Falls, guys. That's an awfully long way."

Hank draped a consoling arm across Ally's shoulders. "Duchess was pregnant, about to deliver. She could have been trying to make her way home to San Angelo to deliver her puppies, and ended up here."

Her expression thoughtful, Ally turned into Hank's embrace. He squeezed her, then let her go.

"You hear about that sometimes," Ally murmured. "Dogs surmounting impossible odds—and doing whatever they have to do to get home."

More than one movie had been made about this kind of true life event, Hank knew.

"And it could have happened in this case," Kurt said as he checked Duchess. Finding everything in order, he put his stethoscope back in his bag. "Pregnant dogs have a desire to nest, and a lot of them instinctively go off in private to deliver. But it's also possible Frannie Turner could have gotten the information elsewhere. Everyone in the community is talking about it. And they're all telling their friends and family. So it's possible this woman is trying to pull a scam on us."

Ally's brow furrowed with emotion. "So now what?"

Kurt sighed. "Apparently, Frannie didn't tell her sister-in-law the dog was missing, because she had enough to deal with and Frannie didn't want her to get upset with her. The sister-in-law is a very serious professional dog breeder, she claims. Now that Frannie knows we found the dog and that the puppies are all okay, she's not afraid to tell Talia Brannamore." He locked eyes with Hank and then Ally. "So Frannie told me she would call Talia in Nashville, and see if she can't get us some sort of proof."

"How long is that going to take?" Hank asked, impatient to get this resolved before he or Ally became any more emotionally involved with Duchess and the pups.

Kurt stood. "She's already done it. I spoke to the breeder right before I got here. Talia Brannamore reiterated everything Frannie already told me, but said she doesn't have any proof with her. It's all at her house in San Angelo. And she won't be back there until December 23. Talia offered to drive through Laramie on her way home, since she'll pass right by here, and see Duchess. If her story is true, and Duchess is hers, then the retriever should immediately recognize her. If not, and we think a fraud is being perpetrated...well, I've already talked to my brother Kyle, and we'll have someone from the sheriff's department ready and waiting."

"But you think it might be true, don't you?" Ally asked, clearly upset.

Kurt shrugged. "All I can tell you is that the woman from San Angelo was really concerned about her pregnant dog being lost and not knowing anything about it. She is exceedingly grateful to you and Ally and the vet clinic, and prepared to compensate us all for our troubles."

Which went to confirm the value of golden retrievers, Hank thought.

He cast a sideways look at Ally. Her face had a crushed expression that mirrored his own feelings and tore at his heart.

He watched her kneel down and pick up Gracie, cradle her tenderly. He knew he'd do anything to make Ally happy. "What about the pups?" he asked.

Kurt knew where this was going. He shook his head. "They're all spoken for, every last one."

Hank swore silently to himself. "Including the runt of the litter?" He had to make sure.

Kurt nodded and confirmed grimly, "Gracie, too."

Ally sat in the kitchen, devastated, while Hank walked his cousin out. She had known this could happen. She had just been hoping that it wouldn't....

Hank strode back in, an old-fashioned hatbox, emblazoned with his name, clasped in his hands. Wordlessly, he set it on the table and came around to where she was sitting. He knelt in front of her, like a knight before a queen, and covered her hands with his warm ones.

Ally lifted her head. How easy it would be to depend on him this way. And how foolish. Since she wasn't staying, and he wasn't about to leave, and the sale of the ranch still stood between them...

Hank searched her face. "Are you okay?"

Embarrassment heated her cheeks. "Why wouldn't I be?" she countered grumpily.

"You've gotten attached to Gracie."

Against all common sense, she reminded herself unhappily. "And you're attached to Duchess. And we always knew this would happen." She drew a deep breath, then added honestly, "I wished it wouldn't. I just hoped I'd be able to find a way to keep the littlest one. But that's not going to happen," she said, the bitterness of old coming back to haunt her. Like every other situation at Mesquite Ridge, this event had a bad ending. For her, anyway...

Hank looked into her eyes as if he shared her heartache. "You can get another puppy," he murmured softly, as if there was no place on earth he would rather be.

She gripped his hands, drawing on his strength despite herself, and blinked back tears. "I know," she said thickly.

But it wouldn't be the same, Ally knew. *Just like making love with another man won't be the same. Not after you.*

With effort, Ally pushed her melancholy thoughts away. Hank was right—she could get another puppy. Someday. In the meantime, she had four days left in Laramie. She wasn't going to let the bleakness of her future life ruin what she had today. She was going to do what she'd never been wise enough to do before. Enjoy the here and now, and forget about whatever tomorrow might bring.

Swallowing, Ally nodded at the box in Hank's hands, determined to try to get back in the holiday spirit and be cheerful if it killed her. "What's that?"

"My mom sent it over. Kurt almost forgot to give it to me."

Okay, that told her absolutely nothing, except that his mother apparently liked fancy hatboxes, and this one looked as if it had been around for a while. In fact, there was even a little dust on it. "Aren't you going to open it?" Ally prodded.

Hank shrugged, as maddeningly determined as she was impatient to learn more. "Sure. If you want." He flashed her a grin that upped her anticipation even further. "That is—" he leaned forward intimately, more than ready to lend a little sensual distraction "—if you're ready to do *your* usual thing and get your bah, humbug on."

Hilarious. "Can't wait, cowboy." Ally dared him with a glance. "Do your best to get me in the spirit."

Hank chuckled as if it were already a fait accompli. He took the lid off the hatbox. It was filled with a breathtaking array of amazing and unique ornaments. Some wrapped in tissue, some not. He picked up a ceramic Western-boot-wearing Santa Claus driving a sleigh filled with presents. "I got this one when I was five."

Ally could imagine him hanging it on the tree, as an adorable little boy. "Cute," she murmured, intrigued by this glimpse into his holidays past.

Hank fingered a Nutcracker soldier and reflected fondly, "This came from Dallas the year I turned eight. Mom and Dad took the whole family to see the ballet at Christmastime."

The wooden figure was exquisite, even without the beautiful memories. "So everything in here has special meaning."

He nodded, then gathered the box in one arm, took her by the hand with the other and led her into the living room.

Belatedly, Ally realized there were electric lights

on the tree. Hank had to have put them up. When, she wasn't sure.

Chuckling at her surprise, he leaned over and plugged in the cord. The tree lit up with a rain of tiny sparkling lights.

He reached for the box and fished out an ornament with a picture of him as a gap-toothed first grader on it. He walked over and hung it on the tree they had yet to decorate. "When I was a teenager, I found this photo hideously embarrassing."

Ally sauntered closer. "And now?"

He brushed his thumb across her cheek. "It brings back memories. Good ones." He paused. "I guess this isn't so great for you, though." He started to remove the ornament. "Maybe we should just stick to the decorations I bought at Neiman Marcus."

Ally looked over at the shopping bag he had brought home days before. "We can use those," she told him happily, returning to the hatbox full of memories. "But let's use these, too." It was fun, hearing his stories. Learning about his childhood made her feel closer to him in a way she hadn't expected.

Hank studied her with concern. "It's not really fair to have a tree for us that says everything about my childhood and nothing about yours, though."

For us. She liked the sound of that.

Ally raised a hand, promising cheerfully, "We can rectify that. Wait here." She darted upstairs, anxious to surprise him, too. She came back several minutes later with a cloth-covered shoebox, and opened the lid. Inside was a collection just as unique.

His dark brow furrowed. "I thought you said your family didn't celebrate Christmas."

Ally sent him a wry look. "They didn't." She unwrapped a paper chain and another of artificial popcorn and cranberries, aware she was sentimentally attached—to every ornament of her youth, as he was to his. She smiled, belatedly realizing that "Christmas" was found in the unlikeliest of places. Like here, with Hank.

"But the teachers at school did," she continued, surprised to find herself eager to share her past with Hank. "And when I was younger, we made stuff in art class, too." She had tucked it all away, in the very back of her closet, where it would be safe.

Hank's eyes locked with hers.

"I used to get it all out and look at it over the holidays," she confessed.

He gathered her in his arms, intuitively giving her all the comfort and reassurance she needed. "That's…sad."

She had thought so, too…until now. "Not really." Ally had a brand-new way of looking at things. She lifted her chin. "Not when you consider how much joy these little trinkets brought me."

Tenderly, he drew a knuckle across the bow of her lips. "So there is a heart inside that Grinch exterior, after all."

Ally grinned and wound her arms about his neck. Playfully, she went up on tiptoe. "Just don't tell anyone about it."

He regarded her in a way that left no doubt they would be making love again very soon. "Not to worry," he whispered. "Your secret is safe with me." As if to prove it, he captured her lips in a kiss that was so unbearably tender it had her melting against him. "Although," Hank drawled finally, smoothing a palm down her spine, "you may not be able to keep it secret much longer...."

Ally chuckled and splayed her hands across the warmth of his chest. "Just decorate the tree!"

An hour later, they had all the remnants from their youth hanging next to the beautiful glass ornaments from Dallas's top department store. It was an eclectic tree, rife with meaning. Ally knew she had never seen anything more beautiful.

Hank stepped back to admire the pine. He braced his hands on his hips. "All we need now is something for the top."

Suddenly, Ally wanted to do more than just be dragged into participating. "Why don't you let me handle that?"

"Sure?" Hank teased her with a kiss to the brow. "Wouldn't want to ruin your rep as a holiday curmudgeon."

She rolled her eyes. "Trust me, there's very little chance of that!"

"I don't know...you're looking awfully happy right now."

Her heart pounded against her ribs. "I'm feeling awfully happy." Which was odd, given the fact that she was about to lose the puppy and the mama dog she had fallen in love with. Closer still to unwillingly forfeiting her job and selling the home she'd had since birth. By all rights, she ought to be flat-out miserable tonight, and crying her eyes out. She wasn't. There was only one reason for that.

He knew it. And was coming closer once again, to claim her. Fully, this time. Hank took her into his arms, lowered his mouth to hers. Their lips were just about to touch when his cell phone rang.

Hank grimaced, looking very much like he didn't want to answer the call. Then again, it was late, and generally people didn't phone at eleven at night unless it was important....

He let her go reluctantly. "This will just take a second. Hank McCabe..." He listened intently, frowned some more. "You want to meet *now?*" he asked, his tone incredulous. "Of course...I understand. Time is of the essence. Fifteen—twenty minutes okay? See you then." He ended the call. "I've got to go into town."

"Let me guess." The words were out before Ally could stop them. "Lulu again?"

To his credit, Hank didn't back away from the facts. "She's an integral part of my plan to buy Mesquite Ridge."

Ally's heart sank. "I heard she got a lot of money in her divorce settlement."

Hank acknowledged that with a brief nod, but did not comment, before once again glancing at his watch. "I've got to go." He paused, the inscrutable look coming back into his deep blue eyes. "I'm not sure how long this will take."

Jealousy and anger twisted inside her. "Don't worry." Ally flashed the most nonchalant smile she could manage. "I won't wait up."

Hank was out the door a few minutes later.

Ally paced the room. The tree that had seemed so festive moments earlier appeared flat and unexciting now.

She guessed the old saying was right—beauty was

in the eye of the beholder. The question was, how did Hank see Lulu? As his savior?

Ally didn't have a big bank account. If she did…

But she didn't. She might not even have a job.

She glanced at the clock again. It was late, but chances were, Porter was still up. She went to get her phone. Seconds later, her call went through, and her colleague answered on the first ring. "Hey, stranger," he said. "About time you returned any one of the half-dozen calls or email messages I left for you."

"Sorry. I've been a little busy. How are things with you?"

"Glum. The current job market in Houston is bleak. I might have to go back to Phoenix, where I grew up."

"Do you have a lead?"

"On several things, as a matter of fact. With all the retirees still moving to the Sun Belt for their golden years, the demand for financial analysts and advisers is growing every day. I can give you the name of the recruiting firm I'm using. It might not be so bad if we both got jobs and moved there at the same time."

To Arizona? "I don't know, Porter. I'm a Texas girl, born and bred…." To date, she had never thought much about it. But now…? "I'm not sure I want to live anywhere but the Lone Star State."

"Look. You don't have to decide anything tonight. Just send in your résumé and a cover letter to the contact I emailed you this morning. Think of it as insurance. Chances are, if a firm in Arizona gives you an offer, you won't lose your job in Houston."

Chances for success were definitely better if they had multiple options, instead of just the one. Ally forced herself to be practical. "I like the way you think."

Porter chuckled. "Thank you."

She paced back and forth. "Any further word on the layoffs?" Unlike her, Porter always had his ear to the ground for workplace gossip. If there was something to know, her friend would be aware of it.

"Nope. Just that the new management intends to keep a skeleton crew on to manage the transition, and the rest of the cuts are going to be massive, and brutal."

Which meant, Ally told herself sternly, she *had* to be practical. She couldn't just follow her heart....

She thanked Porter for the info. They chatted some more and then hung up. Restless, she took care of Duchess and the puppies. By the time she had finished, it was well after midnight, and there was still no sign of Hank.

He was not off making love with Lulu. Or looking for a liaison. Lulu was probably just using her connections to help Hank find the additional financing he needed to be able to make an offer on Mesquite Ridge.

But on the off-off chance that Hank was out doing something that would signal the end of Ally and him... She figured she better do as Porter advised and develop a much better plan B.

Hank tiptoed in at 3:00 a.m. Ally had said she wouldn't wait up, and she hadn't. She was fast asleep on the living room sofa, an angelically peaceful look on her face—and what appeared to be a half-finished quilted Christmas stocking in her hands.

Hank considered picking her up and carrying her to bed, but knew he'd wake her, and then he'd want to make to love to her. Trouble was, given the time and where he'd been, it was unlikely that Ally would welcome his advances.

So, he figured, as he went upstairs and got one of the blankets off her bed and covered her up, this would have to do.

Kissing her would have to come later.

In the meantime, he needed a little shut-eye himself. He had a lot to accomplish and a short amount of time to get it all done, if he were to make Ally's dreams come true and give her a truly merry Christmas, to boot.

Chapter Thirteen

The sound of footsteps jerked Ally from her reverie. Her heartbeat accelerating, she turned to see Hank striding toward her, two steaming mugs in hand. He greeted her with a cheerful smile. "You're up bright and early."

And you, Ally thought, as she put the fabric samples she had been studying aside, *got home awfully late.*

Determined to keep her hurt feelings to herself, she waved off his offer of a fresh cup. "Thanks." She forced herself to be polite as she rose from the living room sofa. "I'm already at my limit." For caffeine and a lot of other things....

A knowing look on his face, Hank set the beverage he'd brought for her on an end table, safely out of harm's way. "In case you change your mind," he said casually.

Not likely, now that another potential investor was in the picture, Ally thought, with unprecedented resentment simmering deep inside her.

Ally had *promised* herself she would never again get in a situation where the acquisition of land took precedent over everything else. The fact that Hank could ditch her on a moment's notice at eleven o'clock at night, when they'd been close to making love again, proved that he felt otherwise. Clearly, the ranch was more important to him than the two of them.

So Ally had no choice. She had to take a step back from the fierce attraction she felt for Hank, and think about what was in her best interests.

It didn't matter how capable and kind he seemed, standing there in the morning light. Or how good he looked and smelled, fresh from his shower. She could not allow herself to forget her own need for long-term financial security, throw caution to the wind and make love with him again.

Not when his obsession with acquiring the ranch had him putting Mesquite Ridge first, her second. Or maybe, considering Lulu Sanderson's involvement, even third...

Hank inclined his head at the bolts of fabric scattered across the living room. "What's all this?"

"I'm still planning to put the ranch on the market on December 24."

Ally ignored the shadow that passed over Hank's face. This was business—not personal, no matter how much he might want her to think otherwise.

Deliberately, she pushed on. "The broker from Premier Realty, Marcy Lyon, is coming out to do a walk-through inspection and take some photographs for the MLS listing on the 22. She and I will nail down the final asking price at that time, which as you know could be quite a bit higher or lower than the tax appraisal Corporate Farms is using. I want it to be higher, of course, so I'm trying to do everything I can, within the constraints of my budget, to get the place looking the best."

Hank glanced around in admiration. "You've already had the place painted, and made draperies as well as slipcovers for all the furniture in here."

"We still need splashes of color to brighten up the space. And I don't want to buy any more fabric—I'd prefer to use the remnants from my mother's sewing room. So I'm trying to figure out which to use for pillows and a throw. I'm even thinking about making a wall hanging or two, since we don't really have any art, and the walls are looking a little bare. It would be easy enough to do."

Hank pointed to several bolts of colorful cloth with a splashy modern art motif. "I don't know if you want my opinion, but I like those."

Ally nodded. Call it coincidence, but they were the ones she had chosen, too.

Hank stepped closer, his expression intent. "Look, I know we said we wouldn't talk about the offer I'm planning to make on the ranch until I get everything pulled together—"

She cut him off with a quick lift of her palm. "It's still a good idea."

Hank gave her a steady, assessing look. He *wanted* to confide in her. What did she want? The answer to that was easy enough. She wanted to protect her heart and get her life back on a secure track once again.

"Are you sure?" he asked finally.

Ally nodded. It hardly mattered whether Lulu was drawing on her handsome divorce settlement and personally loaning Hank the money he needed to make a down payment on a mortgage, using her business school connections to line up another investor to help him out, or going in on the ranch with him. All options left Ally feeling like a third wheel. It didn't matter whether she wanted to be with Hank or not. She couldn't live like that again.

"Well, I must say," Marcy Lyon concluded when she had finished the tour of the property, "you have done an incredible job in a short amount of time, fixing up the interior of the ranch house."

Ally had to admit it looked better. The soft gray walls and gleaming white trim showed off the wide plank floors. Ivory slipcovers covered a multitude of sins on the aging furniture. Antique Texan accessories, throw pillows and fabric wall hangings provided color throughout. And of course, there was the Christmas tree she and Hank had decorated. It still lacked something on top, and Ally reminded herself she still needed to take care of that.

"Unfortunately, it's not enough," Marcy said reluctantly. "The plumbing, electrical and roof are all forty years old. There's no dishwasher or disposal. The kitchen is nice and big, but the linoleum floors and counters are terribly dated, and the appliances are ancient. The bulk of the acreage is in similarly bad shape." She sighed with regret. "This puts Mesquite Ridge squarely in the category of a fixer-upper, and lowers the price a good ten percent. That, combined with the commission you'd have to pay on what should be a two point five million dollar property—but currently isn't—minus the existing mortgage debt... At the end of the day you'd have very little."

Ally felt her heart sink. "So in other words, the last offer I received from Corporate Farms..."

Marcy looked her square in the eye and put her pen back in her briefcase. "Is really unbeatable, if money is your only criteria."

Ally watched her continue to pack up her belongings. "And if it's not?"

She closed the clasp on her briefcase with a snap, then pressed her lips together. "May I be blunt?"

Nodding, Ally said, "I need you to be as direct with me as possible."

Marcy began to pace. "You can't expect to sell to Corporate Farms—knowing full well they intend to drive everyone else out of business so they can create an outfit bigger than the King Ranch right here in Laramie County—and think it will be okay."

"If I were to do that..." Ally swallowed and looked the real estate broker in the eye "...I'd never be able to come back, would I?"

Marcy shook her head. "I don't see how you could."

Hours later, Hank walked into the living room where Ally sat beside the Christmas tree. Duchess was curled up next to her. The puppies were sleeping in a comical heap across her lap. It was a blissful scene, except for the faintly troubled look in Ally's eyes.

Hank tossed his leather jacket over the back of the chair and loosened the knot of his tie. He wished he could tell Ally about the meeting he'd just been to. But like everything else about the negotiations he was involved in, the details were top secret until the deal was set. And that wouldn't be for another thirty-six hours.

In the meantime, though...moments like this didn't

come along all that often. He took out his cell phone, determined to capture the moment. "Hang on a minute. I've got to get a picture of this."

For a second he thought Ally might burst into sentimental tears, which was not surprising, given how attached she had gotten to all the dogs. Then she got that fiercely independent look in her eyes he knew so well. She mugged dramatically, then picked up Gracie and held her to her chest. She used her other hand to soothe the equally hyperalert Duchess. "Since when are you into taking pictures?" she chided.

The walls were coming up around Ally's heart again, higher than ever. Hank wanted to tear them down.

"Since I found the perfect Christmas card photo." *And the perfect woman.* "And because," he added honestly, "this is something I want us all to remember for a long time to come."

Some of the fight drained out of Ally. "You really think the dogs are going to remember?" she asked softly, pressing a kiss on top of Gracie's head.

The pup opened her eyes and looked up at Ally.

If Gracie wasn't focusing on Ally's face, Hank decided, she was darned close.... Certainly, there was love and affection reflected on her cute little mug as she snuggled there.

Realizing Ally was still awaiting an answer to her question, he said, "I'm sure the dogs will recall all the love and attention they've received from us. In fact," he predicted, working to disguise the small catch in his throat, "I think they are going to be as sad to leave Mesquite Ridge tomorrow as we will be to see them go."

To his chagrin, Ally noticed the unusual huskiness in

his voice. She made another face and teased, "I didn't think ranchers got emotional about stuff like this."

For some, the acquisition and loss of pets was a normal part of the ebb and flow of ranch life. Something accepted without much thought. For Hank, dogs were part of the family. Which was why he'd been thinking about getting one as soon as he had his own ranch.

"What can I say?" He shifted angles to make sure he captured the tree and the fireplace in the next frame. Smiling, he joined their makeshift family. Holding the cell phone out in front of him, he took a photo of all of them together. "You bring out my sentimental side."

This time Ally's smile was from the heart. "And your familial one," she added softly.

That was true, too, Hank noted. Never had he wanted to have a family of his own more than he did right now, with Ally, Duchess and Gracie...

Whenever she let her guard down, Ally seemed to want that, too.

Silence fell as they looked into each other's eyes. Ally sobered, as if suddenly recalling all that still remained unsettled, all that could drive them apart. She was right to be concerned, Hank admitted reluctantly to himself. It was time to have a serious discussion, at least about the things they could talk about at this juncture.

Such as her meeting with Marcy Lyon.

Hank pocketed his phone once again. Figuring this was one conversation best had with no distraction, he helped Ally return the puppies to the warming box, next to Duchess in the whelping pen. The warming box was situated next to the mother dog. When they'd all settled down to sleep once again, Ally motioned for Hank to follow her.

"So how did your meeting go?" he asked, while they walked back into the living room.

She sank down on the sofa, propped her feet on the coffee table and released a long, slow breath. "Premier Realty's appraisal did not come out as I had hoped."

Hank tensed, not sure whose side he was on—hers or his. Maybe both… He sat next to her, being careful to give her plenty of room. "How bad was it?"

Ally passed a weary hand over her eyes. "So bad Marcy is refusing to list the ranch for me, because she doesn't want every bit of profit I might make from the sale of the property to go toward her commission." Briefly, she explained, then looked over at him and shook her head in exasperation. "What kind of person shoots themselves in the foot professionally that way?"

Hank replied frankly, "The kind who lives in Laramie, Texas. Neighbors here help each other out. They don't take unfair advantage for personal gain."

"Like Corporate Farms would."

Hank nodded, knowing he would give anything to find a way to keep Ally in his life. Even his dream of one day owning this ranch, if that's what it would take. Because she was worth any sacrifice to him. The question was, what was he worth to her?

She released a beleaguered sigh and turned toward him, tucking one foot beneath her, her other knee nudging his. Her green eyes were full of strength and wisdom. "I'm a financial analyst." She shifted closer, the fragrance of her hair and skin inundating his senses. "I know the smart thing to do, fiscally, would be to accept CF's deal and not look back."

Hank gazed at her thoughtfully, really wanting to understand her. "And yet…?" he prompted softly.

She tensed, seeming on guard once again. "They'd destroy the house, the barn and everything that is familiar about this place."

And that, Hank noted, was something Ally couldn't bear. He reached over and covered her hand with his. "I thought you hated Mesquite Ridge."

Her fingers grasped his and she bit her lip. "I did, too. At least I thought I did." She paused to look deep into his eyes. "But now that I've been here again and started fixing up the house, I'm remembering some not so bad times." She shrugged. "Like sewing with my mother. Learning the ins and outs of finance and bookkeeping with my dad. As much as I hated their frugality, I have to admit no one could stretch a dollar better than the two of them." Ally pushed her free hand through her hair, mussing the silky strands. She shook her head, her eyes glimmering moistly. "I feel like I have no good options."

Unable to bear seeing her in so much distress, Hank shifted her onto his lap and wrapped his arms around her. "That's not true. You have me. I am this close—" he held his index finger and thumb half an inch apart "—to being able to help you." *This close to being able to tell you everything I feel...everything I want us both to have.*

She scowled briefly. "Please don't say that," she begged, splaying her hands across his chest. "Really. I can't bear any more half-baked promises. Not tonight."

Tenderness swept through him. Not sure when he had ever felt such devotion, he shifted her closer still. Heaven help him, he wanted to make love to her here and now. And one day soon, their time would come.

"Then what can I do?" he asked quietly.

The caution that she'd been feeling the last few days, about the two of them, fled. She leaned into him and allowed herself to be vulnerable to the undeniable sparks between them once again. "Help me to forget I may soon have to sell the only real link to family that I have left. Or that tomorrow I'm going to find out whether or not I'm going to be laid off from my job." Her voice cracked emotionally. She looked at him with raw need. "And that Duchess and Gracie and the rest of the puppies are going to be taken away...."

She was facing tremendous loss, Hank knew. But she wasn't going to lose him. Not if he could help it. And lowering his mouth to hers, he set about to show her that.

One kiss turned into two, then three. She shifted around on his lap so she was straddling him. The softness of her breasts pressed against his chest as she nuzzled his neck.

Hank unbuttoned her blouse, eased it off and divested her of her lacy bra. She shuddered as he palmed her nipples, teasing them into tender buds. His hands drifted lower, to release the zipper on her skirt.

Deciding the sooner there was nothing but pure heat between them the better, he shifted her again, so she was on her feet. And then she took the lead, stripping sensually, helping him do the same. She touched and kissed him with a wild rapture, pushing him toward the edge. In a haze, he suddenly found himself sitting on the sofa again, with Ally straddling his lap.

"Now," she said determinedly, tangling her fingers in his hair.

"Not until you're ready." He held her wrists in one hand, using his other to touch, stroke, love. She quivered, as he kissed her again, vowing to make this last, to make it so incredible she would never want to pull away. Her skin grew flushed, her thighs parted to better accommodate his. And then she was wet and trembling, ready, wanting, needing, and Hank was lost in a completeness unlike anything he had ever known. His heart pounding, he caught her hips. Brought her flush against him. Ally closed around him, her response honest and unashamed. Surrendering entirely, she took him deep inside her, resolutely commanding everything he had to give. And when she would have hurried the pace even more, he held back, making her understand what it was to feel such urgent, burning need.

Until there was no doubt that this holiday season, the two of them had every dream fulfilled, in their lovemaking, in each other. Until she was giving him every ounce of tenderness and passion she possessed, just as he was to her.

For the first time Hank knew what it was to come home to where the heart was, to have every detail of his future happiness laid out in front of him, his for the taking.

He wanted to tell her how he felt. But with the business of the ranch still between them, he knew he had to wait. So Hank tried to show her instead, with kisses full of longing, touches full of need. Until she was shivering with pleasure, until she drew him toward the brink and was crying out hoarsely as he thrust inside her, the friction of their bodies doubling the pleasure. Her hands were on his skin, and his were on hers, and nothing mattered but the two of them. Their mouths and bodies meshed until every bit of her was sweet and wild and womanly. And all his... Beautifully, magically, wonderfully his.

All they had to do was make it another thirty-four hours.

Until late Christmas Eve.

When he would finally be able to tell her the truth.

And give her the security and sense of belonging she had always craved.

Chapter Fourteen

Ally clapped a hand over her heart and stared at the litter. Her pretty face glowed with a happiness that would have been hard to imagine just two weeks before. "I can't believe it, Hank! They're actually *standing*."

"Before they fall over, that is." Hank chuckled as the puppies—all roughly three pounds each now—struggled upright, tottered and then fell, only to get right back up again. It seemed once Gracie had the idea, all her bigger littermates wanted to follow her example.

"It's going to be so quiet here without them," Ally mused tenderly.

Even quieter without you, Hank thought. *If you choose to leave. I'm still hoping a Christmas miracle will happen and you'll decide not to return to Houston, after all.*

Pushing his own concerns aside, he asked, "Have you heard about your job yet?"

Ally paled. "Word was supposed to be sent out via email at seven this morning."

Hank glanced at his watch. "It's seven-thirty."

She acknowledged this with a slight dip of her head. "I know. I should check. But…" she lifted her slender shoulders in a shrug "…I'm afraid to look."

Hank knew it was his job to lessen the tension. He flashed her a consoling grin, and drawled, "You know what they say…"

"I'm sure you're going to tell me," Ally replied, mirroring his deadpan expression.

"Burying your head in the sand doesn't give you anything but grit up your nose."

She burst out laughing. "And here I thought you were going to go all Churchill on me and say something like—" she lowered her voice to a booming alto "—Now, Ally, there's nothing to fear but fear itself!"

"That, too." He moved a strand of hair from her cheek, and tucked it behind her ear. "Why don't you have a look?" he encouraged gently. For her sake, he hoped she got what she wanted—continued employment and a steady salary coming in. "I'll have the champagne ready."

She looked as if she was going to need a hanky instead. "I'm going to be fired," she worried out loud.

Hank shook his head. "Not if they're smart."

Ally gave him one last glance, then swallowed and went to the desk. She switched on her laptop computer and brought up her email. Waited impatiently, her hands trembling slightly all the while. Finally, she drew a long bolstering breath, typed in a command, then another. And promptly burst into tears.

Hank swore silently to himself and reached for the tissue box.

"Porter lost his job," Ally sobbed. She accepted the tissues he handed her and wiped her face. "I kept mine."

Hank was ambivalent, to the say the least, since this meant she would be leaving Laramie—and him. His need to be a decent and chivalrous human being demanded that he once again put his own concerns aside, and congratulate and wholeheartedly support Ally on her career success. "Well, that's good, isn't it?" he countered enthusiastically.

Ally's face crumpled. She slumped back in her chair and wearily ran a hand over her damp eyes. "It means I have to be back in Houston for an 8:00 a.m. managers meeting on December 26."

Which meant she would be leaving Christmas Day, if not sooner, just as she had initially planned. Not so good. Still, Hank didn't want to be a jerk. "Congratulations," he said, meaning it with every fiber of his being.

"Thank you." Ally closed her eyes and exhaled slowly, looking even more distressed. Finally, she straightened. "I have to call Porter."

"I'll manage things here," Hank promised as another round of puppies stood, wobbled and fell into a wiggling pile.

Ally stepped outside on the wraparound porch to speak in private.

Just as she finished, Talia Brannamore arrived. Ally greeted her, then brought her inside.

Hank had been prepared to loathe the breeder who'd managed to put Duchess in the care of someone so obviously incompetent. Who could lose such a precious dog who was about to give birth? But it was clear Talia

Brannamore had been through a little bit of hell herself. Her face was haggard with fatigue, her middle-aged body drooping.

Duchess thumped her tail in recognition and panted happily when she saw her owner, but didn't rise to greet her, as Hank would have expected her to do after such a prolonged absence.

Talia shook her head at the puppies tumbling over each other in an effort to get to their feet and stay there. She knelt and picked them up one by one, examining each in turn. "The nose is a little short on this one," she noted with a discerning frown. "I don't like the look of these ears. Now this one…this one is darn near perfect. And what happened here?" Talia stopped when she saw Gracie, who weighed in at only two and a half pounds, instead of the three sported by all her littermates. "What a little runt she is!"

Ally's jaw dropped. She squared off with the woman unhappily. "I don't know how you can say that! I mean… she's on the small side, but she's absolutely beautiful!"

Talia sighed. "Only because you know nothing about show dogs. This one would not win Westminster. Now this one…" she picked up a particularly robust male puppy "…would." The breeder set the puppy down with barely a pat of affection. She rocked back on her heels. "Fortunately, most of my customers aren't interested in showing their dogs. They just want their pet to look like he or she could be competitive enough to win first place." That said, Talia Brannamore looked back at Gracie and shook her head in obvious disappointment.

"If you don't want her, I'll take Gracie!" Ally blurted.

Again, Talia shook her head. "I can't do that. These dogs have all been presold for months now. And even though they won't be able to go 'home' for another seven weeks, I've promised their new owners they'll be able to come and visit their puppy on Christmas Day. So I've got to talk compensation with you, and then load them up and get going."

Saying goodbye to all of them was tough, even for Hank, but saying goodbye to Gracie was heart-wrenching. Ally's lower lip trembled and tears rolled down her face as she kissed the smallest puppy on the head and then gently put her in the flannel lined warming box with her littermates. The box was plugged into the power outlet in Talia Brannamore's station wagon.

The breeder patted the blanketed cargo area. "Come on, Duchess, let's go."

The retriever looked at Talia and then Hank, and went to stand next to him. Taking his hand in her mouth, she tugged him toward the back of the station wagon.

She seemed to be urging him to get in with the puppies.

Then Duchess went to Ally and gently mouthed her hand, doing the same.

Ally cried all the harder.

The lump in Hank's throat got even bigger. "Well, I'll be darned. She wants us to go with them," he muttered in awe.

"Honestly," Talia said, exasperated. She patted the cargo bed vigorously and commanded, "Duchess! Inside! Now!"

Duchess gave another last long look at Hank and Ally, then did as ordered. She settled next to her puppies, as if knowing this was where she had to be. The breeder shut the back, then turned to them. "Thanks again. Y'll have a merry Christmas now!" She got in and drove off.

As the station wagon went down the lane, they could see Duchess press her head against the window, looking back at them.

Hank had grown up around animals. He knew that there was a cycle to things, and this cycle had ended—at least for him and Ally. It still hurt almost more than he could bear. He turned to her and could tell at a glance that it was all she could do not to run after the station wagon and beg Talia Brannamore to let all the dogs stay.

He felt the same way.

On top of that, he was about to lose Ally, too! Talk about yuletide misery. She apparently felt it, too, for she pivoted, saw his eyes gleaming with moisture, and promptly lost it.

There were times, Ally knew, when a person needed to be held. And right now she needed not just to be held, but for *Hank* to hold her. And he knew it, too. She thrust herself into his arms. He caught her to him and buried his face in her hair, offering low, consoling words and the sweetest solace she had ever felt. Then the tears came, in an outpouring of grief she could not seem to stop.

Ally cried because they'd lost the dogs they both loved so much. She cried because she had kept her job, and that meant she had to leave. She cried because she wasn't quite sure where she stood with Hank. And most of all, she cried because for the first time in her life she felt like she just might belong somewhere, with someone. And she wasn't sure that was going to last, either. All she knew for sure was that she was drenching his shirt, and that he made her feel so safe and cared for. And that he probably thought she was an utter fool, for reacting so emotionally around him…again.

Sniffing, Ally forced herself to pull herself together and draw back. She dabbed at her eyes. "They're going to be fine," Hank told Ally firmly as they walked back into the ranch house together.

"Of course they are," Ally agreed.

Hank laced a protective arm about her waist. "Duchess wasn't our dog to begin with."

Ally shrugged out of her jacket. "We knew that from the outset."

Hank went to tend the fire in the grate. "Looking out the window that way was just Duchess's way of saying goodbye to us."

Ally battled a new flood of tears.

Hank paused, abruptly looking as utterly bereft as Ally was feeling. Ally drew a bolstering breath, aware her hands were shaking. She wrung them together. "I'm not sure what you're supposed to do in a situation like this."

Hank replaced the screen on the fireplace. "I know what we do in the military when we lose a comrade— and in this case," the corner of his lips crooked ruefully "—we just lost 'twelve' of 'em. We raise a glass in our lost friends' honor." He rubbed his chin with the flat of his hand. "The only problem is I think I drank the last beer several days ago, and since it's only eight in the morning, I doubt any of the bars in town are going to be open. Although I guess we could hit the grocery store…"

Ally didn't even want to think what the talk would be

if she and Hank showed up together, looking for even "medicinal alcohol" at that time of morning.

And while she was soon leaving, to go back to her job in Houston, Hank would have to stay and face— not just the gossip—but the million and one questions from his parents.

"I think I might know where there's a bottle." She dragged a chair over to the cabinets and stepped from that onto the countertop. Sidling carefully, she opened the very uppermost storage cabinet, above the sink. Inside, wedged in the very back, was the bottle—just where her mother had put it, the day the gift from a grateful client had arrived.

Ally removed it and blew off the thin layer of dust. "Voila! Peppermint Schnapps!"

Hank wrinkled his nose.

Happy to have something that would ease the sorrow in her aching heart, if only temporarily, Ally waved off his disdain. "Buck up, cowboy! Beggars can't be choosers."

She turned to hand off the bottle and found Hank's hands anchored securely around her waist. He lifted her down, as easily as if she weighed a feather. "You're right," he acknowledged, looking like a marine, ready for action. "In this case, a drink's a drink."

Her heart racing, for a completely different reason this time, Ally handed the pint to Hank. He ripped off the seal, took off the cap. Sniffed. His expression perplexed, he offered the bottle to her. "Is it supposed to smell like this?"

Ally dutifully inhaled the mixture of peppermint-scented vodka. "I don't know," she said with a shrug. "I've never had it."

He grinned. "Me, either."

It didn't matter how tough life was, Ally noted. Being near Hank always made her feel better. "Well, let's give it a try." She got down two water glasses, the nearness of him and the intimacy of the moment filling her senses. "You want it over ice or straight up?"

His eyes darkened seductively. "Straight up, probably while holding my nose."

Ally wrinkled her nose at his joke, glad for the distraction of their 'toast'. She poured an inch in each glass.

Hank lifted a brow. "That's a little stiff."

Moving closer, Ally breathed in the masculine fragrance of his skin and hair. "I can handle it."

He met her gaze and their fingers brushed as he accepted his drink.

He lifted his glass, his deep blue eyes glittering with ardor. "To Duchess and Gracie and the rest of the cute little darlin's. May they have all the happiness they brought us."

"Amen to that." Ally touched her glass to his and took a hefty drink. The liqueur burned on its way down. She coughed a bit while Hank grinned, then poured another inch for both of them. They lifted their glasses again. "And to Mesquite Ridge," Ally toasted softly, wanting this said. "I'm glad I came back, after all."

Two hours, a good portion of the pint—and a plate of Christmas cookies later—Hank and Ally were lounging side by side on the living room sofa. They'd pulled off their boots and had their feet propped up on the coffee table. Hank had put a CD of Christmas music on, turned the lights on the tree and built a fire in the grate.

The whole scene was like something out of a holiday movie. Ally felt her heart swelling with joy.

As she tilted her head slightly to the left, to look around, the top of her cheek brushed the hardness of Hank's shoulder. She reveled in the contentment. She still missed the dogs—and knew he did, too—but it still felt so right, being with him this way.

Like they could handle any challenge that came their way, as long as they stuck together...

"I know I didn't make that many changes, but the ranch house seems so different now," she murmured.

Hank nodded and shifted position slightly, so the natural thing for Ally to do was let her head rest on his broad shoulder. "It's much nicer."

Relaxing all the more, she cuddled against him and admitted, "It makes me want to keep going. You know, redo the kitchen—at least the countertops, floor, and appliances—and bring in some better furniture, like the kind I have in Houston."

"So it'll feel even more like home to you," Hank guessed, regarding her in a reverent, possessive manner.

Ally studied his expression—aware she hadn't dared share the solution forming in her mind with anyone just yet. "You know, don't you?"

Blue eyes crinkling, he looked over at her as if he wanted nothing more than to make love to her, as thoroughly and ardently as he had the evening before. He took her hand in his and kissed the inside of her wrist. "Know what?"

Ally tingled with a longing for him that went soul deep. She savored the warm seduction of his touch. "That I'm having second thoughts about selling the house," she explained.

His expression sobered.

She pushed on. "Not the ranch land—that still has to go. But I'm beginning to think I might want to keep the house and the barn and ten acres or so around them. Just sell the other three thousand nine hundred and ninety acres."

The joy she had expected to see on his ruggedly handsome face did not materialize.

Hank took a moment to absorb what she'd revealed, then replied in a low, implacable tone, "Corporate Farms is going to want the whole thing."

Determined to do the right thing, for everyone involved, Ally retorted, "Corporate Farms is going to want a lot of things they aren't going to get."

Hank went very still. "You've decided not to sell to them?"

Ally's stomach fluttered with a thousand butterflies. "I'm not doing anything until I see what all my options are." And that included whatever it was Hank—and/or possibly Lulu Sanderson—were getting ready to propose to her.

Hank nodded with a mixture of approval and relief. "The important thing is, you don't have to rush to make a decision now."

"That's true." Ally traced the knee of her jeans. "Now that I know I still have my job, I do have some time." And the opportunity to develop the plan of her own, that had been brewing ever since Marcy Lyons had set her straight on the financial inadvisability of a traditional sale by broker....

"And we do need to sit down together and have a serious talk about it," Hank stipulated, smiling broadly, as if he had a secret. "Say, tomorrow at noon?"

Ally wanted to do that, too. She only hoped that he would be as open to a nontraditional arrangement as she was, at this point. Because she knew now, more than ever, that he was the one who should run cattle on Mesquite Ridge. A twinge of uncertainty tightened her middle. Would the ranch finally help change her luck—and bring her happiness at long last?

She searched Hank's expressive blue eyes. "You're okay with the two of us having a business meeting on Christmas Eve?" If anything could tempt fate…

He captured her hands with his. "When it's this important to both of our futures, absolutely."

His words hinted at a permanence Ally found very exciting.

"But right now," Hank continued tenderly, using the leverage of his grip to bring her even closer, "I have something even more important to ask." He shifted her onto his lap. "I know you're due at work on the 26… and I respect that. But I'm hoping you'll stay and spend Christmas with me."

For the first time in her life, Ally found herself looking forward to celebrating the holiday, with nary a bah humbug in sight. "I'd love to." She smiled and reached for the buttons on his shirt. "In the meantime, though, we have much more important things to do…"

Hank groaned in pleasure as she undid them, revealing his powerful chest and spectacular abs. While her hands explored the chiseled contours and warm satiny skin, he bent his head and slowly kissed her neck. "Looks like the celebrating is starting early…."

And celebrate they did, with tender kisses and hot caresses. And a roll in the sheets that was completely devoid of words—and utterly glorious.

Ally had never realized lovemaking could be so incredibly fulfilling. Never knew touch alone could communicate so much! Or guessed that anyone could make her feel so warm and safe, and so wanted and revered. Was it any wonder she was driven to take their pleasure to a new plateau, and make love over and over again?

Before long she was giving herself over completely, tempting him to do the same. Until at last she knew what made their connection so special. It wasn't just that she had finally given her whole heart and soul to Hank. It was that he made her feel he had fallen impossibly, irrevocably in love with her, too.

Chapter Fifteen

Ally awakened slowly. Late afternoon sunshine poured across the rumpled covers of the bed. She could hear the shower running across the hall. Knowing she had never been so thoroughly loved, she stretched languidly. Then burrowed even deeper in the sheets, the crisp percale shifting smoothly across her bare skin.

A minute later, the water shut off and the shower curtain was swept back.

Ally opened her eyes and propped her head on her upraised hand. Smiling, she watched Hank saunter into the room.

Towel knotted low on his waist, he padded barefoot to the bed. As he sank down by her side, his towel-clad hip nestled warmly against her thigh. "How's your head?" he asked, running a hand down her arm.

Beginning to regret the morning lazing around, imbibing peppermint schnapps, but not what happened afterward, Ally groaned. "Throbbing. Yours?"

Hank grinned. "Better since I took some aspirin."

He lifted a staying hand, then went back to the bathroom. He returned, bottle of aspirin and water glass in hand. "This will help."

Ally took two pills before lying back among the pillows, as eager to make love again as she had been the first time. She waggled her eyebrows at him. "So would not getting up at all."

Briefly, Hank looked tempted. Very tempted. "We'll have to work on that part later." He bent and kissed the curve of her shoulder. "We've got an open house to go to tonight." He straightened while she was still tingling. "Remember?"

At his parents' ranch.

His eyes spoke volumes as they locked on hers. "I really want you to be part of my family's annual Christmas gathering."

Two weeks ago, Ally would have been totally intimidated by the notion of going to Greta and Shane McCabe's open house. Now she was looking forward to it. Hoping that someday she would be part of the loving clan…and not just an invited guest. The telling expression on Hank's face indicated he felt that way, too.

Bursting with joy, Ally flung back the covers. "I'm headed for the shower right now."

An hour later, they were heading out the door.

"One question," Ally said, when they arrived at their destination. She knew what their relationship felt like in private, but in public she needed to be clear—in case questions arose. "As far as everyone else is concerned…

are you just my ride for the evening?" Or was he as ready as she was to go public with their romance?

Hank's gaze drifted over her before returning ever so slowly to her face. He made no effort to hide the emotion brimming in his eyes. "Are you kidding?" He pulled her close and kissed her tenderly. "You're a lot more than that, Ally Garrett. You're my future."

And you, Ally thought, *are mine.*

Smiling, he took her hand and led her toward the front door.

Moments later, they were mingling inside.

Ally couldn't help but note that Lulu Sanderson kept catching Hank's eye. Every time the divorcée did she flashed a secret smile. The confident way Hank looked at her in return told Ally there was *something* going on between him and Lulu.

Pushing aside the niggling feeling of uneasiness, Ally continued making her way among the guests, at first with Hank, then by herself after his father asked for his help bringing in more firewood.

Hank's mother appeared at Ally's side. Looking as beautiful and put-together as always, Greta engulfed her in a hug. "How are you doing, darlin'?"

Ally basked in the easy maternal affection and smiled back. Greta would be a dream mother-in-law. Not that anyone was anywhere close to talking marriage yet.

"Good," Ally replied. *At least I was before we walked in the door and I saw whatever-it-is going on between Hank and Lulu again.... Whatever he's chosen not to share with me. Again....*

Greta arched a silver-blond brow. "That son of mine treating you right?"

Ally noted the matchmaker's gleam in her eyes. Obviously, Hank's mom had either been told or figured out on her own that Ally and Hank were romantically involved. That had to be a good sign, didn't it?

Greta clasped her arm and leaned in close to confide, "Just so you know, honey…I haven't seen Hank this happy in years. And it's all due to you. So keep up the good work. It's about time someone put a spring in that boy's step and a light in his eyes."

I hope it's all due to me, Ally thought, looking at Lulu, who was standing next to a group of her old high school friends at the buffet table. But what if it wasn't? What if the real reason behind Hank's happiness was the ranch? And the fact that she couldn't sell it via the traditional route, and had decided not to sell to Corporate Farms?

Oblivious to the troubling nature of Ally's thoughts, Greta checked out the fast-diminishing spread on the buffet with a frown. She propped her hands on her hips. "Speaking of loved ones, have you seen my husband lately?"

Ally nodded, glad to talk about something else. "He stepped outside a few minutes ago with Hank, to get more firewood."

"Would you mind getting Shane? Tell him to meet me in the kitchen when he does. I need his help carving the brisket."

Ally nodded. "No problem."

Given the crowds of people, she figured the easiest way to reach him was to go out the front door and walk around. Ally grabbed her coat and headed outside. She was halfway around the porch surrounding the entire first floor when she heard the rise in men's voices.

"I don't understand why you won't take our money, if the Garrett ranch is what you want," Shane said, sounding as if he had very little patience left.

Hank harrumphed. "I don't need it, Dad. I've worked out everything on my own."

"Then the rumors going around town are true?" Shane demanded, sounding even more upset. "You *are* going to marry Lulu Sanderson for her money."

A brief silence followed. "If I was going to marry anyone for her money, I'd marry Ally Garrett," Hank snapped. He was obviously exasperated. "But that's not necessary with the plan I have."

Of course it wasn't, Ally thought, reeling backward in shock. She was ready to give Hank everything he could ever want, without so much as a promise of a ring on her finger. But Hank didn't know that yet.

Deciding the conversation was over, she started forward once again, only to hear Shane McCabe say, "But Lulu is involved in this plan of yours…."

The grim note in Shane's voice stopped Ally in her tracks once again.

"Not that it's any of your business," Hank retorted, just as tautly, "but yes, Lulu is an integral part of my future plans, too."

Ally's heart sank. She ran a trembling hand over her eyes.

"You have to see you can't have Ally and a deal with Lulu, too," his dad argued.

"I don't see why not," Hank scoffed, confident as ever.

"It'll never work," Shane insisted with the paternal wisdom for which he was known.

"Yes," he argued, as tears misted Ally's eyes, "it

will, Dad. The real question is when are you going to start believing in me again—with the trust and faith you gave me when I was a kid?"

And when, Ally mused, was she going to learn she would always—*always*—take second place to the family ranch?

"I do believe in you, son," Shane insisted.

"Then why are you standing here tonight, trying to loan me the down payment and whatever collateral I need to purchase Mesquite Ridge?" Hank countered bitterly.

And why wouldn't he take the offer? Ally wondered. Surely receiving money from family was better and more honorable than whatever it was Hank had cooked up with Lulu Sanderson.

"Your mother and I want you to be happy," Shane soothed. "We want you to have kids. You and Ally seem like a good match."

Ally leaned against the side of the house. *I thought so, too.* Obviously, she'd been wrong. Otherwise Hank would have confided some of this to her.

The voices came a little closer. "Lulu and I are a good match, too, Dad. Just not in the way you'd expect."

Or want to hear, Ally thought.

Realizing she had witnessed enough, she marched briskly on around the corner of the house. Both men took one look at her face and realized she'd overheard enough to be deeply disturbed. Knowing she had to talk to Hank privately first, Ally said quietly, "Shane? Greta is looking for you. She needs your help in the kitchen."

He nodded briefly at Ally, his glance conveying a thousand apologies as well as compassion. For Shane, too, knew what it was like to be emotionally shut out of

Hank's life at precisely the moment when Hank should have been opening up the most. To family, friends and especially the woman in his life. The woman he had pretended meant everything to him! Not, Ally thought miserably, that Hank had ever come right out and said he loved her, either. What if he didn't? What if it was just passion keeping them together? A passion that might not last?

Ever the gentleman and congenial host, Shane said, "I'm sorry if I misstepped or have in anyway said or done anything to make you uncomfortable here this evening." Shane cast another meaningful look at his son. "I was only trying to help."

There was no question of the elder McCabe's gallantry. Ally dipped her head in acknowledgment. "I know. I appreciate what you were trying to do, sir." Even if Hank didn't.

With a last rueful look at his son, Shane went inside. Ally stood facing Hank. She put her wounded feelings aside and faced him like the savvy businesswoman she still was. "Is it true that Lulu Sanderson is going to be an integral part of the deal you're proposing to me tomorrow?"

Hank shrugged and ambled up the steps toward her. To her amazement, he now appeared to be annoyed with her! "I told you I've been talking business with Lulu."

Ally warned herself to resist jumping to further conclusions. "I thought—hoped—you were just getting advice from her, or making use of her considerable connections in the venture capital and banking community, since she went to an Ivy League business school and worked in the financial sector before she came back to take over her dad's restaurant."

Hank stepped closer. It was clear from the look on his face that he wanted to tell her everything but for some reason still couldn't. Or still wouldn't. Frustration welled up inside Ally, as potent as hurt. "I've given you no reason to mistrust me."

Hadn't he? "Those glances Lulu has been giving you all evening say otherwise."

Hank's jaw set with the resolve of an ex-marine. "I've told you before. You have no reason to be jealous."

Ally threw up her hands. Her feelings had been constantly dismissed and disregarded by her parents. No way was she letting it happen to her again.

She regarded Hank coldly. "I have every reason, given how happy Lulu is and how *unhappy* I am right now."

"It's just business."

How many times had her parents told her that, while excluding and ignoring her? How many times had she been expected to just go away quietly and wait for the crumbs of their attention? "Then why can't you tell me about it right now?" Ally countered with a burning resentment she could no longer contain. "Why are you treating me the way you're treating your parents and heaven only knows who else?" Ally ignored Hank's dissenting frown and rushed on miserably. "By only telling us what you feel we have a right to know at any given time, and yet still expecting us to magically understand what is going on in your mind and your heart?"

Hank's spine stiffened. "When you really care about someone, you take things on faith," he returned gruffly.

Like Lulu apparently was?

"Your dad is right," Ally warned flatly. "You can't

have intimate relationships with both Lulu and me simultaneously."

Hank folded his arms in front of him deliberately. "I know what you're thinking and you're wrong, Ally. Lulu and I are just friends."

Maybe not physically…at least not yet…

Ally set her jaw and took a stance. "I saw the way Lulu's been smiling at you all evening, Hank."

He lifted a hand. "She's excited!"

Jealousy flared inside Ally. "I bet!"

Hank's eyes narrowed. "I need you to believe in me, Ally."

No doubt he did, Ally thought. But he wasn't the only one with requirements for personal happiness. "And I need a life where I don't feel excluded by ranch business, the way I did when I was growing up!"

More to the point, *she* had wanted to be an integral part of Hank's efforts to purchase and build up Mesquite Ridge. Not Lulu. Ally had even, through clever financial analysis, found a way to do so that would meet both their monetary needs. For all the good it had done them.

Ally gestured dismissively. "Whatever the deal with Lulu is, I won't accept it."

Hank scowled. "I've spent days working on this," he warned.

How well Ally knew that! "I don't care. It's pulling us apart, and you have other options."

A muscle ticked in his cheek. He stared at her as if she were a stranger. "You're not even going to give me a chance to lay out the proposal for you tomorrow at noon?" he asked incredulously.

"Not if the plan involves the participation of Lulu Sanderson or any of her money or ideas." Because there was no way Ally was playing second fiddle to another woman, or being shut out by Hank and Lulu in the way she had been emotionally shut out by her folks. Especially over ranch business.

Hank studied her a long moment. His expression was grave. "You're serious."

"Dead serious," Ally stated bluntly.

Anger flashed in his blue eyes. "I wish you'd made this clear a lot earlier."

"Me, too," Ally said bitterly, as the tears she'd been holding back spilled over and ran down her cheeks. "Because if I had," she choked out, unable to hide the depth of her distress any longer, "you and I never would have made love. We never would have come here together tonight."

"You can say that again." Hurt and resentment scored his low tone.

With effort, Ally gathered her dignity. "But not to worry, Hank. We won't be leaving together. Because whatever this was—" *though it had felt like the love of a lifetime* "—is over."

Her heart breaking, Ally turned on her heel and walked inside. She got her purse, her coat, and walked back out, to call a cab. Looking every bit as disappointed and disillusioned as she felt, Hank made no move to stop her.

"I figured you'd show up here sooner or later," Jeb McCabe said.

If anyone could understand the mess he found himself in, Hank figured it was his oldest brother. "Can I bunk here tonight?"

Jeb beckoned him in. "Ally kick you out?"

"No."

Jeb ambled into the kitchen and broke out the beer. "She sure left the open house in a huff."

Hank removed the cap on his and took a long drink. He tensed at the memory. "You saw that, huh?"

"See, that's why I'm married to my ranch." Jeb rummaged around and brought out a hunk of summer sausage, too. "Women are just too much trouble."

Hank pulled up a chair. "You wouldn't believe that if you'd spent the last two weeks under the same roof with Ally Garrett."

Jeb smirked. "While pursuing Lulu Sanderson on the side."

Not his brother, too! "For the last time, there's nothing romantic going on between me and Lulu!"

"Then why is Ally so jealous?" Jeb opened a can of nuts and tossed a handful in his mouth. "'Cause I saw the way Lulu was looking at you and the way Ally was looking at Lulu. Not good, little bro. Not good at all."

Hank felt like a man who was fast coming to the end of his rope. "Lulu and I have a business deal in the works," he explained for what felt like the millionth time. "One I'm not at liberty to discuss. And won't be until the final details are set."

Jeb shrugged. "So tell Ally that."

Hank munched glumly on a slice of sausage. "I did… sort of. It didn't help. She feels excluded."

Jeb took another pull of beer. "Then call off the business deal."

Hank rolled his eyes. "I can't. Not if I want to buy Mesquite Ridge." And he did.

Jeb smiled like the carefree bachelor he was. "Sure you can. Just accept Dad's offer."

Hank froze. Was there no end to his humiliation to-night? "You know about that?"

His brother sighed. "For the record, I told Dad not to do it. That you'd only be insulted."

Obviously, their father had not listened. "As would you have been," Hank muttered, still fuming over having been treated like a snot-nosed kid who couldn't put a business deal together if he tried.

"True." Jeb leaned forward in his chair. "Although maybe Mom and Dad wouldn't hover over you so much if you talked to them more, let 'em know what's on your mind. And the same goes for Ally. 'Cause you can't be really close to someone unless you can confide in 'em."

Enough with the greeting card sentiment! "You sound like Ally," Hank grumbled, downing the rest of his beer.

"So?"

A goading silence fell. "It's not that easy." Hank returned his brother's level gaze. *Not for me anyway. I don't like showing weakness. Don't like being forced to open up.*

"I know that." Jeb stood and clapped a fraternal hand on Hank's shoulder. "I also know if you want to feel understood by family and/or the woman in your life, you're going to have to start disclosing one hell of a lot more than you have been."

Ally was astounded to see Hank's little sister on her doorstep at nine the next morning, a gaily wrapped basket of baked goods in her hands.

"May I come in?" Emily asked.

Ally hesitated. "If you're here to talk about Hank…" She'd already spent a sleepless night crying her eyes out.

She didn't want to start sobbing all over again, and she was fairly certain it wouldn't take much to set her off. Perhaps the mere mention of the scoundrel's name...

Emily walked in. "And Christmas."

Ally blinked. Now that she and Hank were no longer hooking up, she did not expect to be included in the McCabes' yuletide celebrations. Unable to help herself, Ally grumbled, "What does the holiday have to do with anything?"

"I know what Christmas means to Hank—celebrating the end of one chapter of your life and moving on to the next, with hope and joy in your heart."

Ally had planned to do just that...before the dirt had hit the fan. When she'd overheard Hank's argument with his father, she'd realized that Hank could have gotten the money to purchase the ranch from Shane all along—he just hadn't wanted to do it that way. Even if it meant aligning his fortunes with another woman, and shutting out the woman he seemed to love...

"But to me," Emily continued gently, "Christmas is all about giving—even when you feel you can't. It's about finding the courage to make that leap of faith that will transform your life." She paused, letting her words sink in for a moment, then pleaded softly, "Don't go back to Houston just yet. Stay another day or two and give your own Christmas miracle a chance to happen."

Ally thought about what Emily had said for the rest of the morning.

By noon, she knew what she had to do.

She left the silent, lonely ranch house and drove to town.

Luck was with her. Lulu Sanderson was standing

at the cash register at Sonny's Barbecue, looking gorgeous as ever as she rang up preordered smoked hams and turkeys.

Lulu smiled at Ally. "If you're looking for Hank…"

That, she thought nervously, would come later. She swallowed and looked the other woman in the eye. "I wanted to speak to you first."

Lulu murmured something to her dad, and another employee, then stepped out from behind the counter. She escorted Ally through the restaurant and kitchen, then out the service entrance. The delicious scent of mesquite-smoked meat emanated from the giant iron smokers located behind the building.

Suddenly all business, Lulu said, "Look, I know the time I've been spending with Hank has caused some trouble between the two of you, but he's been helping me on a really important business deal."

"Just as you've been helping him."

"Yes." Lulu sobered. "I wanted to speak to you about what was going on, but Hank asked me not to. You see, there were reasons we had to keep everything between us quiet."

Trust me, Hank had said… *Believe I can find a way to purchase the ranch.*

The only question was, did Ally still *want* to sell the ranch to Hank? Or anyone else?

Oblivious to the conflicted nature of Ally's thoughts, Lulu paused. "As of nine this morning, that's no longer the case."

Here was her chance, Ally thought. She could get Lulu to tell her everything Hank wouldn't, and stop feeling excluded. Or she could demonstrate the faith she had in Hank and his integrity.…

Ally held up her palm. "That's not going to be necessary."

Lulu leaned forward anxiously. "Are you sure? Because in retrospect, *especially* after last night, I realize how this all must have looked…."

And still looked, in fact. The only thing different was Ally's attitude.

"Hank will tell me what he wants me to know when he wants me to know it." *In the meantime, I'm going to draw on all the patience I possess and wait for that to happen.*

She drew a deep breath and extended her hand in the age-old gesture of peace. "Right now, I just want to offer my sincere apology. I haven't been very friendly to you and I'm sorry."

Lulu shook her hand warmly. "Apology accepted, and one given in return."

And just that quickly they were on their way to being what Ally had never dreamed they could be in a million years—friends.

Hank thought about the things Ally and his brother Jeb had said all night. By morning, he knew they were right. Ally had every reason to be upset with him. So did his parents.

If there was ever going to be a change for the better, it had to start with him. He called his parents and asked to meet them at their ranch.

"I know you've been worried about me," he began, as the three of them sat down to talk. "And a lot of it is my fault. In my efforts to be the kind of stand-up, I-can-handle-anything sort of guy I was raised to be, I haven't been very forthcoming about a lot of things."

He paused, looking them both in the eye. "I realize that has to change."

His parents welcomed his confession. "We're at fault, too," Greta said quietly, reaching out to take her husband's hand. "In our efforts to protect and help you, your father and I realize we've been in your business a little too much."

Shane nodded. "We should have trusted that you are capable of starting a ranch and running your own life—without our interference."

Hank didn't want to appear ungrateful. "I know you're both here for me, in whatever way I need, whenever I need it. And I appreciate it."

"We just don't want to let you down," Greta said.

Shane concurred. "Not ever again."

Hank grimaced. "About that." He knew it was past time he took his parents step by step through the decisions he had made. To his relief, his parents were equally candid. By the time they had finished their heartfelt discussion, Hank understood his parents as well as they understood him. The tension between them was gone.

They promised to maintain their transparency, then hugged and said goodbye.

Relieved that it had gone so well, Hank headed for his next destination. He turned into the driveway leading to the Mesquite Ranch just in time to see Graham Penderson come out of the house. The agent shook hands with Ally as if they were sealing a business deal, then got into his car.

Hoping that didn't mean what it looked like, Hank returned the other man's wave of acknowledgment and then parked in front of the ranch house.

Ally was still on the porch, looking radiant in a cranberry-red dress and black suede boots. His heart in his throat, Hank approached. "Do you have time to talk to me?" he asked.

She nodded, looking as reserved as he felt. "Come on in."

In the foyer was a case of champagne, with a gift card that said "Merry Christmas from Corporate Farms." Beside it was a manila folder holding what looked like legal papers.

Had she sold the ranch? At the end of the day, did it matter?

Ally waved a hand. "I haven't sold Mesquite Ridge, if that's what you're wondering."

Relief mixed with the anxiety he felt about their future. "But Corporate Farms is putting the pressure on," Hank guessed, following her into the living room. At once, his eyes were drawn to the angel atop the beautifully decorated tree. It was as lovely and delicate as the woman who had put it there.

Ally reached out and took his hand. "They presented me with yet another bid, two percent higher than the last one."

Hank's throat closed. He looked at her with all the hope his heart could hold. "And?"

Ally's green eyes were steady, but her lower lip trembled. "I told them I was no longer interested in selling the house and the barn."

Which meant she hadn't changed her mind—she was keeping her link to Laramie County.

"Graham said both had to be part of the deal," Ally continued in a rusty-sounding voice. "I said, 'No way.'"

Hank clasped her fingers tightly. "So it's over?"

Ally regarded him shrewdly. "He'll be back, just like you said, until the land is sold. Then he'll look elsewhere."

Here was his chance to show her what she meant to him. What he cared about, and what he didn't.

And most important of all, to say what he should have said when she had been upset the evening before. "First off, I want to apologize because you were right. I *should* have talked to you earlier about my plans, even if they weren't completely formed...."

Ally matched his steady gaze, with obvious regrets of her own. "And I should have trusted you—even without detailed explanations," she said softly.

She meant that, Hank realized with gratitude. His spirits began to soar. Suddenly, the future was looking a lot brighter. Once everything that had kept them apart was out of the way, that was. Knowing a lot more than a simple apology was required to completely fix things here, he pushed on, "Second—about Mesquite Ridge... and the way you feel..."

Again, she cut him off, this time by going up on tiptoe and pressing her index finger against his lips. Ally looked him right in the eye. "I've talked to Lulu," she said softly. "Whatever the two of you want to do in terms of business is fine with me."

Hank eyed her in surprise. "You're serious."

Ally released his hand. "You need a partner."

"Yes," Hank agreed, catching her about the waist and pulling her flush against him, "I do." He looked down at her tenderly. "And that partner is you."

Ally splayed her hands across his chest. "I don't understand." But for the first time, she seemed willing and ready to listen, with a completely open mind and heart. Encouraged, Hank continued.

"Lulu plans to expand her father's barbecue place into a state-wide chain. She's already selected the locations and she's got venture capital lined up, to begin construction immediately."

Ally's eyes widened. "You're part of that?"

Proud of what he had negotiated, he explained, "I'm supplying the mesquite to fuel the smokers. Hopefully, it will come from your ranch. That is, if you agree to lease me the timber rights to the property." Hank pulled papers from his pocket. "That way the land will be cleared at no charge or bother to you. And I'll get enough money from the harvesting of the mesquite to provide the down payment I need to make a serious bid on the ranch and/or the timber rights." He locked eyes with her. "But if you don't want to do that, then Lulu plans to make a deal with you directly. In either case, you'll have the option to do a controlled burn and get rid of the mesquite permanently, hence increasing the value of the land for ranching or keeping it producing indefinitely, for harvesting."

Ally listened intently to everything he was saying, but he couldn't quite read her expression. "In the meantime," he continued, "you'll have a buyer for your wood, a steady stream of income and a way to pay the mortgage and the taxes on Mesquite Ridge for as long as you want to stay." He handed her the proposal he had meticulously drawn up, down to the last penny. He hoped it was enough. "It's all here, in black and white."

Ally stared at the numbers as if he had just given her the best gift she had ever received in her life. "This is very generous of you."

And selfish. "I want you to be happy and safe and free from financial worry," Hank said sincerely. And most of all, he wanted her to stay....

Ally looked at the papers and began to laugh. "You're not going to believe this," she admitted ruefully. "I've got a proposal all printed out, too."

She went to get it, came back and thrust it into his hands, her cheeks flushed with excitement. "I was going to let you live here and run a herd of cattle for me, in exchange for land."

Sounded good, Hank thought. Very good. And generous, too.

"Every year, you and I would split the profits on the cattle, fifty-fifty. Instead of a salary, I'd pay you in acreage. At the end of thirty years, you'd own it all. Or sooner, if you could pull together the cash." Before he could express his delight, Ally added quickly, "Except for the ranch house, that is." Firmly, she continued, "I've decided I want to hold on to this. It's part of my heritage."

Hank stared at her in wonder. "You really have changed your view of Mesquite Ridge!" And maybe ranching in general.

She looked at him with the affection he'd been craving. "Although it often felt to me that the land meant more to my mom and dad than I did, you've shown me it doesn't always have to be that way. You can own a ranch and make it your home and still put the people you love first in your life."

"Agreed. But your idea is good, too. Maybe there's a way we can combine our two proposals, and come up with something even more solid. In the meantime..." Hank put both sets of papers aside. He wrapped his arms around her and pulled her close. "We have a few more things to discuss."

She sent him a glance that started a flood of memories, both tender and erotic. "I'm not going back to Houston. I resigned my position."

Hank gazed into her eyes. "You're sure?" he prodded, wanting more than anything for her to be happy— even if it meant he had to commute, via helicopter gigs, to see her.

Ally nodded. "My home isn't there anymore, Hank. It's here."

She couldn't have given him a better Christmas present if she'd tried. "Does that mean I'm getting kicked out?" he teased.

"Depends." Her green eyes went misty again. She moved closer still. "Do you want to share the space with me?"

Wary of asking for too much too soon again, Hank paused. Being roommates or live-in lovers wasn't what he wanted. Unless it was all she was ready for. "You're talking about living together?"

"A little more than that, actually. I love you, Hank. I love you with all my heart."

Hope for the future mixed with the joy he felt. "I love you, too," he told her, then paused for one long, sweet and tender kiss. He looked deep into her eyes. "More than I ever dreamed was possible..."

Ally grinned as contentment swept over them. "Which is why," she informed him as her take-charge nature reasserted itself once again, "when all this ranch business is done, I'd like us to make it official."

"You want to get married?" He grinned, triumphant.

Ally tilted her chin, stubborn as ever. "Got a problem with that, cowboy?"

"Not at all!" Hank laughed with delight. "I like a woman who knows what she wants and goes right after it."

Ally rose on tiptoe and kissed him sweetly. "I like the same kind of man."

"My answer to your proposal is yes then." Hank danced her backward, stopping under the mistletoe. Clinging together, they made up for lost time with long, lingering kisses.

"I can't believe it," Ally murmured finally, when at last they drew apart and turned to admire their tree. "It's not technically even Christmas for a few more hours, and I've already got everything I ever wanted. Except…" she gave a heart-wrenching sigh "…one thing."

Hank listened in the silence of the ranch house and read her wistful expression and knew immediately what it would take to make life in the ranch complete.

"A dog of our very own," they said in unison.

Epilogue

Seven weeks later...

Ally was in the ranch house kitchen, trying to decide what to make for dinner, when Hank strolled in. His hands were full, a grin as wide as Texas on his face.

She gave him a facetious once-over and propped her hands on her denim-clad hips. Unable to completely stifle a laugh, she chided with mock censure, "Seriously? The mistletoe and Santa hat again? It's almost Valentine's Day!"

Hank waggled his brows and closed the distance between them in three lazy strides. He set the hat on her hair, lifted the sprig of greenery above her head, and paused to deliver a long, sensual kiss that robbed her of breath and warmed her heart.

Her toes curled in her boots.

With a look of pure male satisfaction on his handsome face, he drew back and drawled, "Cupid won't be here with his bow and arrow for another week. But you're right." He bent and kissed her again, ever so tenderly this time. "That is something to anticipate. We'll have to put our stamp on that holiday, too. In the meantime—" Hank blazed a steamy trail from her ear to her throat "—every day is Christmas, with you by my side."

Hank was right about that, Ally thought, as she clung to him lovingly.

Finally, he drew back, his midnight-blue eyes serious now. He put the mistletoe aside and clasped her in his arms. "Besides, if this is the only thing we ever disagree about, we're in pretty good shape, wouldn't you say?"

Ally nodded, and stated unequivocally, "We're a very good team."

After confessing their love, and pledging their commitment to one another, they had easily forged a deal regarding the ranch that implemented both their ideas and benefited them each, from a business and financial perspective. Hank had helped Ally set up an office in town, where she could give others financial advice. He had cleared more land, sold the mesquite and used the proceeds to buy two hundred head more cattle.

Most important of all, they'd agreed on a wedding venue and date, and had married a week ago in a private ceremony on the ranch, with family and close friends as witness.

"Except for one tiny thing," Ally added after a moment.

An inscrutable look came into Hank's eyes. "A dog."

"I want an older one," she reiterated the discussion they had been having nearly every day in some form or another since Duchess and the puppies had gone home with Talia Brannamore.

Hank exhaled, no more willing to budge on this particular issue than she was. "And I think we need a puppy," he said firmly.

They squared off, both silent and yet unable to stop smiling. "Does it really matter what age the dog is," Ally asked finally, "as long as the one we adopt as ours is sweet and lovable?"

Hank winked. "And fluffy and golden…"

Ally laughed. She lifted a hand in a gesture of peace. "Okay, so we do agree on a breed."

"It's definitely got to be a golden retriever," Hank said firmly, then looked at his watch. "What do you know?" he drawled, as a familiar pickup truck turned up the lane toward the ranch house. He peered out the window. "It's time."

Time for what? Ally wondered, but didn't ask. Hearing scratching noises on the floor above them, Ally pushed Hank toward the door. "Better go see who that is," she said hurriedly.

He shot her a perplexed look over his broad shoulder. "I already know who it is. It's my cousin Kurt."

Probably here on some vet business regarding Hank's cattle, Ally thought. "Still…" Hearing another sound, she gave her husband a nudge.

No sooner was Hank through the portal than she raced upstairs.

Into the sewing room.

Where her "gift" was on her feet, sticking her nose out the window.

Ally adjusted the big red bow around her neck and patted her head. "Come on, honey. It's showtime!"

Together, they headed down the stairs.

Before they reached the bottom, Ally heard the truck start up again and drive off.

Seconds later, Hank walked in.

His jaw dropped as he saw who was standing at Ally's side.

"Duchess?" he said hoarsely.

Ally could have sworn there were tears in his eyes.

She gaped at the bundle of fluff with the big red bow in Hank's arms. "And Gracie!" she cried ecstatically.

The nine-week-old puppy squirmed and jumped free. She ran to her mother, gave Duchess a quick greeting, then made a beeline for Ally.

Ally dropped to her knees, and the adorable puppy leaped into her arms, burrowing close.

Duchess rushed toward Hank. He hunkered down on the floor to give her a proper greeting, and the mama dog climbed into his lap so enthusiastically she practically knocked him over. Whimpering eagerly, she licked him under the chin.

Gracie did the same to Ally, while the two humans laughed and cried in unison. Finally, the pup and her mama climbed off them. When Gracie started to circle, Hank jumped to his feet and scooped her up in his arms. "Oh no, you don't, sweetheart. We're taking this outside."

Ally looked at him in confusion as he shepherded all four of them out the front door to the yard.

He set Gracie down on the grass. She circled again and got down to business.

"Oh!" Ally said.

"House-training," Hank explained with a grin. "We'll get the hang of it."

She smiled and went to stand next to him as mother and pup romped together in the grass.

"Wow, she has grown so much!" Ally noted jubiliantly. "From less than a pound at birth…"

"To nearly nine pounds now," Hank said.

Ally turned to him. She clasped his forearms and searched his face, aware that this truly was a miracle, one she never had thought would be possible. "How did you manage to get her? I thought Gracie was already spoken for."

"She was," Hank admitted, sobering. "But after a lot of begging and pleading I managed to convince her would-be owner to take another golden, from another championship litter, in Gracie's place."

"Good move! This is my best present ever."

"I'm so glad." Hank paused. "How did you get Duchess? Because I tried to buy her, too, but was told by the breeder in no uncertain terms that she was not up for adoption."

"I knew how much you loved each other, so I called Talia the day after she was here. She told me this was Duchess's second litter and that she was retiring—since it's not healthy for a golden to have more than two litters in a lifetime. So I arranged for her to come here. Only Duchess couldn't leave until all her puppies were weaned and old enough to go to their new homes."

"Which was today," Hank murmured.

Ally nodded. "That explains where I was this morning."

"And where I was this afternoon. I picked Gracie up, took her over to the vet clinic for a checkup and her second round of vaccinations. Kurt wanted to keep her for a short while—just to make sure there was no reaction, and to let the techs in the office play with her a bit…."

Ally beamed. "Because she's so adorable!"

"Absolutely. Just like you." Hank kissed Ally again. "And then he followed me out to the ranch and kept Gracie in his truck at the top of the lane, while I came in to make sure you were ready for your surprise."

Ally watched the pup and her mother nestle together contentedly on the lawn. She shook her head, marveling at their many blessings. "So now we have two dogs."

Hank grinned, still looking a little stunned by their belated Christmas miracle. He wrapped his arms around Ally and hugged her close. "Looks like."

She rested her cheek on his shoulder. "I couldn't be happier."

He stroked a hand lovingly up and down her spine. "Me, either, Mrs. McCabe."

Ally grinned and drew back to look up into his face. "You really have made all my dreams come true," she told him seriously. The ranch that had been the bane of her youth was now the source of all her joy.

"For now," Hank stated, the fierce affection he felt for her reflected in his eyes. "There will be plenty more fulfilled wishes to come."

Brimming with hope and joy, Ally knew that anything was possible. She looked at Hank with all the love she possessed. "And plenty more Christmases to celebrate."

* * * * *

HARLEQUIN®

SPECIAL EDITION

Life, Love and Family

A VERY MAVERICK CHRISTMAS
The conclusion of
*MONTANA MAVERICKS:
20 YEARS IN THE SADDLE!*
by *New York Times* bestselling author

Rachel Lee

Who's that girl? is the question on the lips of everyone in Rust Creek Falls this holiday season. Julie Smith is searching for the answer to that very question. She doesn't know her real name or anything about herself—just that she might discover more in Rust Creek Falls.

*Available December 2014
wherever books and ebooks are sold!*

Catch up on the first five stories in
MONTANA MAVERICKS: 20 YEARS IN THE SADDLE!

*Million-Dollar Maverick by Christine Rimmer
From Maverick to Daddy by Teresa Southwick
Maverick for Hire by Leanne Banks
The Last Chance Maverick by Christyne Butler
The Maverick's Thanksgiving Baby by Brenda Harlen*

www.Harlequin.com

HSE65856

***

The whole time he worked, he was aware of her—the pure blue of her eyes, her skin, dusted with pink from the cold, the soft curves as she reached over her head to hand him the end of the light string.

"That should do it for me," he said after a moment. In more ways than one.

"Good work. Should we plug them in so we can see how they look?"

"Sure."

She went inside the little structure at the entrance to the village, where she must have flipped a few switches. They had finished only about half, but the cottages with lights indeed looked magical against the pearly twilight spreading across the landscape as the sun set.

"Ahhh. Beautiful," she exclaimed. "I never get tired of that."

"Truly lovely," he agreed, though he was looking at her and not the cottages.

She smiled at him. "I'm sorry you gave up your whole afternoon to help me, but the truth is I would have been sunk without you. Thank you."

"You're welcome. I can finish these up when I get here in the morning, after I take Joey to school. Now that I've sort of figured out what I'm doing, I should be able to get these lights hung in no time and start work on the repairs at the Lodge by midmorning."

She smiled at him again, a bright, vibrant smile that made his heart pound as if he had just raced up to the top of those mountains up there and back.

"You are the best Christmas present ever, Rafe. Seriously."

He raised an eyebrow. "Am I?"

He didn't mean the words to sound like innuendo but he was almost certain that sudden flush on her cheeks had nothing to do with the cool November air.

"You know what I mean."

He did. She was talking about his help around the ranch. He was taken by surprise by a sudden fierce longing that her words should mean something completely different.

"I'm not sure I've ever been anyone's favorite Christmas gift before," he murmured.

She gave him a sidelong look. "Then it's about time, isn't it?"

***

Hope Nichols was never able to find her place in the world—until her family's Colorado holiday attraction, the Christmas Ranch, faces closure. This Christmas, she's determined to rescue the ranch with the help of handsome former Navy SEAL Rafe Santiago and his adorable nephew. As sparks fly between mysterious Rafe and Hope, this Christmas will be one that nobody in Cold Creek will ever forget!

Don't miss THE CHRISTMAS RANCH
available December 2014, wherever
Harlequin® Special Edition books and ebooks are sold!

SPECIAL EXCERPT FROM

(H) HARLEQUIN®
TM

~American Romance®

*Looking for more all-American romances like the one
you just read? Read on for an excerpt from
Cathy Gillen Thacker's LONE STAR CHRISTMAS
from her* **McCABE MULTIPLES** *miniseries!*

Nash Echols dropped a fresh-cut Christmas tree onto the
bed of a flatbed truck. He watched as a luxuriously outfitted red SUV tore through the late November gloom and
came to an abrupt stop on the old logging trail.

"Well, here comes trouble," he murmured, when the
driver door opened and two equally fancy peacock-blue
boots hit the running board.

His glance moved upward, taking in every elegant inch
of the cowgirl marching toward him. He guessed the sassy
spitfire to be in her early thirties, like him. She glared while
she moved, her hands clapped over her ears to shut out the
concurrent whine of a dozen power saws.

Nash lifted a leather-gloved hand.

One by one his crew stopped, until the Texas mountain-
side was eerily quiet, and only the smell of fresh-cut pine
hung in the air. And still the determined woman advanced,
chin-length dark brown curls framing her even lovelier face.

He eased off his hard hat and ear protectors.

Indignant color highlighting her delicately sculpted
cheeks, she stopped just short of him and propped her hands
on her slender denim-clad hips. "You're killing me, using
all those chain saws at once!" Her aqua-blue eyes narrowed.
"You know that, don't you?"

Actually, Nash hadn't.

Her chin lifted another notch. *"You have to stop!"*

At that, he couldn't help but laugh. It was one thing for this little lady to pay him an unannounced visit, another for her to try to shut him down. "Says who?" he challenged right back.

She angled her thumb at her sternum, unwittingly drawing his glance to her full, luscious breasts beneath the fitted red velvet Western shirt, visible beneath her open wool coat. "Says me!"

"And you are?"

"Callie McCabe-Grimes."

Of course she was from one of the most famous and powerful clans in the Lone Star State. He should have figured that out from the moment she'd barged onto his property.

Nash indicated the stacks of freshly cut Christmas trees around them, aware the last thing he needed in his life was another person not into celebrating the holidays. "Sure that's not Grinch?"

Look for LONE STAR CHRISTMAS
by Cathy Gillen Thacker from the
McCABE MULTIPLES *miniseries from*
Harlequin American Romance.

Available December 2014
wherever books and ebooks are sold.

www.Harlequin.com